Pay a call to the most seductive

address in London and meet

the Rakes of Cavendish Square....

Praise for the Novels
of Tracy Anne Warren

"Warren delivers . . . a truly satisfying romance."
— *The New York Times Book Review*

"An exceptionally entertaining Regency historical [that] offers readers a delectable combination of lushly elegant writing and lusciously sensual romance."
— *Chicago Tribune*

"Warren's emotionally wrought protagonists are beautifully portrayed." — *Library Journal*

"Impeccably written . . . a thrillingly romantic, intrigue-infused tale." — *Booklist*

"Zippy yet soulful . . . deeply relatable characters and strong writing." — *Publishers Weekly*

"Tracy Anne Warren dazzled me once again. . . . She knows what romance readers enjoy."
— Romance Junkies

"A fairy-tale-like story with characters full of personality, depth, and humanlike qualities . . . a fun adventure for all types of romantics." — Once Upon a Romance

"Sexy and wildly emotional . . . should be on the top of all historical romance lovers' to-be-read lists."
— Joyfully Reviewed

"Warren's wickedly wonderful and witty romances enchant readers and have made her a shining star."
— *Romantic Times*

"A rich book full of elegance, desire, and romance. Tracy Anne Warren sketches a magnificent tale that grasps hold of the reader. . . . This is one impressive read that I will always remember."
— Coffee Time Romance & More

TRACY ANNE WARREN

The Bedding Proposal

THE RAKES OF CAVENDISH SQUARE

A SIGNET SELECT BOOK

SIGNET SELECT
Published by the Penguin Group
Penguin Group (USA) LLC, 375 Hudson Street,
New York, New York 10014

USA | Canada | UK | Ireland | Australia | New Zealand | India | South Africa | China
penguin.com
A Penguin Random House Company

First published by Signet Select, an imprint of New American Library,
a division of Penguin Group (USA) LLC

First Printing, March 2015

ISBN 978-0-451-46922-9

Printed in the United States of America
10 9 8 7 6 5 4 3 2 1

For Leslie—always and again

Chapter 1

"This party is duller than a Sunday sermon," Lord Leopold Byron complained, with a sigh.

From where he stood with his elbow crooked idly atop the fireplace mantelpiece, he surveyed the other guests. Not for the first time, he wondered why he'd bothered to accept this evening's invitation; the only amusing activity was drinking, and he could have done that anywhere. At least the champagne was a palatable vintage. Taking consolation from the thought, he drank from the crystal flute balanced in his other hand.

At the opposite end of their host's mantelpiece stood his twin brother, Lord Lawrence Byron. Given that they were identical, Leo supposed they must make a picture, particularly dressed as they both were in black silk evening breeches and black cutaway coats with crisp white shirts, waistcoats and cravats.

Lawrence looked at him and raised an eyebrow, its color two shades darker than his golden brown hair, which fell past his jaw; Leo also tended to wear his hair slightly long. "Just be glad you aren't actually in church," he said.

"If I were, at least I'd be able to catch up on my sleep. Rather handy, being able to doze off with my eyes open; fools the vicar every time. Tough to do standing up, though."

"I can manage in a pinch, so long as there's a convenient wall to lean against. Last time I tried it, though, I started snoring. Great-aunt Augusta caught me and boxed my ears."

Leo chuckled in sympathy. "She may be pushing eighty, but the old gal can still pack a wallop."

Lawrence nodded. "I'll wager she could make even the great Tom Cribb shake in his boots."

Both men grinned for a moment at the image of their formidable aunt taking on one of England's fiercest boxers.

"You can't expect London to be terribly exciting this time of year," Lawrence said, "what with most of the *Ton* off at their country estates. I don't know why you didn't stay at Braebourne with everyone else for another few weeks."

"What? And leave you rattling around Town all by yourself? I know you've taken it into your head to actually do something with your legal studies, but coming back to London early in order to set up your own practice? It's beyond the pale, even for you."

Lawrence gave him a wry half smile. "At least one of us values his education. I happen to like the law; I find it fascinating. And might I remind you that you also studied the law, same as me?"

"Just because I earned a degree in jurisprudence doesn't mean I want to spend the rest of my life pitching my oars into legal waters. You know I studied the law only because I couldn't stomach anything else. Now that the war's over, the military holds little appeal. As for taking ecclesiastical orders—" He broke off on a dramatic shudder. "Not even Mama can see me in a vicar's collar with a Bible tucked under my arm."

Lawrence laughed. "*No one* could see you in a vicar's collar with a Bible under your arm. The very idea is sacrilegious."

"You're right," Leo said. "I prefer to live a gentleman's life, as befits the son of a duke. And thanks to some sound financial advice, courtesy of our inestimable brother-in-law, Adam, and our brother Jack's friend Pendragon, I can afford to do so, even if I am the fifth youngest of six sons."

"Only by two minutes," his twin reminded. "You know, I've always wondered if the nursemaid didn't switch us in our cribs and I'm actually the elder."

"Not likely, considering I'm the brains behind the majority of our greatest schemes."

"The brains, are you? I'll admit you've got a God-given flair for making mischief that few others can match, but I'll thank you to remember who it is who always manages to talk our way out of the thicket when we land ass-first in trouble."

"You do have a knack for turning a story on its head." Leo drank more champagne. "Which leads me back to this career nonsense of yours. You invested successfully with Pendragon, same as me, so I know you don't need the blunt. Why, then, do you want a job? You know as well as I do that gentlemen don't engage in trade."

"It's not trade. The law is a perfectly honorable profession," Lawrence said as he fiddled with his watch fob; it was a gesture Leo knew always indicated defensiveness on his twin's part. "As for my reasons, it keeps me from being *bored*—unlike you."

Leo rolled his eyes. "God, save me. Next you'll be telling me I should join you in chambers and hang my shingle up next to yours. Or worse, take up a cause and run for Parliament. I can see it now: the Right Honourable Lord Leopold, standing on behalf of Gloucester." He shook his head, smiling at the absurdity of the idea.

But his twin didn't return his grin. "Might be good for you. You're five-and-twenty now. You could do with some purposeful direction."

"The only direction I need is to be pointed toward a fresh glass of wine," Leo said, tossing back the last of his champagne. "That and a proper bit of entertainment."

"A woman, you mean? Maybe you shouldn't have broken things off so soon with that pretty little opera dancer you were seeing over the summer. She was a prime bit o' muslin."

Leo scowled. "Oh, she was pretty enough and most definitely limber, but after a couple of weeks, the attraction began to wear thin. Outside the bedroom, we had absolutely nothing in common. Her favorite topics were clothes and jewels and the latest amorous intrigues going on backstage at Covent Garden. It got so that I had begun making excuses not to visit her."

He paused and briefly drummed his fingers against the mantelpiece. "I knew enough was enough when she started hinting that she wanted to quit dancing so I could take her on a tour of the Continent. As if I'd consign myself to spending weeks alone in her company. I'd rather be clapped in irons and paraded naked through the streets than endure such tedium."

Lawrence chuckled. "I hadn't realized the situation was quite so dire."

"That's because you were too busy with your own flirtations." Slowly, Leo turned his empty glass between his fingers. "No, if I wanted to set up another mistress, she'd have to be someone unique, someone incomparable, who other men would go to great lengths to possess. Someone like—"

And suddenly, from across the room, a woman caught his eye.

Her hair was as dark as a winter night, upswept in a simple yet refined twist that showcased the delicate, creamy white column of her throat. Around her neck hung a plain gold chain with a cameo that nestled between her breasts like a cherished lover. Despite the surprisingly modest décolletage of her silk evening gown, the cut served only to enhance the lush curves of her shapely figure, while the brilliant emerald hue of the material cast no illusions regarding her sensuality and allure.

He knew who she must be, of course. He'd heard talk that she might make an appearance tonight—none other than the infamous Lady Thalia Lennox.

Ever since the firestorm of scandal that had erupted around her nearly six years earlier, she'd become both disgraced and notorious. Even he, who had been no more than a green youth reveling in one of his first years about Town, had been aware of the uproar at the time.

The gossip had ignited first over her much-publicized affair, then exploded during the divorce proceedings that followed. Divorces were virtually unheard of among the *Ton*, and extremely difficult to obtain due to the necessity of three separate trials and an Act of Parliament. Nevertheless, her cuckolded husband, Lord Kemp, had sued against her and been granted a termination of their marriage.

And while a taint of scandal continued to trail Lord Kemp even to this day, the proceedings had turned Lady Thalia into a social outcast. Once a darling of the *Ton*, she now dwelled along the fringes of genteel respectability, invited out only by those who either were dishonored themselves or simply didn't care what anyone thought of them—or so said the gossips who continued to relay stories of her alleged exploits.

This evening's supper party was hosted by a marquess who was separated from his wife, lived openly with his mistress and most definitely didn't give a fig about other people's opinions.

Frankly, his host was one of the reasons Leo had attended tonight's revel, as Leo had assumed the party would be wilder and more amusing than it had turned out to be thus far. But now that he knew Thalia Lennox was among the guests, his expectations for a lively evening were reinvigorated.

"You were saying? Someone like who?" Lawrence asked, picking up on the sentence Leo had never finished.

"Her." Leo set his glass aside.

Lawrence's gaze moved across the room. "Good Lord, surely you aren't thinking what I think you're thinking?"

"And what would that be?" he said, not taking his eyes off Thalia, who was conversing with an elderly roué who couldn't seem to lift his gaze higher than her admittedly magnificent breasts.

"We were discussing women, and, if I'm not mistaken,

that's the scandalous Lady K. over there. You must be out of your mind to even consider making a play for her."

"Why? She's stunning. One of the most enchanting women I've ever beheld. And I believe she goes by her maiden name of Lennox these days."

"However she's called, she uses men like toys and discards them once they're broken, to say nothing of the fact that she's several years your senior."

Leo couldn't repress a slowly forming grin as he turned to his twin. "Just look at her. She can't be that much older, even if she has been married and divorced. As for her using me like a toy, I look forward to being played with. Anywhere. Anytime."

Lawrence shook his head. "I'll be the first to admit she's attractive, and I can see why you'd be tempted, but do yourself a favor and find another opera dancer. Or better yet, go visit one of the bawdy houses. You can slake your thirsts there without causing any lasting damage."

"Ah, but where is the challenge in that?" Leo said. "I want a woman who can't be had simply for the price of a coin. A spirited female with some good solid kick to her."

"The only kick you're going to get is in your posterior when she boots you out of her way. My guess is she won't look at you twice."

Leo raised a brow. "Oh, she will. Care to wager on it?"

Lawrence narrowed his eyes. "All right. Ten quid."

"Make it twenty. Ten's hardly worth the effort."

"Twenty it is."

They shook, sealing the bet.

Lawrence stepped back and crossed his arms. "Go on. Amaze me, Don Juan."

Leo brushed the sleeves of his coat and tugged its hem to a precise angle. "Take the carriage home if you get tired of waiting. I'm sure I'll be otherwise occupied tonight."

With that, he set off in search of his quarry.

I should never have come here tonight, Lady Thalia Lennox thought as she forced herself not to flinch beneath the leering stare of Lord Teaksbury. She didn't believe he had met her eyes once since they had begun conversing.

Old lecher. How dare he stare at my breasts as if I'm some doxy selling her wares? Then again, after nearly six years of enduring such crude behavior from men of her acquaintance, one would think she would be well used to it by now.

As for the ladies of the *Ton*, they generally looked through her, as if she were some transparent ghost who had drifted into their midst. Or worse, they pointedly turned their backs. She had grown inured to their snubs as well—for the most part, at least.

Still, she had hoped tonight might prove different, since her host, the Marquess of Elmore, had known his own share of personal pain and tended to acquire friends of a more liberal and tolerant persuasion. But even here, people saw her not for the person she was, but for who they assumed her to be.

Ordinarily, she tossed aside invitations such as the one for tonight's supper party—not that she received all that many invitations these days. But she supposed the real reason she had come tonight was a simple enough one.

She was lonely.

Her two friends, Jane Frost and Mathilda Cathcart— the only ones out of all her acquaintance who had stuck by her after the divorce—were in the countryside. They had each invited her to join them at their separate estates, but she knew her attendance at the usual autumn house parties put each woman in an awkward and difficult position. Plus, neither of their husbands approved of their continued association with her, their friendship limited to occasional quiet meals when they were in Town, and the back-and-forth exchange of letters.

No, she was quite alone and quite lonely.

Ironic, she mused, considering the constant parade of lovers she supposedly entertained—at least according to the gossip mavens and scandal pages that still liked to prattle on about her. Given their reports of her behavior, one would imagine her town house door scarcely ever closed for all the men going in and out—or perhaps it was only her bedroom door that was always in need of oil for the hinges?

She felt her fingers tighten against the glass of lemonade in her hand, wondering why she was dwelling on such unpleasantness tonight. Better to put thoughts like those aside, since they did nothing but leave the bitter taste of regret in her mouth.

A hot bath and a good book—that's what I need this evening, she decided. That, and to tell the old reprobate still leering at her to take his eyes and his person somewhere else.

If only she hadn't given in to the temptation to wear emerald green tonight, perhaps she wouldn't have ended up being ogled by a loathsome toad like Teaksbury. But she'd always loved this dress, which had been languishing in the back of her wardrobe for ages. And honestly she was tired of being condemned no matter what she wore or how she behaved. *In for a penny, in for a pound,* she'd thought when she made the selection. Now, however, she wished she'd stuck to her usual somber dark blue or black, no matter how dreary those shades might seem.

Ah well, I shall be leaving shortly, so what does it really matter?

"Why, that's absolutely fascinating," Thalia said with false politeness as she cut Teaksbury off midsentence. "You'll have to excuse me now, Lord Teaksbury. After all, I wouldn't want to be accused of monopolizing your company tonight."

Teaksbury opened his mouth—no doubt to assure her that he didn't mind in the least. But she had already set down her glass, turned on a flourish of emerald skirts and started toward the door.

She had made it about a quarter of the length of the room when a tall figure stepped suddenly into her path, blocking her exit. She gazed up, then up again, into a boldly masculine face and a pair of green-gold eyes that literally stole her breath. The man sent her a dashing, straight-toothed smile, candlelight glinting off the burnished golden brown of his casually brushed hair in a way that only increased his appeal.

Saints above, she thought as her heart knocked hard inside her chest, her pulse leaping as it hadn't leapt in years—if it ever had at all.

Schooling her features so they revealed none of her inner turmoil, she gave him a polite nod. "Pardon me, sir." She waited, expecting him to step aside.

Instead, he executed an elegant bow. "Allow me to introduce myself. I am Lord Leopold Byron. My intimates, however, call me Leo."

Arrogant, isn't he? Well, she'd met arrogant men before, many times.

She gave him a long, cool stare. "Do they? How nice for them. Now I must insist you step aside. We haven't been properly introduced. As you ought to know, a gentleman never speaks directly to a lady with whom he is not acquainted. Pity one of your intimates isn't here to do the honors. Good evening."

She took a step to the right.

He matched her move, impeding her path once again. "Shall I go find our host, then?" he asked pleasantly. "I'm sure Elmore would be happy to affect an introduction. Frankly, though, it seems like a great lot of bother, particularly since we are conversing already."

Reaching toward the tray of a passing servant, he picked up two glasses. "Champagne?" he offered. Smiling that devastating smile again, he held out one of the crystal flutes with its golden draught effervescing inside.

Audacious as well as arrogant. That and handsome in a sinful way no man had a right to be.

Call me Leo, indeed.

She didn't know whether to be annoyed or amused, particularly since she was sure part of his strategy in waylaying her was to provoke a strong reaction. Still, she found herself accepting one of the proffered glasses, if for no other reason than to give herself time to steady her nerves.

"Since I doubt you'll volunteer your name, not without Elmore's aid at least," Lord Leo continued, "I suppose I must try guessing on my own. Lady Thalia Lennox, is it not?"

The wine suddenly turned sour on her tongue.

Of course, she realized, she ought to have known that he was only playing games and knew her by reputation.

Everyone in the *Ton* did, it seemed—even if they wouldn't associate with her any longer. "Then you have me at even more of a disadvantage than I realized."

"Not at all, since we have only just met and need time to learn about one another."

"I am sure you've heard all you need to know about me. Divorce trials will do that for a woman. Now, if you'll—"

"If you're concerned I mind a sheen of scandal, I don't. I've weathered a few of them myself over the years, so such matters make no difference to me."

He'd been embroiled in scandals, had he? Vaguely she remembered mention of various members of the Byron family involved in deeds that had shocked Society at one time or another. But none of their acts had made any of the Byrons outcasts. And being that Lord Leo was a man, the *Ton* was, of course, more apt to forgive, no matter how serious the trespasses might have been.

As for his "over the years" remark, he didn't look old enough to have weathered all that many scandals. In fact, just how old was he? Certainly not her own one-and-thirty, even if he had the confidence of a man in his prime.

Regardless of scandals and age, she had no interest in setting up flirtation with a stranger. "It has been ... interesting meeting you, Lord Leopold, but I really must be going."

"Why? It is early yet. Surely you can remain a while longer?"

"Truly, I cannot," she said.

He gave her a shrewd look, as if he saw right through her excuses. "Afraid you might enjoy yourself? Or are you worried I'm going to stare down your dress like Teaksbury?"

Her mouth dropped open before she could recall herself.

"It was rather hard to miss that crass display of his," Lord Leo remarked. "The man's a boor. It's a wonder he wasn't actually drooling. Not that I can entirely blame him, given your irresistible feminine charms. Still, were I to feast my eyes upon you, I promise it would leave you in no doubt of my sincere admiration."

Slowly, his gaze dipped down, moving gradually over her body in a way that felt almost like a caress.

When he met her eyes again, his own were alight with unrepentant desire. "You are the most exquisite woman I have ever beheld. Even a god would find himself tempted by you."

A hot flush burst over her skin, shocking her with its force. Only barely did she resist the urge to reach up and cover her hot cheeks with her hands. The sensation was truly singular considering she hadn't blushed since her girlhood and her first London Season.

Experienced women did *not* blush.

Yet this outrageous lord with his heart-stopping smile and velvety voice roused emotions in her that she hadn't realized she still possessed.

"Now," he said, "why don't we go somewhere more private so we can get even better acquainted? I have my coach just outside. And please, I insist you call me Leo. As I said before, all my intimates do."

All his bedmates, he meant, his meaning clear.

Without even knowing what she intended, she flung the contents of her glass up into his face, champagne splashing everywhere.

He blinked wine out of his eyes, a stunned expression on his wet face.

"You and I shall *never* be intimates. Good night, *Lord Leopold*."

Spinning around, she marched toward the door.

As she did, she caught sight of a man standing across the room—a man she would have sworn was Leopold Byron had she not known he was still dripping somewhere behind her. Her step wobbled slightly as her mind worked to figure out the unexpected anomaly.

Twins? Good God, are there two of him?

And his brother was laughing, making no effort at all to contain his mirth.

Well, let him laugh. Impudent beast, just like his sibling.

As for the rest of the guests whose stares pierced her from all directions, she was used to such scrutiny.

The entire incident would be in tomorrow's papers, of course.

But what do I care? Tossing champagne into a man's face was nothing, not compared with what she'd been through already. For when you've known the worst, the rest was naught but a trifle.

Leo withdrew a white silk handkerchief from his waistcoat pocket and dried his face as he watched Thalia Lennox disappear from view with a final flourish of her green skirts.

Lawrence appeared at his side moments later, his grin so wide it was a wonder it didn't split his cheeks.

"Well, that went swimmingly," Lawrence said, with a hearty chuckle. "Had her eating right out of the palm of your hand, at least until she decided to give you a champagne bath!" He laughed again. "You owe me twenty quid. Pay up."

"I will when we get home." Leo wiped briefly at his sodden cravat before giving up.

"What on earth did you say to her anyway? I knew she'd rebuff you, but not with quite so much enthusiasm."

Somewhat begrudgingly, Leo provided him with a brief recounting.

Lawrence erupted into fresh gales of laughter, so loud the outburst drew every eye.

"Oh, do shut up, won't you?" Leo told his brother with a grumble. "I think there might be one scullery maid in the kitchen who hasn't heard you."

Rubbing moisture from the corners of his eyes, Lawrence did his best to silence his mirth, though his lips continued to twitch. "My condolences for your loss." He laid a consoling hand on Leo's shoulder. "You know what your trouble is?"

Leo sent him a baleful look. "I'm certain you shall be happy to illuminate me."

"You're too used to being fawned over by women. When was the last time one of them turned you down? You were what? Fifteen?"

"Thirteen," Leo countered, unable to repress a grin.

"Remember that gorgeous little chambermaid at Brae-bourne? She never did let me steal more than a kiss."

Lawrence's eyes twinkled with clear recollection. "She let me steal two."

Leo shot him a fresh glare.

"Never say you weren't warned," Lawrence continued. "I told you the ex–Lady K. would knock you down and kick you into a convenient corner. From now on, stick to more accessible, and appreciative, females."

Leo considered his twin's remark. "I do not believe I shall."

"What! But surely you've had enough?"

"No," he said, his gut tightening with the knowledge that he wanted Thalia Lennox, now more than ever. She'd said they would never be intimate, but he'd learned long ago the mistake of saying never, since fate had an interesting way of turning matters on their head.

"She may have eluded me tonight, but our paths will cross again. And when they do . . ."

"You're deluded, that's what you are," Lawrence said.

Leo grinned. "No, just determined. Now, how about making our excuses to our host and finding some company with a bit more fire in their blood? Fancy a game of cards or dice? I know a prime hell we haven't tried."

Lawrence's eyes brightened. "By all means, lead on, brother mine."

Slapping a hand across his twin's shoulder, Leo led the way.

Chapter 2

Four mornings later, Thalia sat at the writing desk in her small study and added a last few lines to the letter she was penning to her friend Jane Frost. Satisfied after a quick final perusal, she laid her quill aside. She then sanded the ink dry and folded the missive into a neat square before sealing it with hot wax from the nearby candle, which she blew out the moment the task was complete.

Once, she would have thought nothing of letting the taper burn down to a nub, but the past few years had taught her the expense of items such as candles and the wisdom of frugal living.

Actually, despite her straitened circumstances, she counted herself lucky that she was able to live in a decent part of London. Were it not for the small unencumbered legacy that had been left to her by her maternal grandmother, which included the furnished London town house and enough money to maintain it, she would have had nothing. But to her everlasting gratitude, the bequest had somehow miraculously escaped inclusion in her marriage settlement.

Gordon had seen to it that she hadn't received so much as a farthing from him in their divorce, and had kicked her out of his family's massive ancestral residence in Grosvenor Square with nothing but the clothes on her back that dreadful June day so many years ago.

Her lady's maid, Parker, had taken pity and, with the help of a footman who'd had a soft spot for Parker, had spirited out a couple of trunks of Thalia's clothes a few days later. Even so, she hadn't gotten so much as an additional handkerchief after that, not even the jewels that had been hers prior to her marriage.

Under the law, everything she'd owned belonged to Gordon, down to the last hairpin and thimble. Sadly, that had included a string of hundred-year-old pearls that had been passed down to her from her great-grandmother. She'd pleaded with him for their return, but he'd laughed and said he'd sold them, along with all the other "unwanted baggage" she'd left in the house. He hadn't wanted her possessions, but spiteful to the end, he'd made sure she didn't get any of them back.

The luxurious emerald green dress she'd worn to Elmore's party the other evening had been one of the gowns packed inside that long-ago trunk of clothes from her maid. The dress had been involved in a sea of trouble then and it had caused her nothing but trouble again.

Call me Leo.

A memory of Byron's velvety voice rang inside her head once again, warm and silky as a caress.

She shivered, her eyelids sliding a fraction of an inch lower. He really had been arrestingly handsome and surprisingly charming—at least until he'd made his outrageous proposition to her.

But why was she thinking of Lord Leopold anyway? It's not as if she would be seeing him again. Time to move along, just as she always did.

She gave herself a hard shake.

He was nothing but an impudent rogue bent on sowing a fresh crop of wild oats. Well, he would just have to sow them with someone else, since in spite of her reputation, she didn't dally with men.

Rising from her chair, she brushed a quick hand over the skirt of her day dress, then crossed the room to give the bellpull a tug.

Ten minutes passed before a discreet knock sounded at the door. A stoop-shouldered old manservant in black livery entered. His hair was as wispy and white as dandelion fluff, his body so thin as to be almost skeletal, even though Thalia knew he ate three hearty meals a day down in the servants' hall.

"You rang, milady," he said on a gruff croak that sometimes reminded her of a bullfrog.

"Yes, Fletcher," she said, "I have a letter to mail. Has the postboy been by yet?"

"Nay. He should be here soon enough, though. I'll see this is added to the others going out."

"Excellent." She smiled and held out the letter for him to take. "And would you inform Mrs. Grove that I shall be going out this afternoon and would like an early dinner on my return. I shall be attending an auction at Christie's. Please ask Boggs to ready the coach so that we may leave by eleven o'clock."

"Of course, milady." Fletcher executed a stiff bow. "I'll see to it immediately."

She knew "immediately" would be some while, but that was all right. Fletcher moved as quickly as his old bones could take him and she'd allowed plenty of time for her journey to the auction house on Pall Mall.

Once Fletcher left, she went to her desk and picked up the catalogue for that afternoon's sale. Within its pages was a listing of all the items for sale, together with descriptions and ink renderings of the most interesting lots.

She kept an eye on the London auction houses in hopes that she would stumble across some of her old possessions. Of course she couldn't afford to buy back the truly expensive pieces such as her jewelry and silverware, but every once in a great while one of the less costly bits showed up.

So far, she'd managed to reclaim a flowered Sevres teapot and four matching cups and saucers whose provenance showed they had once "belonged" to Lord Kemp.

She'd also bid for and won a ladies' sewing basket with an embroidered motif of blue birds, lilacs and lily of the valley on its cushioned top. She'd recognized the basket instantly, since she had done the needlework herself—her tiny initials were still on the inside-right corner, exactly where she'd placed them.

And lastly, she'd bought a small oil painting depicting

the village near her parents' country estate that had once adorned the wall of her childhood bedroom. She'd paid rather more for it than she'd wished, but the painting had been worth every farthing, since seeing it brought a smile to her face each and every morning when she woke.

Now there was another possible item to recover.

She'd found it in the current Christie's catalogue and, from the description, strongly suspected the keepsake was one of her "lost" belongings. A porcelain Meissen trinket box made in the last century, it had a pair of hand-painted black-and-white kittens in a basket on its top—just like the one her father had given her as a gift for her fifteenth birthday. She'd been crushed to lose the piece, so she was cautiously excited that it might be hers once again.

Assuming the bidding didn't go too high.

At a previous auction, there had been a pair of silver and ivory hair combs that she had desperately wanted back. But the auction price had started high and quickly escalated far beyond the bounds of her meager budget. If the porcelain box proved to be the one her father had given her, she prayed that today's audience would be packed full of dog lovers who had no interest whatsoever in the precious little cat trinket box.

Brimming with nervous excitement, she went to make ready for her departure.

Two hours later, Leo Byron walked slowly along the rows of numbered auction items that had been set out for prospective bidders to peruse prior to the official commencement of the sale. He held a copy of the Christie's auction catalogue rolled up in his hand, his selections having already been made before he'd ever set foot past the door.

In spite of that, he always made a point to personally view any items he was thinking about purchasing, rather than taking anyone else's word for their condition or authenticity. Not that he doubted Christie's integrity, since it was quite justifiably regarded as the premier auction house for arts and antiquities. But to his way of thinking, a man needed to judge matters for himself. That way if he made a mistake, he had no one but himself to blame.

He'd come today specifically to bid on a fifth-century B.C. Athenian red-figured water jar depicting a scene from the Trojan Wars. Signed by a known maker, it was a beautiful example of the period and would make an excellent addition to his collection. There was a small Grecian marble sculpture of dancing nymphs that he rather liked as well and planned to acquire if the price was right.

After inspecting the jar and the sculpture, he moved on, surveying the other items being displayed. He found a Sevres vase with crimson roses painted on a cobalt blue ground that he thought his older sister, Mallory, would enjoy. It was a mid-eighteenth-century estate piece, so not yet an antique, but he decided it would make a fine present nonetheless.

He also came across a porcelain trinket box with cats upon its top that immediately put him in mind of his other sister, eighteen-year-old Esme. She was a devoted animal lover, so the small box, with its sweet little black-and-white kittens, was certain to charm her. A mere trifle—he doubted the bidding would be anything but lukewarm at best, making it an easy purchase.

He was heading toward the adjoining room where the auctioneer's lectern and rows of chairs had been arranged for the sale when a white feather from a woman's bonnet caught his eye. He looked more closely and felt a thrill warm his blood.

It was Lady Thalia Lennox in the flesh.

And what fine flesh it was, although he couldn't see nearly enough of it, clothed as she was in a rather ordinary day dress of blue worsted. The dress didn't become her half so well as the emerald green evening gown she'd worn the night they'd first met. Even so, there was no concealing her beauty, her skin creamy white, her lips like petals, her hair as dark and lustrous as an ermine's pelt.

He imagined what that hair might look like spread in loose waves over a plump white pillow, her caramel eyes sparkling while her rose-colored mouth curved in sensual anticipation as he lowered himself to join her between the sheets.

He'd thought of her frequently over the past few days, wondering when he might have another chance to see her. Providence, it seemed, had decided to smile upon him. And luckily, there was no champagne anywhere in sight, so he didn't need to worry about another dousing—a first even for him.

Smiling to himself, he started toward her, aware she hadn't seen him yet. She appeared lost in her own inspection of the goods up for auction, perusing the items as he had already done himself.

She also appeared to be alone. Or had she come with a lover and the man was off finding them seats while she amused herself here for a final few minutes before the sale began?

Either way, he didn't plan to squander the chance to speak with her. After all, who knew where it might lead?

Thalia walked slowly along, studying the auction items. She'd already located the kitten trinket box and had known immediately that it was the one that used to be hers. She hugged the knowledge to herself, hoping that when she left the auction today, the box would once more be safely in her possession. She had just the right spot for it too, inside her grandmother's glass-fronted rosewood cabinet that she kept in her upstairs sitting room.

Of course there were other antiques and collectibles that she would have loved to bid on as well, including a splendid landscape painting of the Dover cliffs with a seascape so realistic she could almost smell salt in the air. But the opening price was far too dear and she stalwartly refused to give in to the temptation to spend more than she could afford. A painting here, a bejeweled pin, a vase or a silk fan there, and she soon wouldn't have the money to pay the tea seller for her favorite Ceylon black or for a new supply of paper and ink from the stationer. The little keepsake was more than indulgence enough.

She was admiring a set of ornate silver chargers that

she would once have thought nothing of buying when she sensed someone watching her. She turned her head and looked straight into a pair of vivid green eyes rimmed in gold.

Beautiful, unforgettable eyes.

Lord Leopold Byron sauntered toward her, a faint smile on his attractive mouth.

She cursed inwardly. It was too late to pretend that she hadn't seen him and walk away. Drawing a breath, she prepared herself for the encounter.

"Lady Thalia." He stopped and made her an elegant bow. "How do you do?"

"Lord Leopold," she said, her words calm and cool.

His smile didn't waver in the slightest over her lack of enthusiasm. "What happy luck to find you here."

"Really?" She arched a brow. "I was thinking just the opposite."

Rather than take exception, he casually ran the catalogue through his free hand as his smile widened. "The auction looks to be a fine one. Mr. Christie should be pleased by the turnout."

Lord Leopold was right. The salesroom was filled with patrons with more wandering in all the time. It threatened to be what was known in the vernacular as a sad crush.

"A great number of bidders generally makes for a lively time," she observed, "although I might wish for fewer folk so the prices don't go impossibly high."

"Yes, big crowds tend to be bad for a bidder's pocketbook. And on what have you come to bid today, Lady Thalia?"

The question was innocuous enough, but the warm cadence of his voice moved through her with a strange power, as if they were sharing a secret. Something private, even intimate. And as she had already told him, there was never going to be anything intimate between the two of them.

"That is for me to know, Lord Leopold, and me alone. Now, if you'll excuse me."

She turned to move away.

"Are you headed in the direction of the main sales-room?" he asked. "If so, allow me to escort you."

Her brows creased. "Thank you, but no. There are still a few minutes left before the bidding begins and I have not yet looked at all the goods up for sale. Please do go on without me."

But he made no effort to move.

"As a gentleman," he said, "it would be remiss of me to leave you on your own. Unless you are here with a friend? Is someone joining you?"

He gave her an expectant look, clearly interested in her answer.

Her frown deepened and she wondered whether she should lie. But as soon as she took a seat, he would know the truth, so what was the point?

"No, I am attending the sale unaccompanied, except for my maid, of course," she said. "But I am quite familiar with the interior of this auction house and have no need of escort. Pray absolve yourself of any sense of obligation."

She turned then and walked on, hoping he would take the none-too-subtle hint and be on his way.

But of course he did not, strolling along a few steps behind her.

She stopped and pretended an interest in a black-lacquered Chinese vase that had to be one of the most hideous pieces she'd ever seen.

He stopped too.

Steadfastly, she refused to look at him, an exasperated breath escaping her lips.

"Ugly, isn't it?"

She nearly looked around, but caught herself at the last second.

"That vase is absolutely monstrous," he continued, when she didn't respond. "Makes you wonder what Christie was thinking not just chucking it straight into the nearest rubbish bin."

Her lips twitched, but she forced herself not to smile.

"Maybe he's hoping some of the bidders will be blind. That way the winner won't mind purchasing something so repellent it would give a sewer rat the shudders."

"It's dreadful but not *that* dreadful," she said, unable to silence the remark.

Lord Leopold met her gaze and raised a single golden brow.

A laugh escaped her mouth. "You're right, it is atrocious. But useful. A bouquet of roses would brighten it considerably."

"It would probably make the petals wilt."

Before she could stop herself, she laughed again.

He smiled, his teeth white and straight, his eyes twinkling in a way that made him even handsomer than he already was. "I presume it's safe to say neither of us will be bidding on that particular piece?"

She nodded. "Yes, quite safe."

"The auction will be starting soon. Again, may I escort you to the salesroom so we can find seats?" He offered his arm.

"My maid is saving one for me."

"Then shall I escort you to your maid?"

She hesitated, wondering how she had found herself in the position where refusing him would seem churlish. But letting him show her to her seat didn't mean she had to continue their association. Quite the contrary, since they would part soon enough.

"If you wish, Lord Leopold."

"I do."

She laid her hand on his coat sleeve, the walnut brown superfine wool smooth and soft beneath her fingertips, his arm firm with muscle.

Slowly, they began to walk.

"Lady Thalia, I hope you will allow me to apologize for my behavior on the occasion of our last meeting."

"Our *first* meeting, you mean."

"Exactly." He gave her another one of his winning smiles. "My only excuse, if there is one, is that I was bewitched by your beauty and quite lost my head. There was also the goodly amount of spirits I'd consumed prior to our conversation. It may have loosened my tongue a bit more than it ought."

She sent him a wry glance from under her bonnet.

"Alcohol is often a convenient excuse for untoward behavior."

He winced visibly. "Ouch. I deserve that, I suppose. Although you also have room to make an apology, as I recollect."

"Me?" Her gait slowed, her gaze meeting his. "For what do I have to apologize?"

"A certain glass of champagne perhaps."

"Oh. That."

He chuckled. "Yes. That."

They strolled on.

"I've quite forgiven you," he continued in an even tone, "even if you did ruin a perfectly good cravat. My valet had to discard the one that you doused. Apparently wine stains don't come out."

A faint smile played across her lips. "A great loss, I am sure. Pray send me a reckoning and I shall have a replacement cravat sent round to your address."

"I would much rather you agree that we may start over. Act as if we had met only today." He stopped and turned toward her, taking her hand inside his own. "Allow me to introduce myself. Lord Leopold Byron at your service, ma'am. And you are?"

"Someone who didn't wish to be introduced the first time."

His beguiling smile widened. "Your name, fair lady?"

"You know who I am."

He waited, clearly expectant.

"Lady Thalia Lennox. There, are you satisfied?"

"Not yet, but I hope to be in the very near future."

She sent him a warning look. "Careful, Lord Leopold, or I may find myself in need of another glass of champagne."

He laughed, then made her an elegant bow. "May I say what a pleasure it is to make your acquaintance, Lady Thalia."

She shook her head. "You, Lord Leopold, are absurd."

"Ah good, your barbs aren't quite as sharp. We're making progress."

"I wouldn't count on it."

"Now that you've agreed to forgive me and begin again—"

"I haven't agreed to anything," she said, trying to conceal the fact that she did find him rather charming in spite of her better judgment. But she wasn't interested in men. They were nothing but a great deal of trouble.

"Of course you did," he insisted.

"No, I did not. And you presume a very great deal on so short an acquaintance."

"Which is exactly why we need to take the time to get to know each other better. I suggest now."

"I suggest never. The auction is about to start. We should be finding our seats."

He held out his arm again for her to take.

Instead, she nodded toward the main salesroom and the rows of occupied chairs. "I see my maid waiting just there. Thank you, but I can manage to walk the last few yards on my own."

"If I accompany you, we can sit together. I am sure another chair can be located for your maid."

"Good-bye, Lord Leopold," she called in an amused singsong before she set off into the fray of eager bidders.

Leo wanted to go after her, but he realized he'd pushed her enough for one day. Any more and she might bolt completely. It was curious, but for a woman of her experience and reputation, she was strangely reserved. It was as if she lived behind a carefully constructed wall, letting others see no more than glimpses of the real woman beyond.

He'd assumed she would be more openly flirtatious, more coyly inviting despite their inauspicious introduction at Elmore's party last week. Rumor had it that she was wild and wanton, and that she had a string of lovers whose identities were the stuff of whisper and conjecture.

But there was no lover here today, he realized as he took a seat in one of the last unoccupied chairs. She really was here with her maid, doing nothing more than attending an auction, rather than engaging in some clandestine liaison.

Then again it wasn't her days that concerned him but

rather her nights. Nights he planned to be spending with her in bed in the very near future. For now, he would have to content himself by watching her from afar—or at least from a few rows behind and to her left.

She sat in profile, her long, sable eyelashes brushing lightly over her cheeks when she blinked, her straight nose, refined cheekbones and delicately rounded chin cast in lovely angles beneath the brim of her chip-straw bonnet.

On what was she planning to bid? he wondered. Some pretty little objet d'art, he supposed.

Then one of Mr. Christie's senior auctioneers stepped up to the podium and, with the forthright echo of his gavel, began the sale.

Thalia sat in her chair, resisting the temptation to bid as item after item was offered up to the eager crowd. There were dishes, vases, candlesticks and oil lamps; desks and dressers, paintings and portmanteaus, boxes and baubles and far too much more to contemplate. There were even some ancient antiquities from a small but impressive grouping that drove the bidding to eye-popping heights.

Lord Leopold was among those select few gentlemen with the means to bid on even the priciest of items. And he was crafty, hanging back until it seemed the sale was all but concluded, then swooping in with a couple of last-minute bids that decisively squashed the hopes of the final competitors.

She'd recognized the rich, brandied cadence of his voice the instant he spoke, and looked over her shoulder to discover Lord Leopold seated a few rows behind. Until then, she'd refused to look, not wanting to encourage him by seeking him out in the crowd—even if she had been aware that he was seated somewhere nearby.

When he made his first surprise bid, everyone in the room looked, so she was only one of a multitude. Yet his eyes found hers immediately as if he had been waiting all this time for her to turn her gaze upon him.

And he didn't look away, his eyes locked with her own in spite of the fact that he was still engaged in the bidding. He smiled with open pleasure when the gavel descended and the auctioneer announced him the winner. It was an expression of victory, satisfaction and command, and it shot straight through to her marrow.

She faced forward again, her fingers knotted in her lap.

Luckily, her maid didn't notice her reaction, her own head bent over her sewing, since she had absolutely no interest in the auction proceedings themselves.

Lord Leopold bid again—on a marble sculpture this time—but she refused to look. Instead she listened to the action, his voice the only one she really heard as he won once again.

The auction moved on, more items coming and going as she waited for the kitten trinket box to make an appearance. Then finally, there it was. She sat up straighter in her chair, her attention riveted.

"Next we have item number one hundred and eight, Meissen, hand-painted porcelain box with cats," the auctioneer said in his clear voice. "The bidding will open at twenty pounds. Who will give me twenty? Twenty? Anyone twenty?"

No one spoke, Thalia among them, since she knew better than to take the auctioneer's opening bait.

"Five pounds, then, for this exceptional Meissen box with its sweet pair of moggies? Do I have five pounds?" the auctioneer said, quartering the bid.

A man in the second row raised the numbered card with his bidder number.

"And I have five, thank you, fine sir. Who will give me five and a half? Five and a half . . . Do I have five and a half?"

A man on the opposite side raised his hand.

And on it went at a frenzied pace. Still, Thalia held back, pulse hurrying beneath her breasts as she waited for the right moment to jump in.

"I have ten . . . and a ten . . . and ten—"

Thalia lifted her card. "Fifteen," she said in a carrying voice.

The auctioneer smiled. "Fifteen! Excellent, madam.

Fifteen it is. Do we have fifteen and a half? Fifteen and a half . . ."

She held her breath, leaning forward onto the edge of her seat as she waited to see if the leap in price would be enough to scare off the other bidders. She hoped so, since she'd planned on bidding no more than twenty and would feel quite pleased if she could come away with it for less.

Two of the bidders had dropped out already. The last—another woman—sat with a frustrated expression, her round florid face turning even ruddier, red eyebrows scrunched together like a pair of badly knotted ribbons. She hesitated, clearly warring with herself over the price.

"Fifteen going once, going twice—"

"Sixteen."

The voice that rang out was new and distinctly male. To her shock, Thalia realized the man's identity without even having to look. And yet she couldn't stop herself from turning her head.

Lord Leopold looked straight at her.

"Sixteen from the gentleman in the back," the auctioneer cried. "Ladies, do we have seventeen?"

The redhead with the bad eyebrows frowned so hard it was a wonder her face didn't crack; then she shook her head.

She was out.

It was up to Thalia. She hesitated only a fraction of a second, then raised her bidder's number. "Seventeen."

"Eighteen," Lord Leopold said.

Thalia's jaw tightened. What was he doing bidding on her kitten trinket box? What possible use could he have for such a thing? Then it occurred to her. Was this his revenge for the other night? For her refusal of his overtures and the champagne she'd tossed in his face?

So much for wanting to start over.

"Nineteen," she said, the word hard and precise.

He barely waited for the auctioneer to confirm her bid before he spoke. "Twenty-five."

A little ripple of reaction went through the crowd, all eyes affixed to her and Lord Leopold.

Silently, she cursed.

Twenty-five? More than she wanted to pay. More than she could afford, if truth be known, since twenty pounds had been her top bid from the start. Yet it galled her, the idea of giving in to him, of letting him take something that belonged to her by rights and that had been stolen from her once already.

"Twenty-five going once, going twice—"

Was she really going to let him have her box?

"Thirty," she said, throwing aside the last of her common sense.

Renewed murmurs echoed. Then all was silent as everyone settled down, waiting for the next bid. Even the auctioneer paused for an extra moment before diving back into the action.

"Do we have more than thirty, my lord?" Christie's man asked. "Thirty-one? Will you go to thirty-one?"

And Lord Leopold's eyes met Thalia's once more, his own fierce and enigmatic as if the two of them were engaged in a battle that went far beyond the present moment.

She shivered, reading the barely concealed desire in his eyes. He wanted her; of that she had no doubt. And she sensed that he always got what he wanted, whether it be a porcelain trinket box or a woman who had taken his fancy.

"Fifty," he said in a deep, smooth voice.

Her shoulders sank.

It was over. She couldn't possibly pay more than that and he knew it. Fifty pounds was more than her cook's yearly salary, more than the cost of the coal she used to heat the house and the kitchen from autumn to spring, more than her allotment for food and sundries combined.

"Fifty once, fifty twice . . ." The gavel came down. "Sold."

She looked down at her hands, clenched tight in her lap. Fury and disappointment warred within her, knowing her father's lost gift was lost yet again.

And all because of Lord Leopold Byron.

She didn't know yet what game he thought he was playing, but he was in for a sad awakening and his own rude disappointment. She knew all about being a man's pawn and it was something she'd sworn never to be again.

Rising to her feet, she signaled to her maid. It was time to leave.

She didn't look at him, careful to keep her gaze directed straight ahead as she walked out of the salesroom, head held high.

To her relief, he didn't follow. But she knew her reprieve was only temporary. It was simply a matter of waiting for his next volley in this battle of wills they had begun.

Chapter 3

"Would you look at that?" Lord Lawrence Byron said two afternoons later.

He and Leo were finishing a late nuncheon in the study. Lawrence was ensconced in his favorite armchair near a sunlit window, Leo seated at a nearby table.

They had moved into their new bachelor quarters in Cavendish Square a few months earlier. The town house was far larger and much better appointed than their previous lodgings. It also gave them enough privacy that neither felt inconvenienced by the other's routine—although being twins, and close in a way only brothers could be, they never really minded each other's company.

"Look at what?" Leo asked absently as he ate the last few bites of an excellent beef pie.

"At the trio of Pocket Venuses who just came out of the house next door at"—Lawrence cast a glance toward the clock on the mantelpiece—"two o'clock in the afternoon."

Leo wiped his mouth on a napkin, then leaned over to look out the window at the females in question.

The trio of women—two blondes and a redhead—were giggling and talking as they climbed into a waiting coach in a colorful flurry of skirts. "They're pretty, to be sure, but why the interest? Beyond the obvious, of course," Leo said.

"Because I happen to have seen them arrive last night and they have only now emerged."

"Spent the night, did they? All three?" He waggled

his eyebrows and laughed. "You're just cranky because Northcote didn't invite you to the party."

"What party? Far as I could tell, they were the only guests."

Leo whistled. "You've got to hand it to him. He certainly knows how to enjoy himself."

"You and I know how to enjoy ourselves. Northcote is . . . well . . . the man is a complete reprobate."

Leo laughed again. "Complete, hmm? What does that make us? Partial reprobates?"

"Very funny," Lawrence said.

Leo smirked. "I don't have to worry, do I? You aren't in danger of turning Methodist on me or anything?"

Lawrence gave a derisive snort. "Hardly."

"Then what's with spying on Northcote? If you aren't careful, old Lady Higgleston will be complaining that you're trying to steal her thunder as the biggest pair of prying eyes in the neighborhood."

"Nobody could have a bigger pair of prying eyes than Lady Higgleston. Her front curtains twitch more than an aged beggar with the palsy. You know she has to have seen those playthings of Northcote's come trotting down his front steps just now. She'll probably be up all night writing the details to every Tom, Dick and Harry in a two-hundred-mile radius."

"I doubt the old girl knows any Toms, Dicks or Harrys, considering her general opinion of men." Leo grinned and leaned back in his chair. "It's really rather decent of Northcote to pull the limelight off us. Maybe we should send him a present. Box of French letters, do you think?"

He and Lawrence exchanged looks, then started laughing.

"You never did answer my question about spying on him," Leo said once he'd regained control of his voice.

"No, because I wasn't *spying*. Well, not the way you're implying. I was in here working on a case last night when his light-o'-loves arrived. It was rather difficult not to notice them."

"Oh, I'm sure. You just casually happened to note the time and everything, did you?"

Lawrence shot him a narrow-eyed glare, which Leo completely ignored.

"All I can say is the next time you run into Northcote, why don't you ask the man to be neighborly and share?" Leo said. "Or else invite your own coterie of ladyloves over."

Lawrence leaned back in his chair. "Two for me? One for you?"

"I'm not greedy—you can enjoy all three. I'm pursuing my own quarry at the moment and she's the only one I want right now."

Lawrence's gold and green eyes lit with understanding. "La Lennox, you mean? So you still haven't given up on that hopeless quest?"

"Not a bit. Why would I when I've only just begun? In fact, I'm sending her a little something special."

"Apology presents already? I take it this is for something more than the other night at Elmore's? What have you done now to vex her?"

"Vex" was a nice way to put matters, especially considering the expression on Lady Thalia's face when she'd walked out of the auction. She'd looked shocked and furious and curiously wounded.

He shouldn't have done it, he realized. He ought to have stepped back and let her win the bid. But he'd planned on buying the Meissen piece anyway and his natural competitiveness had asserted itself so that he just hadn't been able to resist. Besides, as he'd realized at the time, it gave him an excellent reason to contact her again, which he would not otherwise have had.

"I've done nothing that cannot be repaired," Leo said. "Anyway, her vexation only livens up the game."

His twin laughed. "I doubt she agrees."

"We'll see." Leo laid his napkin aside and got up from the table. "Now as much as I hate to end our conversation, I'm promised to meet with my estate manager. Wants to talk about crop rotation and how best to drain the southern fields for planting next spring. He should be here any minute."

"Ah, Brightvale. When you won it at the card table, I

bet you never imagined all the things you'd have to learn about property management, tenant relations and farming. Gives one new respect for our Ned."

"Believe me, he has my full respect and admiration. I thank my lucky stars that I wasn't born the duke. That's more responsibility than I'd ever want on my shoulders. Our brother wears the mantle well."

"Oh, I think you could take it on if you were put to the test."

"Me? The hedonistic wastrel? The unrepentant rake? I trust you won't be bandying that opinion about to any of our acquaintance or you'll have my reputation in tatters."

"What reputation?"

Leo grinned. "My point exactly."

"Will there be anything else, milady?" her maid asked after she set the tea tray on a small table in Thalia's study.

"No, thank you, Parker, this looks excellent."

While her maid let herself out of the room, Thalia went to the tray and poured a cup of hot, fresh Ceylon tea, steam curling upward from the beverage in misty tendrils. She added a splash of milk, then selected one of the butter cookies that Mrs. Grove had added to the tray. She bit off the end, the sweet golden crumbs melting deliciously against her tongue.

Rather than return to her desk, where the household account ledgers were stacked alongside a pile of bills and receipts in need of her attention, she carried her tea over to the window and gazed out at the garden beyond.

The tree branches were a riot of orange, yellow and red, fallen autumn leaves strewn in sere layers over the gravel walkway and small patches of grass. The neatly trimmed evergreen hedges were going dormant in preparation for the coming winter, the black wrought iron garden bench already too cold for sitting.

She would need to have the gardener come again to clear away the leaves. It would be a far easier matter to spare the money for his services now that she hadn't bought the Meissen trinket box.

Her fingers tightened on the cup handle, her mouth firming into a hard line. Regardless of how many times she told herself that the outcome of the auction was all for the best, that anyone might have outbid her and that she needed to put it all in the past, anger still flared inside her each and every time she thought of Lord Leopold Byron.

Clearly he'd known she wanted the Meissen piece and yet he'd decided to go toe-to-toe with her, upping the bid again and again with an arrogant surety that he would win.

At least it had cost him fifty pounds.

Of course to him fifty pounds was probably pocket change, an amount he could afford to lose on a whim and forget without a second thought. He'd been born into one of the wealthiest, most influential families in England and was now apparently rich in his own right in spite of being a younger son. No doubt he was used to getting everything he wanted, including his own way.

She scowled and drank her tea.

Oh well, she thought, determined to put the whole thing out of her mind. Pretty as it might be, the trinket box was just a decorative whimsy. As for the sentimental value, she would simply have to remember the day her father had given it to her and all the memories that had come afterward. No one could take that from her.

And she'd lost worse, she reminded herself. Much, much worse. Wounds that cut clean through to the soul and left scars that would never fully heal. Considered in that light, losing the trinket box was nothing more than a minor disappointment.

Suddenly, a quiet meow came from the other side of the glass, interrupting her thoughts. Thalia looked down to find a pair of round, green eyes gazing hopefully at her out of a furry brown-and-black-striped face.

"Hera," she said, smiling. "Have you been out in the garden stalking squirrels again?"

The cat gave her a look of complete innocence and meowed again.

"Well, come in." She set down her cup, then twisted

the latch and opened the window. "Gotten chilled, have you?"

With a sinuous grace, the cat moved inside and leapt down onto the floor on silent paws. She circled around Thalia, brushing up against her skirts.

Thalia closed the window, then bent down to stroke the cat's sleek coat, eliciting rumbling purrs. "You're getting fur all over my skirts, you know. Parker will purse her lips like a lemon and complain about you when she sees the mess you've left."

Hera made another circuit around Thalia's skirts and meowed one more time.

"Oh never mind, she'll just have to understand," Thalia said. "What's a little cat hair between friends?" She petted Hera again and earned a head nuzzle into her hand. "I need to see to some correspondence. Care to join me?"

Thalia walked toward her desk. The little tabby followed and was up on the desk before Thalia had time to take a seat. Hera settled in one corner atop a pair of leather-bound books; it was a routine that was comfortable and familiar to them both.

Thalia regarded the account books and bills with a baleful eye. Then sighing in resignation, she reached for the first bill.

She'd been working for nearly half an hour when a tap came at the door. Glancing up, she saw her butler hovering near the threshold.

"Yes? What is it, Fletcher?"

He came forward slowly, a box held in his wizened hands. "A special delivery for you, milady."

"Really? How unusual." With the exception of holidays and her birthday, she never received gifts. "Did the messenger say who sent it?"

"There is a card, I believe." Fletcher set the package with its gaily tied, gold satin bow in front of her on the desk. Quietly, he withdrew.

She eyed the package for a moment, admiring the sophisticated elegance of the wrappings. Even more inviting was the nosegay of fresh purple violas secured underneath the ribbon; she touched the little flowers, finding their petals velvety soft.

A curious tingle of suspicion went through her, but she ignored it and tugged free the bow. After taking an extra moment to set the nosegay carefully aside, she lifted off the lid.

And there it was, nestled inside a protective cocoon of crumpled vellum and white silk—the Meissen trinket box. She recognized the tiny painted kitten paws and ball of red yarn first before she peeled back the silk to reveal the rest.

A silent inhalation of breath caught in her lungs, her heart giving an odd knock inside her chest.

She didn't need to open the card to know who had sent the gift. But she reached for it anyway, unfolding the paper to see what was written inside.

> *My Dearest Lady Thalia,*
>
> *Please accept this token of my esteem. I could not keep it, knowing that you would cherish it more.*
>
> *Ever Your Servant,*
> *L.B.*

She sat unmoving for a long moment, digesting his words and the fact that the trinket box, *her* trinket box, was in her possession once again.

After laying down the card, she reached for it. With utmost care, she lifted out the delicate piece of porcelain. She hadn't been able to touch it at the auction, not the way she'd wished, not holding it as she did now in a full, open, unhindered way. Reverent and admiring. The little box was exactly as she remembered, the paints just as bright, the expressions on the kittens' faces just as sweet and mischievous as ever.

She ran a fingertip over one feline back, memories crashing over her in waves. Then she sighed aloud, longing coursing through her with an almost tangible ache.

Oh, how she wished she could carry it upstairs to her keepsake cabinet and place it inside.

But a present such as this quite naturally came with strings. If she kept it, Lord Leopold would expect more. First supper, perhaps, then attendance at a play or maybe a drive in the park. Next an invitation to her town house.

Then finally into her bed.

She had no doubt what it would mean if she accepted this gift. He'd bought the trinket box for fifty pounds and if she took it, he would be buying her as well.

But she was not for sale.

Calling forth every ounce of resolve at her disposal, she set the porcelain with its familiar kittens inside the box, tucked it back into its nest of protective silk and vellum and replaced the lid. She secured the ribbon around the package again and tied it neatly, though not with the same expert skill the original wrapper had used.

She stood and crossed to ring the bell.

Fletcher appeared a short time later, almost as if he had known she would have need of him again.

"See that this is returned." She held the package out to him. "The sender's name is Lord Leopold Byron. I presume you can locate his address here in Town?"

"Certainly, milady. Consider it done."

"And be careful. The item inside is fragile."

Fletcher nodded. "Of course. The utmost care shall be taken."

It was only after he had gone that she noticed the nosegay of flowers. Another token from Lord Leopold, something else she could not accept. Picking them up, she moved to her wastepaper basket. But even as she reached to toss them inside, she stopped. They were so pretty and it had been such a very long while since she'd had fresh flowers in the house—another unnecessary extravagance.

What is the harm? she thought, stroking one of the petals again. Even overprotective mamas of innocent young girls had no objection to flowers. And heaven knew she was no naive, innocent young debutante.

Flowers meant nothing.

Carrying them back to her desk, she went to find a vase.

Early evening darkness obscured the dressing room windows as Leo finished tying a last knot in his cravat. He was promised for dinner and cards tonight with a group of his cronies. There would likely be further gambling and carousing afterward, but in spite of his justifiably wild reputation, he didn't frequent brothels. Far too great a chance of picking up one of the unspeakable diseases that made the rounds in such establishments. He insisted on women of a better class who were clean and healthy. And if truth be known, he'd grown tired of quick, meaningless couplings. He preferred knowing any woman he took to his bed.

Turning, he allowed his valet to assist him into his black evening coat. The servant had just picked up a brush to remove any lingering specks of lint when a knock came at the door.

One of the footmen stood on the threshold. "Pardon me, my lord, but this was just delivered for you."

Leo eyed the small lidded box, recognizing it instantly by its familiar gold bow. "Was there a note?"

"No, my lord," the servant told him. "Just the package."

"Set it over there," he said, gesturing toward a small table.

The servant did as instructed, then withdrew.

Leo waited until his valet left before he opened the box and peered inside.

Well, damn, so she sent it back.

Here he'd hoped his offering would please her, since she'd clearly wanted the little porcelain piece. Her expression had been one of acute disappointment after she'd lost the bidding to him. So despite his original plan to give the trinket box with its kitten duo to Esme, he had known he would offer it as a token to Lady Thalia instead.

But apparently she was having none of it, her attitude toward him as remote and unyielding as ever. At least her rebuff hadn't been cold and wet and from a champagne flute this time.

Well, he hadn't expected that his pursuit of Lady Thalia would be easy. After all, any prize worth attaining demanded an extra measure of effort — and she was most definitely a worthy prize.

Reaching into the box, he withdrew the Meissen piece. He would keep it for now and be patient. The day would come when Lady Thalia wanted both him and his gifts.

Chapter 4

"Here we are, milady," the coachman said a week later as he held open the carriage door.

Thalia gazed out at the immense Jacobean mansion that was located in the still countrified west side of London. The great house gleamed like a beacon of stone and glass in the waning autumn light. Even at this time of year, its exceptionally well-tended grounds, with their prized dahlia bushes, were a sight to behold.

She had never been to Holland House before but knew of its stellar reputation as a gathering place of Whig politicians, intellectuals and artists. Many agreed that it even rivaled the celebrated salons of Continental Europe for its influence and gracious style.

She'd been surprised when she'd received the invitation to attend this weekend's gathering. Once, many years before, she had received another such invitation to join Lord and Lady Holland at their estate, but she had refused. At the time, she'd been sunk too deep in scandal and despair to wish for company. Her pride had also stopped her from accepting what she'd seen then as an act of pity.

Now she realized that she might have been foolish to assume that to have been the Hollands' only motivation, particularly given the social disgrace they themselves had endured. After all, she and Lady Holland shared something unique. They both had the dubious distinction of knowing what it was like to be divorced and cut off from polite society. Unlike Thalia, however, Lady Holland had been fortunate enough to escape a bad marriage in exchange for a happy one. The Hollands might be outcasts from the high sticklers of the *Ton*, but no one could dispute that theirs was a love match.

I wonder if I might have found a sympathetic ear all those years ago? Maybe I still might.

But it was curiosity, rather than a need for kindred spirits, that had led her to accept their present invitation.

That and her old nemesis—boredom.

She could spend only so much time writing letters to absent friends or curled up on the sofa with her cat and a book from Hookham's lending library before madness began to set in.

Then there was the loneliness—the other pitchforked devil on her shoulder.

A weekend in the country, among interesting people, had seemed an excellent restorative. And maybe if she was very lucky, she would make some new friends. She could use someone new in her life.

For reasons she couldn't begin to fathom, thoughts of Lord Leopold Byron popped into her head. She'd heard no more from him since she had returned the trinket box. She'd thought he might attempt to contact her, try to persuade her to reconsider her refusal to accept his gift. But there had been nothing—no notes, no visits, no further tokens of his supposed admiration. Apparently he'd given up his pursuit.

Which was just as she wished it, of course.

So why was he still on her mind?

Aware that her coachman was still waiting for her to alight from the carriage, she allowed him to help her down. At the same moment, the Hollands' butler and a pair of liveried footmen emerged from the house and hurried forward.

"Welcome to Holland House," the black-clad butler said with a genial smile. "If you will come inside, the housekeeper will show you to your room. Lord and Lady Holland will be receiving guests in the drawing room at seven."

"Thank you."

Taking one last look at the beautiful grounds, Thalia followed the servant into the house.

Three hours later, Thalia stood inside the luxuriously appointed drawing room.

She had met Lord and Lady Holland on her entrance. The middle-aged couple was all gracious smiles and kind words. They had put her immediately at her ease, despite Lady Holland's reputation for having a blunt tongue and rapier wit.

"You know, Lady Thalia," Lord Holland remarked while they chatted, "I believe you and I are distant cousins through the Lennox side of the family. Considering the connection, we ought to have done this far sooner."

Thalia smiled. "You are right. I wish that we had. The fault, I fear, is my own."

"Not a bit. You are here now, so that is all that counts."

Knowing there would be plenty of time to become better acquainted over the next couple of days, Lord and Lady Holland had moved on to greet their other guests. Thalia recognized a few of the numerous attendees, including the former prime minister and several lauded artists and writers.

"Champagne?" a footman inquired.

Thalia accepted a glass from a silver tray. As the servant moved away, she wondered how much longer dinner would be. She'd had nothing but a cup of tea and a small sandwich since breakfast and she was starved. She laid a hand on the waist of her blue velvet evening gown and hoped her stomach wouldn't disgrace her by rumbling.

"If I stop to offer my felicitations, will you promise not to throw that drink on me?" a silvery male voice said from behind her.

Thalia turned and met the bold green-gold eyes of Lord Leopold Byron.

"I forgot to pack extra neckclothes," he continued, "and have enough only to get me through the next three days."

Her heart thumped. *Lord, what is he doing here! So much for not seeing him again.*

Yet there he stood, looking tall and elegant in formal black and white. His gold embroidered waistcoat made a perfect foil for the dark golden brown of his hair. He smiled a moment later, the movement lighting up his entire face.

Seeing that smile hit her, as it always did, like a quick poke to the solar plexus.

My, but he's handsome. And what a simpleton I am for noticing.

She sent him an arch look, suddenly out of sorts with him and herself. "You may offer your felicitations if you wish, Lord Leopold, since I cannot prevent you. As for the drink, I never make promises I'm not certain I can keep."

Rather than take offense, much as he had at their last encounter, he laughed, his deep-set eyes alight with humor. "Then I shall take care to be on my guard, ready to stand clear at a moment's notice."

"Have a lot of experience with that, do you?"

"Only with you, curiously enough." He smiled with roguish amusement. "I never did get that neckcloth you promised me. Perhaps I shall have to demand another sort of recompense while we are here together. A dance perhaps?"

"Will there be dancing? In that case, I shall have to make sure my card is completely filled."

He grinned. "Come now, I thought we'd laid down arms last week. I like to consider us a good way along the path to being friends."

"Then you must have a much shorter path in mind than I do."

"I did give the Meissen box to you, if you'll recall. You are the one who decided to refuse it."

"Because it was vastly improper of you to give it to me in the first place."

He gave her another slow, wicked smile. "Have you not yet realized, dear Lady Thalia, how vastly improper I am?

Just say the word and we can be vastly improper together."

She stared for a long moment, unable to decide whether to toss another flute of champagne in his face or just laugh.

Humor won the day.

She gave a wry laugh. "What an amazing optimist you are, Lord Leopold."

"I'm a fatalist as well. Only see how providence keeps setting us in each other's path?"

"Providence has nothing to do with it."

"Are you sure?" he insisted. "How else do you account for us finding ourselves here together?"

"Invitations from Lord and Lady Holland perhaps?"

"Touché," he said, awarding the point to her. "Still, this party does give us another opportunity to further our acquaintance."

"And what makes you think I have any wish to know you better? Find another woman on whom you can work your wiles. One who will be dazzled to receive your attentions."

He gazed into her eyes. "Ah, but therein lies the rub." His voice deepened, pitched for her ears alone. "I don't want anyone else. I have my sights set squarely on *you*."

Her heart beat faster, unwanted tingles racing over her skin, though she was careful to let none of her reactions show on her face.

"As for my attentions," he went on, "I think you are far more receptive to them than you care to admit."

"Then you are delusional as well as overly optimistic."

He leaned closer, his height causing her to tip back her head. "Agree to spend time with me and we will see which one of us is deluded," he said. "Why do we not begin now? Let me take you in to dinner, where we can continue this highly illuminating conversation."

She shook her head. "I'll grant you one thing, Lord Leopold: you do not lack for confidence. What a pity for you that I am promised to accompany someone else to the dining room tonight."

His eyes narrowed. "Tell me who it is and I shall make certain he relinquishes his seat to me."

She shook her head again. "Lady Holland wouldn't allow it. Now, shh, the gentleman approaches."

Thank heavens for her hostess, Thalia thought, Lady Holland having already chosen a gentleman to accompany her in to dinner. In addition to the usual protocol concerning such things, she was attending the party alone and had need of a reliable escort. Having a prearranged partner made everything so much easier, particularly now that she knew Lord Leopold was one of the guests.

"Mr. Hetford," she said, putting far more enthusiasm into her greeting than she would normally have done. "His lordship and I were just talking about you and here you are."

Hetford sent her a mildly surprised look, his rounded features and bushy brown eyebrows putting her in mind of a grouse. "Good things, I hope?"

"Only the best." Thalia gave Hetford another fulsome smile that caused him to blink repeatedly as if he'd looked directly into the sun. She slipped her arm through his. "I see that Lady Holland is leading the procession into dinner. Shall we follow?"

"With pleasure." Hetford smiled widely.

Perhaps rather too widely.

She resisted the urge to sigh, aware she would have to be careful not to encourage him further during the meal. She certainly didn't need Hetford chasing after her too.

Looking up, she met Lord Leopold's eyes.

Rather than glowering, however, he looked amused, as if he was fully aware of what she was doing. Somehow the knowledge disturbed her more than if he'd simply been jealous.

"If you will excuse us, Lord Leopold," she said in a deliberately lighthearted voice.

"Indeed, Lady Thalia. You may be excused." He angled his large body so that his mouth was near her ear. "For now."

A shiver trailed down her spine.

Ignoring the reaction, she turned her back and let Mr. Hetford escort her from the room.

"Still winning her over, I see," Leo heard a voice say, one that sounded remarkably like his own. "You've got her trotting at your heels like an adorable Yorkshire terrier. Is Lady Thalia from Yorkshire, do you think?"

Leo swung around to face his twin. "Don't be such an ass."

"I believe there is only one of those in the room tonight and I'm looking at him."

"If that's the case, then find a handy mirror. You'll be able to see him again."

Lawrence laughed. "When you said you had business at Holland House, I ought to have known she was involved. And here I was hoping you had decided to take an interest in politics after all."

"Everyone is going in to dinner," Leo said, ignoring his brother's last remark. "We should join them."

Lawrence nodded. The two of them started forward.

"Since you aren't making any real progress with Lady Thalia," Lawrence said after a minute, "maybe I ought to try my luck with her. If she doesn't care for one twin, perhaps the other will do."

Leo stopped and grabbed hold of Lawrence's arm. "Don't you dare. She's out of bounds to you, do you understand? I am not sharing."

His brother's eyes widened. "Here now, there's no need for that. I was only joking."

Leo forced himself to loosen his grip. He wasn't sure where the sudden burst of fury had come from, but without warning, the emotion had burned through him as hot and quick as a fireball. A curious sensation, really, since he wasn't used to being jealous, especially not of his own brother.

"Yes, well, I knew that," he said stiffly.

"Good." Lawrence beat a hand over his abused coat sleeve to remove the creases. "I wouldn't want to have to hurt you."

"As if you could." Leo made a disdainful noise. "Remember the black eye I gave you when we were ten?"

"Remember the bruised ribs I gave you?"

His side twinged for a moment with ghostly pain. Yes, he remembered, along with various other rough-and-tumble brawls they'd had over the years—most of them nothing more than good-natured horseplay.

"Thalia wouldn't have you anyway," Leo said.

"Oho, so she's Thalia now, is she? Are you making more progress with her than I thought?"

"Enough. These things take time."

"True, but how long are you prepared to wait? At the rate you're proceeding, it may take an eternity."

Leo cuffed him. "I should never have told you I was going to be away for a few days. I ought to have packed my bags and departed without leaving so much as a note."

"That would have been most unbrotherly of you. I would have worried."

"No, you wouldn't. Not for a week at least," Leo stated.

"Four days. Even if you're off carousing, you always manage to surface long enough to send word that you're still among the living. After four days, I'd feel obligated to start a search."

"I'd do the same for you, though I wouldn't wait more than two. You're far too responsible not to leave a note. Must be the barrister in you."

Lawrence's step slowed and he moved to one side to allow a last trickle of guests to funnel past them into the dining room. "I do have one more question, though."

Leo arched a brow. "Oh, only one?"

Lawrence brushed off the sarcasm. "How many favors did you have to call in to get Lady Thalia invited to this party?"

Leo stilled. "Why do you think I had anything to do with it? Maybe she was already on the guest list."

"Do give me some credit. The Hollands have a cadre of regular guests who visit and she isn't one of them. Which leaves your mark stamped all over the matter. Does she realize?"

"No." Leo's jaw tightened. "And you aren't going to tell her."

"What do I get for staying silent?"

"Continued good health. Promise you'll hold your tongue."

Lawrence shrugged and crossed his arms over his chest. "I don't know. Seems there ought to be something in it for me."

"You're a bastard, do you know that?"

"Guess that makes two of us, then, seeing as we once shared a womb."

"Fine. You can name your price later."

Lawrence grinned, his arms falling to his sides. "I'll hold you to that, you know."

Leo glared at him. "Come on. If we're any later, we'll cause a scene."

"It wouldn't be the first time." Still chuckling, Lawrence followed Leo into the dining room.

Chapter 5

Over the years, both before and after the divorce, Thalia had endured the watchful gazes of a great many people—most particularly men. But never in her life had she found herself the focus of two individuals who looked exactly alike, down to the last eyelash and dimple. Even their mannerisms were the same!

Yet there they sat opposite her, the Byron twins, one at either end of the Hollands' long, magnificently decorated dining table. Neither man was impolite enough to stare directly at her, of course, but still she felt their unique gazes on her at all too frequent intervals.

Clearly one brother is as impertinent as the other, she decided as she stabbed the tines of her fork into the excellent fillet of beef on her plate. *Really, they ought to keep their eyes to themselves.*

But why was she letting the Byron twins bother her? It wasn't like her to be troubled by such things—or rather such men.

Inclining her head, she nodded at something Mr. Hetford was saying. She had discovered that maintaining a conversation with him didn't require much work; the man never seemed to stop talking except to draw breath.

The gentleman on her left wasn't much better, but for the opposite reason. Despite being a poet of some repute—she actually owned a copy of his latest book of sonnets—he had curiously little to say for himself. It would seem he preferred to let his verse do all his talking.

As a result, she had plenty of time to watch the Bryon brothers when they weren't busy watching her.

At first, she'd puzzled over which man was which. After all, they truly were identical twins. But the longer she studied them, the more confident she became that she could distinguish the one from the other.

Lord Leopold's brother—she still didn't know his given name—seemed the quieter of the two, taking more time to listen to his dinner companions than did Lord Leopold. He also had an interesting habit of running the tip of one finger along the table edge in between courses. Yet it was his eyes that had given the game away. They weren't quite as green as Lord Leopold's—with rings that were more the golden hue of a stalking cat. And unlike his brother, he didn't look at her with desire, but with curiosity instead.

As for Lord Leo, his green-gold eyes gleamed with a sensual hunger every time they fixed on her. In those moments, she found the force of his gaze almost shocking in its intensity. It was as if he would much rather be feasting on her than on his dinner.

A fine tremor ran just under her skin at the thought, her fingers tightening on her fork again.

"This might seem an impertinent question, Lady Thalia, but is there some . . . well . . . connection between you and Lord Leopold Byron?" Mr. Hetford asked, his question abruptly riveting her attention.

She met his gaze. "No. Why would you imagine that?"

Unless he had noticed the way Lord Leopold and his brother had been watching her. And if *he* had, then who else had?

"Well, it is just that . . ." Hetford's words trailed off.

"Yes? Just what?"

Why didn't he simply come out and say what he was thinking instead of all this hesitation? It was amazingly annoying.

"I did wonder why Lady Holland asked *me* to take you in to dinner."

"And why would she not?"

"It is . . . um . . ."

She ground her teeth. "Yes?"

"It is my understanding that you were invited here at the express wish of Lord Leopold. When I saw the two of you talking earlier, it did make me wonder whether you and he might have—how should I put this?—an arrangement?"

Air rushed from her lungs. "I beg your pardon?"

"Yes, from what I understand, he approached one of Holland's closest cronies and specifically requested your inclusion in the festivities here," he continued. "The person who told me said the information wasn't supposed to go any further, but since it applies to you directly, I didn't see the harm." A row of small lines creased Hetford's brow. "You don't mind that I mentioned it, do you?"

She sent him a warm smile, one that caused him to blink several times in a row. "Of course not. I am glad that you did." Underneath the table, her fingers curled into a fist, her nails biting into her skin.

So Lord Leopold had made arrangements, had he? Why, that impudent, arrogant scoundrel. How dare he manipulate her in such a brazen manner? The gall of exposing her to ridicule and speculation when Lord knew she'd had more than enough of that to last her a lifetime.

Long practice was the only reason she managed to keep her features calm, a serene smile on her lips despite the fact that her dinner was turning to acid in her stomach. Quietly, she laid down her fork and let the footman remove her plate.

As for Lord Leopold, she refused to cast so much as a single glance his way. If only she had it all to do over, she would have thrown tonight's glass of champagne in his face when she'd had the chance, after all.

Or maybe poured it over his overinflated head!

Of course everything made sense now about the invitation. She'd wondered at Lord and Lady Holland's sudden wish to include her in one of their gatherings. If only she'd put more thought into their possible motivations.

Or rather Lord Leopold's motivations.

Did he think she wouldn't find out? Or did he just not care? Surely he must have considered how word would spread. Or was that his plan? Did he imagine that if everyone thought she was his mistress, she would unbend in her opposition to him and agree to the arrangement in truth?

Well, he was in for a rude awakening on that score. See if she spoke a civil word to him for the rest of the party.

Even so, a frigid rebuff on her part didn't seem adequate enough recompense. She'd refused him numerous times already and he'd brushed it off like a duck feathering aside raindrops. No, she would need to do something more. Exact some appropriate measure of revenge. One he would not soon forget.

But what?

Hetford shifted in his seat, angling his body ever so slightly closer. "So . . . um . . . are you and Lord Leopold . . . that is . . . are you friends?"

Lovers, she knew he meant.

"No," she said in a frosty voice. "We most definitely are not."

"Ah." A small silence fell. "Then perhaps you and I might take time to further our own acquaintance."

Her fingernails dug into her palms again. She summoned another pleasant smile. "We could, but aren't you married, Mr. Hetford?"

"Well, yes, but that need not deter us."

Now she wished she could pour wine over *his* head. Loathsome man.

"True, but what if your wife were to hear rumors?" she asked.

"She's at our country estate with the children. It's unlikely she'd hear anything."

Thalia paused as if she were considering his suggestion. "Then again, word does travel, even when one doesn't wish it to. Terrible shame if she were to receive a letter from some anonymous individual, telling her how you've really been spending your autumn here in the city."

He scowled.

"Then too there is your father-in-law. Did he not play an active and influential part in helping you win your seat in the House of Commons? Close, aren't they, your wife and her father?"

He flinched, then scrubbed a finger against the side of his cheek. "Yes, very close."

"Then I doubt he would like hearing rumors about you and me." She sighed and shook her head. "No, I think it best if we say no more on this subject. Or any of the others we've been discussing tonight for that matter. Agreed?"

His eyes narrowed, his skin mottled with an odd mix of red and white. After a moment, he gave a jerky nod.

She smiled. "Good. Ah, look now, I believe they are about to serve the cheese and sweet."

But Hetford wore a sour expression that made her doubt he was in the mood to partake of either. Deliberately, he turned his attention toward his dining partner on the other side.

Without thinking, she glanced up and into the vivid green and gold of Lord Leopold's eyes. Her pulse beat out a traitorous tattoo that warned her to look away. Instead, she met his boldness with boldness of her own, lifting a brow in sudden confrontation.

His lips curved. Slowly he raised his glass and took a drink. She did the same, an idea forming in her mind as the cool liquid passed over her tongue and down her throat.

The action allowed her to break away, her lashes sweeping down to conceal her expression. And in that instant, she knew exactly what she was going to do.

Leo watched Thalia from where he sat on the opposite side of the dining table. She'd surprised him when she'd met his gaze and held it. For a moment, there had been a definite measure of sensual challenge in her eyes before she had looked away, much to his disappointment.

By Christ, what a beauty she is, he thought.

Leaning back in his chair, he once again admired the pale creaminess of her skin and the lustrous sheen of her updrawn hair, which lay as dark as a raven's wing against her head. Her mouth was lush, as ripe and sweet as cherries. He'd been craving a taste of her ever since he'd sat down for the meal. What he wouldn't give to get her alone.

One of the footmen laid the next course in front of him.

Across the table, another servant did the same for Thalia. Fruit and cheese were arranged on her plate. He didn't bother looking to confirm that he had received the same.

A new vintage of wine was poured. He raised the drink to his lips.

Thalia picked up her fork and sank the tines into a grape. She lifted the fruit to her mouth. Rather than eat it, though, she ran the grape slowly along her bottom lip, back and forth, then back and forth again.

Arousal pulsed through him, blood warming in his veins.

Her eyes met his again—hers a warm, sultry brown that reminded him of the sleekest, softest mink.

Her tongue slid out and swirled around the grape, then she began sucking on it, moving it between her lips.

He turned instantly hard, feeling as if her tongue were swirling around his shaft instead of the fruit. Beneath the table, he fisted his hand against one taut thigh.

She didn't look away as she ate the grape, then reached for another. She slowly licked that one too.

His erection gave another painful throb.

Siren, he thought. She certainly knew how to torment a man. He looked forward to returning the favor one of these times soon. He could almost hear her breathy little gasps of pleasure now.

Reaching out, he picked up his glass of wine. With his eyes still locked on hers, he raised the goblet in a silent salute, then tossed back the contents in a deep, single swallow.

She blinked, her tongue stilling for a moment on the grape before she popped it into her mouth and chewed.

A dozen footmen soon arrived to clear the course from the table. Then it was time for the sweet.

Leo eyed the array of sugary treats laid before them, including a particularly creamy-looking chocolate mousse. He nearly groaned as Lady Thalia reached for her spoon.

He was going to need more wine.

Chapter 6

It was working even better than she'd imagined, Thalia realized as she picked up her spoon.

Maybe a little too well.

From across the table she felt Lord Leopold's jewel-bright gaze move over her like a slow caress. His eyelids were heavy with undisguised desire as he leaned casually back in his chair, drinking his wine and watching her.

What had begun as a game had taken a quick turn into dangerous waters. But she wasn't going to back down now. He deserved every bit of torment she could dish out. Then again, the devil didn't look as if he seemed to mind. In fact, he seemed to be enjoying himself despite all the other people in the room.

Well, she would see if she could rattle his indomitable composure with this next course.

Dipping her spoon into the chocolate mousse, Thalia brought the confection to her lips and ran her tongue around it in long, slow gliding licks. She took her time, savoring every melting bit before she stuck the spoon into her mouth and sucked against it in a way that momentarily hollowed out her cheeks. The creamy sweet melted delectably in her mouth. She slid the spoon out again, then paused to run the edge of her tongue around the perimeter of her lips in a slow, wet glide.

Lord Leopold's eyes widened ever so slightly and he swallowed, his Adam's apple moving up and down beneath his cravat. He shifted fractionally in his chair. A distinctly predatory expression came over his face as if he wanted to vault across the table and drag her out of the room so he could have his way with her.

An unexpected shiver went through her, warmth curling in her veins at the thought.

Truthfully, she hadn't realized how easy it would be to arouse him. In spite of her reputation as an unprincipled temptress, this was the first time she'd ever tried to tease a man sexually. Gordon had never inspired such amorous play and after the divorce, she'd kept well clear of entanglements with men despite their best efforts to attract her. She was tired of being manipulated. She'd had more than enough of being controlled to last her a lifetime.

Which was why she was going to teach Lord Leopold a much-deserved lesson. By the time this party was through, he would be grateful to see the last of her. And she would be equally grateful to be rid of him.

Sliding her spoon into the mousse once more, she ate another bite at a slow, tortuous pace, aware of Lord Leopold's keen gaze upon her.

Then she laid her spoon aside and smiled across at him, deciding she'd made more than a satisfactory start to her plan.

Leo relaxed in his chair, paying only partial attention to the conversation around him. The ladies had withdrawn, leaving the gentlemen to their port and cigars. He supposed it was for the best, since he wasn't sure how much more of Lady Thalia's teasing he could have withstood.

When Lady Holland had signaled for the women to leave the dining room, he'd been of half a mind to follow. He was sure there would have been some way to single out Lady Thalia, then convince her to find a secluded spot where they could tryst. Or better still, retire upstairs to one of the bedchambers.

At this very moment, he could have had her lying naked and writhing beneath him amid warm silken sheets. Her little gasps of pleasure sounding in his ears as he sank himself deep into her aching flesh, her long arms and lush white thighs wrapped tightly around him.

Presuming, of course, that she really had changed her mind and was now receptive to his amorous overtures. Clearly, she was playing games; he just wasn't sure yet what kind.

A short while later, Lord Holland drank a last swallow of port, then suggested all the men adjourn to the drawing room to rejoin the ladies. As Leo stood to leave, Lawrence came up beside him.

"Interesting evening so far," Lawrence remarked. "I eat my words about Lady Thalia ignoring you, no pun intended considering we just finished dinner."

Leo shot him a glance, then started from the room. Lawrence fell into step at his side.

"Couldn't help but notice the ... umm ... performance she put on during dessert," Lawrence said in a low voice. "I half expected the air to combust between the two of you and melt everyone's pudding."

Leo's skin warmed at the memory, a slow smile moving across his lips. "She does have a way with a dessert spoon, doesn't she?"

"That she does." Lawrence smiled briefly before his expression sobered again. "Look, I won't waste my breath trying to warn you off her again, since I can see you're determined to seek out the devil in your own way."

"You know me and the devil," Leo quipped. "We're old friends."

"Be that as it may, you need to remember that there's far more to a woman than the comeliness of her face."

"I am well aware of the many and varied facets that make up the feminine half of humanity. You're not turning philosopher on me, are you?"

"No, just doing my duty as your brother. By the way, I've decided to return home in the morning."

"But we only just arrived."

Lawrence shrugged. "This is your show. You'll enjoy yourself far more without me around."

Leo smiled. "Come to think, you're right."

"I always am."

After entering the drawing room, he and Lawrence separated—Lawrence to find a few of his friends, while Leo went in search of Lady Thalia.

He found her seated on a gold damask sofa between a pair of gentlemen who were avidly vying for her attention. A lighthearted laugh rippled from her throat at something one of them had just said.

Leo came to a halt before her. She didn't bother to look up, her interest apparently fixed on the man's next words. The fellow murmured something in her ear that sent her into gales again.

Leo ignored his rivals and made her a bow.

She took a sip from the glass of ruby-hued cordial in her hand and responded to a new remark, this time from the man on her left.

Leo's jaw tightened. So she was back to ignoring him again, was she? Blowing hot, then cold, in whatever game she had now decided to play.

"Lady Thalia," Leo said in a voice with too much authority to be dismissed.

A long moment passed before she raised her caramel brown eyes to his. "Lord Leopold."

"I was wondering if you would accompany me for a stroll in the garden?"

He wanted her alone, wanted to know exactly what she'd been about toying with him tonight and what she was planning on doing next. He, on the other hand, wanted to kiss her—long and hard and deeply enough to find out if she still tasted like chocolate mousse.

"A stroll?" she said. "Now? Thank you, my lord, but no. I'm afraid it's far too cold."

"Then I shall have one of the footmen fetch your cloak." He refused to be daunted.

"It is October. I do not walk out in October."

"You didn't seem to mind the other day when we attended the Christie's auction together."

Her sofa companions' ears seemed to perk up at that bit of news.

Her dark brows furrowed. "We did not attend *together* and the event was held indoors."

"Still, we had a most entertaining conversation," he said affably. "Very well, if you won't come out to the gardens, then let us take a tour of the house. The Hollands have an excellent picture gallery."

Her luminous eyes glittered. "So I have heard. Another time perhaps. I am quite comfortable where I am."

Stubborn minx. Thought she could tease him, then brush him aside, did she? She needed to learn that he was every inch as stubborn as she and then some.

"All right, since you insist, I shall join you here," he said.

Unfortunately, the only unoccupied chair was several feet distant. With his hands tucked behind his back, he stood as she inclined her head to continue her conversation with the other two men.

Leo fixed his gaze on Wilcox, a redhead with badly freckled skin and pale blue eyes. Wilcox glanced up at him, then away, looking distinctly uncomfortable that he was being watched. He responded to something Thalia said, but his words lacked the proper focus and enthusiasm as if his thoughts were elsewhere.

He reminded Leo of a cornered hare, while Leo, in this instance, was the fox.

"Wilcox," Leo said, breaking into the conversation a minute later, "Lady Thalia could do with another refreshment. Why don't you go get her one."

Wilcox met his eyes, an entire row of the freckles disappearing into the sudden creases on his forehead. "I beg your pardon?"

"No need to beg my pardon, it is Lady Thalia who is parched." Leo stared, using his height and muscled physique to add power to his intimidating expression.

"There is no need—," Thalia began.

Leo didn't look away from Wilcox. "She's waiting. You don't want to disappoint her, do you?"

Wilcox swallowed, a mixture of outrage and alarm on his face. For despite being older than Leo by several years, he was no match when it came to a battle of dominance.

Wilcox rarely took on a fight and, as everyone knew, still did the bidding of his domineering mother. Perhaps that's why he had yet to marry, because she had yet to approve of a bride. She certainly wouldn't like it if she knew he was flirting with the notorious Thalia Lennox.

Wilcox's weak chin trembled as he decided whether to tell Leo to go straight to hell. Suddenly, Wilcox looked away—the staring duel apparently done. Huffing out a breath, Wilcox stood, executed a stiff bow and stalked away.

Casually, Leo turned his sights on Lady Thalia's other companion, Lord Stanley. He'd seen him a few times over the years at White's Club, but they were no more than passing acquaintances. Stanley was stocky with a head of thick black hair and had far more confidence than Wilcox could ever hope to muster. At the moment he looked amused, leaning back against the sofa while he waited to see what Leo's next move would be.

Leo considered trying to intimidate the other man, but decided a more direct approach might be in order.

"Take yourself off too, Stanley. I'd like a word with Lady Thalia and you're rather a gooseberry at present."

Stanley raised a brow, his lips twitching as if he was deciding whether to be annoyed or further entertained. He angled his head toward Thalia.

"Lady Thalia, what do you think? Shall I go or would you prefer that I remain and send this wayward ruffian off instead? I'd advise you not to be alone with him. He has a dreadful reputation, you know."

As did Stanley. Everyone knew the man was an unapologetic womanizer. Then again, maybe that's why Thalia was sitting here with him on the sofa.

Leo scowled at the idea.

"She'll hardly be alone, seeing that we're in the middle of a crowded drawing room," Leo said. "Now, trot on after Wilcox and find some other lady to importune."

Stanley laughed. "Shall I do as he demands, Lady Thalia? It's completely up to you, although I readily admit that Byron and I have put you in a bit of a fix. Which one of us shall it be? I await your pleasure."

Lady Thalia's lips thinned, her eyes moving between

them as if she wished she could send both of them packing.

"Thank you for your concern, Lord Stanley," she said after a moment, "but I fear there will be no peace if I do not give in to Lord Leopold's demands. We shall have plenty of time to talk again before the party ends."

"I look forward to the occasion." Stanley stood and made her a bow. "Byron."

Leo nodded but said nothing else. As soon as the other man was gone, Leo dropped down into the vacated spot next to her.

Rather than scoot away, Lady Thalia held her place. "I knew you had an overabundance of gall, but I had no notion you could behave like such a barbarian."

He smiled. "Of course. How else do you think my ancestors have managed to hold on to a dukedom for the past three hundred years? Knowing how to vanquish one's enemies is a trait that runs strong in the Byron bloodline."

"I don't believe Mr. Wilcox and Lord Stanley count as enemies."

"They do if they stand in my way where you are concerned. I won't brook another man coming between us."

She turned her cordial glass slowly in her hand. "And what makes you imagine there is going to be an *us*?"

He leaned closer, his voice low. "The way you enjoyed your dessert this evening perhaps? It has put all sorts of imaginings into my head and left me thinking just how I would like to enjoy *you*."

Her lashes swept low for a moment before she looked up again and met his gaze. Her eyes were dark and mysterious, full of secrets. Quite suddenly he found himself wanting to learn them all.

"I think you read rather more into my actions than was actually there," she said lightly. "I have a passion for chocolate, that is all."

"What about the grapes?"

"Those as well."

He stared for another moment, then laughed. "Well,

if you put that much enthusiasm into a dish of sweets, sweetheart, then I cannot wait to see where else your passions lie."

"I am not your *sweetheart*, Lord Leopold, and you are not to say such things. Someone might overhear."

"You're right. Are you sure you wouldn't care to take that stroll in the gardens, after all?"

"Yes, quite sure. As always you presume far more than you ought. Now, I see a spare seat at the whist table. If you will excuse me, I am going to play cards."

She stood, taking a moment to set her cordial aside.

"But wait, don't go. We haven't settled anything between us yet."

She turned and met his eyes. "No, we haven't."

On a swish of blue velvet skirts, she strolled away.

He could have followed and acted the barbarian again by turfing another one of the players out of his chair to join her at the card table. Instead, he leaned back against the sofa cushions and contemplated his next move.

Good Lord, what have I started? Thalia wondered as she slid into the open chair at the card table and offered quiet greetings to the other players.

She'd known Lord Leopold had a forceful personality, but she'd had no idea that he could be so intimidating. He'd chased Wilcox off like a naughty pup. As for Lord Stanley, she wondered if it might have come to far more than words if he'd been unwilling to cede the field. She had the distinct feeling that in a fight Lord Leopold could best any opponent he faced.

But he wasn't going to intimidate or defeat *her*. This was her game and she would control it.

Control him.

With his natural arrogance, he didn't even seem to realize that she was the one leading him where she wished and not the other way around. But it served her purposes to let him think he was the one doing the seducing.

Tonight continued to be a promising beginning to her instructive lesson for Lord Leopold, and it wouldn't do to be seen as giving in to him too abruptly, not after all her previous rebuffs. She would let him think she was gradually succumbing to his wiles; then when he least expected, she would turn the tables. Exactly what that entailed she wasn't quite certain of yet. But she would think of something when the time was right.

Accepting her hand of cards, she focused her attention on the whist game.

Chapter 7

Leo mounted his roan stallion the following morning, taking a moment to draw in a deep breath of the leaf-scented air. The sun shone down from a nearly cloudless sky, forecasting an excellent, unseasonably warm autumn day for an outing.

A hunt had been arranged for the guests and a few local neighbors, including a viscount who was the current master of foxhounds. All around Holland House's main drive, horses and riders were being readied. The pack of hounds was brimming with tail-wagging excitement, the dogs giving an occasional bark of anticipation for the chase to come. Servants moved among the assembled guests, offering tall cups of spiced punch and squares of fruitcake.

Leo was pleased to see that Lady Thalia was to be one of the party. Due to hunting's physically demanding nature, many ladies preferred not to participate, especially hampered as they were by the necessity of riding side-saddle. But Lady Thalia looked eager for the challenge, a smile on her face as she allowed one of the servants to help her mount the horse she would be riding.

She looked as bright and beautiful as the clear day, attired in a surprisingly sensible habit of navy blue serge with polished brass buttons sewn down the front. The style looked slightly out of fashion, but the well-made cut suited her to perfection. Her shining mahogany hair was pulled into a neat twist at the back of her head, topped by a tall black riding hat.

Now settled on her horse, she took a few moments to

arrange the drape of her long skirts before straightening, the reins held confidently inside her small gloved hands.

He walked his stallion forward, maneuvering around several other riders so that he could slip into an empty spot at her side. Her mare shifted and chuffed out a breath at his stallion's arrival. An answering shiver rippled through his own horse's sleekly muscled flanks.

Leo understood the feeling, his chest and groin tightening in instant reaction to Lady Thalia's nearness. The sensation grew more intense as he caught the faintest hint of lilac drifting elusively in the air—there one instant, gone the next.

Had she bathed in lilac-scented soap this morning, he wondered, or else smoothed a couple of drops of perfume onto her skin as she dressed? Either answer put all sorts of wicked ideas into his head.

His hands tightened briefly on the reins before he forced away the thoughts. "Fine morning for a hunt," he remarked.

She turned her head, her dark eyes unfathomable. "Indeed, the weather is excellent for such sport, even if a tad warm."

"Holland's gathered a good group."

They both paused to survey the large number of horses, riders and dogs that were assembled.

"Lord and Lady Holland are known for their entertainments. One could expect no less from a hunt held on their estate." Her mouth tightened briefly before easing again.

"I was pleased to see you aren't the timid sort and will ride out for the start."

"Oh, I'll be there for more than the start. I love to ride and shall stay on the field as long as I can manage. As for the jumps, the higher the better, I say."

He frowned. "Boldness is an admirable trait, but it's also best to remember that an unfamiliar course can be dangerous."

"Do you doubt my ability to ride, Lord Leopold? It may have been some while since I rode to hounds, but you will find I am no novice when it comes to sitting a horse."

"I only meant that I do not wish you to come to harm, Lady Thalia."

"Don't worry. I learned how to take care of myself a long time ago."

With that, she set her horse in motion and cantered away.

He followed, determined not to lose her.

He had just drawn abreast of her again when the horn sounded the call to release the fox and the hounds.

Tallyho. The hunt was on.

With a kick of his heels, Leo sprang into action, Lady Thalia at his side, as everyone set off.

Thalia surged forward into a fast run, giving her mare her head as dozens of riders took to the field. Clots of green turf kicked up under churning hooves as the yards fell away behind them. It wasn't long before the pack separated into the leaders and those who tried to keep pace.

She settled into a position at the rear of the lead group, letting herself savor a sense of freedom she had not felt in a very long while. She didn't ride in London nearly as often as she might have liked, since maintaining a riding mount was a luxury she could ill afford. Occasionally, she took one of the carriage horses out to the park, but city riding was disappointingly tame compared with the sensation of flying over a grassy field at a rough gallop. She'd missed this, being able to ride a fine steed through the countryside. The divorce had denied her such opportunities, so this one came as a rare treat.

Lord Leopold rode next to her, his powerful stallion easily keeping pace with her own spirited mare. She tossed him a look and increased her speed, wondering if she could shake him off.

But he stuck with her like a burr, catching up as though nothing had changed. The pair of them pelted onward, correcting course with the other riders as the horn blew to signal a fresh sighting of the fleeing fox.

One by one, members of the lead pack separated, some making a jump over a large tree trunk laid out across a wet ditch, while others took a safer, longer route around.

She headed straight for the fallen tree.

Lord Leopold followed.

As the obstacle grew closer, she gathered herself to make the jump, using her reins and her left knee to set her horse into the correct gait. She tightened her other knee around the pommel to anchor herself more firmly in the saddle. Out of the corner of her eye, she saw Lord Leopold make his own adjustments as he readied his mount.

And then they were airborne, sailing high and wide of the tree and ditch. He landed first with a slight splash of mud; she came next.

As the two of them rode onward, she couldn't contain the laugh of pure exuberance. She glanced over and met Lord Leo's jewel-bright gaze. He grinned back, displaying his set of even white teeth, his features alive with a kind of unrestrained pleasure.

Her heart pounded, and not just from the exertion.

After another quarter mile or so, the pace slowed to a canter, then again to a walk. The fox, it seemed, had temporarily eluded the hounds, the dogs having lost the scent. The whippers sent them out to locate it again.

"You're a smashing rider, Lady Thalia," Lord Leo said, leaning forward in his saddle.

She patted her horse's neck. "The lads in the stable gave me a good hunter. She's got a fearless heart."

"As do you. I was a little concerned when you headed straight for that jump, but I see that I needn't have worried."

"My father had me on a horse before I could walk. Riding is easy. I wish I could indulge myself this way more often."

"I would be happy to make arrangements for you to do so. I know several landholders not far from London who would have no problem letting you ride on their property. The Hollands are not the only ones who hunt, you know."

For the second time he was offering her something she truly longed to accept. But just as before, his offer came with conditions. Conditions she had no intentions of fulfilling—not that she planned to let him know that at present.

"What an interesting notion," she said. "You do know how to cast out tempting lures."

His eyes darkened. "And have you decided to reel this one in? You have but to say yes and I shall see it done."

Howls from the dogs suddenly filled the air and the horn sounded again, relieving her of the need to answer. "Look," she said, "we're off again."

And indeed they were, the pack having apparently relocated the scent. Thalia urged her mare into action, while Lord Leo did the same with his mount.

As before, he kept pace at her side, their horses flying fast over the rolling, tree-laden hills and down slick shallow valleys. A series of hedgerows rose up, forcing the riders to spread out as they made the jumps either solo or in small groups. By the time she and Lord Leo cleared them all, the leaders and the pack had disappeared from view.

"This way," Lord Leopold said, gesturing to his right, "it ought to give us a chance to catch up."

She nodded in agreement and followed.

The pair of them pelted into a nearby wood, winding their way through the trees and shrubbery. When they finally emerged, Thalia saw that they were in a small clearing, bordered on the opposite side by a tall green thicket that stretched as far as the eye could see.

"We could try going over," she suggested, tapping her riding whip impatiently against her knee.

He shook his head. "It's too high. Even if we could clear it, there's no way to tell what's on the other side. We might land on a steep slope for all we know."

"Or find nothing more dangerous than a flat field." Still, he had a good point. Without knowing the territory, it was a foolish risk to take. "Shall we ride the hedge line and see if there's a break ahead?"

He nodded and off they set. But after another five minutes without finding a good place to cross, they drew to a halt again.

He tapped his riding crop against his thigh. "It's

useless—the hounds must be long gone by now. I don't hear them anymore, do you?"

She listened, the only sound the soft susurration of the wind.

"No. It's back to Holland House, I suppose," she said, disappointed.

He paused. "Not necessarily. I noticed a meadow with a pretty stream not too far back. We could stop there for a time."

"And why would I want to do that?"

"Because it's a beautiful day, far too nice to stay cooped up inside." He gave her one of his most engaging smiles. "If we return now, the ladies might compel you to join them in some activity. Fan painting, for instance? Somehow I don't see you as being in the mood to indulge your artistic side."

"Not if it involves desecrating fans. What a ghastly thought."

His smile widened. "It is rather, isn't it?"

She knew she should refuse him. She could always retire to her room until the hunt breakfast commenced. No one would trouble her despite the threat of fan painting. Yet this seemed a good opportunity to engage with Lord Leo. She'd decided to teach him a lesson and he'd never learn anything if she didn't take the necessary steps.

"Very well, Lord Leopold," she said softly, "lead me to your meadow."

Chapter 8

"Oh, how beautiful," Thalia declared several minutes later as she surveyed the expanse of verdant green meadow. A narrow stream wound at the base of a gentle slope, while hawthorn, blackthorn and rowan trees, laden with colorful autumn berries, stretched their limbs toward the blue sky above. "It must be even more breathtaking here in the spring and summer when the wildflowers are in bloom."

It is beautiful, Leo thought, *but not as beautiful as you.*

He secured his reins, then sprang lightly from his horse. "Shall we stretch our legs for a few minutes?"

She hesitated briefly, then nodded. "A stroll might be pleasant."

"Ah, so *now* you'll take a stroll with me," he said in a teasing voice.

"If you aren't careful, I might change my mind."

He came forward to help her down. "Then I shall make certain to do nothing to provoke you."

"I might as well make my way back to Holland House now, then, since I'm certain you'll have difficulty keeping that promise."

He gave a slow smile. "Allow me to try at least. After all, anyone who rides with the nerve you do can surely take on a small risk."

"I don't believe you and 'small risk' have any business being mentioned in the same sentence."

He laughed, then reached up to assist her. "Enough. Let us enjoy the beauty of our surroundings."

"I am fully capable of dismounting on my own," she told him in a light tone.

"I am sure you are, Lady Thalia, but I will aid you nonetheless." Gently, he laid his hands at her waist. "Besides, I have no intention of wasting an opportunity to get my hands on you."

Before she could protest, he tightened his grip and lifted her from the horse. He held her against him for long, long moments, savoring the sensation of her soft, warm body pressed to his. "You're light as a feather. I could hold you like this all day."

"Could you?" she asked, her eyes a rich, melting brown. "Are you really that strong?"

"Indeed. I have impressive stamina as well."

She lifted a single dark brow. "How interesting, Lord Leopold." Her voice was as silky as the chocolate mousse she'd taunted him with the evening before. "You may put me down now."

What he wanted to do was kiss her. Take her fully into his arms and capture her mouth for a long, heated joining that would leave her aching and moaning with need.

Of course, she'd probably slap him if he tried. Still, it might be worth risking her ire. But he had promised not to provoke her—for now at least.

Reluctantly, he set her down.

She stepped back, then reached down to secure the long end of her riding habit so that she would be able to walk unimpeded. Without giving him time to offer an escort, she started across the meadow.

With a shake of his head, he followed.

Thalia willed her heartbeat to slow, grateful for an excuse to put some distance between herself and Lord Leopold. Not that he was allowing her much distance, his long-legged stride giving him more than an unfair advantage when it came to catching up. Still, she kept her gaze fixed ahead, her interest seemingly all for the bountiful wealth of autumnal flora bursting with life around her.

For a moment when he'd had her in his arms, she'd thought he was going to kiss her. Her heart picked up speed again at the memory, wondering what it would have been like if she'd let him.

Disappointing, most likely.

In her experience, the reality of kissing never lived up to the fantasy. Poets wrote all variety of odes and sonnets about the transcendent ecstasy of a lover's kiss, but she'd never found the act to be anything above moderately pleasant.

Her former husband used to tell her she lacked a woman's proper passion. Then again Gordon had never had much use for kissing, saying that it mostly amounted to a lot of useless bother. Still, she'd tried to please him, especially in that first tenuous year of their marriage. By the second and third years, she'd been relieved when he'd stopped making any effort in that regard. As for sex, well, that was another golden tale turned to dross. More than her innocence had been stolen on her long-ago wedding night; her rosy dreams for the future had crumpled to dust as well.

Once again she thought of her ironic reputation as a carnally voracious seductress who devoured men like candy. Lord Leopold probably believed that her refusals were part of some elaborate ploy she was using in order to make their eventual bed play more exciting. Only there wasn't going to be any eventual bed play.

Won't he be blue-deviled with disappointment when he finds out? she thought. But that's what he'd get for pursuing a woman who didn't wish to be pursued.

"Look, a crab apple tree," she said, breaking the silence between them. "And it's full of fruit. My mother used to have jars of jelly made up every autumn. It was one of my favorite treats at the breakfast table. I haven't eaten it in years."

"Then perhaps we should apply to Lady Holland and ask if we could harvest a basket or two. It would be easy enough to have the fruit sent on to London. I presume your cook would have no problem finding a recipe."

"I'm sure not. But I would rather you didn't ask any more favors of Lord and Lady Holland on my behalf."

She gave him a pointed look. "I believe they have been importuned enough for one visit."

"I see someone has been telling tales," he said, not pretending to misunderstand. "Who?"

"What does it matter who?" She walked a few steps away, then turned to face him again. "Suffice it to say I know and that I was not pleased to learn how you arranged matters so I would be here for this party. The breadth of your arrogance never fails to amaze me, Lord Leopold. By now half of the company believe I am your mistress, while the other half has only to hear the rumors to believe the same."

A frown settled on his smooth forehead. "I only wanted the chance to see you again. You don't make it easy, you know."

"You're right, I do not. But I have been considering the matter and despite my better judgment, I find your persistence . . . intriguing. It makes me wonder just how far you might be willing to go."

"Go?" He arched a golden brow.

"Hmm," she said in a low murmur, "in your quest to make me your lover in truth. Perhaps a small test is in order."

He cocked his head. "What sort of test?"

"I was going to wait until after we returned to London, but perhaps here in the country is better."

His eyes darkened. "What exactly did you have in mind?"

"A rendezvous. Somewhere we can be private, away from prying eyes, while I decide if I want to take matters between us any further."

He spread his arms and smiled. "I am yours to command. We are alone now. Shall we begin here?"

"No, this won't do." She shook her head. "We'll be missed if we stay away much longer. I'll send word to let you know when and where we will meet. By the way, you don't shock easily, do you, Lord Leopold?"

His smile widened to a wolf's grin. "I don't shock at all."

"Good." She reached out and ran the tip of one finger along his warm, close-shaven cheek. "Be prepared for some sport. That is what house parties are for, is it not? Entertainment and sport."

His green-gold eyes flashed. "How right you are."

Thalia turned away, her heart thundering at her bold words and her even bolder plan.

She'd taken three steps toward the horses when he wrapped his hand gently but firmly around her upper arm. He drew her to a halt and turned her to face him. "Before we return to Holland House, I believe a token is in order, something to seal the start of our new relationship."

Her heart gave a swift, hard beat. Outwardly, she sent him a cool look. "We have no relationship. Not yet."

"Oh, but we do. Otherwise, we wouldn't be standing here alone in this meadow making plans for a secret rendezvous. I want a little taste of what's to come. I deserve that much for my patience, particularly after the performance you put on at dinner last night."

Ah, yes. The chocolate mousse.

She wanted to tell him he deserved nothing and was going to get exactly that. But if she showed her hand now, her whole scheme would collapse and she would find herself back at the beginning.

She forced a smile. "What exactly did you have in mind?"

"Nothing elaborate." He moved closer. "Just a kiss to tide us over."

She bit back a curse, wishing she could put him off. But from what she'd learned about Lord Leopold, he wasn't the sort to be gainsaid, particularly now that she'd given him reason to believe she returned his interest.

"But waiting will only heighten the anticipation," she said, laying a restraining palm on his chest. "We should resist for now."

He slid an arm around her waist. "I don't want to resist. I've been resisting since the night we first met. I say we indulge ourselves instead."

He tugged her another inch forward so that her body was pressed flush against his.

"Yes, but the first kiss is always so memorable," she improvised. "Better to save it for our rendezvous, where we will have time to explore our desires at will."

"I would rather explore our desires now." He skimmed a knuckle over her bottom lip, then caught her chin between two fingers. "You are exquisite, you know."

He didn't give her the chance to voice another excuse as his mouth lowered swiftly to meet her own.

She fought her natural instinct to stiffen, aware that any reticence on her part might give the game away. *It's a kiss,* she told herself, forcing her body to relax. *How bad can it be?*

Silently, she prepared to endure.

To her wonderment, the sensation of his mouth wasn't unpleasant. In truth it was quite the opposite, as tendrils of pleasure radiated through her like a warming sun. His technique was assured and bold with a relaxed confidence that demonstrated his skill in the sensual arts. For a man of his age—for *any* man, come to that—he certainly seemed to know a great deal about kissing.

He angled his head and deepened their embrace, teasing and coaxing and nibbling at her lips as he encouraged her to open to him.

She hesitated, knowing what came next. Kissing in the French style had never been one of her favorite activities, yet suddenly she found herself curious to see how it would feel with him. Lord Leopold had surprised her so far. Maybe he would surprise her again.

She parted her lips and braced herself for the invasion. But rather than a rude, rapacious shoving of tongue, he eased forward slowly, doing nothing more than gliding the tip of his tongue along her bottom lip before touching it to the tip of hers.

She shivered, hot and cold tremors running gently under her skin. He flicked his tongue lightly and slid in a fraction deeper, pausing to give her time to respond as he sought her willing participation.

Without thinking, she gave it, the sensations as delicious as sliding between a set of warm silk sheets on a cold winter night. Her eyelids drifted closed as their tongues tangled further in a warm, wet pas de deux. Suddenly she was kissing him back, her fingers clutching the material of his jacket as she pressed her body closer.

His palms slid over the length of her back to her waist, stroking there for a time before going even lower. All the while, his mouth moved against hers, each subsequent kiss deeper and darker than the one before, his touches both tender and demanding in ways she'd never known. He took the giving flesh of her buttocks into his hands and gave a gentle squeeze, then rocked their hips together. She gasped softly, feeling the hard length of his erection, even through the heavy cloth of her riding habit.

His kisses turned frenzied, his breathing quickening as he imitated with his tongue what he obviously wished to do to her body. And she responded, taking what he gave and craving more.

He moved up to cup one of her breasts, testing its feminine weight and fullness as his thumb sought out her nipple. Despite its covering, the traitorous bit of flesh peaked immediately, her body clearly enjoying what he was doing to it.

His lips worked in a hot slide along her throat, scattering kisses down, down until he came to the collar of her riding jacket. He reached to unfasten the buttons, pressing their hips even more tightly together as he sought to free her from her clothes.

And she nearly let him, imagining how it would be to have the wet heat of his mouth on her naked flesh, her breasts bared to the sight of his beautiful eyes and wicked tongue, her skirts tumbled high as he lowered them both to the ground and fit himself between her willing thighs.

But then she remembered other times, other hands, and broke their kiss, her thinking mind jolting back to life. She pushed against his chest, struggling suddenly to free herself from his hold.

Immediately, he let her go.

His eyes had turned a virid green; he was so consumed with desire that the pupils had all but crowded out the gold. "A good beginning," he said with husky satisfaction. "Next time will be even better."

Her fingers curled trembling at her sides, leaving her grateful for the concealing nature of her voluminous skirts. Her heart pounded improbably fast, her body not feeling at all like her own. For the first time, she wondered if she had made a dreadful mistake, letting him take the liberties she had allowed.

Because, she realized with sudden worry, he might be right about the next time being better.

And if it was . . .

No, she must rid herself of him once and for all. It was imperative that she find the means to stop him from continuing his pursuit. For if he did not, the risk just might prove too great to bear.

Chapter 9

It was half past midnight when Leo dismissed his valet from his guest bedchamber. He was comfortably attired in a long robe of soft brown cashmere, a pair of supple leather slippers on his feet. After picking up the small glass of brandy he'd poured for himself, he crossed to settle into an armchair positioned near the cozily burning fire. A log popped in the grate, red sparks flashing upward before the flames calmed again.

He opened a book and settled the volume on his lap. But it wasn't the words inside that held his interest. His thoughts were all for Lady Thalia, just as they had been for the whole of the day.

And what a long day it had been.

With activities scheduled one after another, beginning with the hunt breakfast to which he and Thalia had returned after their ride, there had been virtually no opportunity to speak with her. Something or someone always seemed to keep them apart. Even when the gentlemen joined the ladies after dinner, he had found Thalia otherwise engaged. If he hadn't known better, he might have thought she was avoiding him. But maybe she was simply being cautious, not wanting to add to the speculation already swirling around them.

His thoughts went once more to the kisses they had shared in the meadow, his blood heating with pleasure and anticipation for their next encounter. He couldn't wait to be alone with her again. Could barely contain his need to have her in his arms. She was everything he had dreamed of and more. Yet her kisses had surprised him.

For an experienced woman there was a curious reticence to her touch, an emotional reserve he had not expected. Still, she had warmed to him after those first few moments, her natural passions turning her pliant and inviting. Those fleeting moments with her had further whetted his appetite. He'd wanted her before. Now he craved her with a hunger that bordered on obsession. Only imagine how much better it was going to be once they were together fully and without restriction.

Ignoring the desire that hummed through him like a live charge, he forced his gaze back to his book, searching for the paragraph where he'd left off. But even after he'd started reading again, he couldn't concentrate, his mind still on Thalia.

He glanced at the clock on the mantelpiece, wondering how soon everyone in the house would be abed. What if he went to her now rather than waiting for their upcoming assignation? She might not thank him for it, though, especially if he got caught outside her bedchamber door.

She'd made it plain that she did not approve of the efforts he'd used to get her invited to Holland House. Yet if not for his scheming, she might never have agreed to see him again, let alone change her mind about the two of them forming a liaison. From his perspective, any temporary disapproval on her part was well worth it.

He yawned and laid his book aside. If he wasn't sneaking off to her room, he supposed he ought to go to sleep. He quaffed the last of his brandy and had just stood when a quiet rap came at the door. He tensed, sudden anticipation racing through him.

Was it possible? Could Thalia have come to him?

Instead, he found a maidservant waiting on the other side. She held out a note. "Pardon me, my lord, I was asked to deliver this to you prompt-like."

He accepted the folded piece of cream-colored vellum. "Thank you."

The girl curtsied and walked away.

Leo stepped back and closed his door. He lifted the letter to his nose, catching a trace of lilac on the paper. Thalia hadn't come to him in person, but at least she had sent a note. Exactly as promised.

He broke the seal with eagerness.

> *Meet me by the pond near the great oak tomorrow at four.*

It had no signature. Then again, it didn't need one.

Smiling, he crossed the room and tucked the note inside his book, knowing that tomorrow could not come soon enough.

Thalia set off from the Holland House stables the following afternoon, mounted on the same spirited mare she'd ridden to hunt the day before.

She was already a few minutes late for her tryst with Lord Leopold. The ladies had taken longer than planned to return from a "wilderness" sketching expedition in the nearby woods, putting her behind schedule by the time they all strolled back to the house.

Once there, ladies and gentlemen alike had separated for a few hours of rest in their rooms before dinner. With the house quiet and the servants occupied with their duties and their own meal belowstairs, it was an easy thing to slip away unnoticed.

Even so, she'd nearly changed her mind.

Yesterday's kiss had shaken her. She hadn't expected to like it so much. Nor had she thought to find herself dwelling on the embrace again and again, wondering what it might be like to share another with him.

She'd sensed before that Lord Leopold could be dangerous; now she knew it for a fact. Which was why she had decided to keep their appointed rendezvous in spite of her qualms. She couldn't afford to let matters progress any further between them. She'd learned through great pain and suffering what it was to be at the mercy of a man. She'd vowed never to let herself be put in such a circumstance again. If that meant resorting to desperate measures, then desperate measures it would have to be.

Lord Leopold wanted her and she needed to find a way to change his mind. So far cold champagne and even colder refusals had done nothing to lessen his interest. Hopefully what she had planned this afternoon would put an end to his pursuit of her once and for all, as well as teach him a much-deserved lesson about the need to respect a lady's wishes.

As for their rendezvous spot, a helpful groundskeeper had told her about the pond and the great oak where she and Lord Leopold were to meet. The gray-haired servant described the area in enthusiastic detail, expounding on the beauty of the foliage and the secluded nature of the freshwater pond.

She'd thought it sounded like the perfect location. And it was, she realized as she rode the last few yards toward the spot. The giant tree stood fifty feet tall, exactly as described, its branches now bared for the autumn. The pond lay close by, glimpses of its blue waters visible through a thick surround of smaller trees and evergreen shrubs.

Nearby, a horse stood tethered to a low-hanging branch.

Lord Leopold was waiting.

He walked forward as she drew her mare to a halt; sere leaves of gold and red crunched quietly under his boots. He smiled and reached up to lift her down from her horse. She didn't resist this time, but let him wrap his strong hands around her waist to ease her from the saddle.

Just as he'd done the day previous, he took his time, letting her body slide against his own for long, long moments before finally allowing her feet to touch the ground.

Quivers gathered low in her belly, her breathing not entirely steady in her lungs. She ignored both reactions and stepped away before he had a chance to lower his head and kiss her.

"Come back," he said in a silky voice as he reached out to bring her near again. "I haven't said good day to you properly yet."

"You haven't said good day to me at all," she admonished gently. "But here is not the place for pleasantries, at least not of the sort you have in mind. Let us move closer to the pond where we will be unseen. We can talk there."

He nodded, then reached for the reins of her horse to lead the animal forward.

While he secured her mare not far from his own steed, Thalia made her way toward the pond. The surrounding foliage did indeed create an atmosphere of privacy, the greenery a lush barrier that protected those enjoying the pond from the prying eyes of casual passersby.

Just as it had been yesterday, the weather was unseasonably warm, more suited to a summer day than one in the autumn. She hadn't even needed to wear a cloak, the lightweight, short-sleeved tan pelisse she'd chosen earlier more than adequate for the task. It went well with her forest green day dress. She supposed she ought to have changed into her riding habit again, but there hadn't been time; the loose-fitting gown suited her purposes better anyway.

She was studying the water, her mind full to the brim with thoughts, when a pair of long male arms caught her around the waist. Lord Leopold spun her around before she could gather her senses, his mouth taking hers without so much as a word. His touch was every bit as delicious as she remembered, passionate and inviting in ways that surprised her still. She gave in to the pleasure for a short while, then forced herself to pull away.

Because however tempting his kisses might be, she couldn't forget her purpose. Not now. And certainly not for a fleeting taste of passion with some arrogant rakehell who would forget her two minutes after he got her into his bed.

For as charming and persuasive as Leopold Byron might be, she had no illusions about the fact that he considered her a prize to be won. Not much different really from the fox they had chased the day before. She had no intention of being anyone's prey—not ever again.

He thought he knew her, but all he knew was the rumors, not the real woman inside. He didn't want the true Thalia Lennox, who strove to maintain her pride and integrity as a lady in spite of her public shame. Instead he wanted the fantasy—the lascivious seductress and unprincipled divorcée who supposedly devoured men like sweetmeats. What he longed for was a woman who did not exist. But shortly he was going to find out that he wasn't going to get either Thalia—the real one or the fake.

Wearing a false smile, she laid a hand on his shoulder. "Now, now, let's not rush things. We only just arrived."

"Yes, but our time is limited before we have to return." He leaned down to steal another kiss. "Let's not squander it."

She turned her head away so that his kiss landed on her jaw instead of her mouth. "We won't be squandering anything. I chose this location for a reason, you know. I thought we could have a little fun first."

"I believe that's what we're already doing." His arms tightened around her again.

Slowly, she shook her head. "I mean a different sort of fun." Lifting up on her toes, she kissed him just below his ear. "The naked sort," she whispered.

She felt his body tense with obvious desire.

"Exactly the kind I like best." His eyes gleamed. "What did you have in mind?"

She stroked her fingertips along his smoothly shaven cheek and watched his eyelids turn heavy. "Hmm, with the weather so clement, I thought a dip in the pond would be nice."

"A dip in the pond would be very nice." He smiled, his hands moving toward the fastenings on her dress.

Quickly, she stepped out of his hold and danced back so that she was out of his reach. She waggled a finger. "Not yet, Lord Leopold. You first."

"Me?" He arched a fine golden brow.

"It's all part of the excitement. I don't care for surprises, so I want to see exactly what I'm getting. Undress yourself."

His eyes widened briefly; then he grinned. "As you like." His fingers went to the buttons on his waistcoat.

As a healthy male in his prime, he exuded supreme confidence. It rolled off him like a tide, natural and without restriction. He didn't look away, but instead held her gaze as he began to strip—boots first, then the rest. He preened, corded muscles flexing without the slightest inhibition as he removed one piece of clothing after the other. They landed in a pile in the grass until he stood bare from head to toe.

Another part of him stood proudly unashamed as well, his erect shaft jutting out from his body with a length and girth that would have been impressive by anyone's standards. She had always considered her former husband an attractive man—on the outside at least—but he'd never looked like this.

Lord Leopold was quite simply mouthwatering.

Her pulse beat up into her throat; she was tempted in spite of herself. But indulging her unexpected case of prurient interest wasn't part of the plan. Steadying her resolve, she gave herself a firm mental shake.

"Turn around," she said, twirling a pair of her fingers in the air for encouragement.

His grin widened. "But of course, my lady."

He held his arms out from his body and turned. The view from that angle was even better, his taut buttocks and long muscled legs practically begging to be caressed.

He turned to face her again. "Well, do I meet with your approval?"

"Most assuredly," she murmured with complete truth.

"Your turn," he said, setting his fists on his hips. "I can't wait to see what's under those skirts of yours. Do you require assistance disrobing? I've been told I perform admirably as a lady's maid."

She had no doubt that he knew his way around the intricacies of feminine attire, considering all the women he must have bedded.

"I am sure you do," she said, "but I would rather do it myself. Why don't you go ahead into the water. I'll join you there in a minute."

He crossed his arms over his chest. "But I'd rather watch."

"You can watch next time. I am a lady, after all. I don't want to reveal all my charms at once."

For a moment, he didn't look convinced. Then he shrugged. "Very well. But don't take too long."

"Oh, I shan't."

She waited, watching as he waded into the pond. "Go out farther," she told him when he stood submerged to the hip. "I want to know how deep it is."

He nodded and used his strong arms to propel himself forward. He stopped at the center and spun around, treading water. "You're not undressing," he called.

"I will in just a moment. Can you touch the bottom?"

"No."

"Why don't you dive down and see how deep it is? I want to make sure we don't have to worry should we forget ourselves while we're . . . playing."

Even from a distance, his eyes gleamed with desire. Then, slick as a fish, he disappeared beneath the surface.

She sprang into action the moment he vanished from sight. Racing as fast as she could, she bent and gathered up his clothes, rolling them all into a tight bundle, which she tucked beneath her arm. Without sparing another glance in his direction, she ran for the trees.

She had just untethered both horses when she heard Lord Leopold call her name in the distance. Working as fast as she could, she tied the bundle of clothes to the back of her saddle, then thrust her foot into the stirrup. She wasn't used to mounting a horse without assistance and faltered as she struggled to lift herself up. If he caught her, there would be hell to pay.

The realization gave her the strength she needed in order to climb onto her horse. Her heart rabbited in her chest, her breathing labored.

Suddenly, he jogged out from behind the tree line, his wet hair plastered to his head, his naked body glistening from his swim. "Thalia, what are you doing?" His confusion was plain.

She wheeled her mount around to face him. "I am leaving."

"What? Why?" He looked shocked.

"If you had been paying attention, you would know why. You ought to have listened to me when I told you I wasn't interested in being your bed partner."

A heavy frown settled on his brow. "You aren't? Then what for Hades' sake has all this been about?" He waved an arm toward the pond behind him.

"A lesson, Lord Leopold. Since you refuse to take no for an answer, I thought a more overt demonstration of my wishes was in order. I've tried to be polite, but you persist in your unwanted pursuit of me."

"It is not unwanted." His eyes flashed.

"See? You are doing it again. Listen to me closely. *I-do-not-want-you*," she enunciated, "so stop chasing after me."

"Really? That's not what your body and your kisses say."

She brushed off any truth to his words and continued on. "You've shamed me, first at Lord Elmore's party and again here at Holland House by insinuating to everyone that I am your mistress. Rumors are as good as the truth and I am tired of being lied about and manipulated. You embarrassed me, so I have decided to return the favor by embarrassing you. Enjoy the humiliation, my lord."

His scowl turned black with sudden suspicion. "What humiliation? Get down from that horse. We will talk."

"No, I am done talking. Enjoy the walk. It's only a couple of miles back to Holland House."

Before he could get close enough to reach up and grab the bridle, she wheeled her horse around. Raising her riding crop, she brought it down hard on the buttocks of Lord Leopold's horse, sending the startled animal into a frenzied gallop. She had no doubt the stallion would run all the way back to the stables. She gave her own horse a sharp kick and sent the mare charging forward.

"Thalia, come back here!" Lord Leo bellowed.

But she rode on, forcing herself to ignore his furious shouts of outrage.

Chapter 10

Of all the endings to his afternoon, Leo had never expected to find himself walking stark naked through the open countryside back to Holland House. How he was going to present himself once he got there, he had no idea. He could only imagine the wide-eyed stares and titters over his arrival.

If he was lucky, maybe one of the servants could be persuaded to fetch him some garments while he concealed himself behind a convenient bush. Or even better, perhaps the assembled company would still be in their rooms dressing for dinner and he could sneak upstairs unobserved.

Somehow he doubted he would be that fortunate—exactly as Lady Thalia had intended.

Hell and damnation, he still couldn't believe what she'd done—most particularly taking his clothes! He remembered the way his temples had throbbed with fury and disbelief when he'd gone back to the pond and realized they were gone.

At least she left my boots, he thought as he tramped along the path, leaves and stones crunching under his heels. *I must look a complete fool.*

Also exactly as she'd planned.

Just wait until he got back. She might think she'd delivered the last salvo, but he wasn't the only one who would learn a lesson today. Precisely what he planned to do once he confronted her, he didn't know. But this wasn't over between them.

Doesn't want me, does she?
Liar.

He'd tasted the passion on her lips, knew he hadn't imagined her pleasure or her longing for more.

And she was going to get more—a lot more. But first he had a score to settle with the deviously clever Lady Thalia.

He walked on, grateful that he hadn't encountered anyone so far. If the trees hadn't been barren of leaves, he might have tried snapping off a weak limb to use as concealment. But she'd plotted her revenge well, leaving him no choice but to make the journey back in nothing but his altogether.

For his own part, he didn't care a jot about being naked, having never suffered from an overabundance of modesty. But other people might not feel the same. There was also the uncomfortable fact that he was growing chilled, gooseflesh beginning to pop out over his skin now that the sun was sinking lower in the sky.

He'd been walking for another five minutes when a cottage came into view. A brown-haired woman stood in the rear yard, tossing handfuls of grain to a small flock of chickens, while a toddler played with a wooden toy on a nearby patch of grass. Not far away, freshly washed laundry hung on a line, the clothes waving slowly to and fro in the modest breeze.

Among the items was a man's shirt and trousers, the answer to his current dilemma. Even if the shirt was the only thing that fit, at least he wouldn't be completely bare-arsed naked any longer—shockingly attired, yes, but not naked.

But how to acquire them?

He considered the straightforward approach of just walking up to the woman, explaining his situation and asking to borrow the clothes—with the promise that she and her family would be more than generously compensated once he was back in his proper element and in his own clothes again. But there were far too many things that could go awry with that plan, he decided. Once she got an eyeful of him, she might not stay long enough to hear him out as she ran for the cottage and barricaded herself and her child inside.

His only other options were equally unappealing. The first being that he would continue on to Holland House exactly as he was, or the second, that he would wait until the woman wasn't looking and take the clothes.

He balked at the idea. A gentleman no matter his difficulties did not stoop to thievery. It was wrong, plain and simple. Yet if he took the clothes, just long enough to make his way back to Holland House, then promptly returned them, was he actually stealing? It was more a case of borrowing really when you thought about it.

He cringed, knowing his rationalization was exactly that. But thanks to Thalia—blast her outrageousness—he was in a real fix and had to consider all his options, honorable or otherwise.

Yet what real harm was there in using the clothes for a couple of hours? If all went well, the woman wouldn't even notice they were missing. And he would send the garments back, freshly washed, with a note of thanks and money attached for their use. Seen in that light, she and her husband might regard the entire incident as a kind of unexpected boon.

He weighed his choices, watching her from behind the tree.

She finished feeding the chickens, then walked over and scooped the little boy and his toy up off the ground. Tucking the child against her hip, she went into the house, the door swinging shut with a bang.

Now was his chance. If he wanted the clothes, he had better make a dash for them while the opportunity was ripe. He weighed his options one more time, cast another quick look around and ran.

He reached the clothesline and yanked the trousers out of their pins. He'd just taken hold of the shirt as well when the back door to the cottage slammed open on its hinges again. Only it wasn't the woman who came out into the yard this time.

It was a man—a huge, massive bull of a man with a barrel chest and arms that looked as if they could bend steel. His hands were the size of hams and curled inside one of them was a rifle. He raised the weapon to his shoulder and took aim.

"What in the hell do ye think ye're doin'?" he bellowed. "Ye believe ye can come up to my home, naked as the day God made ye, and help yerself to my clothes?"

Leo held out a hand. "No, no, it is nothing like that."

Technically, it was exactly like that, but there were mitigating circumstances. If only the bull-sized man would put down his weapon and let him explain.

"I've had an unusual mishap, you see, and lost my clothing while swimming in one of the nearby ponds," Leo began. "I'm borrowing these only until—"

"Borrowin', my left eye. Ye're a thief an' I don't hold with thieves. Ye're indecent to boot."

Leo held up the trousers in his hand. "I wouldn't be if you'd permit me to put these on. I am a guest of Lord Holland's and will recompense you for their use."

The man didn't lower the gun by so much as an inch. "Liar too, I see. Drop the rig and step back."

Leo's hand tightened on the material. "If you would simply see reason, I am sure some accommodation can be reached. How much for the clothes? I will purchase them from you outright."

"Purchase them!" The farmer barked out a humorless laugh. "Don't see no pockets ne'er ready coin on that bare skin of yers. Nay, ye stay where ye are, while my older boy goes for the constable."

Leo scowled. "There's no need to involve the law. Send word to Holland House and you will see that I am telling you the truth. My name is—"

"Don't care what yer name is. Now sit down and wait while Mull is called." He gestured toward the ground with the end of his rifle. "I want 'im to see ye, jus' as ye are, so there's no mistaking the situation."

Leo glanced beneath him at the damp grass, the thin green stalks underlain by patches of sticky mud and a scattering of moldering leaves. It looked cold and uninviting and he had no intention of sitting on it, especially naked. "I would prefer to stand."

"Ye sit or ye'll get a taste of the wrong end of Bess here."

"I will thank you not to threaten me," Leo said in a voice hard with authority. "Put *Bess*, as you call it, down."

In answer, the farmer lifted the gun barrel higher.

Leo studied the other man, searching for potential weaknesses. On initial inspection, there didn't seem to be any, particularly since the farmer was the one holding the weapon. But weapon or no, Leo wasn't about to wait around for the local constabulary to arrive.

Considering how unwilling the other man was to listen to him, he didn't hold out much hope that Mr. Mull would be any more accommodating. Leo was vulnerable enough standing here in nothing but his boots. He wasn't taking the chance of being tossed that way into a gaol cell.

"Look, there is no need for all this," Leo said. "Why don't I just give you back your garments and be on my way?" In a gesture of apparent concession, he let the clothes drop onto the grass. "See? No harm done."

"No harm? 'Course there's harm." The man bristled. "If I let you go, ye'll be after one of me neighbors next. Now, enough of yer prattle. Shut yer gob and sit."

Leo said nothing for a long moment, then gave a conciliatory shrug, as if he was giving in. "As you like."

Certain he'd won, the cottager shifted his stance, the weapon finally lowering a little.

Springing into action, Leo charged the other man. Reaching him in seconds, Leo curled his hands around the wooden stock and pushed the rifle up and away, wrestling for possession.

But the big bull held fast, every ounce as strong as he looked. They hadn't struggled for long when suddenly the gun went off. The bullet flew skyward, the reverberation from the shot traveling the length of Leo's arms.

Leo wasn't the sort to back away from a fight, but he also knew when retreat was the better choice. Hoping surprise would gain him a much needed advantage, he shoved the gun hard toward the farmer, then abruptly let go.

He ran, pushing himself as fast as his legs would carry

him toward a stand of trees not too far in the distance. He might not be able to outwrestle the bull-sized farmer, but he knew he could outrun him.

He was nearly to his goal when pain suddenly burned like a brand through his arm, the echo of a rifle shot sounding behind him seconds later. He glanced down and watched as blood ran hot and wet over his skin. Scarlet droplets pooled at his fingertips before splattering in the grass.

Rather than stop, he ran faster, even more determined to escape now that he was injured. He finally reached the shelter of the trees, only then pausing long enough to catch his breath. But he knew he didn't have time to waste. The farmer and his son, and whomever else the man could round up, would be after him soon.

He would have to tend to his wound later.

Cradling his injured arm against his chest, he pushed on. If he could just reach Holland House, he would be safe. As for arriving naked and bleeding, well, it would only add to the drama of his harrowing tale and raise the tally against Lady Thalia Lennox.

Checking quickly behind him to make sure they weren't already in pursuit, he set out again in what he hoped was the right direction.

Thalia was almost to the Holland House stables when she slowed her mount. The mare whickered softly, shaking her head with a jingle of the tack as they came to a halt in the middle of a grassy field.

Thalia supposed Lord Leopold was walking back by now wearing nothing but his boots. He must make quite a picture, all that finely wrought flesh exposed for all the world to see — assuming he wasn't concealing himself behind every tree and bush along the way. Yet somehow she knew that he was far too proud a man to hide. Instead he was probably striding confidently forward, moving as if he were just out for a stroll regardless of the reaction he would most certainly provoke if seen by some unsuspecting local.

She frowned and caught her lower lip between her

teeth, thinking of the predicament she'd put him in. She ought to be pleased, puffed up with self-satisfaction for a job well done. Her scheme had worked exactly as planned. She'd wanted to humiliate and humble him, to make him so angry that he would never want to speak to or look upon her again.

So why did she feel troubled?

Why was guilt souring in her stomach like a piece of unripened fruit?

She'd wanted to teach him a lesson. Instead, she wondered if she was the one in need of tutelage. Had she been unforgivably cruel? And if so, what was she going to do to make amends?

She sat unmoving for a few seconds more, then heaved out a breath and signaled for the mare to turn around and ride back the way they'd come.

Thalia was about halfway to the pond when a sharp crack splintered the air. She'd attended enough autumn shooting parties to recognize the sound of gunfire. Her heart sped faster, a strange, sick fear rising in her chest.

It could be anything, she thought. A hunter perhaps or shooting practice. It didn't need to have anything to do with Lord Leopold.

Yet somehow she knew it was.

A harsh gasp rattled in her throat when she saw him, one of his arms bathed in a wash of crimson as he came out of a small grove of trees at a stumbling run.

"My God," she cried as she urged the horse toward him.

He stopped and looked up, the waning afternoon sun glinting off the threads of gold and amber in his hair. He looked beautiful despite his injury, like a warrior who'd just battled a mighty foe.

"Lady Thalia?" he said, clearly surprised to see her. "What are you doing here?"

She ignored his question as she kicked her stirrup free and jumped down from her mount, running to him as quickly as her skirts would allow. "My lord Leopold, what has befallen you? Have you been shot?"

"Yes, and likely to be again if we don't leave." He cast a worried glance over his shoulder.

"What do you mean?"

He shook his head. "Never mind that now. Let's get on your horse and ride for Holland House."

Favoring his wounded left arm, which was obviously too painful to use, he went around to pick up the reins of her mare using his right. The animal backed up, turning suddenly fractious at the scent of fresh blood. He calmed her as best as he could, then gestured to Thalia. "You mount first, then I'll come up behind."

"All right, but we should bind your arm first so you don't lose any more blood. I have your clothes with me as well. You can get dressed too."

"We'll worry about both of those things later. For now, get on the horse."

She stiffened and was opening her mouth to disagree when a huge man emerged from the trees. A frightful scowl darkened the stranger's face, one paw-sized hand clenched around a rifle. A lad of ten or eleven trotted at his heels. Without hesitating, he and the boy made straight for them.

"Accosting women now, are ye, ye blackguard?" the big man called. "Step away from her or it'll go even worse for ye than it already has."

Thalia stared in horror.

"Ye're safe, ma'am," the man said reassuringly. "He won't hurt ye."

From the corner of her eye, she saw Lord Leopold do as instructed, clearly trying to separate himself from her so that she would be out of the line of fire. Without a moment's hesitation, he'd chosen to place himself in further danger to protect her.

The selfless act warmed her down to her marrow, something unexpected shifting in the vicinity of her heart. Rather than let him continue to move away, she stepped sideways so that she was once again standing between him and the gun.

"Hurt me?" she told the large man derisively. "Do not be ridiculous. Lord Leopold would never hurt me." And curiously, in that moment, she knew it was true. For all his rakish ways, she realized that Lord Leopold was the sort of man who would never resort to violence against a woman, or any creature weaker than himself.

"It is you, sir, who are cause for concern," she continued, her tone blistering. "Put that gun down immediately."

The man stopped abruptly, the boy at his side.

"Thalia, don't," Lord Leo said quietly. "You'll just antagonize him. Step away and let me handle this."

But as before, she ignored him, her attention fixed on the other man. "Are you the one who shot Lord Leopold?" she demanded.

"Wot?" Thick eyebrows rose skyward.

"You heard me? Did you shoot and injure this gentleman?"

The large man bristled. "He's no gentleman—he's a thief. He were tryin' ter steal the clothes right out of me own yard."

"Well, of course, he was, given that he had lost his garments and had need of new ones. And I am sure he was not stealing them as you claim, but rather borrowing them until such time as he could repay you for their use."

"Exactly what I tried to explain, but you refused to listen," Lord Leopold said to the farmer. "As you can see, the lady has no difficulty in her understanding of the situation."

The big man's eyebrows bunched with renewed anger. "'Ow were I ter know you was some high-nob lord when ye ain't wearin' so much as a kerchief around yer nethers? 'Sides, ye're the one what ran off when I told ye I was callin' fer the constable."

"No doubt because you were holding that gun on him," Thalia stated, interceding before the men could come to further blows, verbal and otherwise. "You still are holding it by the way. Did I, or did I not, tell you to put that weapon down? Do it now."

The farmer flushed, ruddy anger darkening his skin. But to the surprise of them all, he did as she commanded, laying the rifle carefully into the grass.

"Thank you," she said. "Lord Holland will be informed of everything that has occurred here. As magistrate, it will be up to him to decide what is to be done, though I rather doubt he will be pleased to hear that you tried to kill one of his houseguests."

The color drained out of the huge man's face. "I didn't try ter kill 'im. Just winged him. He's all right, ain't he?"

"He's gunshot and bleeding, so he most certainly is not all right. If you are done threatening his lordship and me, I should like to tend to his wound and get him back to Holland House so that he can receive proper medical attention. Young man," she said turning her attention to the boy, "have you a blanket in your house?"

"Aye," the boy said.

"Then pray run and fetch it while I see to Lord Leopold."

After the boy ran off, the farmer turned to follow.

"Not you," she said. "Once I've done binding his lordship's wound, you are going to assist him up onto my horse."

"That's not necessary, Lady Thalia," Lord Leopold said quietly. "I can see to myself."

But one look at his wan complexion told her he was not nearly as steady and robust as he claimed. "Sit down, Lord Leopold, before you pass out."

"I never realized before quite how bossy you are."

"I am sure there are many things you have not realized about me. Now please, sit down."

"Hand my trousers to me first. Then I'll gladly oblige."

Oh. He was right. In the midst of all the turmoil, she'd nearly forgotten that he was unclothed. He was shivering as well, she saw, the setting sun and falling temperature only adding to his discomfort.

Hurrying to the mare, she pulled the bundle of clothes off the saddle. Her hands trembled, suppressed tension coming to the fore now that the danger was over. But she could collapse in a quivering heap later, once she was alone. Right now, Lord Leopold had need of her.

She returned to his side. "Here." She shook the bundle free, then held out the trousers.

"Are those his clothes?" the farmer asked.

"Never you mind," she said over her shoulder before turning back to Lord Leopold. "Can you manage?"

"Of course."

But he couldn't, his wounded arm too stiff and painful to be of much use. In the end she knelt down and helped him into them—he fastened the buttons on his own, however, using only one hand.

Next she retrieved his cravat. "This will have to serve as a binding for now," she told him as she tied the soft linen tightly above the wound to slow the bleeding. Once done, she wound the rest around his arm as best she could.

The boy suddenly appeared with the blanket, a woman with him.

"What has happened?" she said, a toddler set at her hip. "Is this the man who was in our yard? Thomas said he's Lord something or other and one of Lord Holland's guests. Oh, Joseph, what 'ave ye done?"

"Hush, Mary," the big man said. "Let's get 'em on their way, then we'll see wot's wot."

"But—"

"I says not now."

Mary fell silent.

The rest of Lord Leopold's clothes were impossible to put on, since his shirtsleeves were too narrow to fit over the makeshift bandage. Thalia draped the blanket over his shoulders instead, then urged him toward her mare.

Lord Leopold was looking grayer by the moment. Circles of pain rimmed his eyes and his balance was not entirely steady. Nonetheless he insisted on trying to mount her horse on his own once she was settled. But getting seated behind her as he hoped to be proved impossible, and in the end he was forced to rely on the aid of the man who'd put him in this predicament to begin with.

She made no complaint when he wrapped his good arm around her waist. "Hold tight, Lord Leopold."

He did, pressing his chest to her back, his body far too cold for her liking.

It was with immense relief that they set off, Thalia urging the horse forward at a gentle gait.

Neither of them spoke for a time.

"Thank you," Lord Leopold said in a low voice.

"For what?" she murmured.

"For coming back. You were magnificent, the way you faced down that lumbering brute. Stupid, but magnificent."

"I am not sure if that's a compliment or an insult, but I'll take it regardless." She paused. "I am sorry."

"For what?" His words were slightly slurred, his weight resting more and more heavily against her.

"For leaving you in the first place back at the pond. It was wrong and I should not have done so."

"Got you in my arms, didn't it?" He tucked his chin on her shoulder, his cheek against her own. "One arm anyway."

A minute later, she felt him sway.

"Don't you fall off."

"Won't." He tightened his hold on her waist, then sagged some more. "Just going to rest."

"We're nearly there." At least she hoped they were, since early evening darkness had fallen. But the horse seemed to know her way, so Thalia wasn't concerned about reaching their destination. It was Lord Leopold who worried her.

"My lord?"

He did not answer.

"Leopold?"

Had he lost consciousness?

But shortly afterward, as they rode out of a grove of trees, she saw the lights of Holland House. She released a pent-up breath, grateful that help would soon be at hand.

Chapter 11

Thalia couldn't sleep; Lord Leopold was on her mind. Try as she might, she couldn't shake the memory of his ashen face and the expression of pain he'd worn when he'd been helped off her horse and led into the house and upstairs.

The pair of them turning up together with Lord Leopold injured and weak from blood loss had sent a flurry of shock through the household. It had also sent the guests into full gossip mode just in time for them to convene in the drawing room before dinner.

While the physician had been sent for, she had told Lord and Lady Holland what she knew about the shooting, careful to leave out any mention of having been at the swimming pond and her role in Lord Leopold's missing clothes. She'd concocted a story about going out for a ride and discovering his riderless horse—with his clothes tied in a bundle to the saddle—and how she'd then ridden on only to discover him injured. She wasn't sure if the Hollands entirely believed her version of events, but if not, they were too polite to say.

As for Lord Leopold, he'd been taken up to bed, where hopefully they hadn't asked him more than a few cursory questions before leaving him to the ministrations of the doctor.

What had Lord Leopold told them? She supposed it would serve her right if he'd given an unvarnished accounting of the truth. Still, she rather hoped he had twisted his story enough to keep matters private so that the truth remained solely between him and her.

How is he? she wondered.

She'd taken a bath and eaten dinner on a tray in her room, unable to face the other guests. She'd received no further word about Lord Leopold's condition; not even her maid knew how he was faring.

Telling herself it was really none of her concern, she had gone to bed. But after a great deal of tossing and turning, she finally gave up.

She lit a candle and picked up her book, hoping a bit of light reading would help her drift off. But after five minutes, she tossed it aside and reached for her robe.

Fastening the tie at her waist, she went to the door.

Leo dozed against the warm, clean sheets, the ache in his arm keeping him from sinking into a peaceful slumber.

He'd refused the dose of laudanum the doctor had pressed on him; he hated the stuff and had done so ever since he'd fallen—or rather jumped on a dare from Lawrence—from a second-story window at Braebourne as a boy. He'd been trying to land in a nearby tree at the time and had actually succeeded until the limb he was standing on snapped and sent him plummeting to the ground. He'd dislocated his shoulder. Even now, he remembered the pain and how violently sick the laudanum had made him. He'd vowed never to take it again; the pain was far preferable.

He shifted, catching sight of the red stain beginning to form on the white cloth bandage wrapped neatly around his upper arm. His wound was seeping, exactly as the doctor told him it would.

There had been no bullet to dislodge, the shot a clean one that had gone straight through. Another few millimeters and the bullet would have hit bone, putting him at risk of losing his arm—or at least the use of it. As it was, the doctor had doused the wound with liberal amounts of fresh water, then brandy that had burned like fire. Now it was simply a matter of putting up with the discomfort until it healed.

The doctor had also recommended bleeding him, but Leo decided he'd already lost enough blood for one day and refused the treatment. He'd never held with the idea of letting blood to remove ill humors; he'd known far too many people weakened by the procedure, fatally so in the case of his late father.

Leo was drifting back into another shallow doze when the door latch gave a quiet snick. After the door closed again, a figure moved toward him, illuminated by the low candlelight. He peered through his lashes and saw a woman, but not just any woman. It was Thalia.

He closed his eyes again, his pulse gaining speed. He worked to regulate his breathing, drawing in her light floral scent. She stopped when she reached his bedside. Even with his eyes shut, he could sense her studying him.

By rights, he ought to be angry with her given everything that had happened. She'd tricked and manipulated him, stolen his clothes and put him in a situation that had resulted in his being shot.

But she'd also returned to find him, fearlessly faced down an armed brute of a man in his defense, then led him to safety. And she'd apologized.

Considering that, how could he be cross? If anything, he felt gratitude and a grudging admiration. She was what was known in the vernacular as a formidable woman. Brave, resourceful and clever. And he liked her all the more for it.

She'd wanted to give him a disgust of her. But her gambit had failed, since he was more determined than ever to have her in his bed. She'd told him she didn't want him as a lover, but if that were true, then why was she here in his room—alone, at night? And in her dressing gown no less.

Maybe this injury of his might not be such a bad thing after all, assuming he could work it to his advantage.

One minute passed, then two, as she stood at his bedside. Finally she gave a soft sigh and began to turn away.

He moved against the sheets as if he were just waking and opened his eyes. "Hmm, is someone there?" he asked in what he hoped was a sleepy voice. "Who is it?"

She swung around and stepped back into the small circle of candlelight near his bed. "Pardon me. I didn't mean to wake you."

"No matter. I've been drifting in and out." He looked at the curtains that were tightly drawn over the windows. "What time is it? It must be late."

She tucked her hands against the folds of her dressing gown. "It's after two. I just . . ."

He'd never heard her tongue-tied before. He found it rather endearing. "Yes, just what?"

"I wanted to check on you, that's all. See if there might be anything you need."

He needed all sorts of things, but none of them seemed particularly prudent until his arm had a chance to heal. "Still feeling guilty for getting me shot?" he said, unable to resist teasing her.

She bristled. "I did *not* get you shot, at least not intentionally. How was I to know you'd get caught stealing clothes and be chased by a lunatic with a gun?"

She crossed her arms over her breasts.

He stared at their lush roundness for a long, appreciative moment before forcing his gaze upward again. "Maybe because you're the one who left me naked in the first place? It was bound to cause trouble."

"Yes, well, I've already told you I'm sorry." She frowned. "I should not have come. If you have need of anything, ring the bell for one of the servants."

She turned to move away.

Before she could, he reached out with his good hand and caught hold of her wrist. It was narrow and fine-boned, delicate for so resilient a woman. "Don't go," he said in a soothing voice. "We've quarreled enough for one day, do you not think?"

She stood motionless and made no effort to free herself. At length, she raised her eyes to his. "Yes." She gestured toward his bandaged arm. "What did the doctor say? Shall you recover or might there be . . . permanent damage?"

"I lost a fair amount of blood and needed stitches, but with proper rest and care, I should heal."

Actually the doctor had told him he should be back to most of his normal activities in a few days, so long as he kept the wound clean and the dressings changed regularly so that infection did not set in.

"Are you in a great deal of pain?" she asked, her eyes filled with compassion.

"Some," he said, his voice deliberately soft.

"What have you taken for it? Is it time for another dose?" She glanced around, obviously searching for a medicine bottle.

"No. I'll be . . . fine." His voice sounded even weaker.

He paused, wondering whether he was overplaying his hand. But apparently not, since she just kept looking at him, her dark eyes soft and gentle in a way he'd never seen. He closed his own so as not to betray himself.

"I should let you rest," she murmured after a minute.

"No." His fingers tightened around her wrist. "Stay. I like your company."

"Do you?"

"Surprisingly, yes," he said in a teasing voice. Cracking open one eye, he caught sight of a faint smile hovering on her lips. It made him want to smile back—that and kiss her. "Please honor me with your companionship, if you would be so kind."

"How am I to respond to that? You make it rather hard to say no."

"Then don't. Say no, that is."

She shook her head. "Very well, let me get a chair." She moved to free her wrist from his grasp.

Instead he pulled her closer. "Sit here on the bed next to me."

"I couldn't, my lord—," she protested.

"Of course you can." He tugged again until, with some reluctance, she sat.

He relaxed more deeply against the sheets. "Good. That's good." With a fingertip, he traced the satiny skin on the inside of her wrist. "Do you not think after everything that has passed between us that you might call me Leo? We're here together alone, you in your robe and me in my drawers. And don't puff up—you've seen me naked, after all. And stolen my clothes. Not to mention coming to my aid when I was at a decidedly low ebb. Surely we are beyond formality at this point?"

She arched a brow. "I have found that a measure of formality never goes amiss. Besides, were I to start using your given name, it would only encourage you and as we both know, you have no need of that."

He laughed, then groaned when a fresh stab of pain shot through his arm.

Her eyes softened again. "Are you certain there is nothing I can bring you to ease your hurt? Surely the doctor left a sedative of some kind."

"He tried, but I didn't want it. Laudanum and I don't mix well."

"A glass of wine, then? Or brandy?"

"Later perhaps. Right now, there are other things I'd like better."

"Leo—," she said in soft warning.

"See how easy that was? Say my name again just so I know you've got the knack of it."

"I should go."

"What? And desert me again? You did leave me out in the wilds, naked and defenseless, if you'll recall."

She lifted a single dark eyebrow. "I don't think anyone would ever describe you as defenseless."

"And yet, here I lie, gunshot and in pain."

She studied him briefly, a new frown creasing her forehead. "I already told you I am sorry. What more can I say?"

"Nothing. But you could *do* something to make it up to me."

"Such as?"

"Admit that you aren't nearly as indifferent to me as you claim."

"Lord Leopold—"

"Leo," he reminded. He slid his fingers along her arm, gratified by the answering tremor that rippled just beneath her skin. "Spend some time with me after we return to London. Two weeks in which we can get to know each other better. If, at the end of that time, you still wish

to be quit of me, I shall cease my pursuit and never trouble you again."

"Two weeks, you say?"

He nodded. "But you can't shut me out like you did before. You have to give me a fair chance to show you just how compatible we can be."

"And if I refuse?"

"Then I shall continue to chase you, even more ruthlessly than before," he said, his words filled with unmistakable intent.

"That hardly seems fair."

"Neither was being shot by an outraged cottager who didn't like finding a naked stranger purloining a few of his clothes from the laundry line."

"Borrowing, remember?"

"I did offer to pay him outright, but as he pointed out, I had no money on my person at the time."

Her expression grew troubled. "Have you spoken with Lord Holland about the incident? Is the man to be jailed?"

Leo shook his head. "No. I am not pressing charges."

"But he shot you!"

"He did. Were I not who I am, though, a wealthy aristocrat with a powerful family and influential friends, the law would likely see his actions as justified. I *was* stealing from him no matter my real intent."

"He ought to have accepted your word as a gentleman, even if you were unclothed at the time."

He smiled at her protective outrage. "Perhaps. But you have to admit it isn't every day a naked aristocrat wanders into a farmer's back garden looking for a pair of breeches to cover his bare buttocks."

Her eyes rounded briefly before a smile crept over her mouth.

"At least he was only a middling shot," Leo remarked. "Just think how you would feel now had he killed me."

Her cheeks paled, all amusement disappearing from her face.

"Two weeks with me, Thalia," he urged. "Then I shall absolve you completely and never mention it again."

"Fine," she said on a hastily exhalation, "you can have your two weeks. But don't think that means you will be spending them in my bed."

"A tumble on the sofa would serve just as nicely," he said with a wicked smile.

She cuffed him on the shoulder.

"Ouch. Injured here, remember?"

"Sorry," she said, looking genuinely contrite.

He closed his eyes again and worked to look even wanner than he felt, deciding it couldn't hurt to fan the flames of her guilt a bit more.

"Are you certain you won't take a glass of brandy?" she asked.

He peeked out from beneath his eyelashes, and felt a little guilty himself. She really did look upset.

"No. I just need to rest." He paused, a small silence settling between them. "So when shall I call at your town house?"

"When you are well. But understand something. This time together will not change my mind about becoming your mistress."

He hummed low in his throat. "We shall see."

"I do not want a lover, Lord Leopold," she said with exasperation.

He traced the length of her forearm again, then caught her hand, threading his fingers through hers. "But I wouldn't just be your lover. I would also be your friend."

And I do want to be her friend, he realized. *I want to discover everything there is to know about the beautiful, mysterious woman who is Lady Thalia Lennox.*

For a long moment, surprise and confusion shone in the rich caramel of her eyes, as though no other man had ever said such a thing to her.

Then it was his turn to frown.

"I really do need to go," she said. "And you need to rest."

But he tightened his hold again. "Not yet. There's one more thing I require before I can sleep."

"What might that be?"

"A kiss. To make it all better, as they say."

"I don't think a kiss will heal the bullet hole in your arm."

"No, but it can't hurt it either."

Her lips twitched; then she gave a grudging laugh. "You are incorrigible, Lord Leopold."

He grinned. "Leo. Now, let's have that kiss."

"This is a very bad idea."

"It's an excellent idea. Look upon it as an act of mercy."

She shook her head, then sighed. "Close your eyes."

He shifted beneath the covers, his pulse racing faster, as fresh arousal awoke inside him.

"Eyes," she reminded softly.

Dutifully, he closed his lids.

And waited.

He was beginning to think she was going to renege when she leaned over and pressed her lips to his forehead, her touch as warm and smooth as rose petals.

"There," she murmured, easing away. "All better."

His eyelids lifted. "Hardly."

And before she could slip away, he wrapped his good arm around her and pulled her against his chest. The impact sent a new jolt of pain through his wound, but he didn't care. Her lips were just too sweet to resist.

"Leo," she warned. "Remember what I said."

He smiled. "Fancy that. You called me Leo."

Then he was kissing her, taking her mouth with a gentle, insistent pressure that made his blood heat and his body ache with a different sort of pain altogether. He waited for her to protest. But instead, softly, slowly, she began to kiss him back.

What am I doing? Thalia wondered as a hazy, languorous warmth stole through her. *Why am I letting him kiss me, this man I do not want?*

Yet even as the thought flickered through her mind, she knew it was a lie. For as imprudent and insane as it might be, she could not deny the attraction she felt for him.

Nor the pleasure of his touch.

Kissing him was lovely, more than lovely, better than the most decadent whipped confection or the sunniest spring day. She'd never known anything quite like it in her life—a curious realization considering that she had been married and was far from a virginal innocent.

Yet perhaps in this she still had much to learn, his touch now, as before, a quiet revelation. How easy it would be to let him go further. How simple to forget time and place, and allow herself to slide down into the bed beside him.

As if hearing her thoughts, he deepened their kiss, parting her lips to ease his tongue inside. He licked her as if she were indeed a treat, using long, luscious strokes that made her toes curl in her slippers and fire sizzle in her veins.

He threaded the fingers of his good hand into her long, loose hair to caress her scalp and the nape of her neck. She arched, unable to deny the pulse of pleasure that rushed through her with a wild beat. Down he went, fingertips moving over her throat and collarbone and shoulder, then lower to steal beneath the edges of her robe.

Finding her breast, he cupped it through her nightgown, along with the traitorous peak that nestled wantonly into the firm flesh of his palm. Smiling against her mouth, he flicked his thumb over the aching point and made her shudder. He was about to do it again—and she was about to let him—when a log popped in the fireplace.

The sound brought her back to her senses.

She jerked, abruptly breaking away.

"There," she said, hating the breathless quality to her voice, "you have your good-night kiss. Now you can sleep."

He quirked a dark golden brow but didn't stop her when she slipped out of his hold. "Thank you for the kiss. It was perfection. As are you." Reaching out, he recaptured her hand and pressed his mouth to her palm. "As for sleep, I fear it may yet elude me, but I shall try."

Thalia said nothing. Instead, she got to her feet on unsteady legs and made her way to the door. When she stood on the other side in the darkened hallway, she clutched a fist against her chest, aware of the swift, almost painful rhythm of her heart.

He'd said he might not sleep tonight.

She knew she would not either.

Chapter 12

"You rang, milady?"

Thalia looked up from where she sat at her desk in the study. She had returned to her town house nearly a week ago, glad to be back in the familiar confines of her own home. Her tabby cat, Hera, was asleep nearby, curled up inside a wooden tray full of correspondence.

"Yes, Fletcher," she said, laying down her quill pen. "I wanted to inform you that I am expecting company this afternoon. Lor—" She paused, the name sticking suddenly in her throat. She cleared it before continuing. "Lord Leopold Byron will be paying me a call. See he is shown into the drawing room and advise me of his arrival."

The butler's white eyebrows rose high on his wrinkled forehead. As a rule, she didn't receive gentlemen callers, especially not the kind who had sent her a gift that she had been sorely tempted to keep rather than send back. But Fletcher had too many years in service to show any further reaction whatever his opinion might be.

"Shall I ask Mrs. Grove to have a tea tray standing ready?" he inquired.

She frowned. She hadn't really considered the social niceties of Lord Leopold's impending visit. Actually, since her return to Town, she'd been trying not to think of it—or him—at all, which sadly had proved impossible.

Much of the time, especially at night, thoughts of him were all that seemed to go round and round in her head—that and the impulse to scold herself for agreeing to his impossible arrangement. But of all the scenarios she had considered, whether to have the tea tray sent up had never occurred. Still, being polite never went amiss.

"Yes, have Mrs. Grove make up a tray," she said.

Maybe food would prove a useful distraction. Men loved to eat. If she filled him up with enough crumpets and tea, perhaps she could scoot him back out the door before he quite knew what had happened—one of their fourteen days together done.

Two weeks!

Guilt or no guilt, what had she been thinking when she'd agreed to his terms? He had been shot and she had apologized; that should have been enough. What she ought to have done was stand firm and say no, especially when it had come to that last kiss, which should never have happened at all. But as she reminded herself, the allotted two weeks would pass quickly and then she would be able to put him out of her life once and for all. He'd promised to leave her alone once their time together was over, and she planned to hold him to that pledge.

Now she just had to get through it.

She also had to make sure there was no further kissing or touching. She'd been weak, allowing him to take liberties. But she would not be weak again.

"Thank you, Fletcher," she said, dismissing the butler. "That will be all for now."

He withdrew quickly for a man of his advanced age. No doubt the entire household would know about Lord Leopold's impending call within the next ten minutes. But they were bound to know about him regardless once she let him set foot over the threshold.

Luckily her servants gossiped only among themselves and not outside the house. Most of them had come with her from Lord Kemp's household after the divorce and they were fiercely loyal. She had nothing to worry about on that score.

As for her reputation, it was ironic that the rumor mill would finally be right. For years her detractors had claimed that she entertained men in her house; now she really would be guilty as charged. Although it didn't seem quite fair to count one man as *men*. Then again, when it came to London Society, one was all it took to be painted with a brush of shame.

A pair of green eyes stared at her from atop her stack of letters. "What?" she asked the feline. "You weren't there. He didn't give me any choice."

Hera blinked, her expression oddly knowing. Then the cat lifted a paw and began to groom her fur.

"What is *that* supposed to be?"

Leo glanced over at his twin from where he stood in the entry hall of their town house. He accepted his great-coat from a footman before dismissing the man. "What does it look like?" he said to his brother. "It's a sling."

Lawrence made a small show of walking around him, his gaze roving over the empty rectangle of black cloth tied with a knot at the back of Leo's neck. "Yes," Lawrence said, "but why are you wearing it? It's not as if you have need of its support."

"Of course I have need. I was shot, if you will recall."

Lawrence crossed his arms over his chest. "How could I forget? I leave you to spend a few days at Holland House and you return home amid a flurry of lurid stories about how you went out to take a swim only to return shot, half-naked and slumped over Thalia Lennox on the back of her horse. The betting at the clubs is rampant that she shot you as the result of a lovers' quarrel, then thought better of it. But, of course, I know the truth."

Leo grimaced. "Wheedled out the truth, you mean."

To his immense irritation, Lawrence was the one person on earth to whom he could not successfully lie. Not only did they look alike; they often thought alike too and knew each other's tells. His twin couldn't deceive him either, so he supposed they were even. Still, he could have done without the needling he'd endured since revealing the actual sequence of events.

"I'd have had it out of you one way or the other," Lawrence said. "Just be glad Mama and the rest of the family have no idea what really transpired."

"And they never shall, shall they?" Leo said in a menacing tone.

Lawrence chuckled, then made a twisting gesture across his lips as if turning a lock and throwing away the key. "You know I always keep your secrets."

"Only because I keep all of yours."

Lawrence shrugged with easy agreement. "So why bother with the sling when your arm is only a bit sore?" Suddenly, he held up a hand. "No, wait, I just realized. You're going to see *her*, aren't you?"

"What if I am?" Leo slid his arm inside the cloth so that it was secured against his chest; one sleeve of his greatcoat dangled empty.

"Playing for sympathy, hmm? Just don't slip up. She won't like it if she finds out you're trading on her guilt."

Leo smiled. "I'm already trading on her guilt. How else do you think I got her to agree to spend the next two weeks with me?"

Thalia paused in front of the closed drawing room door. She brushed a few stray cat hairs off the skirt of her eggplant merino wool gown, then smoothed quick fingers over her hair to make sure no stray wisps had come unanchored from their pins. Taking a deep inhalation, she opened the door and walked inside.

Lord Leopold turned from where he stood next to the window, late autumn sunlight making the gold strands in his hair shine brighter among the brown. His cheeks were dusted with healthy color and he looked a great deal steadier than he had the last time she had seen him. Of course, he'd been lying flat on his back in bed the last time she'd seen him, but she could tell that the past few days had wrought an improvement.

Her gaze went straight to the black cloth sling he wore around his injured arm. She frowned, wondering if his wound was still hurting a great deal.

"Good afternoon, Lord Leopold," she said walking farther into the room; she left the door ajar at her back. "I must say I was surprised to receive your note this morning informing me that you would be paying a call. It has only been a few days since you left Holland House. I thought surely you would remain home for a while longer, recuperating from your injury."

She took a seat, then gestured for him to do the same.

Rather than taking the chair she indicated, he sank down onto the cushions beside her on the sofa. "I probably should still be resting, but I feared that if I put off a visit much longer, it would invite you to change your mind about our arrangement."

She met his eyes, noticing the twinkle in their green-gold depths. "Believe me, the thought did cross my mind," she said. "But men are not the only ones who can be honorable. I gave you my word and I will abide by it. Why else do you imagine you are sitting here in my drawing room?"

He smiled slowly. "Why else indeed?"

A quiet tap came at the open door; then Fletcher shouldered his way inside, bearing a laden silver tea tray.

Thank heavens for Fletcher and his forethought in suggesting that Mrs. Grove prepare something for her and Lord Leopold, Thalia mused. The repast would make an excellent diversion.

"Here, let me help you," Lord Leo said to the elderly servant, rising automatically to his feet and walking forward.

"But your arm, Lord Leopold," Thalia said. "You mustn't strain your injury."

Lord Leo stopped, looking curiously nonplussed. "Ah, yes, my injury." He frowned.

"Not to worry, milord," Fletcher croaked in his thready voice. "I've been carrying tea trays for nigh on fifty years. I can manage this one just fine."

And although he was visibly slow and the china cups rattled in their saucers, the old man completed his task without spilling so much as a drop of tea or leaving a splash of cream on the tray.

"Shall I serve, milady?" the butler asked with great dignity after he'd straightened as much as his old back would allow.

"No, I shall take over from here. And please thank Mrs. Grove. This all looks most excellent."

Fletcher bowed, casting a long, appraising glance at Lord Leopold before he withdrew.

Lord Leo waited until the servant was gone before reclaiming his seat. "Should he still be working? He looks as if he ought to be pensioned out."

Thalia busied herself arranging a selection of sandwiches and sweets on a plate. "He may not be young, but Fletcher is an excellent butler and serves me admirably. If he wished to retire, I would support his decision, of course, but he is a proud man and insists on earning his keep."

She handed him the filled plate and a fork. "His sister and her family live in the countryside. They have offered to take him in, but he says he would rather be put on a spit and roasted alive than spend his last years with them."

Leo gave a brief laugh. "That makes quite an image."

"It does rather, doesn't it? Personally, I believe he stays for me."

"Oh? How so?"

Reaching for the urn, she poured the tea. "He was my butler when I was Lady Kemp. In spite of his many long years of service with his lordship's family, which go back to the late Lord Kemp's time, Fletcher did not take my ex-husband's side in the divorce. When I was asked to leave my former home, Fletcher came with me and has been in my employ ever since. He has become as dear to me as family and will always have a home here, if that is his wish. I feel the same about the rest of my staff. They are all very kind and loyal and I could not do without them."

She looked at Lord Leo for a long moment, then stared down at her cup. Why had she had told him all those things? she wondered. It wasn't like her to be so forthcoming, especially to a stranger.

Except Lord Leo wasn't a stranger, she realized, not anymore.

She scowled and drank her tea.

"I am glad you are in such good hands," he said. He bit

into one of the small, crustless sandwiches she had put on his plate. "And talented ones as well," he remarked once he'd swallowed. "This is delicious. My compliments to Mrs. Grove."

Thalia smiled. "I shall tell her you approve. Just wait until you taste her shortbread. It is quite the best I have ever eaten."

Finished with his sandwich, he picked up a narrow rectangle of sugar-sprinkled pastry and bit in, his teeth white and even. "Hmm, you are right again," he told her. "My own cook is quite adept but not as good as yours, though don't tell mine that I said so. Mrs. Grove's cooking gives me even more reason to look forward to our coming weeks together."

He smiled, his eyes sparkling like gemstones.

Her heart fluttered in her chest in an annoyingly girlish way. But she wasn't a girl, she reminded herself. She was a mature woman with far too much experience to let herself be swayed by a handsome face and a winning smile.

But oh, what a smile it is.

Two weeks of this—of him—how was she going to manage?

Irritated, she bit into her own piece of shortbread and slowly chewed.

"Tattersall's is selling off Lord Drovner's stables tomorrow morning," Lord Leo said after a short silence. "I was wondering if you might enjoy accompanying me. He had acquired some prime horseflesh before his bankruptcy, so there might be some good buys to be had."

"Drovner has gone bankrupt? How?" She set down her plate.

"Gambling, I believe. I heard he recouped his lost fortune by way of some highly lucrative shipping ventures only to turn around and lose it all again at the card tables. Rather imprudent of him, I would say."

"Well, he never did have a lot in the way of brains. Too much hair and not enough sense."

"How apt, particularly given the considerable amount of pride he actually does take in his hair."

"Lud, you're right." She leaned closer. "Does he still wear that horrible pomade?"

"The one that smells like a pine bough?"

"Exactly," she said. "I always thought it a wonder that a bird didn't land in it and try to build a nest."

"Or a squirrel, perhaps, in need of a place to hide acorns."

He grinned and she grinned back, and for a moment she forgot all the reasons it would be foolish to let herself like him.

Unless it was already too late.

Do I like him?

The question danced along the edges of her mind.

"So are we in agreement?" he asked. "Shall I come round tomorrow morning and pick you up?"

She stared, forcing herself out of her reverie. "Oh, for the sale, you mean?"

"Yes. The sale," he repeated, looking faintly amused. "Would you care to accompany me? It would count, of course, toward our two weeks together."

When he put it that way, she supposed it would be foolish to refuse. And she had to admit that a chance to see the horses from Drovner's stable sounded quite exciting. Not that she could afford to purchase any of them, but still, that didn't mean she wouldn't enjoy viewing some excellent horseflesh.

As for being seen publicly with Lord Leopold, well, she supposed it made no difference at this point. Anyone who cared to notice had probably already seen his coach parked outside her town house and knew he was even now inside her home. So what did it really matter? Then too there was all the gossip from their adventures at Holland House. . . .

"Yes, all right," she said. "What time?"

"Eight thirty, if that's not too early. The sale starts at ten, but I thought it would give us a chance to inspect the stock first without feeling rushed."

"I am an early riser. Eight thirty is most acceptable."

He settled back against the sofa. "Excellent. And how interesting that you are not given to sleeping late. I wake up with the sunrise most days myself. We're even more compatible than I thought."

"Many people awaken early. It hardly signifies."

"Perhaps not at present," he drawled in his smooth baritone. "But later, I have every confidence, it will signify a very great deal."

She didn't pretend to misunderstand his barely veiled innuendo. "Then you suffer from an overabundance of confidence, Lord Leopold."

A laugh came from his throat. "One can never be too self-assured. It's rather like having money, I have found. And it is 'Leo,' remember? No more 'lords,' not when we are alone."

"Hmm, so you've said. More tea, *Lord Leopold*?"

He reached down and placed his hand over hers where it lay in her lap. When she tried to slip free, he captured it firmly inside his own. "I'm going to hear you say my name again, often and of your own volition. I look forward to those sunrises when you will whisper it in my ears, over and over again."

She yanked her hand loose. "I thought you understood that our arrangement does not include any bedroom activities."

"I do. Still, you can't expect me not to at least try to change your mind." He held up his good hand before she could say anything in response. "Fine, fine. I'll behave for now. So what shall we do for the rest of the afternoon?"

"Who says 'we' are doing anything further this afternoon?"

"You promised to spend time with me."

"I am. I've fed you tea and biscuits. You may leave whenever you like."

Instead he remained seated and smiled. "Do you play chess? If so, we could have a game."

"You want to play chess?" she said, unconvinced.

"Well, I can think of other things to do." He paused, his gaze drifting briefly upward toward the ceiling before returning to hers. "But since you've ruled that out, I thought chess would suffice. I considered cards instead, but there's this arm of mine. One hand and all, makes it a bit difficult to draw and discard."

She frowned, once again eyeing the black cloth sling he wore. He must still be in pain. She caught her bottom lip between her teeth in an old gesture of guilt, then let it go the moment she realized what she'd done. "I have a set here somewhere. In the library, I think. It's been a long time since I played."

"Good. You'll be easier to beat."

She studied him for a time; then, to her surprise, she laughed.

Chapter 13

"Congratulations, Lord Leopold, on a splendid acquisition," Thalia told Leo the following morning as they stood among the crowd gathered in the auction yard at Tattersall's. "That is one of the most beautiful pair of matched grays I have ever seen. Well done. Well done, indeed."

Leo grinned down into her caramel eyes, not sure which pleased him more — the fact that he'd just won the bid for the grays or that Thalia was smiling at him, more at ease and happier than he had ever seen her look. He gazed at her and decided it was Thalia.

She'd been ready and waiting when he'd called on her promptly at eight thirty. Much to his approval, she was dressed in a dark green kerseymere day dress and a sensible pair of brown leather half boots. She'd donned a warm brown pelisse and hooked a small reticule over her wrist before accompanying him to his waiting coach.

Despite their early arrival, the sales yard had been filled with prospective buyers and curiosity seekers all there to inspect and banter noisily about the horses on view. Thalia had lit up from the moment her feet touched the ground, clearly delighted to be part of the action.

She'd surprised him, as she had done repeatedly since their very first encounter. He knew she rode well and enjoyed horses, but once they began considering individual animals, he quickly realized that she had a keen understanding of all things equine.

"Oh, my father was horse mad," she explained when

he inquired further. "Really, it was the only thing the two of us could talk comfortably about when I was growing up. We used to drive my mother crazy, discussing breeding lines and conformation and which horse had the best chance of winning the derby in a particular year.

"I never really thought about all the things I was learning—I just took it in like children do and didn't question. I was sixteen and on the verge of womanhood when Papa died. I still miss those talks with him."

Leo had thought of his own father in that moment, understanding what it was like to lose a parent at a young age. He'd only been seven when he'd learned first-hand about grief and death.

He'd been glad when Thalia continued talking.

"After that," she said, "my mother saw to it that I focused on what she considered proper feminine matters such as clothes and dancing and preparing me for the Season. She wanted me to make an advantageous marriage, you see." She gave a self-deprecating shrug. "Well, I hardly need discuss how that turned out."

Hampered by the sling he was still wearing, he'd wrapped his good hand around her elbow, then slid it through so their arms were hooked. She hadn't resisted, returning to their discussion of the horses up for auction as they strolled along.

Once the sale began, he'd settled for bidding on the grays, while she had seen a beautiful little mare that had made her sigh with longing. Despite his encouragement, she'd refused to bid. She'd also refused to let him bid on her behalf.

"You ought to have let me buy that roan filly for you," he said now as they began to make their way back to the coach. "It would have been my pleasure."

She paused. "Thank you, but I do not accept gifts from gentlemen."

Does she not?

Most women adored gifts, particularly from lovers. But in spite of her lurid reputation, he was beginning to wonder if there were any lovers. He certainly hadn't seen evidence that he had rivals. And now that he had gained access to her house and spent some time alone with her, he found himself questioning the stories he'd believed about her when he'd started his pursuit.

So who precisely was the real Lady Thalia Lennox? And what was the truth of her past and the circumstances that had led to the demise of her marriage?

"If not gifts, then would you at least allow me to buy you a hot chocolate at Gunter's? I trust you can have no objection to that?"

Her dark brows furrowed. "Not to the chocolate, no, but Gunter's is . . . well, I no longer frequent that establishment."

Because of her divorce, she meant. Because she didn't feel welcome among the members of the *Ton* who gathered there to eat ices and sip tea.

He knew that she was ostracized by Society. Realized that she wasn't invited to parties and entertainments with the people who had once called themselves her friends. Her former husband had suffered no such harm and was warmly greeted at all manner of Society events. Supposedly, Thalia had had an affair: the justification for her disgrace. In the *Ton*'s eyes, Gordon Kemp was the wronged party. But Leo wondered now if he really was.

Whatever Thalia may or may not have done, Leo couldn't believe that the blame lay solely with her. There had to be far more to the story than what was readily visible on the surface.

But for now, he wanted to take her out for a simple cup of cocoa. And the idea that she wasn't "allowed" in Gunter's, well, it made him angry. He didn't bother pretending not to understand her hesitancy.

"The last time I checked, Gunter's was a public establishment. If we wish to dine there, it is nobody's business but our own."

Her eyes widened slightly before they took on a look of sad resignation. "Yes, but it is not somewhere that a woman such as myself goes."

"I fail to see why not. They serve ladies and gentleman and you are a lady. You have every right to visit their premises. I presume you have never been refused service?"

"No, but I have not gone there in years."

His jaw tightened in what his family would have recognized as his mulish streak. "Then it is long past time you did."

"It will cause an uproar—"

"Let it. What do either of us care for the opinions of a bunch of staid old harridans and disapproving ape leaders?"

"It is more than old harridans and ape leaders. Believe me, I know." She laid her hand on his sleeve. "Leo, it is most kind of you to defend me in such a way, but I reconciled myself to my particular situation ages ago. To be honest, it is wearisome being snubbed and stared at. I would much rather drink chocolate with you at my town house. Let us just go back there."

He looked into her eyes. "I don't believe in taking the coward's way out."

"No, there is nothing of the coward in you, Lord Leopold. As for me, I have learned to choose my battles. Besides, Mrs. Grove makes better hot chocolate. Ices are Gunter's specialty. If we want to stage a rebellion, we ought to do it in the summer."

He studied her for another moment, then relented. "I am going to hold you to that, you know. You and me and ices at Gunter's and Society be damned."

She smiled, but said nothing further.

With her hand still on his arm, he started them toward the coach once more.

"You know," he said, "it just occurred to me that perhaps you don't want to be seen with me in public."

Her eyes flashed up to meet his. "If that were true, I wouldn't have come out with you this morning. I am sure someone noticed us together."

"Of course they did. It's not every day I escort the most beautiful woman in London to a horse auction."

She shot him another look, the caramel hue of her eyes turning warm. "Trying to flatter me, Lord Leopold?"

"If it will help win your favor, then undoubtedly."

As she had done the day before, she laughed. The sound made his chest swell with pleasure. Maybe drinking hot chocolate alone with her at her town house was the better plan, after all.

"You are right," Lord Leopold said nearly two hours later. "Mrs. Grove's hot chocolate *is* better than Gunter's." His china cup made a faint clink as he set it onto its saucer.

He'd positioned the saucer on a nearby tea table so he could drink using only one hand. Still, he looked decidedly uncomfortable at times as he dealt with all the restrictions to his movements.

She'd asked him earlier how his injury was faring. He'd given her a curt smile and said only that it was healing. She'd decided to prod no further on the subject, since men could sometimes be touchy about such matters.

"I shall once again convey your compliments to her," she said, setting aside her own cup. "Mrs. Grove beamed like a girl yesterday when I told her how much you enjoyed her sandwiches and sweetmeats."

"Well, the praise is entirely genuine," he said. "You don't suppose she could make up nuncheon for us, do you? It's been hours since breakfast."

"But you just ate chocolate and biscuits."

"A delicious appetizer." He laid a hand on his flat, waistcoat-covered stomach. "Are you not hungry?"

"No, not terribly. But I would be a poor hostess if I did not feed a guest who is in need of a meal."

She rose and crossed to the bellpull.

She was making her way back to the sofa when she heard an odd cracking sound. Without warning, her ankle slid sideways as the heel of her half boot collapsed beneath her.

"Oh!" She reached out instinctively to steady her balance, and stumbled, catching the edge of her gown beneath her other foot. She pitched forward, her muscles tightening instinctively as she began to fall.

A pair of strong arms reached out and caught her. She

pulled in a gasping breath and looked up into Leo's eyes as he held her safe and secure. Her breasts were pressed tightly against his chest, her arms curved around his shoulders as if it were the most natural thing in the world. For a long moment she could think of nothing but him and how right it felt to be held in his embrace.

"My heel broke," she said weakly.

"Is that what happened? I thought maybe you'd tripped on the carpet. Are you all right? Are you injured?"

"I don't believe so," she said automatically. Her nerves were still humming from her near fall—and perhaps from something more.

Knowing she should put some space between them, she stepped back.

Pain stabbed through her ankle. *"Ow!"*

"You *are* hurt." Without waiting for her consent, Leo swept her up into his arms and carried her the short distance to the sofa. Carefully, he laid her onto the cushions.

She clenched her teeth against the pain, which began to subside from sharp to throbbing. Leo knelt at her side and reached down to unlace her boot.

It was only then that she noticed his sling, the black cloth dangling empty around his neck. Why wasn't he wearing it? And come to think, how was it that he'd caught her, and then carried her, when his injury still needed to be immobilized?

"Leo, your arm—," she began.

Her words were cut short when a fresh wave of agony speared through her ankle as he drew off her right boot. "Lie still and let me see if you've broken anything," he said.

She gritted her teeth again as he manipulated her ankle with gentle fingers. *"Ow,"* she complained again. "That hurts."

"I am sure it does." He finished his examination, then laid her stocking-clad foot onto a small decorative pillow that he slid underneath it. "It's definitely sprained and already starting to swell. I expect you'll have bruising too, but it's not broken."

"Are you certain? Maybe we should call the doctor."

He reached out and pulled off her other boot, setting it next to its mate on the floor. "We can, but he's going to tell you what I just did."

"How do you know? Are you a physician?"

The edge of his mouth curved. "I don't need to be. Between my twin brother and myself and our six siblings, I've seen more than my fair share of sprained ankles and broken limbs. I know how to tell one from the other."

Just then, a quiet tap came from the doorway. It was Fletcher. "You rang, milady," he said, the butler moving farther into the room. His eyes widened when they fixed on Thalia stretched full-length across the sofa. "My lady, what has happened?"

Leo stood, calm and innately commanding. "Lady Thalia took a tumble and has suffered a sprain. I need some clean cotton bindings to wrap her ankle, a towel, and ice chips secured inside a piece of waterproof leather or oilcloth. Bring those up first, then have a hot poultice of bran mash prepared. Place the poultice into a covered tureen once it's ready so it will stay warm."

Fletcher stared for another moment. "I shall summon the doctor."

"No need. As I told Lady Thalia, I am well versed in these matters." Leo looked at her. "Unless you require something stronger than brandy for the pain? You don't keep laudanum around the house, do you?"

"No." Her lips tightened, remembering his views on laudanum. Truth be told, she didn't much care for the drug's effects either and the doctor would likely press her to take a draught. "I shall follow Lord Leopold's advice," she told the butler. "For now at least."

With a nod, Fletcher left the room.

She waited until she knew they were alone, then fixed Leo with a pointed look. "Do you really know what you're doing? Ice? And a hot poultice?"

"Cold will reduce the swelling and heat relaxes the muscles. I've found that alternating the two brings excellent relief."

She considered, realizing she was familiar with a similar technique for treating horses. She supposed one might not be all that much different from the other. Resigned, she let herself sink more deeply into the sofa cushions.

Her ankle throbbed. "So?" she said, needing something to distract herself from the pain, "you were telling me about your arm?"

"I wasn't, actually." He turned and swept his gaze around the room. "Are you cold? Here, let me get you a wrap. It won't do for you to take a chill."

"I am comfortable enough," she said.

But he ignored her and walked away.

She twisted her head around, frustrated at being trapped on the sofa. "I am speaking to you, Lord Leopold."

"Pray continue," he called from somewhere behind her. "I can hear you quite well."

She swallowed an oath. "I was just wondering if you have you been lying to me?"

A pause followed. "About what?" he said.

"You know full well what. Your injury. Or rather your supposed injury. Clearly your wound is not as severe as you have been leading me to believe. I am beginning to wonder if you were shot at all."

"Of course I was shot. You saw me bleeding, did you not?"

She had. An image of him ashen and smeared with blood flashed through her mind. Unquestionably, he had been wounded.

"Very well. But why the sling if your arm is healed enough to catch me and carry me?"

He returned, the cashmere shawl she kept draped over the fireside wing chair in his hand. He'd removed the sling, she noticed, his "bad" arm hanging naturally at his side.

He leaned down and placed the shawl over her, taking care to tuck it around her arms and shoulders. "Rest," he said. "We'll talk about this later."

"I would prefer to talk about it now."

He met her eyes. "Has anyone ever told you that you are amazingly stubborn?"

"I believe I could say the same of you."

A tiny smile played over his mouth. "See? Yet another thing we have in common."

A scowl creased her brow. "So?" she pressed after another few moments.

He frowned back. "You're right. I haven't really needed to wear a sling. My arm is still sore and the stitches have yet to come out, but the wound is healing quickly. It's just a matter of waiting for my body to recover fully."

"Then why the charade? Why come here pretending?"

"I needed some means of fanning the flames of your guilt," he said, surprising her with his blunt honesty. "You've made no secret of the fact that you are only allowing me to call on you because you feel badly about your role in my shooting. I worried that if you saw me looking far more hale and hearty than you deemed appropriate, you would put an early end to our arrangement."

"Something I still might do. Did you not think I would discover the truth?"

He shrugged. "The risk seemed reasonable, and I thought seeing me in a weakened state might soften your rather formidable defenses. And it worked. Yesterday is the first time I ever heard you really laugh."

"It may well be the last."

"I hope not. I like your laugh." His voice deepened. "And your smile too. I long to hear and see more of both."

Her heart gave an annoying double beat and she looked away. "I ought to kick you out right now." She tried to put some force behind her words, but they sounded hollow, even to her own ears.

"Luckily for me," he said with quiet humor in his tone, "you cannot walk at present and Fletcher is too old to strong-arm me."

She fixed him with a look. "I could still find a way, if I wished to."

He smiled. "I am sure you could."

She said nothing further, plucking at the edge of her shawl with her fingertips. Why wasn't she tossing him out? After all, he'd lied to her and admitted it. She ought to be outraged.

She *was* outraged. And yet . . .

"Don't ever lie to me again," she said with complete seriousness. "There is nothing I find quite so repellent as deception. If I discover that you've told me another untruth, I really will toss you out of my house and make certain you never enter it again."

His expression turned solemn. "You have my word, Thalia. No more lies. I will be honest with you from this day forward. I trust I have your word that you will do the same?"

She studied him, wondering why she was even considering making such a bargain. Men lied; it was as simple as that. Heaven knew she had learned that lesson in the cruelest of ways. Yet for reasons that escaped her, she believed him.

"Yes," she said softly, "you have my word."

Before he could respond, footsteps sounded in the hallway.

"Your ice and bandages must be ready," Leo said.

He was right, she saw, as Fletcher walked in bearing a silver tray laden with the requested items.

"How are you doing, milady?" the butler asked after setting his burden onto a nearby table. "Mrs. Grove and the rest of the staff are most concerned. She is in the kitchen now, preparing the poultice that his lordship requested."

"Thank you, Fletcher," Thalia told him, while Leo walked over to inspect the items on the tray. "I am resting comfortably. Tell Mrs. Grove and the others not to worry. It is nothing more than a little sprain."

"Time will tell how severe a sprain it is," Leo said, addressing his words to the butler. "Lady Thalia will need to stay off her feet tonight and likely tomorrow as well. Alert the kitchen to have a supper tray sent to her bedchamber this evening—"

"I can eat in the dining room as usual—," she interrupted.

"—and inform her maid to arrange a bolster of feather pillows at the foot of her bed," Leo continued as if she had not spoken. "Her ankle requires elevation tonight to continue easing the swelling."

"Very good, my lord," Fletcher said. "The arrangements shall be made as you request."

Ingrained manners were the only thing that kept her mouth from falling open over the exchange. Thalia didn't know which man she found more vexing, Leo for giving orders to her butler—again—or Fletcher for following them a second time. Still, she said nothing until Fletcher left the room.

"Just because I am mildly discomposed at present," she said, twisting her fingers around her shawl fringe, "doesn't give you leave to order my servants about."

Leo lifted the tray and carried it closer. "I am only doing what needs done."

"So you say. I knew you were stubborn and arrogant, but I didn't realize you were overbearing too."

He shrugged. "Another Byron trait."

"Does your family have any positive qualities?"

"Many," he said, his eyes twinkling. "But we only display them when it is to our advantage."

She gave a soft snort and crossed her arms over her chest. "That I can readily believe. I met your brother once. I believe."

"Oh? Which one?"

"The duke. He was formidable to say the least."

"That's Edward. Although he's lightened up considerably since he married. Claire has a definite way about her and she doesn't put up with his bluster."

"His wife sounds like an excellent woman."

"Yes, you would like her."

Thalia fell silent, aware that she and the Duchess of Clybourne would never meet; they no longer ran in the same circles. Leo looked away, busied himself with the items on the tray. She supposed he must be thinking the same thing.

He turned and leaned over her. "This will work better if we remove your stocking." Without waiting for her consent, he reached for the hem of her dress.

She clamped a hand down on his arm. "What do you think you are doing?"

"Helping you off with your stocking."

"You'll do nothing of the sort."

He arched a brow. "Why not? Modest?"

"No. Just cautious. If anyone is going to put their hands under my dress, it will be me. Turn your back."

"Thalia—"

"Turn your back."

He raised his hands up in mock surrender and did as she bade.

She waited until she was sure he wasn't looking, then sat up so she could pull up her skirts to remove her garter. The moment she did, pain shot through her ankle as her foot shifted sideways against the pillow. *"Ouch!"*

Leo whirled around. "You've hurt yourself."

"It's nothing," she said through gritted teeth. "And you're looking. Turn around."

He took a step closer instead. "I thought you weren't going to lie to me, remember? Stop being obstinate and let me help you. It's not as if I'm the first man to ever see and touch your legs."

No, but it had been a long time, a very long time, since she'd let a man do either of those things. And strangely enough, even that minor intimacy seemed too intense with him. As much as she wanted to refuse, though, her ankle was throbbing like she'd twisted it all over again.

"You're sure it isn't broken?" she asked.

"Quite sure. But that doesn't mean the sprain won't hurt like Hades. Now lie back and let me tend to you."

She hesitated one final moment, then gingerly relaxed back.

She let her eyes close.

They popped back open seconds later when she felt his hands slip under her skirt and travel up her leg with a gliding move that made her skin tingle.

She smacked one hand over the top of his to stop him, clutching it through the material of her dress. "What do you think you're doing?"

"Searching for your garter," he said in an innocent tone. "I'm nearly there, I believe, if you would let me proceed."

"Hmmph. Well, proceed with a bit less enthusiasm."

A grin spread over his face. "I can try, but it might be

difficult. I do everything with enthusiasm, especially when it comes to undressing a desirable woman."

"You are not *undressing* me, at least not in the manner you are implying. You are . . ." She paused, her words trailing off as she tried to think of a way to describe the current situation.

"Yes? What am I doing?" he teased, his grin growing wider.

"Oh, just get on with it and be quick."

"Now, those are words a man never wants to hear."

She stared as his meaning sank in. Then to her consternation, she began to smile. Wiping the look from her face before he could see it, she leaned her head back on the pillow and released her grip on his hand.

As soon as she did, his search recommenced, his big, wide palms gliding upward against her stocking-clad leg. Higher and higher he went, each new touch sending shivers through her body.

She bit the corner of her lip and fought the urge to sigh, the pain in her ankle nearly forgotten.

Moments later, his fingers located her garter. "Hmm, satiny," he said. "I cannot wait to see."

This time she refused to rise to his verbal bait. Instead, she stared intently at a painted medallion of fruits and flowers on the ceiling.

With what seemed a kind of slow torture, he began rolling her stocking and garter down her leg, his fingers trailing after.

The tingles started anew.

He ran one hand along the underside of her knee, then over her calf before he stopped, the thin silk stocking gathered just above her ankle. He slipped the now loosened garter free.

"Pink," he said, holding it up between two fingers. "You never cease to surprise me, Lady Thalia."

"What color did you imagine it would be?"

"I had no idea. That's what makes it doubly interesting." He laid the garter aside, then looked into her eyes. "I shall endeavor to slip this stocking off as painlessly as possible, but brace yourself."

She nodded and fisted her hands at her sides.

Fresh pain lashed her as he eased the stocking past her ankle, but it was over nearly as quickly as it had begun.

"All finished," he said.

Turning toward the tray, he dropped her stocking onto it. Next, he lifted a bath towel and folded it into quarters, then eased it gently beneath her leg and foot.

Again, he left her barely any time to focus on the pain before he carefully placed the ice wrap around her swollen ankle. "How does that feel?" he asked.

She tested the sensation. "Lovely," she said, sighing with relief.

"Good." Leo smiled down at her. "We'll leave it for several minutes until the warm poultice arrives, then switch them around."

She nodded again and let herself sink deeper into the sofa cushions.

Chapter 14

Leo settled a second warm poultice over Thalia's injured ankle, taking extra care not to disturb her.

Twenty minutes earlier, he'd been seated beside her in a chair, softly reading Wordsworth aloud, when he'd glanced up to find her asleep. He'd watched her for several long minutes, the book utterly forgotten in his hands.

Her eyelashes fanned in delicate circles above her rosy cheeks, her lips pink and slightly parted in slumber. Her hands were lax, no longer gripping the fringe of her shawl. Her breathing was deep and even, her pain eased enough to let her rest.

When Fletcher entered the room with a fresh poultice, Leo had signaled him to be quiet, gesturing toward the sofa where Thalia slept. With deliberate silence, the older man had delivered a tureen containing the latest poultice, hot from the kitchen. Then he'd turned his gaze on Leo and studied him with a kind of unfettered curiosity. Leo had raised a brow, but the butler had merely bowed and left the room.

She'd continued sleeping while he removed the leather bag of ice that had pretty much seen its last and laid the new poultice over her ankle, her skin now dappled by a colorful array of bruises. Once this final compress had done its work, he would bind her ankle.

Resuming his seat, he picked up the Wordsworth again and began to read in silence.

*   *   *

Thalia awakened gradually and stared at the ceiling for a few moments before becoming aware of Leo bent over her feet. He was busy wrapping a long length of cotton around her injured ankle in a process that reminded her of a drawing she'd once seen of an Egyptian mummy. Her ankle, she realized, was still quite sore but was no longer smarting as badly as it had been earlier.

She wiggled her toes experimentally.

Leo glanced her way, his brilliant green-gold eyes meeting hers. "You're awake."

"So it would seem." She raised a hand to her mouth to cover a yawn. "Forgive me. It was quite rude to drift off like that."

And quite unusual as well. Generally, she was far too much on her guard to fall asleep anywhere but in the privacy of her bedroom.

He shrugged. "You are not feeling well. An injury can have that effect."

Glancing away again, he resumed his careful binding of her ankle.

She lay quiescent under his ministrations, aware that it was pointless to resist. Besides, she was just too tired.

Of worrying and struggling.

Of arguing and pushing him away.

But mostly she was tired of being alone, exactly as she'd been on the night she'd first met him.

She studied Leo as he secured the last of the bindings, watching the way the afternoon light played with the golden strands in his thick brown hair and the determined set of his jaw as he concentrated on his task.

"Would you stay to dinner, Lord Leopold?"

She wasn't sure which one of them was more surprised, his eyes widening fractionally at her unexpected invitation.

"As I recall, you were desirous of having nuncheon before all this happened. . . ." She waved a hand toward her bandaged foot. "Since that hour has come and gone, it seems only fair that I offer you dinner instead. What do you say?"

His hands dropped to his sides and he straightened, his

eyes all for her. "I should very much like to say yes. But given your current malady, I suppose I ought to help you up to bed, then depart. Although if you wished to invite me to share dinner with you in your bedchamber," he added with a crooked smile, "I might reconsider my good intentions."

She paused for a long moment. "All right."

"All right, what?"

"Have dinner with me in my bedchamber," she said softly.

Her heart gave a queer thump. *What have I just done?* Maybe it wasn't only her ankle she'd hurt; perhaps she'd suffered a blow to the head and just didn't remember.

"I have a small attached sitting room with a very comfortable divan," she said. "I'm sure the servants can arrange something for us there."

A gleam came into his eyes. "In that case, how can I not accept?"

"It is only dinner, you understand," she said, deciding she needed to clarify the point.

"Of course," he agreed calmly.

But then his smile widened—putting her in mind of a cat who has happened upon an unexpectedly plump bird—and ruined the effect.

What am I worried about? It is dinner, nothing else.

But deep down inside, she knew it was a great deal more.

A few hours later, Leo ate a last bite of plum cake with warm brandy sauce, then laid his fork across his empty plate.

"But surely you must concede that Scott's work is often overwrought and unnecessarily dramatic," he said as he leaned back in his chair. "Despite his popularity, I think Scott would do well to continue writing poetry and abandon these efforts of his to write full-length books."

"Not at all," Thalia disagreed, her own half-eaten dessert already pushed aside. "*Waverley* is a fine story. And an author has every right to be overly dramatic on occasion, if for no other reason than to entertain."

"Yes, but does he entertain or just annoy? I suppose you are a devotee of Mrs. Radcliffe's as well?"

Thalia arched a brow from where she reclined on the divan in her sitting room, her bandaged foot carefully elevated on a pair of soft pillows.

After he'd carried Thalia upstairs, her maid had helped her change out of her day dress and into a blue wool dressing gown that was clearly made for comfort rather than style. Her dark hair was pulled back into a long, tidy braid that teased him with the need to slip it free of its ribbon.

He'd smiled to himself at her obvious efforts to discourage any attempts at seduction, despite the fact that it was she who had invited him to join her in her rooms. From the start, he'd realized that an undemanding conversation would go a great deal further than a flirtatious one, so he'd chosen light topics that entertained rather than titillated.

There would be plenty of time later for titillation, he decided. After all, just think of the progress he'd made. Only two days into his two-week campaign and he was already past her sitting room door. How much harder could it be to get into her bedroom and her bed?

He shifted, aware of the half arousal that had ridden him all evening. *Patience,* he told himself, forcing his attention back to the conversation at hand.

"There is no need to be unpleasant," she chided, responding to his question about Mrs. Radcliffe and her writing. "I have read *The Romance of the Forest* and *The Mysteries of Udolpho*, just like everyone else. But you are right, there are other authors who tell a far more compelling story."

"Such as?"

Her chin tilted in unconscious defense. "Jane Austen for one. Her *Pride and Prejudice* is exceptional, witty and amazingly insightful. I also quite enjoyed her latest, *Emma.* The heroine is overly spoiled and meddlesome, but the hero, Mr. Knightley, he is most engaging. A perfect gentleman."

"Is he?" Leo drawled.

"Indeed."

An odd sensation ran through him, one he might have described as jealousy were it not so patently ridiculous. After all, Mr. Knightley wasn't even real.

But Thalia liked this fictional man.

Does she like me?

Given their prior dealings, he wasn't certain he wanted to know the answer.

"Have you read Miss Austen's work?" she asked, completely unaware of his inner musings.

Leo shook his head. "I have heard of her in passing, but have not had the pleasure."

Thalia smiled, her face lighting with excitement. "Then you are in for a treat. I can lend you my copy of either book, if you would like. I do not believe you will find her writing in any way overdramatic."

"Let us hope not, else I consign her to the same purgatory as Scott."

She met his eyes; then slowly her smile deepened and she laughed.

He drank in her animated expression, warmth spreading through his chest at the sight.

"So which fiction writers do you enjoy, Lord Leopold? Or do you not have time to bother with popular literature?"

He reached for his wineglass and took a drink. "I do, if the story is good. Sadly, I often find 'good' to be a relative term."

"Oh dear. I had no idea you could be so hard to please. You surprise me."

"Really? In what way?"

"Well, to the unsuspecting eye, you appear to be little more than a handsome, overindulged young lord, who likes sports, spirits and women."

Rather than take offense, Leo settled further back against the upholstery, enjoying their verbal game far more than he would ever have expected. "You should have listed women first, but do go on."

"The more I come to know you—exactly as you

wished, by the way—I realize that you are not entirely what you seem. You have hidden depths."

"Really?" He swirled the wine in his glass. "I had no idea."

She sent him a look that said she saw right through his self-deprecating humor. "Depths that include the fact that you are obviously an intellectual snob."

He barked out a laugh. "Am I? I believe this is the first time anyone has ever accused me of being an intellectual anything. My professors at university would vehemently disagree."

"Only, I suspect, because that is what you wished them to think. Why is that? Were you merely bored or is there another reason you conceal your obvious erudition? You did promise not to lie to me, remember?"

Some of his relaxed nonchalance fell away. It was time, he decided, to redirect the conversation.

"And I shan't," he said. "But come, how did we start talking about me when there are far more fascinating subjects? Your ankle, for instance? How is it feeling? Still painful?"

Her sable eyebrows drew close. "A bit, yes. I nearly forgot about the pain during dinner, but now that you ask, it has started aching again."

"Then I would advise a spirituous bedtime draught. A hot brandied milk perhaps to help you drift off into a deep sleep. Or would you prefer a buttered rum instead?"

"Neither. I rarely drink anything stronger than wine and I have already had enough of that tonight."

"But you are hurting, so a mug of something stronger won't cause any harm. Listen to Dr. Leo and do as you are told." He stood and crossed to the bellpull.

"You are not a doctor," she said in an amused voice.

He rang the bell. "True. But you've been following my medical advice all day, so why stop now? Have I steered you wrong so far?"

"No, but—"

"Then there is nothing to do except choose. Hot buttered rum or brandied milk? My guess is you'd enjoy the milk more, but it is entirely up to you."

"How generous of you to give me any say in the matter at all," she said, her words dripping with sarcasm.

"It is, is it not?"

She shook her head and laughed. The sound went straight to his loins, making him realize that he didn't need anything but her to warm him up.

"Very well, the milk," she said.

"With a dash of nutmeg?"

"Most definitely."

Chapter 15

More than an hour later, Thalia lay dozing against the divan cushions. Her stomach was comfortably full of warm milk and brandy, the alcohol having done its work so there was scarcely any pain in her ankle.

A robust fire burned in the grate, an indulgence she'd allowed herself tonight because of Lord Leopold's visit. Usually she settled for a modest blaze that died out an hour or two after dinner. Once it did, she would wrap up in a thick woolen shawl to keep away the draughts. But tonight, the room was luxuriantly warm and cozy with no need for extra clothing.

It was so comfortable, in fact, that Hera had broken her usual rule about avoiding strangers and strolled in on silent cat feet. Rather than heading straight for her favorite chair, she'd stopped first to greet Leo, winding around his legs as Hera was wont to do with her.

"How remarkable," Thalia had said. "I've never seen her be so friendly with someone she doesn't know. Generally she hides in another part of the house if I have a visitor. I hope she isn't bothering you."

"Not at all," he'd said as he reached down and ran a palm over the length of Hera's back and tail.

The cat began to purr.

Thalia had watched, knowing something of how Hera must feel. Lord Leo did seem to have a real gift when it came to giving females pleasure.

"Do you have any pets?" she'd asked, hoping her voice didn't sound as strained to him as it did to her.

He glanced up, Hera still purring happily beneath his hand. "Not here in London, no. But my little sister, Esme, keeps a veritable menagerie of animals at Braebourne, so I get my fill of furry company whenever I go back to visit.

"I've considered getting a dog," he said as Hera gave a contented little meow, then moved away to jump into her chair near the fireplace. "Perhaps there will be a likely puppy in need of a home when I go for the Christmas holidays."

"I hope so. Animals are wonderful company and they are never cruel or deceitful. Be kind to them and they will be kind back. If only people were so admirable in their dealings, just think how much better the world would be."

He'd gazed at her then, a thoughtful expression in his eyes.

Luckily, the maid had chosen that moment to knock, entering the room with her hot brandied milk and ending their conversation.

Drifting sleepily now, Thalia lay with her eyes closed, knowing she would need to bid Lord Leo good night soon. Her lady's maid should be able to help her limp into her bedchamber once he had gone. She would ask him to ring for her in a minute.

The next thing she knew was the sensation of two strong arms sliding beneath her. *I must have dozed off,* she realized. "Leo?"

"Keep sleeping," he murmured in a voice as rich and smooth as the hot toddy she'd drunk. His arms tightened as he began to lift her.

"I can manage—"

"Not without difficulty. Now just relax." He straightened, cradling her securely against him.

"But your injury—"

"Is fine. Barely a twinge."

There was a slight edge to his words that made her suspect he was playing down his discomfort, but then he was carrying her and she was simply too tired to resist. Besides, it was lovely being held this way—much more than it had any right to be.

Closing her eyes, she pressed her cheek against the soft wool of his coat and breathed him in, catching traces of linen starch, citrus and a clean, male scent uniquely his own.

Another warm blaze burned in her bedroom fireplace, the sheets and counterpane already turned down on her bed. Leo carried her across the room and laid her carefully onto the mattress.

She sank against the feather tick, her head cradled by a pair of fluffy pillows so soft that she nearly sighed aloud with contentment.

Seconds later, that contentment disappeared, her eyelids popping open as she felt his hand slide beneath the hem of her nightgown and around the bare skin of her calf.

Her gaze locked with his.

"Just settling your ankle on the bolster your maid prepared," he said in way of explanation. "You still have a fair amount of swelling. This should help."

My ankle.

Between the liquor and the relaxation, she'd nearly forgotten about the sprain. Or had the pain dulled because of Lord Leopold? Because he'd driven it temporarily from her mind by the sheer force of his presence?

Her pulse drummed with a deep, visceral beat when she felt his hand lie still against her calf, even though he had finished arranging her foot on the pillows.

"Comfortable?" he asked.

"Enough," she said, willing her heart to slow. Instead it sped faster.

"Do you require anything further? A glass of water, perhaps? Or an extra blanket?"

She shook her head. "No, nothing."

"I suppose I should be going."

"Yes, I suppose you should," she said, suddenly breathless.

Yet he made no move to leave and she did nothing to make him.

"I'll say good night, then. I know you need to rest."

Her lips parted. "I do."

He lifted his palm from her leg; she instantly felt the loss, foolish as it might seem to feel that way.

Without a word, he pulled the covers over her and tucked them in snugly. But rather than step away, he moved closer. Planting a hand on either side of her, he bent near. "I'd stay, if you weren't hurt."

She studied him intently. "If I weren't hurt," she said in a near whisper, "I just might let you."

A light flared deep in his eyes.

She swallowed, wondering what had come over her tonight. Had she really meant to say that? Or was it the brandy talking?

But she supposed she must have meant it, since she'd let Leo past her bedroom door. Injured or not, she could have stopped him if she'd really wished to do so.

"God, you make it hard to go," Leo said, his powerful arms caging her between them. "I suppose I'll have to settle for a good-night kiss. I'll want more once you're better."

And strangely, she thought she might too.

Then he was kissing her, his mouth commanding and persuasive, seductive and eager, as he led her down a path of dark desire and sweeping surrender. But he sought more from her than acquiescence, demanded her full and unqualified response.

Unthinkingly, she gave it, returning his kisses as he coaxed her lips apart and drew her deeper beneath his spell. His tongue circled hers in a slow, wet slide that made delicious shivers chase over her skin and heat spark like lightning in her system.

It was as if she were caught inside a storm, dangerous need crashing inside her as he kissed her with an intensity she was helpless to resist. Blindly, she speared her fingers into his thick golden brown hair, the strands as soft as living silk beneath her touch.

Her mind floated away with the force of her pleasure, making her wonder if this was real or if she was still asleep and dreaming instead.

Then he was seated hip to hip with her on the bed, the bedclothes he'd so painstakingly tucked around her moments ago tossed to her knees. Before she quite knew how it had happened, the tie on her robe lay undone, the buttons on her nightgown unfastened, as he scattered hot, sultry kisses over her cheeks and jaw and along the sensitive length of her throat.

Her fingers tightened in his hair as he moved lower, kissing his way over the flushed, tingling skin of her bare shoulders and chest before burying his face between her naked breasts.

Wild tendrils of desire quivered through her, with want such as she had never known consuming her.

He raised his head and met her gaze, his eyes burning with undisguised lust. "Madame, you are exquisite."

Without looking away, he dipped his head again and licked one of her pink nipples, circling the tip with a warm, wet stroke of his tongue. Then he blew softly, sending a gentle gust of air over her damp flesh to devastating effect before raking his teeth across her taut, aching peak.

She shuddered, then shuddered again as he repeated the process, driving her half-mad as he licked and circled, blew and nibbled over and over again.

Apparently not one to stint, he moved on to her other breast and played there with a leisurely thoroughness that bordered on torture. He teased her nipple with the same sinful magic he'd used before until she thought she might die from delight.

Just when she was sure she couldn't bear another moment of the emotions flooding through her, he cupped her breasts, cradling one in each wide palm, and began to feast in earnest. He hummed low in his throat, making sounds of decadent satisfaction as he opened his mouth and drew strongly upon her.

The sweet suction radiated all the way to her toes, and even more strongly between her legs, where she was wet and aching with need. Gordon used to complain she was frigid and unresponsive; she didn't feel frigid or unresponsive now.

Still, Leo needed to stop. Already his embrace had spiraled far beyond the simple good-night kiss he'd promised. And far, far beyond her ability to control.

Yet just as she was gathering herself to push him away, he leaned up and kissed her again, taking her mouth in a fervid joining that made the last of her good intentions drift off into the ether.

He drew her down, deep where she couldn't seem to find the surface anymore, where her senses ruled unopposed. His fingers stroked her sensitized breasts, while his lips roved in lazy forays across her mouth and nose, cheeks and forehead and chin.

He traced his tongue along the edge of her ear, dipping in like a bee gathering nectar before nibbling just behind in a spot that made her quake. "Whatever you do, don't move," he whispered quietly.

Her thoughts hazy, she could only nod, eager to see where he would go next.

But it wasn't his lips that sought new territory, rather one of his hands that stole soft as a shadow beneath her nightdress. Up he glided, over calf and knee, then across the tender length of her thigh. Higher and higher he roved, fingers gliding and caressing until he reached the V of her thighs, where he paused in search of an even more intimate caress.

Her eyes flashed open and she laid a hand over his, the light wool of her nightgown bunched between them. *"Lord Leo?"*

"Lady Thalia?" He smiled. "Though might I suggest a less formal term of address considering our present situation?"

"Y-you need to stop," she said.

"Do I? Are you sure?" He claimed her mouth again, his kiss turning her feverish and dizzy once more.

Below, he moved boldly to cover her mound, pressing the heel of his palm against her with a gentle yet devastating pressure. "Let me. Just don't move. I don't want anything to hurt." He kissed her again. "At least nothing that won't feel good later."

She trembled, wondering how she had come to such a pass. But then she didn't have time to wonder any longer as his fingers teased her nether curls and found the dampness gathered there. He kissed her again and continued his quest, tenderly stroking and touching her in ways that made it more and more impossible to resist.

She closed her eyes and searched for strength, fighting him, fighting herself.

But it was a useless effort, her hunger too overwhelming to deny. With a sigh, she let her hand go lax as she silently gave him permission to do as he wished.

Gently, he parted her thighs, shifting the knee of her good leg slightly upward so he could fit his hand fully between her legs. He teased her again, rubbing only the outer lips of her feminine core so that she grew even wetter, even more desperate. Her hands fisted at her sides as he continued his passionate assault, each stroke more wicked than the last.

Voluntarily, she edged her thighs open wider and grabbed again for his hand—this time to pull him closer.

"Touch me," she begged.

"I believe that's what I'm doing." He teased her down low again, making her arch against him.

"Ah, ah," he warned softly. "I told you not to move. Your ankle, remember?"

But she hadn't, she realized. She'd forgotten all about her sprain, his touch so enthralling it had driven everything else from her mind.

She forced herself to lie still, biting her lip as she waited for him to continue.

"Good girl," he said. "I believe you deserve a reward."

Slowly, he opened her, parting her like the petals of a flower as he slipped inside. Delving steadily, he eased in one long finger, first to the knuckle, then as far as it would go.

A cry burst from her lips as her inner muscles clenched around him in welcome.

But even that wasn't enough.

She needed more. And he knew it—the devil.

With a smile that rivaled Mephistopheles himself, he waited, watching as they both felt her body grow even slicker around him.

He stirred his finger inside her, circling as he massaged her inner flesh in the most astonishing way. He slid his finger out, then in again to stroke her anew.

Her nipples tightened, throbbing along with the rest of her. As if sensing their need, Leo reached out and took one bud between his thumb and forefinger. He squeezed, ripples of half pleasure, half pain cascading through her as he fingered her harder between her thighs.

Without warning, he added a second digit, filling her, stretching her so that she trembled and moaned.

"Ah, God!" she cried, everything narrowing in that moment to the sensation of his fingers moving over her and in her. He pinched her nipple again, then fondled her breast. He did the same to her other breast as he continued stroking fast and deep inside her.

Suddenly, he added his thumb below where her most sensitive flesh wept for his every touch and then she started to shake.

Rivers of bliss poured through her, pleasure unlike any she had ever known coursing in rivulets through her veins. Her mind grew dull from the surfeit of delight.

Then everything went utterly and completely black.

Leo watched Thalia take her release and thought it was the most beautiful thing he'd ever seen.

She is magnificent.

Her skin was flushed and rosy, her lips parted on a sigh of blissful satisfaction, her eyes closed, lashes inky black against the creamy glow of her cheeks. She looked disheveled and well pleasured, and he should know, since he was the one who had pleasured her.

As for him, his shaft was swollen and throbbing, aching to be as thoroughly appeased as she. But much as he wanted to unbutton his trousers and slide between her milky white thighs to take his ease, he knew she was in much too delicate a state to withstand such vigorous play. He'd pushed the limits as it was—her injured ankle somehow still miraculously tucked in its nest of plush pillows, apparently no worse for their amorous activities.

For now, he needed to let her heal—let himself heal for that matter, since the stitches in his arm had been tugged and tested enough for one night.

But this was only the beginning. And considering how

long he'd already waited, he supposed he could wait a while longer. Especially now that he'd had a taste of her honey.

Lord, she was sweet.

And responsive.

Though strangely, he had to wonder as he watched her doze lazily against the pillows, how sexually experienced she really was.

She wasn't a virgin, of course; that much was clear. Yet she'd seemed so surprised by her reactions to his touch, dawning amazement sweeping over her features as he'd carefully built her desire to greater and greater heights. It was as if tonight was the first time she'd ever truly been aroused. The first time she'd ever found real completion.

If that was true, her former husband must have been a complete lout in the bedchamber. Then again, far too many men were dreadful lovers, concerned for nothing but their own selfish pleasure. When he made love to a woman, he always made sure she claimed as great a share of the satisfaction as he did himself.

He'd lost his own virginity at sixteen to a very experienced, very adventurous widow who'd taught him well the importance of taking care of a bedmate's needs. Increasing his lover's pleasure, he'd learned, inevitably served to increase his own.

He'd put those skills to excellent use in the years since he and his widow had gone their separate ways. He rarely thought of her now—she'd remarried and gone to India, last he'd heard—but he owed her a debt of gratitude for tutoring him so expertly.

Perhaps she was the reason he still preferred older women?

He studied Thalia again, her features ethereally lovely in repose.

What a puzzle she was. A beautiful, mysterious conundrum that demanded to be solved. The longer he knew her, the less about her he really understood.

"Who are you, Thalia?" he whispered, reaching out to brush a wisp of dark hair off her cheek.

She sighed and rolled her head toward him, still asleep.

He wished he could strip off his clothes and climb into the bed beside her. But tonight was not the night.

Soon.

Very soon he would come to her bed, now that they were lovers. And she would find herself satisfied again—well and often.

With gentle efficiency, he smoothed her nightgown down her legs and buttoned her bodice over the glorious breasts he had so enjoyed kissing and fondling. His fingers slowed briefly as he forced himself to fasten the last one before all his good intentions turned to dust.

He stood and reached for the bedclothes, pulling them up to her chin to tuck her in once more. Bending low, he brushed a soft kiss over her lips.

"Leo? Is that you?" she murmured, stirring beneath the sheets.

"Yes." He stroked his hand over her hair. "Sleep. I shall see you tomorrow."

"Tomorrow," she repeated sleepily, her eyelids already drifting closed again.

Smiling, he allowed himself one last look, then turned and left.

Chapter 16

Thalia awakened the next morning with a smile on her face.

She'd slept deeply. Peacefully. Better than she had in too long to remember.

And the dreams.

She'd had the most amazingly wonderful dreams. Lush and vivid and so intense they'd almost seemed real.

Lord Leo had been in them, kissing her and doing all manner of other things that made the blood turn hot in her veins to remember. Things that made her imagination run wild even now.

In response, her nipples tightened into hard peaks, feeling unusually sensitive as they rubbed against the fine wool of her nightgown. And between her legs came a languorous, liquid ache as if her flesh were reliving the delirious sensation of his fingers stroking her deep inside. Stroking her to a pleasure she'd never experienced before.

Her eyes popped open. *Good God, it hadn't been a dream.*

Where was Lord Leo now?

Was he still here?

She sat up abruptly and looked around for him.

As she did, a jab of pain shot through her injured ankle. "Oh," she groaned, sinking back against the pillows again.

Her ankle.

She'd forgotten all about it, exactly as she had last night after Lord Leopold carried her to bed.

She covered her eyes with her hands now as all the rest of the memories flooded back over her. So much for her firm resolve. One simple dinner in her sitting room and she'd been as malleable as clay, letting him touch her with an intimacy that had rocked her to her core.

Despite all the supposed evidence to the contrary, she'd been with only one man in her life. Gordon. The husband who had used and manipulated her. Who had disgraced and ruined her with a cruelty she could scarcely bear to contemplate even now.

After last night, she realized he had done her an even greater wrong, convincing her that she was incapable of passion, unable to derive pleasure from the physical side of her nature. But now she knew he'd lied to her on that score as well.

Because of Leo.

Because he'd shown her there could be more than dutiful subjugation at the hands of a man.

Even so, she wasn't sure what she wanted. Was she ready to let things go further between her and Leo? Did she want to accept him into her life, into her body? She knew it was what he wanted, what he would expect, after everything they'd shared last night.

Yet still she hesitated.

Her life was her own now, for good or bad. Did she want to change that? Did she want to become what Society claimed her to be—a wanton woman?

Up to now, she'd had her pride to carry her through the rough times, even if she was the only one who knew the truth about her virtue. But if she took Lord Leo to her bed, what then? And how would she feel after their affair ran its inevitable course and came to an end?

She was still contemplating the situation when her maid arrived with breakfast. She bade her enter, grateful for the interruption.

Bathed, dressed and fed two hours later, she allowed her maid to help her hobble over to the sofa in her sitting room.

To her pleased surprise, she'd found her ankle greatly improved with most of the swelling gone and only a bit of bruising and soreness remaining. Lord Leo's doctoring skills were apparently as good as he'd claimed. Even so, she wasn't well enough to resume her usual activities. She settled comfortably onto the sofa instead, wrapped up in a warm shawl with a good book in hand.

She'd been reading for nearly an hour when a knock sounded at her door.

It was Fletcher.

"Pardon the interruption, milady," he said, "but a caller has arrived."

Lord Leopold.

She laid her book onto her lap, curious flutters springing to life in her stomach. She'd known he would visit her, but she'd thought he would at least wait until after the noon hour. "Yes, Fletcher. Please show him up."

"Lady Cathcart is the visitor, ma'am," he explained with no outward acknowledgment that he'd noticed her assumption that the caller was Lord Leopold. "I put her ladyship in the downstairs drawing room. I wasn't certain if you were receiving today due to your injury."

"Tilly's here?" Her nerves at seeing Leo vanished. "Yes, of course. Show her up immediately. And bring tea. And sweets. Lady Cathcart never drinks tea without a sweet."

Fletcher smiled. "Very good, milady."

Thalia marked her page, set her book aside and waited for her friend, awash with an entirely different sort of anticipation from before.

"Fletcher says you are hurt," Mathilda Cathcart declared without preamble as she crossed over the threshold on a rustle of elegant dark apricot taffeta skirts. "You poor dear, whatever has happened?"

As blond as Thalia was dark, and as slender and graceful as a willow branch, Mathilda Cathcart was the epitome of everything feminine and lovely. She moved quickly across to the sofa, arms outstretched. "No, no, don't get up."

Bending low, Mathilda wrapped her in a warm embrace, then dusted each cheek with a quick, friendly kiss. Her mother, being half-French, had passed along certain Continental traits to her daughter growing up. And despite the best efforts of her stern English grandmother and her often absent father, Mathilda still clung to a few of her supposed "foreign flaws."

Thalia smiled at her friend and returned her hug. "What a wonderful surprise," she said as Mathilda moved away and sank down into a nearby chair. "But what are you doing here? I thought you were at Lambton until after the holidays."

"Oh, I was, but the house party broke up last week and the place has been frightfully dull ever since. When Henry said he was coming up to London on some parliamentary business, I decided to come too."

"What excuse did you give this time? Or does he even know you're visiting me?"

"He thinks I'm shopping, but as his mother always says, what he doesn't know won't hurt him," Mathilda said, drawing off her gloves. "We all have our little secrets, after all."

Thalia's brows drew close, thinking she detected a thread of strain in her friend's voice.

The two of them had known each other since age eighteen, when they'd both been nervous debutantes embarking on their first London Season. Sensing kindred spirits, they had formed a swift, strong bond of friendship that had withstood their subsequent marriages, the births of Mathilda's three children and—most telling of all—the ravages of Thalia's divorce.

Mathilda's support had never wavered, not once, not even in the face of the most salacious testimony during the divorce proceedings. She'd known that Thalia was the wronged party, whatever had been publicly reported. She'd never even asked for an explanation, although Thalia had told her all the most important parts—the ones that made a difference anyway.

Thalia studied Mathilda. "Tilly, is anything wrong?"

"Wrong? Of course not," Mathilda replied in a not entirely convincing tone. "But what are we doing talking about me when you are the one ailing? What happened to take you off your feet?"

"Nothing so very dreadful," Thalia said, deciding she

could wait until later to probe deeper into whatever was troubling her friend. "It's rather silly really. My bootheel broke and I sprained my ankle."

"Oh, how awful. Did you fall? Are you hurt otherwise?"

"No, someone was there to catch me before I could do any serious damage."

"Someone?" Mathilda's blue eyes twinkled with sudden interest. "Someone who?"

"No one you know," Thalia said, realizing her mistake in mentioning that particular detail. "Oh, look, here comes the tea."

Fletcher made his slow, careful way inside, providing a distraction at just the right moment.

"Don't think this conversation is over," Mathilda said under her breath as Fletcher set down the large silver tray.

"The one we began about you isn't either," Thalia replied.

Mathilda frowned.

They chatted about inconsequential things while the butler laid out plates of sweets, tiny sandwiches and accompaniments. Lastly, he arranged the tea urn in front of Lady Cathcart so she could serve, since Thalia wasn't able to do her usual duty as hostess. Then he withdrew.

"Hmm, these jam tarts are quite the best I've ever had," Mathilda remarked a couple of minutes later. "You must give me the recipe for my cook."

"Gladly. So how are the boys?"

"They're well. Tom went off to Eton this year, you know." Mathilda gave a sad little sigh. "Soon all my babies will be leaving the nest and the nursery will be quite empty. Seems like only yesterday I was rocking them to sleep." She ate another biscuit and drank a quarter of her tea.

"Is that what's wrong? Are you missing Tom and worrying about the day the other boys are off to school as well?"

"Of course, I miss him and dread the day all of them are gone. But no, that is not the trouble."

"So what is it?" Thalia reached out a hand. "You can tell me. Isn't that why you came? So we could talk?"

Mathilda raised her eyes. "I couldn't put it in a letter. It would have made it seem far too real." She took a deep breath. "I think Henry is having an affair."

Thalia paused. "Surely not. He's always been devoted to you. Whatever I may think of him otherwise, I've never been able to fault him in regards to you."

"He doesn't dislike you, you know," Mathilda said. "He finds you amazingly resourceful and brave. It's just . . . well, it's only that he . . ."

"Disapproves," Thalia supplied. "Yes, I know. He is simply watching out for your reputation, not wanting your association with me to taint your place in Society. I quite understand."

"And you should also understand that I don't give a tuppence about such things," Mathilda said fiercely. "You are always welcome at Lambton, however much Henry may worry about raised eyebrows. You ought to have accepted my invitation this past autumn, but you never do. Come for Christmas instead. I would dearly love to have you come for a visit."

"And ruin your holidays? I think not."

It was an old discussion between them; every year Mathilda invited her to her country estate and every year Thalia refused. Her friend Jane Frost did the same. But she couldn't burden either of them with the trouble that would ensue from having such a notorious divorcée in attendance. No, Mathilda's husband was right to discourage their friendship. If Thalia were a better friend to both women, she would have severed ties with them long ago.

Thalia drank the last of her tea, then set her cup aside. "So why do you think Henry is being unfaithful?"

"It's nothing obvious, no scented love letters or midnight rendezvous. But he's been distant lately, preoccupied, and when I ask him what the matter is, he brushes it off. Tells me I am imagining things and that all is well."

Mathilda frowned and bit into another jam tart. "I might almost believe him if it weren't for his frequent trips to London. Business, he says, but it's more. I know it's more. We don't talk the way we used to and he—" She looked away and bowed her head. "He hardly ever visits my bed. I don't think he loves me anymore."

Mathilda burst into tears.

"There, now, I'm sure that's not true." She reached across and squeezed her hand. "He's always adored you. It has to be something else."

"Yes, but what?" she said on a sniff, finding a handkerchief to wipe her eyes.

"Who can tell? You know how men are, silent and all stiff upper lip when they think a woman ought not to know. Look, I haven't the connections I used to, but there may be a way of finding out more."

"Really?" Mathilda brightened, sniffing again.

"I probably shouldn't have said, since I can't promise anything, but I shall do my best. Do you think you can rest easier about it now?"

"I shall try." Mathilda blew out a breath and forced a smile. "And thank you for listening. You are very good."

Thalia laughed. "You are the only one who thinks so."

"Oh, I doubt that." Mathilda took a minute to pour them both fresh cups of tea. "Now what is this about your accident and someone being there to catch you? Who, pray tell, is this someone?"

Thalia hesitated, using the excuse of balancing her teacup to give herself a moment to reply. "It was Fletcher. He caught me just moments after I tripped."

"Fletcher?" Mathilda lifted a skeptical brow.

"Indeed. He is far stronger than he looks despite his age."

"Of course. And the ocean is full of mermaids and soap bubbles." Mathilda laid a small chicken and watercress sandwich onto her plate. "Be forewarned. I shall worm the truth out of you eventually, one way or another."

"But you have the truth. There is nothing more to be said."

"There is plenty to be said, I can tell. But I shall let you off the hook for the time being." Mathilda smiled and bit into her sandwich. "Now, what do you think of the latest gowns in *La Belle Assemblée*? I must have something to discuss should Henry ask me how my shopping excursion went."

They talked for another hour; then it was time for Mathilda to be on her way. It wouldn't do for her to be missed at home whatever issues she and her husband might be having. They were about to say their good-byes when Fletcher entered the room.

"Lord Leopold Byron, milady," he announced. "I did ask his lordship to wait below, since you are resting in your chambers—"

"But I would have none of it," Leo said, finishing the other man's sentence as he strolled inside. "I've come to check on you, Lady Thalia. How is your ankle?"

"Better," Thalia said as she avoided Mathilda's interested gaze. "Thank you for your concern, but you need not have called today, you know."

Especially not with Tilly here.

If only Leo had waited another ten minutes, he and Mathilda would have missed each other completely, she lamented silently. Not that she really minded Tilly knowing about Leo; it was only that she'd wanted to keep him a secret a little while longer. Despite their passionate interlude last night, she wasn't sure if anything more serious was going to happen between them, and she would rather have waited until she decided the future of their relationship before involving her friend.

"Of course I needed to call," he said. "I am acting as your physician, if you remember. I need to care for my patient."

Mathilda's eyes sparkled even more brightly at that remark; Thalia wanted to close her own and groan.

Instead, she looked at Fletcher, resigned to the fact that Leo wasn't going to take the hint and depart. "More tea would seem to be in order," she told the servant. "Or would you prefer something stronger, Lord Leopold?" she added, turning her gaze on Leo.

A smile played over his mouth. "Stronger sounds good, but tea will do for now."

Once Fletcher departed, along with the empty tea urn, Leo sent a glance toward Mathilda, an expectant look on his face.

For her part, Mathilda appeared equally intrigued.

"Thalia," Leo said, "would you be so good as to introduce me to your guest? I would do it myself, but I know what a stickler you are for the proprieties."

She frowned, catching his thinly veiled reference to their first meeting. "Mathilda, allow me to make you known to Lord Leopold Byron. Lord Leopold, this is Lady Cathcart, a very old and dear friend of mine."

"Not so old," Mathilda said with a smile. "Be careful, Thalia, or you will put us both to shame. Lord Leopold, a pleasure."

"The same, ma'am."

They exchanged a bow and a curtsy.

Mathilda spoke first. "I hope I am not mistaken, but I believe I am acquainted with your sister-in-law Lady John Byron? She came to my notice through her beautiful portfolios. I have all her books of flowers and birds, and when I had an opportunity, I begged an introduction through a mutual friend. She is quite as delightful as her paintings."

He smiled. "Grace is extremely talented and one of the nicest people I know. My brother Jack got lucky when he married her. She and my little sister, Esme, are always talking technique when everyone is at Braebourne. Esme is an artist too and amazingly clever with a brush, and I don't say that just because I am her brother."

"In that case, I hope I have the opportunity to view her work one of these days."

Thalia looked down at her linked hands, all too aware that she herself would never have such a chance. Lord Leopold would not be introducing her to any of his wellborn female relations. Nor did she expect him to. She had lost her place in genteel Society the moment Gordon made his accusations against her and sought a divorce.

"So what is this about you being Thalia's physician?" Mathilda asked. "That seems an unusual avocation for an aristocrat."

"Oh, I'm not a doctor, not in the true sense. But I did step in to help after Lady Thalia met with her unfortunate accident yesterday. We were just back from attending a sale at Tattersall's when she stumbled and twisted her ankle. Had her injury been anything more serious than a sprain, I would have called a real physician."

"Ah, the catcher." Mathilda shot Thalia a look of reprimand. "Fletcher indeed."

"Catcher?" Leo lifted an eyebrow.

"Never mind," Thalia interrupted. "Tilly, I thought you needed to be going along. Of course you're welcome to stay if you like—"

"No, no, you're right. I must depart"—Mathilda sent a glance toward the mantel clock—"no matter how tempting it is to remain. A pleasure to have met you, Lord Leopold."

"And you, Lady Cathcart."

She went to Thalia and bent over to hug and kiss her good-bye. "He is divine," she whispered into Thalia's ear so only she could hear. "You must tell me everything in immense detail as soon as may be." She paused. "And don't forget your promise about the other. I shall be waiting on tenterhooks to hear what you discover."

"You will know as soon as I do," she said with a reassuring nod.

Mathilda straightened, smiling past the lines of strain on her face. "I shall call on you again soon," she said in her normal voice. "Do take care and feel better."

"Not to worry," Leo said. "She has orders to do nothing more strenuous than rest and heal. I shall make certain she obeys."

"My, isn't he forceful?" Mathilda remarked.

Thalia met Leo's eyes. "You have no idea."

But he just grinned, as wicked and unrepentant as always.

Chapter 17

"Lady Cathcart seems quite amiable," Leo said once the other woman had departed.

He studied Thalia where she reclined on the sofa, noting again how lovely she looked in a dark blue velveteen day dress and a green woolen shawl. She wore slippers on her feet rather than shoes in deference to her sprained ankle.

"Tilly is quite amiable," Thalia said. "And kind. She has one of the most generous spirits of any person I have ever known. Which is why I am not angry with you for saying the things you did."

"Me?" He laid a hand across his chest, at a complete loss. "What did *I* do?"

"You told her you have been acting as my doctor. A less considerate and discreet individual than she might put all variety of lurid connotations on that."

"Only because you have a naughty mind." Leaning down, he pressed a kiss to her lips before she could protest. "Then again, you may be as naughty with me as you like," he added, winking.

She gave his arm a swat. "Stop that."

"That's not what you said last night."

"Go sit down." She pointed toward the chair. "Fletcher will be along any minute with your tea."

"As you wish," he said. "Before I do, how is your ankle, really?"

"I told you. It is better."

He moved to the end of the sofa and reached for her skirt hem.

"Leo, don't," she said with a hushed warning.

"I'm just going to look at your ankle. Nothing else."

She met his gaze for a long moment, then relented with a nod.

"I'll look at all your other lovely parts tonight."

"There is not going to be a tonight," she said.

"We'll see. There are a lot of hours between now and then." Taking care, he folded her skirt back just enough to expose her ankle. "It does look better. The swelling is greatly improved."

She crossed her arms. "Yes, exactly as I told you. Are you finished?"

"Almost." With gentle fingers, he probed her bruised flesh. "Still sore?"

"Yes! Quit touching. It hurts."

"My apologies. I see you removed the bindings."

"Yes, for my bath."

"Well, I'll bind it for you again after we have tea."

"My maid can bind it." Leaning over, she tossed her skirts back into place.

"*I* will bind it," he said in an implacable tone. "I want it done correctly."

Turning away, he picked up a leftover jam tart from one of the serving plates and ate it as he settled into the side chair Thalia had pointed out to him earlier. "So? How shall we entertain ourselves this afternoon?"

"*We* are not doing anything. You can drink your tea, then leave me to read and rest."

Not at all as I'd imagined, he thought once again. She had such spirit, whatever she may or may not have done in the past. He liked women with spirit.

He liked her.

"I thought after last night you'd be less prickly," he said with an idle tilt of his head. "I see I shall have to find ways to loosen you up again."

She sighed, then looked down, her fingers picking absently at her shawl fringe. She did that when she was nervous, he'd noticed.

Do I make her nervous?

"Leo?"

"Yes?" he drawled.

"About what happened between us. I know you may now presume that we are lovers—"

"We *are* lovers," he said softly.

"Yes, but that doesn't mean we must continue to be. I am not certain . . . that is, I do not know—"

"Did you not enjoy my touch?"

Her eyes met his, their color very brown. "You know I did."

"Then I do not see a problem. So long as we give each other pleasure, then how is it hurting anyone? You are unencumbered and so am I. Or is that what you're trying to tell me? That there is someone else?"

"No," she said with obvious surprise. "There is no one."

A tension he hadn't known he felt eased inside him, followed by a surge of satisfaction. "Good. When I take a lover, I like to keep her all to myself, exclusively. I will expect the same from you. No other men."

"I told you, there's no one." She took a deep breath. "As for the rest, I haven't decided whether I want to be with you—or rather continue to be with you. I need time."

"And you may have it, within reason. There is still our original two weeks—less three days, of course. I won't hurry you. Well, not too much," he amended with a smile. "Besides, I want you fully healed and back on your feet the next time we make love. That way, I can safely tumble you off of them again."

Tiny lines formed between her brows. "Leo, I—"

A faint rattling of china sounded in the hallway. "If I'm not mistaken, our tea is arriving," he said. "You stay where you are. I'll take care of everything."

"Just a small cup for me," Thalia told Leo once Fletcher and the housemaid who had accompanied him laid the fresh service, then departed. "This is the second tea for me today, if you will remember. I already dined with Tilly."

"Then I shall have to do my best to eat heartily from the delicious selection Mrs. Grove prepared," he said. "Her fare is too good to be wasted."

True to his word, he filled his plate, then resumed his seat so he could make inroads.

Slowly, she sipped her hot tea and took pleasure watching him enjoy his own. He ate with the enthusiasm of a boy, yet the refined manners and appetite of a man. And he was all man, whatever his chronological age might be.

At that thought, the nagging question returned, the one she'd been wondering about in the back of her head since the first night they'd met. "How old are you, Leo?"

He stopped eating and met her gaze. "Now, where did that come from?"

"I don't know," she hedged. "I am just curious, I suppose."

Taking up his napkin, he wiped his mouth, then laid his plate aside. "How old do you think I am?"

She regarded him, letting her gaze move over his long masculine frame and the chiseled planes of his handsome face, his green-gold eyes glinting with amused interest as he awaited her pronouncement.

"Eight-and-twenty?" she said, trying for what she hoped was a guess on the younger side. That way she would be pleased when he told her he was older.

"Not a bad estimation. I am five-and-twenty."

Her eyes widened, rounding for a few seconds while she absorbed his unnerving statement.

"How old are you?" he inquired quietly.

She stared at him for a long moment, then set her cup and saucer onto a nearby table. "That is a very rude question to ask a woman."

"You asked me."

"Yes, and you are not a woman."

"I fail to see what difference that makes."

"Well, it does." She tugged at her shawl, abruptly disgruntled.

"I know you are older than I," he said. "I've always

known and I like that. Girls just out of the schoolroom bore me. Mature women don't."

"Mature women," she repeated in a lowering tone. "So I am mature, am I? You make me sound like an elderly matron. You are not helping your case, Lord Leopold."

"And you are not listening to the fact that I find you alluring and beautiful and far from matronly. Your years, whatever they may be—and I do not believe they are much greater than my own—serve only to increase my interest. What are you? Eight-and-twenty? Nine-and-twenty?"

Seconds ticked past while she debated whether to answer. Yet, as he said, what difference did it really make? Their ages were their ages and could not be altered. And it wasn't as if this tenuous relationship they were forming had the least chance of lasting. He would be gone from her life before he turned another year older, so why should she care if he knew her age?

"I am one-and-thirty, nearly two-and-thirty. My birthday is next month."

"One-and-thirty, hmm? Well, you *are* ancient," he teased.

Her lips tightened. "That is not funny."

"No. It's absurd, that's what it is. You are a vibrant, healthy *young* woman, Thalia, who is only now coming into the fullest part of her life. I think you're magnificent. You *are* magnificent. Why else would I have been chasing after you all these weeks?"

"Yes, but—"

"But what?" He stood and came close enough to lean over her, bracing one arm on the back of the sofa and the other next to her head. "You're always looking for an excuse to keep me at bay, but a small difference in our ages doesn't matter, not to me."

"It's more than small," she insisted. "It's almost *seven* years. You were still a little boy being tutored at home when I was saying my wedding vows."

"True," he agreed, his voice smooth and even. "But

just as those vows you took no longer apply, I am no longer a child. I am a man. A grown man, who desires you, a grown woman. Now, I have a question."

"Yes?" she asked warily.

"If our ages were reversed, would it matter?"

Her brows drew together. "What?"

"If I were one-and-thirty and you were five-and-twenty, would you think our age difference to be an impediment?"

She hesitated, considering his fictional query.

Men entered into unions with women younger than themselves all the time. Society even encouraged it—older men being seen as wiser and more capable of caring for a younger partner. She'd even known men old enough to be a young woman's grandfather cheerfully invited by the family to wed their daughter. Many might find that much of an age difference distasteful, but it wasn't disallowed. Men always paired off with women their own age or younger; it's how things were done.

"No," she said, "I would see no impediment."

He met her eyes. "Then why should there be one for us? Why does it matter that you are a few years older than I am?"

When Leo phrased the question that way, a difference based solely on gender seemed ridiculous. And yet it went against everything society deemed right and proper.

She sighed. "Because it does. Because it is the way of the world."

"Then perhaps the world is wrong. Does it feel wrong when I do this?"

Bending near, he claimed her mouth in a slow, sultry kiss that scattered her thoughts in an instant. She closed her eyes and gave herself over to the sensation, knowing it felt too wonderful to stop.

"What about this?" he murmured, feathering his lips across her cheeks and eyelids and forehead before nuzzling the delicate skin at the base of her ear. He traced his tongue around the edge, then blew gently inside.

A shudder rippled through her. "It feels sinful."

He chuckled. "Perhaps. But not because of our ages. I

think we're uniquely compatible." He pressed his mouth to hers again, then caught her lower lip between his teeth for a quick, playful nip. "I think we're perfect. You're perfect. Besides, I've heard younger men and older women make the best lovers. Do you want to know why?"

He is wicked, she thought, unable to break the spell he'd cast over her.

"Why?" she asked dreamily.

"Because a woman in her prime knows exactly what kind of pleasure she wants to receive and a healthy young man has the stamina and enthusiasm to give it to her." He teased her ear again. "Let me give it to you, Thalia."

She turned her head away, not sure where she found the strength. "You said you were going to wait until my ankle is better."

"To make passionate, full-bodied love to you, yes. But I didn't say I wouldn't kiss you. I didn't say I wouldn't do everything in my power to remind you of the fact that you are already mine."

Before she had time to think of an argument, his mouth found hers again. He drew her down fast, taking her into a realm of dark pleasure and unquenchable need. A raw quiver went through her as she reached up a hand and stroked his smooth-shaven cheek.

What strange power does he have over me? And why do I no longer seem to possess the will to stop him?

It had been so clear in the beginning, so simple. He had been no one to her, easy to refuse. But now he was Leo—a man she liked. A man she had no choice but to admit she desired.

Without even realizing her intention, she twined her fingers through his thick, silky hair to pull him closer. He hummed his approval low in his throat as their kiss went from lazy to intense, each new caress more fervid than the last.

Suddenly, he groaned and broke away, resting his forehead against hers. "If you want me to keep my word, I'd better stop. Otherwise I'm going to carry you into your bedroom and take you, sprained ankle or not."

His words yanked her out of her haze. She trembled, sorely tempted to wrap her arms around him and let him sweep her away. But then she saw the afternoon sunlight flooding into the room, noticed the tea tray and her open sitting room door.

She angled her head away. "Yes. We need to stop."

"I was afraid you'd say that."

But he wasn't angry, she noticed, accepting her refusal with a good humor that she found surprising. He pressed one last kiss on her forehead, then went to reclaim his seat.

"This is fun," he remarked as he refilled his cup from the still warm contents in the urn. "I like having tea with you."

Instead of replying, she straightened her shawl.

She and Leo were playing dominoes an hour later—Hera curled up in her favorite chair by the unlit fire—when Thalia remembered her promise to Mathilda.

"Leo?"

"Yes?" He laid a tile on the board.

It was a double six; she didn't have a six.

"I was just wondering," she said, "if you might by any chance be acquainted with Lord Cathcart?"

She reached into the boneyard—the mass of face-down dominoes laid off to one side—and picked one up.

A four. She couldn't play that either.

"Pass," she said.

"Lord Cathcart? You mean Lady Cathcart's husband, your friend who I met earlier today?"

"Exactly."

She waited for him to play.

Of course, he had a six and a three, the wretch.

"No," he said. "I've seen him at Brooks's on occasion, but we do not know one another. Why?"

She frowned and drew another tile. "No reason. It's not important."

His eyes met hers over the board. "I thought we'd agreed not to lie to each other. So, once again, why do you want to know about Lord Cathcart?"

She played the tile she'd just drawn—a three. "Before I do, I want your assurance that you will keep this in strictest confidence."

"Do I seem like the sort who's given to telling tales?"

"No, of course you are not. Still, I should like your promise anyway."

He gave her a long look, half-amused, half-exasperated. "Fine. You have my word as a gentleman. Now what is all this about?"

"Tilly thinks Henry—Lord Cathcart, that is—may be having an affair. But he and Tilly have always had a very strong, loving marriage and an affair just doesn't seem like him."

"Sometimes appearances can be deceiving." He drew a tile out of the boneyard.

"They can, yes." She knew all about false appearances, maybe better than anyone. "But from what Tilly told me, I think it's something else rather than someone else."

"And you were hoping I could help find out?" He played the three he'd just drawn.

She scowled. "Yes, but since you do not know him—"

"I know people. I can make a few discreet inquiries, if you'd like. Assuming you don't feel it will violate my promise."

She paused for a moment, thinking of Tilly's plea. "No, I'm sure I can trust you. Thank you."

His eyes turned serious. "No thanks are necessary. And you *can* trust me, Thalia. With anything. I hope you will remember that."

"I will," she said perfunctorily. Looking away, she studied the board.

Trust wasn't something she did well anymore. She'd faced too much heartache, known too many betrayals to have much faith in the supposed goodness of human-kind.

Yet to her great surprise, she realized she was coming to trust Leo. She had no particular reason to do so. He wanted her, and had made it quite clear he'd do almost anything to have her. Not much reason to trust.

But just as she'd believed him when he promised he

wouldn't lie to her, she found herself believing him in this as well.

Still, it was a great leap. Just as everything else seemed to be when it came to him.

Deciding to put it all out of her mind for the moment, she reached for a fresh tile.

Chapter 18

A week later, Leo sat at his desk in the study, whistling a tune under his breath as his pen moved across the paper.

"What are you so happy about?" Lawrence asked as he came into the room.

Without looking up, Leo added his signature to a letter he'd been writing, then laid down his quill. "Why do you think I'm happy?"

"You're whistling. You only whistle when you're in a particularly good mood."

Leo laughed. "I suppose you're right. I'm taking Lady Thalia to the theater tonight. It took some convincing, but she's agreed."

"I thought she was injured? Sprained ankle, I believe you said."

"I did and it's healed nicely. We made a first outing yesterday in the carriage. It went so well, I convinced her to join me this evening."

"At the theater? Are you planning to use the family box?"

"Of course." Leo's voice hardened slightly. "You can hardly expect us to sit with the rabble in the pit. She *is* a lady, I'll remind you."

Lawrence paused. "Yes, she is. This just seems a bit . . . public. Have things gone that far?"

"Far enough, and soon to go farther. Since when did you become such a stick-in-the-mud? You're worse than Ned at his most dour."

"I'll have to remember to tell our big brother you said that about him when next we meet."

"He's aware of my opinion about his humorless moods and general inability to have fun, though he's much improved since he married Claire. She and the children keep him human."

"They do. Just before we left Braebourne, I caught them all outside on the lawn laughing while he took turns giving piggyback rides."

"I'm sorry I missed seeing that. But I *was* privy to Jack making daisy chains with his girls. Little Ginny had even talked him into wearing one around his neck. Now, that was a sight worthy of a portrait. If only Esme had shown up in time to do a sketch, we could have hung it in the gallery and immortalized it for all future generations of Byrons to see."

Leo and Lawrence shared a pair of identical grins, then laughed.

"But back to your recent spate of stodgy behavior," Leo said.

Lawrence sobered. "Just because I am more circumspect in a few of my choices these days doesn't make me stodgy."

"What about meeting with old Lady Higgleston? I heard she's hired you to represent her in a lawsuit against our neighbor Northcote. If my information is right, she's accusing him of licentious conduct and moral turpitude for holding wild parties in his town house."

"He does hold wild parties in his town house. But I haven't agreed to represent her. I just said I'd talk to Northcote and see if some accommodation could be made."

Leo sniggered. "That's certainly not going to endear you to Northcote or earn you an invitation to his next bacchanal. Sure you shouldn't be representing him instead?"

"I told you I am not representing anyone at present. Just mediating between two mutual neighbors in order to keep the peace."

"Ah, so you're a peacekeeper now too?" Leo stood

and reached out to lift up one of Lawrence's eyelids. "Are you sure you're really my brother? Maybe a changeling got in one night and took his place?"

Lawrence jerked away. "Ha-ha, very funny. And for your information, I have no wish to be invited to one of Northcote's parties."

Leo laughed in earnest. "Liar."

"I'll remind you that you haven't received an invitation from him either."

"Yes, but I have a woman of my own and no need to sate my lust with a bevy of promiscuously inclined beauties."

"Well, neither have I."

Leo crossed his arms. "Really? Do tell?"

"I've taken a new mistress," Lawrence said with a pleased smile. "She's a singer, who recently caught my eye, and we've come to a very comfortable arrangement."

"I had no idea you'd been so busy."

"Probably because you've had one thing—or rather one person—on your mind lately."

"True." Leo grinned.

"Yes, well, I've set my new paramour up with her own cozy little town house a comfortable distance away. It's working out well. Really, Northcote ought to do the same rather than provoking the ire of a prudish old biddy like Lady Higgleston."

An unexpected thought occurred. "Unless that's why he does it? Maybe he *wants* to be provocative?"

Lawrence tilted his head. "Perhaps. To be frank, whatever his intentions, I don't hold out much hope of coming to an amiable solution between the two of them. But it's worth a try."

"Plus, you're dying to see inside his house. Stories say he has naked harem paintings and a vast collection of other erotic art."

"The stories say he has erotic everything."

"If you manage to get inside, I want all the details."

"And in the meantime?"

"In the meantime, I'll be with Thalia."

Dear Lord Leopold,

I am sorry, but

Thalia stopped and drew a line through the words. After a moment, she began again.

I know I promised to join you this evening, however

No, that wouldn't do either.

I am afraid I am not feeling

Well, that was doomed to certain failure. He would see through her excuse in an instant and be knocking on her door in order to check on her health.

Over the past week, he'd become a regular visitor, so she knew the staff would let him in without a second thought. Even Fletcher's initial cool reserve had warmed beneath the force of Leo's cheerful nature and genteel affability. The long and short of it was that in only a few short days, he'd charmed her entire household.

She scowled and glared at the page, which was littered with a sad cross-hatching of black ink; it looked all the worse in the early afternoon sunlight that shone through the drawing room windows. Reaching out, she crumpled the paper into a ball and tossed it into the wastepaper basket.

With resolve, she laid a fresh piece of parchment onto her writing desk and began once again. . . .

My dear Lord Leopold,

Many thanks again for your kind invitation to accompany you to the theater tonight. Unfortunately, I shall be unable to attend.

There, that should suffice, she thought.

Yet as her pen hovered over the spot where her signature would go, she hesitated, knowing it would not suffice. Leo would want—no, likely demand—an explanation. And what was she going to say?

That she was having second thoughts about this affair he wanted.

That she knew by accompanying him tonight she was tacitly agreeing to be his mistress—declaring it not only to him but to Society at large.

And finally that he would expect to come home with her after their outing and spend the rest of the night in her bed.

She closed her eyes, the memory of his kisses sweet on her lips, the haunting sensation of his hands tempting her beyond measure.

And yet was desire enough?

Was it worth all the trouble that might come after?

Her pen was still hovering indecisively over the page when a light tap came at the door.

"Lady Cathcart, milady," Fletcher said. "Shall I show her in?"

"Certainly." She laid down her pen, quietly relieved by the distraction.

"Tilly," she greeted moments later, crossing to wrap her friend in a warm embrace.

"Oh, it is good to see you so improved," Tilly said, glancing down at Thalia's feet as she stepped back. "Is your ankle completely healed?"

"It is. Only an occasional twinge."

She and Mathilda took seats on the nearby sofa.

Mathilda knotted her hands together in her lap. "I had your note. I came as soon as I could."

Thalia had penned Mathilda just after breakfast that morning. "Fletcher, you may leave us. And close the door, if you would be so good."

The butler bowed and withdrew, shutting the door silently at his back.

"Tell me at once," Mathilda urged. "What have you discovered? I want to know and yet I don't. Silly of me, is it not?"

"No, only human. I'm sorry to prolong your anxiety, but I didn't want to put anything in writing should someone else happen to see."

Mathilda nodded. "Very wise."

"Let me begin with the good news. Lord Cathcart is not having an affair."

"He isn't? Oh, thank God." Mathilda's shoulders sagged with relief. "Are you sure?"

"Yes. From everything my . . . friend was able to ascertain, there is absolutely no sign of him engaged in a liaison or availing himself of the services of a bawdy house."

"That's wonderful news. I'm so relieved." A brilliant smile stretched over Mathilda's mouth.

But less than a minute later it was gone, a tiny frown creasing her forehead. "But if he is not having an affair, then where is he going? Why is he behaving as he is?"

"That's the other bit of information my friend learned." Thalia reached out and laid a hand over one of Mathilda's. "Tilly, has Henry mentioned anything about the estate?"

"The estate?" Mathilda looked confused. "No. What has that to do with anything?"

"Apparently he mortgaged the farms and a few other parcels of land. Everything, I understand, that is not part of the Lambton entail."

"But the farms bring in most of the income for the estate. And he's mortgaged them? Why?"

"He made a few investments that have gone badly and he needed the money to cover them. The debt is scheduled to come due in the next couple of months. If the money cannot be found, it will mean the forfeiture of all the mortgaged parcels."

The color drained from Mathilda's face and she took Thalia's hand in a tight grip. "We will be destitute. And the boys. Oh, Thalia, how will I explain it to them? Will there even be enough money to keep Tom in school?"

"You must not despair. You will have Lambton and a bit of land whatever comes."

"And no means of maintaining it. Oh, poor Henry. No wonder he has been so troubled. But he ought to have told me. He should have let me stand by his side. As the vows say, I married him for richer or for poorer."

"I am sure he didn't want you to worry. And there may yet be hope."

Mathilda met her gaze. "How?"

"My friend knows a man who is a pure wizard at finance, or so he says. He told me that if anyone can help, it will be this man. He would be willing to put in a word with him if you agree."

"I'm not sure. Henry is very proud. Then again, this is no time for pride, which I shall convince him of once we speak. But who is this man? And who is your friend?" She tilted her head, a suddenly shrewd gleam in her blue eyes. "It's not Lord Leopold by any chance?"

Thalia paused, wondering whether she should deny it. But Mathilda would find out regardless, especially if she agreed to let him help. She nodded. "I hope you do not mind that I involved him. You did ask me to help."

"You are right, I did. And I thank you, both of you. Henry might take some convincing, but I say yes to Lord Leopold's offer. Please tell him to contact this financial wizard of his—what is his name?"

"Pendragon. Rafe Pendragon, I believe."

"Good. In the meantime, I shall see to Henry," Mathilda said.

Thalia smiled. "I will let Leo know your decision."

"Leo, is it?" Mathilda lifted a brow. "So are the two of you—" She waggled a pair of fingers.

"No! Well, in a manner of speaking. He certainly wants to be."

"And you?" Mathilda asked quietly.

"I—I am not sure."

"Are you not? I couldn't help but notice the way the sparks crackled between the two of you the other day. He fairly smolders whenever he lays eyes on you. As for you . . ."

Thalia crossed her arms. "Yes, what about me?"

"I've never seen you look at a man the way you look at him. You want him. Even more, I think you care."

"Do I?"

I certainly do not want to.

Letting herself feel something more than desire for Leo would be a dreadful mistake, one that could lead nowhere good for either of them.

"It scarcely signifies," she said. "I have no need of a lover and he is far too young for me."

"Is he? I didn't notice his age; he's such a bold, masculine man. And the two of you seem so well suited."

"Well suited or not, I have decided to break things off." A pang went through her as she said the words. "I was just writing to cancel an outing with him to the theater tonight when you called. It's for the best, I think."

Thalia stared down at her lap, fighting the sudden wave of sadness that engulfed her.

"I cannot agree."

She looked up. "What?"

"You and Lord Leopold calling things off. It is a mistake."

"But, Tilly—"

"I know everything you've suffered, how deeply you have been hurt and wronged. But your life is a lonely one, Thalia, and you do not deserve to spend it all alone. I think a lover like Lord Leopold is exactly what you need. Live a little for once. Your critics will condemn you whatever you do."

"You are right about that."

Mathilda leaned forward, her expression earnest. "Forget all the so-called rules. The only question you should be asking yourself is whether or not being with Lord Leo makes you happy. Does it? Does he?"

Thalia's heart beat strongly in her chest, the answer there before she even had to think. "Yes."

"Then do not send that letter. Just tell him yes and let yourself enjoy what comes."

A half an hour later, Thalia stood before the meager fire in her bedchamber, the note to Leo in hand. She studied it, her thoughts and emotions awhirl.

Was Tilly right? Should she throw herself headlong into an affair with Leo?

The gently bred lady inside her said no. The mature woman who'd tasted passion said something else.

Sinful somethings else.

Excitement thundered in her breast, her body warming at the idea of giving herself to him completely. He'd brought her such pleasure already. Only think what more she might find if she just took off the restraints.

And he was delicious. A man any woman would want.

Yet if she did this, she would be everything Society said of her. She would be wanton and wicked in deed, not just in reputation. She would finally be the scarlet woman she'd been branded so many years before.

Yet whom would they be harming? Leo wasn't married, nor was she any longer.

And as Tilly said, hadn't she suffered enough?

She stroked a fingertip over the parchment.

Then, with a sudden flick of her wrist, she tossed the note into the flames.

Turning, she went to the bellpull and rang for her maid.

She had an evening gown to choose.

Chapter 19

"You seem in fine spirits tonight," Leo said to Thalia several hours later as he leaned back in his seat at the theater.

Thalia sat at his side, looking utterly radiant.

She was dressed in an amethyst satin gown that made her skin glow with vitality. Her dark sable hair was swept high to reveal the smooth white column of her throat. A cameo—perhaps the same one she'd worn the night they'd first met—nestled between her full breasts. He wished he could bury his face against their softness and breathe her in.

But that would have to wait for later. At least he hoped there would be a later.

She turned her soft caramel brown eyes on him, her lush ruby lips curved into a tease of a smile. "I am in good spirits. I haven't been to the theater in years. This is a lovely treat. Thank you, Lord Leopold."

"You are quite welcome. When I asked you to accompany me, I wasn't entirely sure you wanted to come."

"I wasn't sure either, but I have since changed my mind. As they say, such is a woman's prerogative."

"Indeed. Might I inquire as to the reason for this change? Not that I have any complaint, mind you."

"You may inquire." She unfurled her fan and waved it languidly before her face. "But that doesn't mean I must answer," she added teasingly. "Look, the play appears to be starting."

And it was, the heavy velvet curtains opening on the

stage below to reveal the players. The performance was *The School for Scandal*, one of Sheridan's most amusing works. But Leo's eyes were all for Thalia, his thoughts centered on her unexpectedly provocative mood.

He couldn't quite put his finger on it, but there was something different about her tonight. Something more relaxed and carefree, as if she had decided to enjoy herself and the consequences be damned. She didn't even seem to mind the curious looks they had been receiving since entering the box together.

Attendance was light given the time of year, but word of their outing would spread nevertheless. He'd worried that Thalia might dislike the attention. Instead, she paid it little heed, laughing and smiling as though they were the only two people in the theater.

What he wouldn't give for them to be alone, since he desperately wanted to kiss her. Perhaps if he played his cards right, he might be able to persuade her to leave during the interval and return to her town house.

His shaft stirred at the idea, memories of their interlude in her bedchamber teasing much more than his thoughts.

He fixed his eyes on the stage, watching the actors with barely any awareness of the play itself. Luckily he'd already seen it, so his inattention would go unnoticed should anyone ask him about it later.

He curled a hand into a fist on his leg and resisted the urge to check the hour on his pocket watch. The time would pass—somehow.

The audience was laughing, everyone's focus on the stage several minutes later, when Thalia leaned toward him. "How are you liking the play?"

"Quite well," he answered, gazing through the low light into her eyes. "And you?"

"It is most enjoyable. But I find this all more wearying than I had imagined. I was wondering if you would mind leaving at the interval?"

It was as if she had read his thoughts, although he hoped she wasn't really all that tired. "No, I don't mind, if that is what you want."

"It is."

Then without any warning, she laid her hand over his where it rested against his leg. "I believe you will find there are a great many things I want tonight, my dear Lord Leopold."

A hot rush went through his blood. He shot her a fresh glance, but she had already turned her attention back to the stage.

She didn't remove her hand, though.

Flipping his hand over, he threaded his fingers through hers, their clasp concealed from view by the dim lighting. Using his thumb, he drew tiny circles on her palm, pleased when he felt a shiver ripple through her in response.

The play continued with frustrating slowness. But he contented himself, knowing that the best portion of the evening was still ahead.

Finally the curtain descended, signaling the start of the interval. He met Thalia's gaze. "Are you still of a mind for us to take our leave?"

Her lips parted on a dreamy smile. "I am. Please, take me home, Leo."

"With pleasure," he said, wishing instead that he could just take her—right then and there.

Keeping his emotions under strict control, he helped her into her evening cloak, then slipped a hand around her elbow to lead her out.

They walked side by side down the hallway, moving silently through the crowd. They were nearing the staircase that led to the exit when a man suddenly appeared in front of them.

Thalia's step faltered slightly, her entire body turning stiff.

Her smile vanished.

The man was tall and stocky with straight dark hair combed back from a long forehead. He sauntered forward, a faint smirk on his face. Some might have considered it handsome in spite of the expression. Leo didn't, sensing the animus beneath the other man's carefully groomed, elegantly dressed facade.

"Thalia, how unexpected to find you here," he said. "I

didn't think you were still in the habit of attending the theater."

She tilted her chin up, her back rigidly straight. Instinctively, she edged closer to Leo.

He tightened his hold on her elbow, bristling with immediate dislike for the stranger—though clearly he was no stranger to her.

"It has been some while since I had the pleasure of seeing a play," she said. "Had I known there was a chance I might run into you, I would have taken care to choose another evening to reacquaint myself with the theatrical arts."

The man laughed, the expression in his ice-blue eyes belying the humor in the sound. "Always so droll. I miss that about you, my dear."

"How unfortunate, since I do not miss anything about you. Now, if you will excuse us."

Leo curved a protective arm around her back, his mind rife with speculation.

"But aren't you going to introduce me to your friend?" the man said. "He does seem a tad young, even for you. Driven to cradle-robbing these days, are we?"

"Whoever you are, sir," Leo said, placing himself between Thalia and the stranger, "the lady clearly has no wish to further her acquaintance. And I have no wish to make yours."

"Oho, a champion. Thalia, I must say I can see the appeal, puppyish though it might be."

"Her name is *Lady* Thalia," Leo said in a hard voice. "You will address her with respect."

For the first time, the man looked at him. "I will address her any way I choose, since she is my wife."

Thalia stared at Gordon, Lord Kemp, and fought the clammy chill that slithered over her skin.

She hadn't seen him in more than five years, so coming face-to-face with him tonight, of all nights, was a shock. He'd aged very little in the intervening years. There were just a few additional lines at the corners of his eyes and some gray hairs now scattered through the black. He'd always been absurdly proud of his appearance and handsome features. But even now, she had no trouble seeing past the pleasant exterior to the arrogant superiority and cruel calculation that lay underneath.

She fisted a hand at her side. "Your wife? Might I remind you, Gordon, that we ceased being husband and wife long ago. You divorced me, if you will remember, in full view of Parliament and the rest of Society."

His lip curled with amusement. "Now that you mention it, I do recall something of the sort. Still, when I think of you, I still regard you as mine."

"Then I would urge you not to think of me at all."

He tossed his head back on another laugh. "As I said before, I miss our little tête-à-têtes. It had quite slipped my mind how amusing they could be."

And how unpleasant.

"So, how are you, Thalia?"

"Thriving." She forced a broad smile and leaned closer to Leo. "Now, I'm sure you don't wish to miss the beginning of the second act, so pray do go on."

"I will *after* I meet your new companion."

The crawling sensation skittered over her skin again, her instincts rebelling against the idea of him even knowing Leo's name.

But Leo was his own man and spoke before she had time to formulate an excuse. "Lord Leopold Byron," Leo stated. "And you are Lord Kemp."

"Indeed. I am acquainted with your brother the duke. We sit together in the House of Lords."

"Really?" he said in a bored tone. "Edward has never mentioned you. But then, there are several hundred lords who sit in Parliament. I'm sure he can't remember them all." Leo glanced away, his expression even more arrogant than Gordon's. In that moment, he looked every inch the son and the brother of a duke.

Leo gazed down at her. "We're done here, I believe."

She sent him a little smile. "Yes, we are."

Together they turned away.

"At least you've picked a protector with funds, Thalia," Gordon called after them. "If you're a good girl, maybe he'll give you some cash and jewelry as payment for your services."

She gasped softly, then looked back. He'd bullied her often during their marriage; she would not let him bully her now. "You mean in order to replace the personal possessions and heirlooms you stole from me, such as my great-grandmother's pearls?"

Gordon's eyes narrowed. "I stole nothing. If your great-grandmother's pearls have gone astray, you've only yourself to blame. You really should learn to take care better care of your belongings, Thalia."

"And you should learn how to be a better liar, Gordon. But we both know the truth, don't we? About everything."

She would have walked away then, but Leo stayed her with a careful touch.

He locked gazes with Gordon. "Apologize, Kemp."

Gordon arched a brow. "For what? I said nothing that requires an apology."

"Tell Lady Thalia you are sorry."

"Or what, you impudent whelp?"

"Or I'll beat you bloody."

"Really? Right here in the theater corridor between acts? Are you sure you want to attract more attention than we are receiving already? I assure you, people will find it even more entertaining than the play."

And Gordon was right, Thalia realized, noticing the small group of onlookers who had gathered to watch and whisper. She needed to stop this before it escalated even further. If not for her own sake, then for Leo's.

"Leo, come away," she murmured, softly tugging at his sleeve. "It's not worth it. He's not worth it."

"Yes, Lord Leopold," Gordon taunted, "do take my former wife's advice and leave. Or has no one ever taught you to mind your elders?"

Leo didn't move, his jaw set at a pugnacious tilt. "Apologize to her."

"My, you are insistent. But then youth generally is. Too hotheaded to know when to give up." Gordon looked around and shared a smile with those assembled.

"Fine, boy. You want an apology? Then you may have one."

Thalia shrank inside, bracing herself, since she knew just how horrible Gordon could be.

"My apologies, Lady Thalia, for insinuating that you are a whore," Gordon said. "I should have been more accurate and called you a slut instead."

Before the words even had time to settle, Leo lunged and wrapped a hand around Gordon's throat, squeezing hard.

Gordon choked and tried to fight back, reaching up with both hands in a vain attempt to break Leo's grip. But Leo held fast and squeezed tighter, clearly the stronger of the two.

Several men rushed forward and locked their arms around Leo, forcing him to release Gordon as they yanked him back and away.

Gordon bent double and gagged, making a terrible hacking sound as he coughed and struggled for air. His face had turned an alarming shade of red, his blue eyes wide with pain and fury.

Leo shook off the restraining arms of the men who held him, then straightened his coat with a sharp downward tug.

Meanwhile, all Thalia could do was watch in horror, wondering how her lovely evening out at the theater had gone so dreadfully wrong.

"I should call you out for this," Gordon rasped.

"Just name your seconds."

"No!" Thalia exclaimed. "Stop this at once."

Both men ignored her.

"I would. Believe me, I'd love nothing more than to put a bullet through you. But you aren't worth the trouble of being forced to flee to the Continent after your death."

"Why do you imagine you would be the one forced to flee?"

Gordon coughed again, taking a handkerchief from his pocket to wipe his florid face. "Begone, puppy. I have had enough of you and my cast-off wife for one evening."

"Coward."

Gordon stilled, his eyes slit like a snake's. "You are trying to draw me out again, but your words don't wound me. Why should they when you are nothing but the latest lover of my cuckolding bride? I finished with her long ago and I am finished with you now."

With that, Gordon turned and walked away.

Leo took a step forward as if to follow. Thalia went to him and took hold of his arm, keeping him in place. "Leo, please," she said in a low voice, "let us go. You have defended my honor and I thank you, but it is over now. Let it stay that way."

"He is vile. How could you ever have been married to such a man?"

"It was not easy. Please, can we not go home? I just want to go home."

He turned his head, looking at her, really seeing her again. "Of course. I should have thought. My pardon."

Despite the fact that the play had now resumed, a few people lingered, watching them with rapt interest.

Obviously aware of the unwanted attention, he slipped her arm through his. Going to the stairs, they went down and out of the theater.

Chapter 20

Thalia and Leo sat in silence during the coach ride back to her town house.

When they arrived, Leo escorted her inside and up to her sitting room, where they found a light supper awaiting them. It consisted of a small pot of beef soup, which sat warming on the fireplace hearth, along with bread, cheese and fruit.

Before her departure, she'd told the servants, including her maid Parker, that they need not wait up, since she would be returning home late. She'd also wanted to assure herself of some privacy with Leo.

But the evening had gone nothing like she'd planned.

Needing something to occupy herself, Thalia ladled the soup into a pair of bowls, then put slices of bread on separate plates. She passed one of each to Leo, who accepted with a quiet word of thanks.

The silence descended between them again.

But she couldn't eat, the soup too hot on her tongue and the bread sticking in her throat. She set her spoon aside.

Leo looked up from where he sat across from her. "Not hungry?"

She shook her head. "No."

"I have little appetite myself." He laid down his spoon.

He sat for another minute, then sighed. "Do you wish me to go?"

Her eyes met his. "No. Unless you want to. I am sorry for tonight."

"What have you to be sorry about?" he asked. "You are not the one to blame. Lord Kemp is the one who sought to sow animosity, not you."

"Yes," she said wryly, "Gordon has always been expert at inciting discord. Even so, it is your name that will be on everyone's lips come morning. How the scandalous Lady K.'s newest lover came to blows with the husband who divorced her."

"Let them talk. I care naught for gossip."

"That is good, since there will be plenty in spite of the lack of Society currently in Town."

She twisted her hands in her lap and looked toward the fire. "I must thank you again for your defense of me. It was quite gallant, even if unnecessary."

"Unnecessary in what way?" he said.

She looked back. "My reputation was destroyed years ago, so nothing said, however dreadful, could sully it further. It was noble of you to take up my cause, though. I cannot recall ever having been so ably championed in the whole of my life."

"Then you must keep very pitiable company indeed." He raked his fingers through his hair. "What would you have had me do? Stand aside while he called you what he called you?"

"Others have turned their backs. Many others. And Gordon has called me worse, and in far more public surrounds than tonight."

"The man is a bastard."

She didn't flinch at his harsh language. "Yes, he is." In far more terrible ways than even Leo realized.

"I suppose it is wrong of me to admit, but I rather enjoyed watching you throttle him," she said. "Not many have the nerve to stand up to Gordon and certainly not with an audience. I am relieved, though, that he refused to duel with you."

The very idea made her ill.

His jaw tightened. "Why? Do you imagine I would have lost?"

"No. I am sure you are highly skilled with either sword or pistol. But I do not trust him to play fair. He uses tricks;

it is his way. He likes to make sure that matters transpire in his favor, whatever the cost."

"Is that what he did to you?"

"What?" she asked, startled.

"Did he trick you, Thalia? For some while now I have found myself questioning the story everyone accepts about your divorce. Were you really unfaithful to him or did something else occur? As for your myriad lovers, I've seen no sign of those either. Tell me the truth. *Your* truth."

She stared at him, quietly astonished. In all this time, no one had ever asked her that question, had ever wanted to know whether Gordon's version of events might not be as truthful as everyone assumed.

Jane and Mathilda had stood by her without the necessity of an explanation; they had known enough about her marriage to consider her blameless, whatever she may or may not have done. As for everyone else, including the few relations she had left, they had accepted Gordon's accusations without a moment's hesitation. They had condemned her and turned their backs.

But now Leopold Byron of all people wanted to hear her side—a side she had not even been permitted to tell during the lengthy divorce trial.

She met his brilliant green-gold eyes, then drew a breath. "No, I was not unfaithful, at least not in the way they claimed."

"Go on," Leo said patiently.

"The man with whom I was accused of dishonoring my marriage was a friend, or so I thought. We talked sometimes, just talked. It was all very innocent, but I made the mistake of being alone with him one evening at a party. He—"

"Yes? What did he do?"

"Held my hand, nothing more. It was a gesture of comfort. My marriage was far from happy, but then most aristocratic marriages are a matter of convenience rather than affection. Mine was no different."

She glanced away. "My spirits were quite low that evening and he and I began talking in the usual way. He took my hand, trying to cheer me. Then suddenly Gordon was there, yelling that he'd caught me in the act, accusing me of cuckolding him. I could scarcely comprehend what he was saying; it was so wrong."

She paused, drawing a shuddering breath. "Everyone came crowding into the doorway to listen to Gordon's hateful rant. I thought my friend would defend me, but he apologized, a look of guilt on his face as if we really had been having an affair. It was only later that I understood."

"Understood what?"

"That Gordon had arranged the entire spectacle. That the man I'd thought my friend was really his pawn. He testified that we were lovers, that he was one of many men with whom I had relations. He painted me a doxy before the entire world. And nothing I said could change anyone's mind. No one asked me anything because no one believed that I might not be guilty."

She hung her head, her hands clenched in a tight, white-knuckled grip. She wasn't even aware of Leo until he took a seat at her side and covered her cold hands with one of his own.

"I believe you," he said. "I believe every word of your innocence."

Then she was in his arms, clasped inside his strong, warm embrace, her face pressed to his shoulder.

"I'm sorry, Thalia." He brushed his lips against her temple. "I would undo it all if I could. Your hurt pains me." He skimmed featherlight kisses over her forehead and nose and cheek, each slight touch driving away a little more of the chill inside her. "But I cannot be sorry you are no longer his wife. For that, I can have no remorse."

Tilting back her head, she looked into his eyes. "I hated being his wife. Make me forget, Leo. Make me forget it all, if only for tonight."

His mouth found hers, softly, slowly. He kissed her tenderly, as if she were made of spun glass and he feared she might shatter.

And perhaps she might, she realized, but not for the reasons he thought.

She was so tired.

Tired of the lies.

Of the loneliness.

And most of all, of denying her own natural human desires.

She'd been branded a harlot yet enjoyed none of the carnal rewards. Until now, until Leo, she had not missed them. Hadn't even wanted them, thinking herself incapable of such needs.

But Leo made her feel, made her yearn as she never imagined she could. He'd given her a taste of pleasure so exquisite it still haunted her dreams, awake and asleep.

And now, tonight, she wanted more.

Closing her eyes, she kissed him back, silently urging him to take things deeper. But his touch remained light, his every move easy and slow, as if time itself had stopped and they were the only two people left in the world.

He dusted silky kisses over her eyelids, nose and cheeks, then down to her chin and jaw, where he placed nibbling little pecks along the length of her throat. His lips settled at the base, nuzzling there before he began drawing on her with a sweet suction that would surely leave a mark.

His mark.

The knowledge made her tremble as fire sizzled through her veins. Her fingers twined in the dark gold of his hair to cradle him closer.

He made a low humming sound of pleasure as she caressed his nape. Scattering kisses, he moved on to a new spot along the upper curve of her breast. He licked her there lightly, then did the same to its twin, leaving behind a damp trail that set her nerves ablaze.

A fresh shudder rippled over her skin, hot and cold, then hot and cold again. Her clothes suddenly felt too tight, too confining, her thin satin slippers irrationally heavy on her feet.

With a restless movement, she kicked them off.

Leo noticed. "Will your maid be along to assist you tonight?"

She shook her head. "No. I told her not to wait up, that I would see to myself."

He smiled, pleased. "Then *I* shall see to you," he told her, a proprietary gleam in his eyes. "Presuming you will let me, that is."

"I will," she murmured. "Take me to bed now, Leo."

He kissed her again, then entwined his fingers with hers to pull her to her stocking feet. Hand in hand, he led her across the sitting room into her bedchamber. He closed the door behind them with a firm click of the lock.

Still holding her hand, he drew her to the satinwood dressing table with its large mirror. Gently, he turned her around so she faced the glass, her back to his front. Their eyes met in the reflection.

He leaned down and pressed his lips to a spot just behind her ear; her toes curled against the soft wool carpet. "Where does she usually begin?" he asked.

"With my jewelry," she said, her breath thin in her lungs.

He came around and reached for the bracelet on her wrist. Unfastening it, he laid it next to the rose-painted porcelain hairpin box on her dressing table.

Her necklace came next.

Moving behind her again, he set his fingers to work, nimbly opening the tiny clasp. She stood utterly still, watching through shuttered lids as he gathered the warmed gold into his palm.

His lips glided over her cheek and temple. Arching her head back against his shoulder, she let him take her lips in a leisurely, openmouthed kiss that left no doubt of his ultimate intentions.

Her eyelids slid closed.

Rather than continue, though, he went to her dressing table again to place the necklace next to its companion. "Gown next?" he said.

Silently, she nodded.

He took a moment first to remove his jacket, leaving him in waistcoat, shirtsleeves and trousers; then he stepped behind her again.

His fingers went to the small buttons on the back of her evening dress. With a deft touch, he began working them open. "I've been wanting to do this since the night we first met."

Her eyes found his again in the mirror, a faint smile on her lips. "Yes, I know. You were horribly forward."

"I was also hopelessly bewitched."

He placed a palm over the exposed skin of her shoulder for a warm caress. "I thought I'd changed your mind that afternoon by the lake at Holland House, but you ran away."

"I did. I'm sorry about that. And for getting you shot."

"I told you before, you are forgiven. Who could possibly have foreseen that farmer and his gun?"

He slid her dress down and off, pausing to let her step free. "But you were right to make us wait. I can see that now."

"Can you?" Her heart beat faster as she stood in nothing but her shift and stays.

He draped her gown over the back of a nearby chair, then returned to unlace her corset. "Yes, I know you now. We know each other. Tonight is going to be amazing."

Tendrils of anticipation spread through her. She knew he was right.

With a speed and efficiency that demonstrated his familiarity with women's undergarments, he pulled her stays free and laid them on top of her dress.

Then he came to stand behind her again, their eyes meeting once more in the mirror. He pulled her gently to him, rocking her slightly against the unmistakable evidence of his erection.

She trembled, then trembled once more as his fingers moved across the thin cotton bodice of her shift to unfasten the buttons there.

Her eyelids drifted closed.

"Open your eyes," he commanded, his voice rich as velvet. "I want you to see yourself, to see us, and how perfectly we fit together."

He waited until she complied before peeling back the cloth to reveal her naked breasts. Cupping them in his wide palms, he ran his thumbs over her nipples. She watched the pink tips tighten, felt their ache down to her core.

"You are so beautiful," he said with unmistakable reverence.

Unable to look away, she watched him fondle her, rolling her throbbing peaks between his thumbs and forefingers, stroking, sliding, before giving them a firm pinch.

She cried out, her head pressing back against his wide shoulder. "Do you like that?" he asked.

"Yes." The word came out on a gasp.

"Good."

Unfastening a last pair of buttons at her waist, he pushed her shift down past her hips. It pooled at her feet. "Kick it away," he told her.

Thighs quivering, she obeyed.

He curved a long arm around her bare stomach and pressed her more tightly against him.

Seeing their reflection in that moment, she was struck by the fact that she was completely naked, save for her stockings and garters, while he was still fully clothed. She waited for him to lead her to the bed.

He shocked her instead.

"Spread your legs," he told her.

Her eyes widened. "What?"

"Your legs. Move them apart." Bending his head, he kissed the side of her neck. "Trust me. I promise I'll take care of you."

And she did trust him. Otherwise she would never have let things go so far, never have given him such power over her.

She hesitated a few seconds more, then obeyed him again.

In the mirror, she watched his other hand slide down, over her waist and hip and thigh. He stroked her inner thigh for a few tantalizing moments, then wove his fingers through the patch of dark curls between her legs.

Her body flushed with heat and longing.

Slowly, he slid one long finger inside her, going deep.

"Hmm, you're so wet already. Practically dripping for me," he said with approval.

His words made her wetter, intimate moisture beading as he inserted another finger beside the first. He stroked, in and out, then in and out again.

The sight and sensation of his touch turned her legs to

jelly. If not for Leo's strong arm at her waist, she knew she would have crumbled to the floor. But he held her steady, relentless as he drove her closer and closer to the edge of insanity.

She moaned and angled her pelvis to draw him deeper still, her head rolling against his shoulder, her eyelids falling shut.

"Keep your eyes open." He stroked her faster, pausing to scissor his fingers inside her with every deep inner touch. "See how beautiful you are as you take your pleasure."

And then she couldn't look away, watching, feeling, as he built her desire higher and hotter. She ached, hunger scraping through her until she felt raw, shaking from the force.

He cupped her with his palm and pressed deeper. As he did, he rubbed with his thumb, doing something so astonishingly pleasurable she thought she might break.

Suddenly, she was crying out, quaking wildly as she toppled over into bliss. Her mind went blank, her limbs too weak to hold her up.

But Leo didn't let her fall. Exactly as he'd promised, she was safe in his arms.

He wasn't done, though, far from it, she realized hazily as he lifted her up into his arms and carried her across to the bed. He laid her against the sheets, the linen cool against her overwarm flesh.

"I forgot to take down your hair," he said, leaning over her for a long, sultry kiss.

Continuing to kiss her, he began sliding hairpins free, dropping them in small clusters onto her bedside table. Once her hair was loose, he drove his fingers into the heavy mass, massaging her scalp as he searched for any overlooked pins.

Tingles radiated downward from her head, the sensation of his fingers unbearably erotic. She shivered and speared her fingers into his hair to draw him nearer. Finding his mouth, she kissed him hard, sliding her tongue in and out with wild abandon.

He moaned and demanded more. Eagerly, she gave it.

Then he broke away, his hands moving to the buttons on his waistcoat.

She watched as he stripped off his clothes, every inch of skin he revealed a profound revelation.

Simply put, Leo was beautiful.

His shoulders and chest were broadly sculpted. His stomach was a flat plane that beckoned to be touched, while his arms and legs were roped with lean male muscle. His hips and buttocks were tight and narrow. As for his shaft, he was heavily erect, thick and long, a bead of moisture glistening on the broad tip.

Before she even knew what she was doing, she reached out and took him in her hand, running a thumb over the drop of his semen. Another one immediately gathered. She rubbed that one too.

A harsh groan rumbled low in his throat, his eyes closing for a second of obvious bliss. "You're going to unman me if you aren't careful," he warned.

"Am I? From what I've seen, that doesn't seem likely."

His eyes gleamed, dark with need. Then he was on the bed, bending up her knees as he fit himself between her legs. He crushed his lips to hers, ravishing her mouth in a way that left her enslaved.

Breath panted from her lips as she slid one leg up over his back. "My stockings," she said, only then remembering that he hadn't taken them off.

"Leave them," he said, palming one of her breasts. "I like the idea of tupping you with them on."

He kissed her again before bending lower to suckle her breasts in ways that drove her mad, using his lips and tongue and teeth until she thought she might drown in the sensations. Hunger coursed through her, stronger than any she'd ever known.

Still, she gasped as he slid a hand beneath her buttocks and thrust heavily inside. It had been a long time, more than six years, since she'd taken a man into her body. She thought she'd known what to expect, but nothing about Leo was ever what she imagined it would be.

Rather than draw back to thrust again, he settled against her more heavily, reaching down to angle her legs higher around him. He went deeper still. She moaned as her body stretched to accommodate his impressive size.

"You're tight," he murmured against her ear.

"It's been a long time."

He brushed her lips with his. "Relax. We have all night."

"I don't think I can do this all night. Can you?"

He laughed, the sensation teasing her inside. "You feel so good I just might try." Then he shuddered, his body and mind clearly at war over the necessity of proceeding.

And she couldn't deny him any longer.

Before she could even think, her body took over, gripping him with a velvet clasp as she arched reflexively, her feet pressing flat against his lower back. She wrapped her arms around him and kissed him hard. "I'm ready," she murmured. "Take me, Leo. Take me now."

At her command, he began thrusting, plunging in and out, faster and deeper, as he plundered her mouth, his hands moving in wild forays over her skin.

She trembled from head to toe and lost herself in the fathomless, pulse-pounding depths of his possession. Her mind went blank, thoughts scattered like petals, aware of nothing but the need lashing her in ever-increasing waves. Aware only of him.

He thrust even harder, deeper, until he'd gone as far as he could go. She held on, her hands sliding restlessly over his back and hips and buttocks, arching high to take everything he could give and more.

Then she broke, a high keening sound filling the air as ecstasy flooded through her, a pleasure so intense that it sank deep into her blood and sinew and bone, where she knew it would stay forever.

A tear slid from the corner of her eye, but it was a tear of happiness.

Of healing.

As if this were her first time all over again and he the only lover she had ever known.

And would ever know again.

She clasped him tighter, pleasure still radiating through her as he claimed his own satisfaction with a shuddering sigh. Smiling, she stroked her hands over him with leisurely caresses, content to luxuriate in the moment.

They lay for an uncertain amount of time, exchanging lazy kisses and murmured words of enjoyment.

"I must be heavy," he said after a while.

She stroked his cheek and rubbed her heel across the dip of his lower back. "No. I like this."

"God," he moaned, his shaft twitching inside her, "I like that too. Do it again."

"What? This?" She rubbed her heel against him again, circling.

His shaft hardened more and he gave a little involuntary thrust. "I think I've created a wanton."

She trailed her hand over his buttocks, then gave the firm flesh a light squeeze. "I believe you have."

He thrust again, his erection stretching her deliciously.

Without warning, he rolled onto his back, taking her with him, still lodged deeply inside. His palms reached up to cover her breasts, which he began to fondle. "I think we *can* do this all night. Shall we give it a try?"

She gave an experimental bounce and laughed, amazed at her sudden daring. "Yes," she said on a breathy sigh as her desire flared hot again. "Most definitely yes, my dear Lord Leopold."

Chapter 21

L eo was gone when Thalia awakened—for the final time, at least.

She stretched her arms over her head, a twinge of soreness making itself known in her thighs and other far more intimate places due to her and Leo's vigorous and enthusiastic lovemaking.

As promised, Leo had roused her at various intervals throughout the night, his prior boasts about his impressive stamina all proving true. But he was more than eager; he was inventive as well, teaching her two sexual positions she'd never heard of with sinful assurances of more to come.

Still, her favorite moments had happened just before dawn when she'd opened her eyes to the sensation of his mouth trailing a line of kisses along her spine.

She trembled blissfully again at nothing more than the memory, recalling how he hadn't stopped when he'd reached the end of her spine but had continued lower. He'd buried his head between her legs to give her the most intimate kisses of her life, bringing her to a climax so powerful she'd had to use her pillow to muffle her frenzied cries of release.

Then improbably he'd done it again, lifting her to her hands and knees and sliding heavily into her from behind to make her climax once more.

She'd lost count of the number of times he'd brought her to pleasure during the night, leaving her delirious and exhausted and so intensely satisfied she didn't know how it could possibly get better. Yet he'd whispered to her that their fun was only just beginning—and she believed him.

Leopold Byron didn't lie.

She shivered deliciously and sat up amid the rumpled bedsheets, late morning sunlight flooding into the room. Her recollection of him leaving was hazy; she'd been so tired. But he'd kissed her, whispering sweet words into her ears as he told her to sleep and that he would see her later that afternoon.

There'd been something about taking her for a drive, she thought. Or was it to a gallery? Either way, she'd find out once he returned, she supposed.

A glance across the room revealed that he'd tidied all her evening clothes before he'd departed, draping them neatly over her dressing table chair. Even her shoes had been carried in from the sitting room and placed side by side underneath.

How surprisingly considerate. How discreet, even though all the servants must realize by now that he had brought her home and spent the night in her room.

In her bed.

She was his mistress now.

No, she corrected. *I am his lover. My favors are given freely out of mutual desire with no financial remuneration involved.*

Mistresses received town houses and carriages, clothes and jewelry and other assorted gifts. She wanted nothing from Leo, only his company. Only his passion, until both of them decided they'd had enough and their affair was done.

Perhaps it was a small distinction in the eyes of the world, but not to her. She was her own woman, independent and self-sufficient, and she would stay that way. Being with Leo did not change that at all. If people wished to think otherwise, she couldn't stop them. It was a hard lesson she had learned well.

But why was she dwelling on such doleful thoughts when she had felt absolutely spectacular only moments ago?

I am going to enjoy this affair, she told herself, *for as long as it lasts. For once in my life, I am going to enjoy myself.*

Enjoy him.

In every wicked, delectable, sinful way possible.

Sliding out of the bed, she padded barefoot and naked across to the bellpull and gave it a tug. She needed a bath and something to eat, since she was utterly famished. Then she was going to dig through her meager wardrobe and find something pretty to wear.

She wanted to look attractive for Leo.

Her new lover.

Smiling, she went to fetch a robe.

"You're whistling again."

Leo jogged down the last of the stairs at his and Lawrence's town house, the tune he'd been accused of harmonizing still on his lips. He offered a final tonal flourish, then looked at his twin. "Am I?"

Lawrence raised an eyebrow. "Which means, I take it, that you had a good evening last night."

"I did, yes." A smile moved over Leo's mouth as thoughts of Thalia replayed in his mind.

"I also presume this good evening was had *after* you got into an argument with Lord Kemp and strangled him in front of several dozen witnesses at Drury Lane?"

Leo strolled into the study.

Lawrence followed.

"I didn't *strangle* him," Leo clarified in a casual tone. "It was more of a corrective throttle." He took the stopper off the wine decanter. "Claret?"

"No, thank you."

Leo shrugged and poured himself a glass.

"Corrective throttle?" Lawrence asked.

"Kemp insulted Thalia. I was correcting him."

Lawrence gave a short laugh. "Gallant of you, I'm sure, but given her history and reputation, insults will unfortunately come her way."

"Well, they had better not come her way around me." He drank a large swallow of wine, his other hand squeezing into a fist. "You'd have throttled Kemp too if you'd heard how he spoke to her. It was unpardonable."

Lawrence sobered. "I'm sure it was. Just don't let your defense of her get out of hand."

"In what way? What do you mean?"

"Just that I heard there was talk of a duel between you and Kemp last night, but that he refused your challenge."

Leo scowled. "You seem amazingly well-informed and here it is only"—he paused and reached for his pocket watch, clicking open the case—"eleven twenty-three in the morning."

"It's the talk of the town—how could I not be well-informed? I had a letter about it over breakfast from one of our friends. It won't be long before the news wends its way to the family."

"Let it wend. Kemp is a villain and a coward. I am only sorry I didn't have a chance to put a bullet in him at dawn this morning."

"I, for one, am glad you did not."

Leo tossed back the rest of his wine. "That's what Thalia says. She told me to let it go."

"Then listen to Lady Thalia. It sounds as if she has a great deal of wisdom."

"She's not what you think, you know," Leo said, meeting his brother's eyes. "She's not what anyone thinks. She's gentle and intelligent and kind. She's quite the most fascinating woman it has ever been my privilege to know."

Lawrence stared for a long moment. "I realize this is none of my business, but just how serious is this . . . relationship between you and Lady Thalia?"

"I'm going to keep seeing her, if that's what you're asking. As for anything more, I don't know. We're taking things as they come and it's still early days yet. Don't worry, it's not as if I'm in danger of falling in love with her."

Or am I?

He stilled, the idea tumbling through his mind. He discarded it seconds later. He liked her, yes. And he desired her—last night was vivid proof of that. But anything more, well, he was looking forward to a heated affair, but the fire between them would burn out soon enough and then it would be over.

They would be over.

An odd constriction gripped his chest. He set down his glass, using the movement to hide his unexpected reaction. He forced a carefree smile that he hoped his brother couldn't see past.

Lawrence gave him another appraising look, then nodded, apparently satisfied. "Sorry. I promised not to meddle, didn't I? Just be a bit more discreet in future, will you? I don't relish having to exile myself in France with you when you do something hotheaded enough to set the law on our tails."

"You're a barrister. So am I, come to that. We'd think of a way out before it came to exile."

Lawrence laughed and relaxed. "I suppose we would. And speaking of the law, I have a visit to conduct."

"Meeting about a new client?"

"No," Lawrence admitted with mild chagrin, "going next door. Northcote has agreed to see me about Lady Higgleston's complaints."

Leo grinned. "Has he, now? That should prove interesting. Fruitless, but interesting."

"And you will be with Lady Thalia, of course."

Leo's grin widened. "Of course. Where else would I want to be?"

"What a pretty day for a drive," Thalia remarked a couple of hours later as she sat next to Leo in his curricle.

Gazing upward, she watched a trio of cottony white clouds lumber past in the pristine blue sky, a flock of sparrows winging this way and that as if they too were celebrating the fine weather. Only the cool, late October temperature offered any sort of challenge, but even that was easily moderated with the help of warm gloves and a thick woolen cloak.

"Are you taking me somewhere in particular?" she ventured as it became increasingly clear that they were leaving the city behind.

"Perhaps," Leo said cryptically. "You'll simply have to wait and see."

"Maybe I don't want to wait. I'm not terribly keen on surprises, you know."

Not any longer at least. She'd had too many unhappy surprises in her life to care much for the experience these days.

He looked into her eyes and reached down to tuck her hand more snugly inside the crook of his arm. "You'll like this one."

"Will I? You'll simply have to wait and see," she said, repeating his earlier words.

Catching the reference, he laughed.

Leo slowed the curricle a short while later and made a turn onto a lane bounded by a redbrick wall with a heavy, black iron gate at the end.

The gate was open. Leo drove through and up to the front of a house made of the same red brick. The door was painted a crisp black, like the shutters that stood sentinel at each window. The grounds were tidy, cleared of leaves and ready for winter, evergreens adding a welcome hint of color.

"Where are we?" she asked.

"Brightvale Manor. I acquired it in a card game a couple of years ago. It comes in handy every now and again when I'm in the mood for a bit of countryside without having to travel too far from London."

"You use it as a love nest, you mean?" she said, an unexpected edge to her voice.

He met her eyes. "No. You're the first woman I've ever brought here."

Her tension fell away and she smiled.

"Shall I show you inside?" he asked.

She nodded. "Yes."

Leo watched Thalia as she looked around the house, pleased that she seemed to like what she saw. He'd changed very little about the manor house or its contents since he'd won it from a boastful sharp who'd thought to fleece him. But his brother Jack wasn't the only Byron who excelled at games of chance. Leo had turned the tables on Brightvale's former owner and won the crucial hand—earning himself the small estate in the process.

Although the house had been in good condition, the grounds had needed work, the tillable fields left unplanted, the gardens overgrown and the tenant houses in a sad state of disrepair.

Originally he'd thought about selling the place. With that in mind, he'd taken it upon himself to make improvements so as to increase the value. But the more he did on the estate, the more he enjoyed the process, and the sense of accomplishment he gained in watching something neglected thrive once more.

Despite his interest in the estate, he rarely stayed more than a few days at a time, leaving the house in the hands of a couple who served as caretakers. But this morning when he'd been considering locations for an outing with Thalia, he'd thought of Brightvale.

Seeing her enjoyment, he was glad now that he had.

"I have one last place to show you," he said, once she finished touring the house.

"Oh? Where is that?"

"You'll see. Or rather you will once I take off your blindfold."

Her dark brows arched. "What blindfold?"

"This one." He extracted a long rectangle of black cloth from his interior coat pocket.

She eyed it with suspicion. "Why do I need to wear that?"

"Because," he said, stepping behind her, "I want what I'm about to show you to be a surprise."

"And might I remind you again what I think about surprises?"

He chuckled. "Just play along. I promise you won't be sorry."

"Very well. If you insist."

"I do." He pressed a warm kiss against her neck, then reached up to tie the blindfold in place. "Can you see?"

"No," she complained. "It's as dark as pitch."

"Good. Take my hand."

"We're walking?"

"We are. And don't worry. I won't let you fall."

"You had better not. I just recovered from a twisted ankle. I don't relish suffering another."

"I shall take utmost care." He linked their hands together and led her slowly forward.

The temperature dropped the moment they left the house, the grass soft beneath their shoes.

"Is it much farther?" she asked after a minute.

"Not much."

Her hand flexed inside his, but she kept walking, relying on him with absolute trust.

Reaching their destination, he opened the door of a small building that Thalia still could not see and led her inside. The air grew warm again—and moist with the scent of earth and vegetation.

"What is that I smell? Flowers?" she ventured.

"Perhaps." He looped an arm around her waist, her hand still in his, and led her a bit farther into the structure. Then they stopped. "Are your eyes closed?"

"They are."

"Keep them closed. I'm going to take the blindfold off and I don't want you to see until I'm ready for you to see."

"My, you are dictatorial today. But then I suppose I already knew that about you."

"And you have a smart tongue. Eyes closed."

"Yes, oh exalted one."

He laughed and untied the blindfold. Taking her shoulders in his hands, he turned her in the exact direction he wanted. "All right. You may look."

Thalia blinked a couple of times as her eyes grew accustomed to the light. Then she gasped as everything came into focus.

Rising high around her stood the clear windows of a glasshouse, the afternoon sunlight that poured inside turning the room as warm as a summer's day. Potted plants grew in a profusion around her—roses and lilies, exotic orchids and bushes replete with lemons and oranges and limes in various stages and colors of maturation.

Yet that wasn't the most astonishing thing. There was also the elegant white-linen-draped table and chairs arranged in an intimate corner. On the table's surface were two place settings of china, crystal and silverware, and on a second smaller table an array of foodstuffs, each one more delectable looking than the last.

"How in the world did you manage all this?" She breathed with amazement. "And so quickly?"

"I sent the servants ahead from London not long after I returned home. It put the kitchen in a bit of a pother for a while, but they came through with their usual remarkable aplomb."

"Clearly."

"Shall we be seated and partake of their efforts?"

Without waiting for her consent, he freed the bow on her pelisse, then reached to unfasten the buttons. She stood quietly and let him take the cloak from her shoulders to hang on a small hook near the door. He added his own greatcoat as well, then took her hand again and assisted her into one of the chairs.

"I gave the footmen leave to wait inside the house," Leo said. "I thought I would serve you myself. That way we can be alone."

A melting warmth spread through her that had nothing to do with the lovely humid heat surrounding them. She drew a deep breath of the loamy, perfumed air and let herself luxuriate in the moment. She couldn't remember the last time she'd been so thoroughly pampered — or so happy.

Her brows creased at the thought.

As she knew all too well, happiness was fleeting. It wouldn't do for her to become emotionally entangled with Leo. She was already in deeper than she'd ever intended. If she wasn't careful, she could see herself falling in love with him.

She glanced down at her hands, folded in her lap, and willed her heart to slow its suddenly erratic beat.

Fall in love with Leo?

The very idea was absurdity.

And insanity.

But it wasn't going to happen. They were only having a bit of fun together. A light, frivolous interlude that would in all probability last no more than a few weeks. Hopefully they would be memorable ones.

Until then, she had a right to be happy, did she not? A right to indulge her senses in whatever ways she chose.

And she chose Leo.

She watched him as he prepared their plates. Studying his hands, she remembered the way they had moved over her body last night in the dark. How they'd touched her with passion, tender and arousing. Sensual tingles raced over her skin, her nipples beading beneath the fabric of her gown.

He'd made her feel more passion in those few brief hours, she realized, than she had felt in the entirety of her marriage. Was it any wonder she was here with him now? That she planned to be with him again, for as long as it suited them both?

As if aware of her scrutiny, he looked up and met her gaze. Finished serving, he set the plate before her. "I hope everything will be to your liking."

"I'm sure it shall."

But it wasn't only the food she meant.

Taking up her fork, she dug in.

Chapter 22

"Hmm, it's so cozy here in front of the fire. A shame we have to drive back to London in the cold," Thalia said with a sigh nearly three hours later.

After their meal, which had been absolutely delicious, she and Leo had walked back to the main house, where they'd settled side by side on the drawing room sofa.

The caretaker's wife, a friendly, cheerful sort of woman, had served them hot tea and tiny sweet biscuits that Thalia had been too full to eat. If the other woman disapproved of Thalia being here alone with Leo, she didn't show it by so much as an extra eyebrow twitch, telling them to ring should they require anything further. Not that it mattered what Leo's servants thought of her, but still, it never hurt to be on good terms with staff.

All in all, it had been a wonderful day.

But it was nearly done, autumn light waning beyond the windows. Even if they left now, it would be full dark before they reached her town house.

Thalia set her teacup aside and mentally prepared herself to leave their warm little nest.

Before she could do more, Leo caught hold of her hand, weaving his fingers through hers. "Why don't we stay here?"

Her eyes went to his. "Stay? For the night, you mean?"

Leaning near, he pressed his mouth to hers for a long, slow kiss that made her toes curl inside her boots. "I'm sure a bedchamber could be prepared," he said. "And we've plenty of food left over from our earlier meal. My cook sent up nearly an entire ham, so we won't starve, even if the larder here proves to be bare. Save for the tea we were served, that is. Tasty biscuits by the by."

"You would know," she teased, resting her head back against the sofa, "since you are the one who ate them all."

"Just replenishing my strength," he said, taking her mouth for another breathless joining. "I shall need it if we hope to repeat last night."

She shivered and slid her fingers up into his hair. "Heavens. Is that even possible?" Her pulse stuttered at the very idea, flashes of their couplings racing through her mind. Her body responded, turning even warmer than it already was.

"I certainly plan to make the attempt." He ran the tip of his tongue across her lower lip, then slid it inside to explore the ultrasensitive lining of her mouth. She gasped and kissed him harder, suddenly in want of more.

"What about you?" he murmured, letting her come up for a trembling breath. "Are you ready to attempt everything again?"

"I am." She trembled.

"Good. Then we'll stay." He slid his hand over her back and waist, then lower, splaying his fingers across her bottom. He gave her rounded flesh a pleasurable squeeze as their mouths locked together for more fervid kisses.

I shouldn't stay, she thought drowsily, drawing him even closer with an arm wrapped around his shoulders.

She had no luggage, no night attire or change of clothes. No brush or hairpins or slippers. Then too there would be her overnight absence from her town house.

Scandalous.

On the other hand, she was behaving scandalously now, wasn't she? Spending the night away with her new lover was something a notorious divorcée would be expected to do. It seemed almost *de rigueur.*

As for her staff, a note could be sent to London so they would not worry when she didn't return. And it was only one night. She rather doubted she would be needing any night attire, not if Leo had any say in the matter.

"Yes," she sighed against his lips. "Let's stay."

*   *   *

Leo awakened hours later, tired but replete. A narrow band of sunlight crept under the sheer draperies, casting the bedroom in a gentle gloaming. At his side, Thalia was slumbering deeply, her head pillowed next to his, one of her legs bent upward between his own.

He considered rousing her. Now that she was becoming accustomed to his touch, she was amazingly responsive. A few passionate kisses, some well-placed strokes and caresses, and her body came alive, instinctively craving the pleasure it hungered for, even if Thalia herself was still learning exactly how to deal with the depths of her newfound desire.

Curious, but when he'd started his pursuit of her, he'd assumed she would be the more knowledgeable one when it came to sex. But in spite of being several years her junior, he was the one teaching her. The one leading her down unexplored paths of sensuality, paths that surprised and delighted—and, yes, shocked—her with the breadth of their power and the completeness of the satisfaction they gave.

Yet he was learning too, taking pleasure from her pleasure, testing boundaries of physicality and need that surprised even him.

And they'd barely even begun their affair. If he could find such extraordinary union with her after only two days, just think what the next weeks would bring.

His shaft stiffened, aching with renewed longing despite the night they'd just spent.

He ought to be exhausted. Instead, he wanted her again.

It would be easy to slide her thigh up and over his hip so she would wake to find him buried thick and deep inside her as he tupped her awake.

He groaned at the very idea, his shaft pulsing with need.

But he'd worked her hard during the night, exactly as promised, taking her repeatedly before he'd shown her another new position that had left her screaming with wild release into her pillow.

She'd sunk into a heavy sleep afterward and he'd followed, holding her close.

But now he was awake again.

Hungry for her again.

He could wait, though, for a little while at least.

Closing his eyes, he willed himself to concentrate on sleep rather than his throbbing sex. He was just drifting off nearly twenty minutes later when a soft knock came at the door.

Scowling, he opened his eyes. Careful not to wake Thalia, he rose from the bed. He pulled on his trousers and shirt, leaving the latter only partially buttoned, then padded barefoot to the door. He found the caretaker's wife waiting on the other side.

"Sorry to awaken you, my lord," she said, keeping her eyes at a respectful level, "but this just arrived from London by messenger. He said it were urgent, so I thought it best not to delay."

Leo took the note. "Quite right. Thank you for bringing it directly to me."

"Shall I put on some tea for you and the lady?" she asked helpfully.

"Not yet. I'll ring should we require anything." Murmuring his thanks once again, he shut the door.

Turning, he broke open the wax seal and began to read. When he had done, he shook his head, unsure whether to laugh or groan. Keeping as quiet as possible, he went to don the rest of his clothes.

Thalia drifted awake to the quiet scratching of what sounded like pen on paper. She forced her eyelids to lift. "Leo?" she said on a whisper.

He stood across the room in front of a small writing desk. He was also fully dressed.

She called his name again.

This time he heard her and turned his head her way. "I'm sorry. I was hoping you'd keep sleeping. I was just writing you a note."

She squinted. "Why?"

"I have to leave immediately for London. My brother Lawrence has landed himself in a bit of a fix and needs my help."

"Oh," she said, pushing her hair away from her face as she tried to shake off her sleepiness. "Is he all right?"

"Yes. At least I think so. I guess I'll find out for sure once I get there."

"Where is there?"

"The Giltspur Street Compter."

"What?" She sat up, the sheets falling to her waist. She snatched them back up to cover her bare breasts. "Your brother is in gaol?"

"So it would appear."

"I shall go with you."

"No, you stay and sleep some more," he said, meeting her eyes. "You must be tired after the night we had."

A sudden warmth curled inside her at the reminder, but she didn't look away. "I am a bit weary, but I'll never be able to fall back to sleep now. Besides, how will I get to London if you leave?"

"I shall return to pick you up, of course."

She gave a small shake of her head. "Who knows how long you will be occupied with your brother? You could be away for hours. No, I shall come with you now."

His golden brown eyebrows drew together in thought. "I suppose I could drop you at your town house first, then go on from there."

"Lord Lawrence would not thank me for the delay. I shall accompany you to the gaol. You can take me home afterward."

He scowled. "Gaol is no place for a lady."

"I'll wait outside."

"In Giltspur Street? I think not."

"No one will accost me, but if you are worried, then I shall accompany you inside. I find myself rather curious to see the inside of a gaol."

"Don't be. They are miserable places."

"Then we must stop arguing and hurry to get Lawrence released. Now, hand me my shift, please."

His jaw worked as if he was deciding which of several rebuttals to make. Instead, he walked across to a nearby chair, picked up her undergarment and handed it to her.

"Turn around," she said, suddenly viscerally aware

that she once again had nothing on while he was fully dressed.

He gave her a disbelieving look. "I have seen you naked, you know."

"I know." She kept hold of the sheet covering her. "Now turn around."

He laughed. "You're being ridiculous."

"And you are wasting time. *Pst-pst.*" She made a turning motion with her fingers.

"Fine," he said after a moment, "but I want a kiss first."

"There isn't time."

He approached, then bent down, taking her face between his hands. "There is always time for a kiss."

Then his mouth was on hers, moving with a leisurely yet determined intensity that sizzled through her like a blistering summer heat. His fingers slid into her hair, massaging her scalp as he kissed her harder.

"We should stop," she said on a breathless gasp. "Your brother—"

"Isn't going anywhere." He smoothed a hand down her arm. "What's another few minutes?"

"Your brother might disagree. Leo, he needs your help."

But her body wished he didn't.

Leo pressed another kiss to her lips, then sighed and eased away. "Put your shift on," he said gruffly. "I'll act as your lady's maid with the rest."

Straightening, he turned his back.

Chapter 23

Beyond the heavy doors of the Giltspur Street Compter, the air smelled of vomit, urine and rank, unwashed bodies. Misery seemed etched into the very walls of the place, human suffering everywhere to be seen inside its shadowy confines.

Yet, as Leo knew, this was nothing compared with the sheer brutality that awaited those unlucky souls scheduled for transfer to the larger, nearby house of incarceration—Newgate Prison. That was where the masses of accused mixed with the worst sorts of criminals—the murderers, thieves and rapists who would likely swing from Tyburn Tree once their trials decreed their fate. Luckily for Lawrence, Giltspur was for lesser, petty crimes or for those who could not pay their debts.

As a barrister, Lawrence usually visited such places to provide counsel to inmates, not the other way around. Clearly, he hadn't been able to argue his way out—although perhaps he'd found himself too embarrassed to try.

"Still glad you decided to accompany me?" Leo asked Thalia, who stood at his side with a handkerchief over her nose. "Has your curiosity been satisfied yet?"

Her brown eyes met his own knowing gaze. Resolutely, she tucked her handkerchief back into her pocket. "It is not something I will soon forget. Let us find Lord Lawrence and be gone from here."

Leo hid a wry grin and followed after the turnkey, who had already received his fee for performing his duty.

In fact everyone who worked here demanded some kind of payment—usually from the prisoners themselves, who found that the more they could afford to pay, the better their accommodations.

Lawrence must have run out of funds, Leo realized, as he and Thalia were led to a rather middling sort of cell.

A couple of prisoners called to them as they passed, one reaching out with grubby fingers, trying to touch the edge of Thalia's skirt. He laughed when she jumped and sidled closer to Leo, who wrapped a protective arm around her waist.

Before Leo could tongue-lash the fellow for his impudence, the turnkey struck the man's knuckles through the bars with the long stick he carried. The inmate howled in pain and disappeared back into his cell.

"Sorry 'bout tha', milady. Milord," the turnkey said as he led them farther along the corridor. "Can't remember last time we had Quality come visitin'. Makes the others restive." He stopped in front of a cell door. "Here we be. Ye say he's yer brother, do ye?"

Leo peered through the bars to the figure who sat hunched on a wooden stool. The prisoner turned his head and met Leo's eyes with ones that were so like his own.

Or rather with one eye, Leo saw, since Lawrence's other was black and swollen shut. Lawrence had a cut lip, another cut along his left cheekbone and a purple bruise that ran the length of his jaw. With his hair mussed and face unshaven, he looked a proper ruffian, rather than his normally well-groomed self. His silk waistcoat was missing, and his jacket and formerly white linen shirt were both ripped and dirty. His trousers had fared slightly better, but not by much. And he still had his boots.

The turnkey blinked and stared between the two of them. "Well, I'll be deuced. Ye two look jus' alike, 'cept fer tha bruises. Guess he is yer kin."

"He is," Leo said in a grave voice. "Open this door at once."

"That'll be an extra two farthings ter let ye go inside," the turnkey stated. His dark eyes widened when he met the glare Leo turned upon him. The older man swallowed nervously.

Leo reached into his jacket and withdrew half a crown. "Tell the sheriff I expect my brother, Lord Lawrence, to be released within the hour whatever the charges. I shall pay any outstanding fines."

The other man goggled, then gave a nod, snatching the coin from Leo's fingers. "I'll tell 'im."

Hands trembling, the gaoler jangled his heavy iron ring of keys, found the one he wanted and inserted it into the lock of Lawrence's cell.

Moments later, Leo and Thalia stepped inside.

The door locked behind them, the turnkey hurrying away.

Lawrence stood and came forward. "Leo, thank God. I wasn't sure if my note had reached you. They're a pack of leeches in here, wanting money for every conceivable thing. Had to trade my gold cravat pin just for the paper, ink and quill. My waistcoat went for the messenger fee. I was afraid I'd have to sell my coat soon if you didn't arrive."

"Well, I'm here now. What in Hades' name happened to you?"

"Long story. Let's just say Northcote got me out on the town drinking last night. We ended up in a rather unsavory dockside pub, then into a brawl with some nasty toughs. All hell broke loose and somehow I ended up here. Northcote's a wild bastard when he fights. Is he here, do you know?"

"I don't. Let's get you released first. Then we can sort out the rest. Do you need to see a doctor?"

"No. It's mostly just cuts and bruises and a sore rib or two. I've had worse."

Leo nodded, remembering well all the worse things Lawrence had suffered over the years.

At his side, Thalia made a compassionate *tsk* low in her throat.

At the sound, Lawrence looked past Leo's shoulder. "Lady Thalia. My pardon for not greeting you immediately. And for my earlier cursing. My manners are somewhat lacking at present, as is my attire."

She sent him a reassuring smile. "That's quite all right, Lord Lawrence. These are rather unusual circumstances, after all. I think a bit of foul language can be excused. And without a valet, the state of your clothing cannot be faulted either."

He smiled, likely for the first time since he'd been tossed inside this cell.

"If you don't mind my impertinence," Lawrence said a moment later, "why are you here, Lady Thalia?"

"Because she insisted on coming with me. She was curious to see the inside of a gaol." Leo crossed his arms and shot her a look. "If I am not mistaken, her curiosity has been satisfied." He met her gaze with a wry challenge. "Unless you would like to go up the street and visit Newgate before we return home?"

Her mouth tightened with annoyance over his teasing, yet she couldn't repress a small shudder at the idea of his suggestion. "Thank you, no. The accommodations here have been more than illuminating."

Leo's lips twitched; then he laughed.

Lawrence joined him moments later.

They rolled to a stop in front of Leo and Lawrence's Cavendish Square town house roughly two hours later. Thalia was seated between the twins, the three of them tucked in as snugly as peas in a pod inside Leo's curricle.

In spite of her misgivings, she had accompanied the brothers to their home rather than insisting that they first drop her off at her own town house. She'd known that Lord Lawrence, regardless of his outwardly brave front, was in a great deal of pain. He was bruised and beaten, exhausted and filthy and, more than anything, in need of care and sleep. She and Leo would get his brother inside and make sure he had everything he required for his health and comfort.

Then Leo could drive her home.

Leo sprang down to the pavement first, then reached up to lift her out.

Lawrence waved off any assistance, climbing somewhat gingerly from the vehicle with a hand clutched against his obviously aching ribs. He looked up at the town house and sighed. "Thank God. It's good to be home."

"Don't thank God," Leo told him in an affable voice. "Thank *me*, since I'm the one who convinced the sheriff to drop the arrest charges against you."

"What I did was in self-defense—"

"Which I explained to him in some of my finest lawyerly exposition since taking part in mock trial proceedings."

"Was that before or after you bribed him?"

Leo shrugged. "We negotiated a rather generous settlement of cash for freedom. If you'd like, I can take you back, so you can argue the case before the judge. I'm sure it will only take three or four days for you to appear at the dock for trial."

"No, I'd rather go inside. Thanks, Leo."

Leo laid a hand on his shoulder. "Anytime. I know you'd do the same for me."

"I'd do anything for you. We're brothers."

"Brothers."

They shared a smile; then Leo turned and reached out a hand to Thalia. She took it and moved to accompany them into the house.

"Byron," a voice called, bringing them all to a halt again.

The twins turned at the same instant, the similarity of their movements almost uncanny.

The man strode closer, then stopped and looked at Lawrence. "Glad to see you made it back in one piece. If you hadn't turned up soon, I would have come looking. Some night, huh?"

"Yes, some night," Lawrence repeated.

This must be Northcote, Thalia realized, the person he'd mentioned earlier.

Compared with Lawrence, Northcote was barely touched, only a single bluish bruise on his left cheekbone. Otherwise, he was impeccably groomed—clean, well dressed and freshly shaven. He was tall, taller even than the twins by two inches at least, and bluntly attractive in an unconventional way. Yet it was his tawny eyes that were his most arresting feature. They reminded her of the eyes of a hawk, a very clever, very keen hawk who knew how to take care of itself, while it skillfully hunted down its prey.

Northcote exuded a lethal combination of sophistication, sexuality and cunning, and woe betide anyone foolish enough to get in his way. Luckily, he now displayed only friendly concern for Lawrence, his drinking companion and neighbor.

Leave it to Leo and Lawrence to have a predatory raptor living one door down from them. Although, as she well knew, the twins were more than capable of being predatory themselves when it suited their purpose.

Leo was more of a lion, however.

Her lion.

Moving closer, she clasped his hand tighter.

He squeezed hers back.

"Sorry we got split up," Northcote continued in his rich baritone. "It was madness after the fight broke out. Are you all right?"

"I've been worse. What about you? You look—"

"Like a man who wasn't just released from gaol an hour ago," Leo interrupted.

Northcote turned his gaze on Leo. "I got home two hours ago from Newgate. I didn't realize Lawrence was still in desperate straits or I would have come to his aid. It would appear I owe him an apology for all the trouble."

Lawrence shook his head. "Don't worry about it. There's no lasting harm done."

"I'm having a party Thursday next," Northcote told Lawrence. "I hope you will attend. And you, Lord Leopold." He turned his penetrating gaze on Leo for a moment before it settled on her. He smiled. "You and your charming companion are welcome as well."

Leo stiffened. "Thank you, but no. Lady Thalia and I have other plans."

Northcote's smile widened as if he was fully aware that she and Leo had no such plans. Then he turned back to Lawrence. "You look done in and I'm keeping you here on the street talking. Go inside and rest. I shall see you anon. Lord Leopold. Lady Thalia." With a short bow, he turned and strode toward his own town house.

"Heavens," Thalia said once Northcote was out of earshot.

" 'Heavens' is an understatement." Leo said.

He scowled after the other man in a way that struck her as being jealous, though he certainly had no reason to be.

He turned to his brother. "So I suppose you're going to accept that blighter's invitation?"

Lawrence grinned despite his split lip. "I wouldn't miss it."

Chapter 24

Four days later, Thalia awakened to the sound of a cold early-November wind rattling the windowpanes and an overcast sky full of clouds that almost certainly promised rain.

What perfectly miserable weather, she thought. But she supposed it was apt, considering what day it was.

Her birthday.

She was now another year older—two-and-thirty.

It was a fact that only added to the oppressive gloominess outside. Then again, she'd long ago fallen out of the habit of celebrating the anniversary of her birth. For her it was a day, just like any other day. She didn't know why she even bothered to remember.

Oh yes, so I can feel the age difference between Leo and me all that much more.

With a sigh, she tossed back the covers and reached for her robe and slippers, sliding into both of them quickly to ward off the chill in the room.

As much as she wished she could crawl back under the covers and sleep for another hour, it was time to be about her day.

Leo had left shortly after dawn, murmuring something about having errands to run as he'd kissed her a drowsy good-bye. She couldn't imagine what errands he might have, but considering the amount of time they'd been spending together lately, she supposed he had been neglecting his business affairs and needed to catch up.

She had accounts and household matters of her own

to which she ought to attend; this morning would be a good opportunity to get a few of them seen to before Leo returned later that afternoon.

Hera gave her a happy little meow from where she lay curled atop a blanket set in the window seat. Thalia went across to pet her, smiling at Hera's answering purrs.

She crossed next to the washstand, pleased when she found the water Parker had left for her still warm in the jug.

Face washed and teeth scrubbed clean with cinnamon tooth powder, she was brushing her hair a few minutes later when Parker gave a quick tap at the door and came inside.

Her lady's maid carried a breakfast tray, a wide smile on her face. Delicious scents drifted to Thalia's nose and her stomach rumbled with anticipation.

"Good morning, milady. I hope you slept well."

"Very well." She took a seat at the small table in her sitting room where she usually broke her fast—although her dining habits hadn't been quite as regulated since she and Leo had started seeing each other.

Her eyes widened when Parker lifted the cloche to reveal a mouthwatering selection of foodstuffs—biscuits, shirred eggs, steak, porridge, stewed apricots, honey, butter, hot tea and milk.

"Gracious. Mrs. Grove has outdone herself. How will I ever be able to eat all this?" Thalia asked.

Usually she contented herself with a simple breakfast of toast and tea, and occasionally an egg and a rasher of bacon if she was particularly hungry. So what was Mrs. Grove thinking to have prepared so much?

Thalia stared down at the plates and bowls, and at the steak in particular. Fresh meat was an expensive indulgence and one she rarely allowed herself these days. Her cook's actions made no sense.

"A big delivery arrived this morning," Parker volunteered as if privy to Thalia's thoughts. "The boy said it was all paid for and to enjoy. Mrs. Grove has been grinning and humming ever since she unpacked the hamper. There was a second basket that came just for the staff. It had a huge ham inside, fresh chickens and all sorts of dried fruits and nuts. Cook says she's going to bake us all some tarts for dinner. If it's all right with you, of course, milady."

"Of course," she said automatically.

Thalia frowned, her thoughts turning over quickly. An extravagant delivery that was already paid for? She didn't need to think long to know who'd sent it.

Leo.

Who else?

She remembered him remarking only the other evening about the small portions of meat served at dinner. While it was true that the end-of-the-month larder had been running lean on rations, Leo should not have sent her hampers of expensive victuals. She would speak to him about it as soon as she had the opportunity, and ask him not to do so again in future.

As for the hampers themselves, it seemed wrong to return the one he had sent for the servants. The staff were all clearly thrilled with the gift and she couldn't see disappointing them by insisting the items be returned. The one for her was another matter and she knew she ought to send word down to the kitchen to pack it up and have it delivered to Cavendish Square.

She gazed again at all the delicious food laid out before her. It seemed churlish and wasteful not to eat it, seeing it had already been prepared. It would just go in the slop bucket if she had it taken back to the kitchen.

And for the rest?

She would keep the hamper, she decided, but give orders to Mrs. Grove that its contents be served only on occasions when Lord Leo was present for a meal. Otherwise she would forgo the offerings.

Picking up her fork and knife, she cut a slice of steak and put it in her mouth. Inwardly, she sighed with delight; it was so tender and succulent. After pausing to pour herself a cup of steaming tea, she set to eating her breakfast in earnest.

She had made excellent inroads into the hearty meal when her lady's maid walked into the sitting room again. This time she was carrying several boxes, two large and one small.

Thalia laid her silverware aside, then patted her lips with her napkin. "What are those?"

"Another delivery. They only just arrived for you, milady. Would you like me to open them?"

She nodded, then stood, saying nothing as her maid moved to the couch and set down the parcels. She watched as Parker untied the ribbon and lifted off the top of the first box.

Inside was an exquisite evening gown; she didn't need to read the card signed with a boldly inscribed *L* to know who had sent it.

Parker held up the garment so that Thalia could take in the full effect of the gorgeous, high-waisted gown of deep rose satin. It had long cap sleeves with sheer white oversleeves, and flounces along the hem trimmed with a row of tiny white rosebuds. The gown looked like something straight out of the latest fashion magazine. She hadn't been near something so new and pretty in over half a decade.

She barely had time to appreciate the beauty of the first garment before Parker laid it carefully aside and opened the second box to reveal another sartorial creation. It was an afternoon dress of blue-green crepe with long, lace-edged sleeves and a deep border of delicate embroidered scallops along the hem.

"Oh, and look," her maid declared as she reached yet again into the box, "there is a matching spencer and gloves. And the most adorable wide-brim bonnet with peacock feathers, of all things. Won't you look a picture in this outfit, milady?"

Wouldn't I, just? Thalia thought with sudden longing. She could imagine Leo's reaction to her in the ensemble. How his brilliant eyes would shine with approval and desire. How pleased he would be to see her wearing the clothes he had bought especially for her.

Clothes he had bought . . .

Parker folded the gown over her arm. "I'll just nip out and give this a press while you finish the last of your meal. I won't be long."

"No," Thalia said firmly. "Please pack everything back

into the boxes and get one of my usual dresses out of the wardrobe. The navy merino, I believe."

"But, milady—"

"And I am finished with breakfast. Please convey my thanks to Mrs. Grove for an excellent repast."

The glow of excitement disappeared from Parker's face and she looked for a moment as if she might argue. Instead she nodded and laid the lovely dress aside, then disappeared into the bedroom.

Thalia's shoulders drooped as soon as she was alone, her gaze returning to the gowns. She moved close and reached out, running her fingertips over a piece of lace edging that she knew was Honiton made.

So soft. So delicate. So pretty.

And so expensive.

Too expensive for her.

With a sigh, she turned away and went to get dressed.

She entered her study almost an hour later, Hera running past her to leap up onto the desk. With rain drizzling outside, the little cat had no interest in venturing beyond the doors today.

She didn't either, come to that.

It was much too cold and dreary to do anything but curl up in her warmest shawl with a cup of hot tea while she saw to the accounts.

Only the room wasn't cold today.

Quite the opposite—it felt warm, she realized as her gaze went to the healthy blaze burning in the fireplace grate. There was a fresh supply of logs laid into the copper bin as well.

She frowned.

The staff well knew that the fireplaces in the house weren't to be lit until nightfall. She would have to have a talk with Fletcher about the situation, no matter how pleasant the study was at the moment.

Hera was clearly luxuriating as well, stretched out with pure feline contentment across her books and papers. Thalia smiled, wondering how she would have the heart to move her; she looked so cute and happy.

She was about to try nonetheless, knowing she'd never accomplish anything otherwise, when she heard a familiar tread at the door.

"Leo," she said, meeting his gaze across the room.

He strode toward her. "Fletcher said you were in here. I told him there was no need to announce me. Seems rather pointless these days, do you not agree?"

Without waiting for her answer, he bent and pressed his lips to hers.

Tingles chased through her, along with a warmth that drove away any last, lingering traces of cold. Her eyes closed as she kissed him back.

"Happy birthday," he murmured, his lips brushing lightly across hers once more.

Her eyes opened on a jolt of surprise. "How do you know it's my birthday?"

Grinning, he straightened. "Let's just say a little birdie told me."

"Might that bird have a name?" She frowned, puzzling over the mystery. Her brow suddenly cleared. "Tilly."

"She was the only one I could think to ask and she proved quite helpful."

"I'm sure." Thalia ran a hand over his lapel. "She pried your name out of me and is extremely grateful for your assistance in putting Lord Cathcart in touch with your financial wizard, Pendragon. The debt on Lambton has been restructured and they are quite saved. I am grateful as well. Thank you for rescuing my friend."

He shrugged. "It was no trouble. Though I wouldn't complain if you wanted to further demonstrate your gratitude," he added, tapping a finger against his cheek.

Leaning up on her toes, she kissed him there, then again on his lips. "Will that do?" she asked a breathless minute later.

"For now. By the way, I sent you a couple of things. Did they arrive?"

She glanced briefly away. "If you mean the food and the clothes, then yes, they did."

With her hands in his, he took a step back and skimmed his gaze over her. "Then why are you wearing one of your old dresses? I had hoped to see you in your new afternoon gown."

"It is still in the box."

"Then go upstairs and change. I'll wait. I want to see you in it."

"No, I can't." She paused, then sighed. "I appreciate the thought. It was very kind of you. But, Leo, you must know that I cannot accept those gowns. I wouldn't have accepted the food hampers either, but Mrs. Grove had other ideas, so it's a bit late for those."

"Good for Mrs. Grove. So why can you not accept the gowns? Are they not to your liking?"

"Of course they are," she said, her chest aching at the disappointment on his face. "The gowns are beautiful. No one could think otherwise. Even so, I must refuse them." She tried to pull her hands from his.

He wouldn't let go. "I do not see why," he said, his voice hard.

"Surely you must. Do I have to say it out loud?"

She saw his jaw tighten. "You do not want my gifts, so yes, I rather think you do."

"I am your lover, not your mistress. Taking those clothes, even taking the hampers of food you sent, they turn our affair into something tawdry. They turn me into a kept woman." She tugged her hands harder this time, setting herself free. "And I will not be a . . . a . . ."

"A what?" he demanded.

"You know what." She hugged her arms around her waist. "A whore," she whispered.

"Thalia!" he said, his outrage clear. Catching her hands again, he pulled her into his arms. "Don't ever let me hear you say something like that again. You are not a . . . you are not that and you know it. I won't even have you thinking such a thing."

"Everyone else thinks it."

"I thought you didn't care what everyone else thinks. They see the lies they want to see, whatever the truth may be. You know that, better than anyone."

"Yes, but—"

"The gowns and other things are birthday gifts, Thalia.

Am I not allowed to get you anything, not even for your special day?"

"I suppose. But it is too much, far too extravagant—"

"Food and firewood and a couple of gowns are too extravagant, are they? I am a rich man. I can afford to be extravagant when I choose."

"Firewood?" She glanced toward the hearth and the blaze burning cheerfully in the grate. "So that's the reason. . . ." Her brows creased. "You should not have sent that either."

He smoothed a hand over her back. "Of course I should. We haven't discussed it before, but I can see that you are sometimes forced to economize. The fires aren't lit half the time and you don't always serve the best cuts of meat at table. And your wardrobe. Pray tell me when you last had a new gown."

She stiffened. "I have no need of new gowns, since I rarely entertain. I manage quite well on the income I receive and have done so very capably for years."

"I know that and I have great admiration for your determination and resolve. But you do without the luxuries. If I want to make your life a little easier, then where is the harm?"

"You know the harm."

"That is your pride talking."

"Some days, it is the only thing I have."

He studied her at length, then sighed. "They are just a few gifts for your birthday, Thalia. Can you not accept them in the spirit in which they are meant? Can you not let yourself enjoy a little?"

Her brows furrowed. "The food and firewood, perhaps, since it benefits the staff as well as me. But the dresses—"

"Will look lovely on you. All you need to do is try them on to see."

"Leo."

"Please." He kissed her, his touch softening her resistance. "What if I promise not to give you anything else?"

"Just today?"

"Exactly. You will agree to graciously accept the

birthday presents I've gotten you and I, in turn, promise not to give you anything else. At least not until Christmas. You cannot deny me Christmas."

Christmas was a little less than two months away. Their affair might well be over by then. So really, would it be so terrible to say yes?

A silence fell between; then she relented. "All right. I shall accept my birthday presents—"

"And Christmas."

"And Christmas. But nothing else. Satisfied?"

A slow smile curved his mouth. "Well enough." He kissed her again.

"Shall I change into my new dress?" she asked, suddenly excited.

"Yes. But before you do, there are a couple more gifts."

"What? But you said—"

"That I am limited to gifts I give you today."

"Maybe I'll take back my promise."

"Can't." He grinned. "Once a promise is made, it cannot be rescinded."

She drew a breath. "Fine. But should you suddenly remember anything more, I shall refuse it."

"If you insist."

"I do." She stepped out of his hold.

Crossing to a nearby table, he picked up a small box she hadn't noticed earlier, and held it out. She took it, admiring the pretty blue ribbon for a moment before she reached to untie it.

Her breath caught when she saw what lay within, hands shaking slightly as she lifted it carefully from its nest of satin and feathers.

The Meissen box. *Her* Meissen box with the pair of frolicking kittens, the one her father had given her so many years ago.

She'd put the beautiful porcelain piece out of her mind, but obviously Leo hadn't forgotten. Now here it was again.

"Oh, Leo," she whispered.

"I've been waiting for the right time to give it to you

again," he said. "You seemed so taken with it at the auction. You do still like it, yes?"

She blinked back moisture in her eyes and nodded. "You cannot know how much. It used to be mine."

His brows arched. "What?"

"My father gave it to me when I was a girl and Gordon . . ."

"Kept it and sold it when you got divorced," Leo finished. "That man is such a bastard."

"Shh, don't ruin the moment. Forget I mentioned him, please. This is . . . wonderful. I couldn't ask for a better birthday present." She cradled the porcelain trinket box in her hand.

"So you're not going to tell me to take it back?"

She shook her head. "It nearly killed me to refuse it the first time. I haven't the strength to do so again."

He slid an arm around her waist. "Nor should you. It belonged to you before and it is yours again, forever."

"Thank you." Threading her fingers into his hair, she urged his head down so she could kiss him.

Leo eagerly complied.

She blinked, a little dizzy by the time he finally let her come back up for air. Taking the trinket box in hand, he placed it back into its protective packaging and set it aside.

"Ready for your last gift?" he asked.

"That's right, I had forgotten there is more. So? What is this final gift?"

"I think '*Where* is the gift?' makes a better question. Do you have an umbrella?"

"Yes," she said, confused by the sudden change of subject. "Why?"

"Because we are going to the stables."

Chapter 25

Leo stood beside Thalia inside the stables, a light, steady rain pouring outside. He watched, studying her face as the groom led her present forward.

"The roan filly!" She clasped her hands to her chest, an expression of wonder spreading across her features. "Oh, she's so beautiful, just as I remember."

"Happy birthday, Thalia."

But just as quickly as it had come, her pleasure faded. "Leo, thank you, but no. Take her back."

"Remember your promise."

"I didn't think you meant to give me a horse. She's far too dear, and I—" She drew him away, lowering her voice so the servant couldn't overhear. "I cannot afford her. The carriage horse I keep is an indulgence already. A riding horse, especially one as exceptional as this, it is beyond my means. Please, do not tempt mc."

"There is no temptation. I shall bear all the cost of her upkeep."

Her mouth firmed. "No. Now have your man return her to the mews at Cavendish Square."

She is so stubborn, he thought. *But I am more stubborn.*

If Thalia would not accept the horse outright, then he would find a less straightforward way to convince her.

"You mistake the matter," he explained, as if that had been his plan all along. "I am not giving her to you permanently. Think of her as a loan."

"What?"

"My little sister, Esme, will be making her debut this spring and she'll need a good horse for Town. I thought you could ride Athena for the time being. Keep her trained and well exercised."

"A groom could do those things."

"Yes, but I want Athena accustomed to a sidesaddle and the feel of a woman's lighter weight and touch. One of my men cannot do that."

Thalia's pretty brows drew close as she considered his words. "I suppose not. Even so—"

"You would be doing a favor, not only for me, but for my sister. Come spring, I am sure Esme will have nothing but praise for your excellent care and training of her new mount. You are an exceptional rider and can make sure the mare is properly gentled. Please, Thalia. Do not make me disappoint my sister."

She frowned harder, then turned her gaze on the mare again. Her features softened, longing plain in her luminous brown eyes.

"It will just be temporary," she repeated. "Only until spring."

He smiled. "Esme will be exceedingly grateful. And do not worry—I will provide for all of Athena's care."

But Thalia wasn't paying attention any longer. Walking slowly forward, she reached out a careful hand and stroked the horse's neck.

Athena whickered softly, puffing out a gentle breath through her velvety nostrils.

"Oh, she's a love," Thalia said with a delighted sigh. "She's got spirit, but she'll be no trouble at all. Will you, girl?"

She patted her again and the horse tossed her head as if agreeing.

Thalia laughed, a wide smile on her rosy lips.

As it had once before, Leo's chest swelled with emotion as he watched her. He drank in her beauty, not just its outward manifestation, but the radiance of the soul he knew lay underneath.

Each day he came to know her a little better.

Every day he wanted to know more, be with her more.

Would a time ever come when he wanted that to stop? Right now, he couldn't imagine it.

Somehow he didn't think he would ever be able to imagine it.

He cleared his throat. "If it weren't for this weather, I would suggest we ride out now. How about tomorrow morning instead?"

She nodded, still stroking a palm over Athena's red-brown neck and shoulders. "Tomorrow morning sounds excellent."

"In the meantime, why don't we go inside and you can try on your new gowns?" He leaned closer so only Thalia could hear. "Then afterward, I can enjoy taking them off of you again."

Her eyes grew dark with sudden desire.

After giving the horse a final farewell pat and receiving a promise from the groom that the mare would get an extra scoop of oats in that night's feed, she let Leo slide his arm around her waist.

Huddled together under the umbrella, they hurried through the rain and back inside the house.

Many hours later, darkness having long since fallen, Thalia lay in bed, warm and replete inside Leo's arms, her head cushioned on his shoulder.

She skimmed her fingers in a lazy arc over his chest, then slowly leaned up to kiss him. "Thank you," she murmured.

"Considering the evening we've had, I should be the one thanking you." He ran a hand across her naked back, then lower to lightly cup her bottom. "But somehow I get the feeling you mean something else."

"What I mean is thank you for today. Thank you for giving me the best birthday I've ever had."

He arched a dark gold brow. "Ever?"

"Yes, ever."

"Not even as a child?"

She shook her head. "Any parties we had were always far more about my mother than me. One year she didn't even invite any children. Just her friends. As I recall, I spent most of the day alone in the nursery with a book and was glad of it."

"How old were you?"

"Seven, I think."

"That's awful."

"Oh, it wasn't so bad." She shrugged. "My parents were often self-involved and thoughtless, but they could be kind as well. I never wanted for anything, not really. And it wasn't as if they did anything so very dreadful. It's not as if they beat me."

"I should think not," he said, his words gruff as if he couldn't even conceive of such an idea.

She looked away, repressing the sudden urge to shiver as other, darker memories came upon her. But just as quickly, she pushed them aside. She wasn't going to let anything ruin these moments with Leo, certainly not the past.

"I just wanted you to know," she said, gazing deeply into his eyes, "wanted to thank you for giving me this one, absolutely perfect day."

His arm tightened around her. "I would give you more. I would shower you with anything you desired, if only you would let me."

She shook her head. "This is enough. More than enough. I learned long ago never to be too greedy. It makes the disappointments that much easier to bear."

"Why do you assume there will be disappointments?"

"Because that is the way life is."

"Not always."

His hand caressed her lower back, sending ripples of pleasure in its wake.

"No," she agreed quietly, "not always."

Reaching up, she pressed her palm to his cheek, his skin faintly rough with a day's growth of whiskers.

But she didn't mind. She liked everything about Leo, even a little bristle.

"Make love to me again," she whispered.

A look of desire came into his eyes; it was an expression she had come to know well.

"Gladly," he said, with husky purpose.

Fitting his mouth to hers, he claimed her with a passionate intensity that quickly robbed her mind of everything but him. She kissed him back, eager and needy, knowing he was the very best present of all.

Her bare skin slid in a sinuous glide against his, her pulse pounding out a wild beat with every new kiss and caress. She met his ardor with her own, demanding, almost greedy, giving and taking until she lost herself in the feverish joy of their union.

She arched, crying out as he lifted her up and over him to bury himself deep inside.

She sighed at the utter perfection, marveling at how right it was with him.

Only him.

And she felt possessed in those moments, changed in some unalterable way as if her very bones and blood were being melted away and re-formed. As if her life was no longer wholly her own and she would be cast adrift without him.

She trembled, suddenly afraid.

But then he surged within her, driving her, forcing the pleasure to a delirious peak that made her body sing and her senses fly free.

And she soared, awash with happiness as she crashed blissfully back down to earth, secure in the unbreakable bonds of his arms.

Leo joined Thalia for her inaugural ride on Athena the following morning. As usual, he'd awakened early and gone back to Cavendish Square to bathe and change clothes. He'd left again straight after, riding his stallion back to Thalia's town house so they could head out together for a morning gallop in the park.

The little roan mare had behaved even better than he and Thalia had predicted, the horse warming immediately to Thalia's skilled yet gentle touch.

Thalia was smiling broadly, her eyes bright with excitement, cheeks pink from the exercise and bracing fresh air by the time they returned to her town house for breakfast.

The two of them indulged in a hearty meal at her dining room table, enlivened by delicious offerings from yesterday's birthday hamper and a seemingly endless supply of enjoyable conversation.

All the rooms in the house were warm now, thanks to the stacks of firewood and a load of coal that had been delivered. And though he had decided not to mention it to Thalia for fear of provoking a fresh argument, another such delivery was scheduled to arrive at Christmastide—more than enough fuel to last her through the winter.

To his amazement, he discovered that Thalia had never visited the Tower of London or seen the crown jewels. So they spent the afternoon touring the great edifice on the banks of the Thames, looking like just another pair of sightseers rather than the experienced city dwellers that they were.

Afterward he convinced her to put on her new evening gown, then took her to the Clarendon Hotel for an excellent meal prepared by the great French chef Jacquiers, former servant of Louis XVIII.

She confided that the experience was another first for her, since she had never before dined out in a hotel with a gentleman or eaten authentic French cuisine that was generally considered as good as the finest fare served in Paris. The sheltered, gently bred ladies of the *Ton*, she told him on the drive home, had no idea what delights they were missing.

"Perhaps there are some benefits to being a disgraced, scandalous divorcée, after all." She smiled and leaned her head against his shoulder. "I never had fun like this when I was married."

But the most fun of all awaited them when they returned for the final time to her town house and went to bed. There in the quiet candlelight, they made exquisite love, feasting on each other while they indulged in a panoply of the carnal pleasures.

He brought her to her peak more than once, loving the breathy little sounds she made as he roused her, and her frantic cries of completion, which he had to smother with hard kisses or into the pillows so she wouldn't wake the house.

His own releases were powerful, leaving him exhausted and satisfied, yet somehow ready for more. He felt bewitched in her arms, whole in a way he couldn't explain.

Their final time was the best of all as he thrust into her with wild abandon, her arms and legs clenched high and tight around his back, her eyes locked with his, neither of them able to look away. He'd shuddered violently as he took his pleasure, her climax still quaking through her body and into his with a force that intensified and prolonged his own.

Later in the dark, he held her and listened to her sleep. He knew he needed to do the same, but somehow he didn't want to give up the moment.

He was too content, too replete.

She made him happy in ways even he wasn't sure he fully understood yet.

For the first time since he'd met her, he wasn't certain of the future. It was still early days in their affair and yet he couldn't see himself growing tired of her.

Or wanting things to end.

Yet what of her?

In so many ways, she was still a mystery to him. For all their closeness, he sensed there was a part of her that she kept bound tightly away.

Hidden and her own.

He wanted to know what that something was, to unlock all her deepest secrets so nothing stood between them.

I will know, he vowed. *With patience I will know everything, know her inside and out.*

He ran a hand over her hair, smiling as she sighed in her sleep and snuggled closer.

Dropping a kiss on her forehead, he closed his eyes and willed himself to join her in the world of dreams.

Chapter 26

Thalia opened her eyes and stretched against the rumpled bedsheets where she lay warm and rested. Rolling her head on the pillow that still bore traces of Leo's scent, she gazed out the window at the white flakes of lightly falling snow.

December truly was upon them, Christmas just around the corner. She couldn't believe how quickly the last six and a half weeks had passed—the most wonderful six and a half weeks of her life.

But tomorrow her idyll would end, temporarily at least, since Leo was leaving to spend the holiday with his family at Braebourne, the Byron family's ancestral estate.

Initially, he'd planned to stay in London and spend Christmas with her, but she'd talked him out of it.

"Your family is counting on you being with them," she'd said. "They'll be hurt if you don't go."

"There are so many of us these days, especially now that all my older siblings have families of their own. I doubt I'd even be missed," he'd answered with self-deprecating humor.

But she hadn't been convinced.

"Somehow I think they'd notice your absence. You're far too dynamic a personality to fade into the background, even if Braebourne is overrun with dozens and dozens of relations." She took his hand. "Go. Be with your family. I will be here when you get back."

He'd frowned. "And what of you? How will you spend the holiday?"

"The same as I always do." She'd shrugged as if it made no difference to her, when in reality she was dying inside at the idea of being alone and without him.

She'd forced a smile. "The staff always makes me a lovely meal and we pull Christmas crackers together. Later, Hera and I usually curl up in front of the fire with a good book and a cup of hot wassail."

"It sounds lonely. I'll stay."

"No, you won't."

As much as she wanted him with her, she didn't wish to tear him away from his people, to cause a rift with his family over her.

"Besides, I forgot to tell you that my friend Jane Frost will be in Town and has promised to drop by for a cup of syllabub that afternoon. I shall be quite entertained."

It wasn't a complete lie, since Jane had written to say that she was coming into the city. But it would be a quick visit just after Christmas and she wasn't planning to stay more than a day or two. She hoped there would be time to meet for a cup of tea.

Thalia hoped so too, but wasn't counting on it, since Jane's husband would be with her and he, like Lord Cathcart, frowned on their continued association.

"Do not worry about me." She'd kept her voice deliberately cheerful. "I shall be perfectly fine on my own. And actually, it may be a good thing, since I've been sadly neglectful of the accounts over the past few weeks." She slid her arms around his neck and pressed her breasts to his chest. "Someone has been keeping me very busy lately."

He'd grinned. "I suppose someone has."

Then he'd kissed her and carried her to bed, even though it was the middle of the day. By the time they'd come up for air, the discussion was forgotten.

But now the day was nearly upon them and he would depart come morning. The thought made her chest ache, agony creeping upon her like a waiting shadow.

She wouldn't let herself wallow yet. She would have plenty of time for that over the next three weeks, since he would be away through the New Year and the Twelfth Night celebration.

Maybe their separation really would be a good thing. She'd become far too dependent on him, living for the hours they spent together, both day and night.

They'd fallen into a routine of sorts, riding each morning before they returned to the town house together to eat breakfast and decide on their plans for the day. He still returned to his house to bathe and change clothes. But lately, he'd been bathing here at her town house and having his valet deliver fresh clothing and other grooming essentials. At the moment, in fact, there was a set of his silver-backed hairbrushes, a razor and strop and shaving soap on her washstand. A spare suit of his clothes hung in her wardrobe and in a small dish on her dressing table there was a pair of gold cuff links.

Small things but incredibly meaningful nevertheless.

She wished he hadn't needed to leave her this morning, that they could have spent every hour of the day together.

And tonight, of course.

But he'd had some last-minute business he'd been unable to put off. So he'd left her to sleep late with promises to return by midday.

As for evenings per their routine, he had dinner with her nearly every night, then took her to bed. They nearly always made love, often more than once. The only exception was during her monthlies when she hadn't felt up to it. But he'd stayed anyway, holding her through the night while both of them slept.

Her bed was going to feel strange without him.

Empty.

Her house too, despite the servants and the warm, sweet, uncritical companionship of Hera.

She sighed and put her hands over her eyes, wondering how she was going to bear his absence.

But she could, knowing he would be back.

And when he wouldn't be?

When the time came and they said their final good-byes?

She let her arms drop to her sides against the sheets and stared again at the falling snow.

She wouldn't think about that day. Not now. Not until it came.

Ignoring the ache in her chest, she sat up and reached for her robe.

"Lawrence and I are leaving tomorrow at first light," Leo told Thalia that evening as they lingered over a dessert of warm apple and raisin tart with brandied cream.

He'd suggested they eat dinner in her sitting room rather than the dining room as was their habit; he'd longed for the warmth and intimacy of her quarters on their last night together.

A frown creased his brows. He ought to be excited about going home to Braebourne. Usually he couldn't wait to walk through its broad halls and beautiful grounds, to spend time with his noisy, exuberant, warmhearted family, who were always ripe for fresh schemes and merrymaking.

But this year he just couldn't seem to muster his usual enthusiasm and the reason was sitting across from him right now.

He gazed at Thalia, taking in her dark-haired beauty as if to memorize it. And perhaps he was. Ridiculous as it seemed, he didn't want to be apart from her, not even for a mere three weeks.

He wished he could take her with him.

But men didn't take their mistresses—or lovers, as he knew Thalia preferred to be called—home to meet their families. Even as open and tolerant as his mother and siblings were, he didn't think they would approve of him bringing the woman with whom he was practically living these days into the midst of their Christmas cheer. As for his uncles and aunts and cousins, well, they would like it even less.

He should have told them he was staying in London. He shouldn't have let Thalia talk him into making the long trip to Gloucestershire and leaving her behind.

"Are you sure you'll be all right here by yourself?" he said suddenly. "I can always send word to Lawrence to go on tomorrow without me."

"Don't be silly. We've been over this before. Go. Enjoy your Christmas at home. I shall be fine."

"Well, if you're sure —"

"I am," she said, her voice firm. "Be with the people you love."

But he was beginning to suspect he was there already. That she was the one he loved above all others.

He held his tongue and drank a swallow of hot coffee instead.

Maybe she didn't feel the same.

Maybe she wanted him to go, to get some separation, since they were together so frequently. Perhaps she was growing tired of him?

He set his cup down with a clink.

"I won't be able to stay tonight," he said. "Mayhap I ought to go. Let you get some sleep."

Some look he couldn't interpret flashed in her eyes before her lashes swept down. "If that is what you'd prefer." Her voice was even, emotionless. "I am sure you could use a full night's sleep as well."

"You're right. I could."

Tossing down his napkin, he pushed back his chair and got to his feet. That's when he remembered, feeling the sight bulge in his coat pocket.

He dug inside and withdrew a slim, black velvet-covered box. "Here. I know you don't want presents from me, but we did agree that Christmas was acceptable. This is for you."

She took it but didn't open the lid. "I have something for you as well. Wait here."

Skirts billowing around her ankles, she hurried from the room into her bedchamber next door. She returned quickly, a rectangular-shaped object in hand. It was wrapped in white paper, a red grosgrain ribbon tied around it in a bow.

"It's not a great deal, but I hope you like it nonetheless," she told him, her words faintly breathless. "Promise you will not open it until Christmas."

He met her eyes. "I promise."

"Well, I—suppose I ought to wish you good night and a safe journey," she said, her hands linked tightly before her.

"Yes. Happy Christmas, Thalia, since I won't be able to say it to you on the day."

"Merry Christmas, Leo. And a very happy New Year as well."

A lump settled in his throat. "Will you miss me at all?" he said harshly.

Surprise lit her eyes. "Yes, of course. Every day."

Seconds ticked past, the very air heavy with the emotion arcing between them.

Suddenly she was in his arms and he was kissing her, pouring everything he had into the embrace. He clutched her to him and lifted her off her feet, ravishing her lips with fervid, almost desperate kisses.

She wasn't far behind, sinking her fingers into his hair, demanding every bit as much as he took. Opening her mouth, she slid her tongue against his with a wet, sinuous glide that made him shudder.

Rocking her against his straining shaft, he hitched her higher into his arms, his hands splayed against her rounded bottom. His hold secure, he carried her to the bedroom.

She bounced lightly against the mattress as he laid her down on her back. Tossing her skirts to her waist, he stepped between her legs, then yanked off his coat before moving quickly to unfasten his falls.

Without any further preamble he was inside her, lodged hard and hot and deep. She clasped him like a velvet glove, one that seemed to have been fashioned expressly for him.

She arched and took more, took everything.

And he gave it back, thrusting inside her until both of them were wild, until she climaxed with a pleasure so intense her fingernails bit into his skin in a way he was sure would leave marks.

Then he claimed his own satisfaction.

He lay over her in the aftermath, waiting for his racing heart to slow. He brushed damp tendrils of hair away from her face and kissed her slowly, softly.

"I suppose I should go," he said after a while.

"Hmm, I suppose you should. You need to sleep, remember?"

"Do I?" He kissed her again, more passionately this time. "I can sleep later."

She curved a leg higher around his waist and kissed him. "So can I."

Thalia awakened in the dark of the night to the sensation of Leo's lips moving against hers. Looping her arms around his neck to kiss him back, she realized that he was fully dressed and leaning over her instead of lying beside her in the bed.

"Sorry to wake you, but I didn't want to leave without saying good-bye," he said.

His features were dimly lit, the room illuminated only by the low-burning embers in the fireplace. Still, she caught a glint of the green in his eyes, memorizing it to think about later.

"What time is it?"

"About four."

Her heart gave a painful squeeze; she tightened her hold. "Then you must go. Be safe."

He kissed her again. "See you in three weeks."

"Yes. In three weeks. Don't forget your present."

"I won't. Thalia, I—"

"What?"

He paused, then shook his head. "Nothing. Go back to sleep and dream happy dreams."

She would dream, but she didn't think they would be happy ones, not with him away. So rather than answer, she kissed him, putting all her passion, all her sorrow at their parting into the embrace.

With a few words, she could stop him from leaving. She could keep him here with her.

But he needed to go and she needed to let him, if only to prove to herself that she still could.

Their kiss ended and then he was gone, the soft reverberation of the door closing behind him all that remained of his departure.

Rolling over, she burrowed under the sheets that still bore his scent and closed her eyes against the moisture gathering there.

Chapter 27

All around Leo drifted the fragrant scents of pine boughs, holly and traces of woodsmoke from a Yule log so big that it would burn steadily throughout the next twelve days.

Yesterday, he and his brothers, Edward, Cade, Jack, Drake and Lawrence, and their brother-in-law, Adam, had overseen its installation in Braebourne's main fireplace. The hearth was so large a full-grown man could stand nearly upright inside it.

Later, as per tradition, a piece of tinder carefully saved from last year's Yule log had been brought out and used to light the new one, officially inaugurating the Christmas holiday. Their mother, Ava, Dowager Duchess of Clybourne, had done the honors as matriarch of the family. It was a special occasion that everyone always enjoyed.

Today was Christmas; the house was filled to bursting with noise and laughter, the entire family gathered in the large drawing room to eat and play games and open presents. The children, many of whom were his own nieces and nephews, had been allowed out of the nursery so they could participate in the festivities. At the moment, several of the older ones were involved in a raucous game of hoodman-blind that had spilled out into the main hall.

The toddlers had been settled together on soft blankets in the middle of the drawing room floor to play with toys under the watchful gazes of their parents and respective nurses.

There were a couple of infants as well, including his

newest nephew, August—Drake and Sebastianne's first child—and Jack and Grace's newest daughter, Rosalind, their fourth child.

They teased Jack on occasion about producing only daughters. But Jack just smiled, saying he liked being surrounded by girls, since women were his favorite of the two sexes.

And Leo could see that Jack was happy and well contented, his wild bachelor days long behind him. After nearly eight years of marriage, he and Grace were still clearly in love.

Glancing across the room, Leo saw them laughing quietly where they sat together on the sofa talking with Cade and Meg and Adam and Mallory, who was heavily pregnant with their second child.

Cade had his arm around Meg; Mallory was resting her head against Adam's shoulder while he absently stroked her rounded stomach; and Jack and Grace were holding hands.

Drake and Sebastianne and Edward and Claire were just as spoony, though Ned, as the duke, did try to maintain a bit more decorum, at least in company. But Leo had seen them together often enough to know the depth of their devotion, the steadfast strength of their love.

He'd always been happy for them but in a bit of an eye-rolling kind of way. Today he felt something else.

Today he felt envious.

He wondered what Thalia was doing.

Was she lonely without him?

Or was she making merry with the friend she'd mentioned?

Had she gone to the other woman's house for syllabub and carols? Were they even now celebrating, perhaps with a whole host of revelers gathered to enjoy the day?

Was he on her mind or had she forgotten him except in passing now that he was away?

He frowned.

I ought to have brought her with me and damned the consequences.

His hand curled into a fist on his thigh.

She could be here at his side right now if she were like the others. No one would dare to say a word if she was his wife.

His breath caught on a quiet gasp, thoughts revolving like a maelstrom, mad though they might be.

Or are they?

"Here, I thought you could do with a bit of Christmas cheer."

He looked up and stared blankly at his younger sister, Esme, and the cup in her hand. "What?"

"I brought you a cup of wassail. I thought it might help cure whatever it is that is ailing you."

She sank down onto the cushions beside him and looked at him out of a pair of dark blue eyes that were much too knowing for a girl of eighteen.

"What makes you think something is wrong?" he asked, accepting the drink.

"Oh, I don't know. Maybe the fact that you're sitting over here in the corner all by yourself. That and the big bearish scowl on your face. It kind of gives you away."

He scowled harder. "It's nothing."

"Obviously, it is something."

"It's nothing I can tell *you*."

"Oh." Her face fell a bit. "Well, that puts me in my place, does it not?"

She started to her feet again, but he stopped her with a hand.

"Sorry," he said. "I don't mean to be a bear, as you put it—leave it to you to pick an animal reference."

"Of course. Animals are the wisest of all creatures. They provide an example for every facet of life."

"There are quite a few humans who might disagree, but we'll leave that debate for another time."

She nodded. "Well then?"

"Well then what?"

"Why are you discomposed, today of all days? It's Christmas. You ought to be smiling and happy."

He showed her his teeth.

Esme laughed, but sobered quickly again. "Are you certain you cannot tell me?"

On a sigh, he leaned back against the cushions. Esme was the last person with whom he should discuss Thalia; mistresses were not something a girl her age should know anything about. And a divorced mistress . . .

Jack or Cade would be better choices by far—any of his other siblings really. Yet oddly enough, Esme was the least judgmental person in the family and also the best listener. She was the most compassionate as well, ready to bind a bird's injured wing or listen to the worries of a scullery maid who'd been scolded by Cook for not peeling enough potatoes.

He drank some wassail, enjoying the flavor of the warm brandy, hard cider, oranges, cinnamon and cloves. "There is someone who isn't here today. Someone I miss."

"A lady?"

"Yes. And do not bother asking her name."

"I wasn't going to."

A brief silence fell.

He drank more wassail.

"Did you not invite her?" Esme asked. "Or is it that she could not come?"

"A bit of both actually. It's . . . complicated."

"Why?"

"Why is it complicated? Because it is," he added at her nod.

"Maybe it doesn't need to be. Do you love her, this woman you miss?"

His frown returned. "I don't know."

"Does she love you?"

His chest tightened, a slightly queasy sensation in his stomach. He set his cup aside. "I don't know that either."

"Then maybe you should find out. Once you do, all the complications may not seem so complex."

"Then again, they still may."

"You are just having a fit of the blue devils today. Come on," she said, reaching for his hand, "come join me for a game of cards. I'm determined to beat Jack and I need a crack hand for a partner."

"Impossible. You know Jack's unbeatable."

"No one wins all the time, not even him. And nothing is impossible, not if you want it badly enough."

"So speaks the naive schoolroom miss."

"Not so naive," she said with a serene smile. "I just prefer to be optimistic, that's all."

"I won't ask what you mean by that first remark for fear of finding myself unduly shocked."

"I doubt there's anything that could shock you."

"You might be surprised. You haven't met our neighbor, have you?"

"No. Is he shocking? In what way?"

"Forget I mentioned him." He allowed her to pull him to his feet. "Let's go get slaughtered at the card table by Jack."

"Yes, let's."

"Another round?" Jack asked nearly two hours later, a gleeful grin on his face as he scraped a huge pile of winnings toward himself across the table.

"No." Leo groaned and tossed down his cards.

"Me either. I've been fleeced enough for one day." Lawrence threw his discards after his twin's.

Edward and Claire did the same, exchanging looks of commiseration.

Leo saw Sebastianne's eighteen-year-old brother, Julien, follow their lead. He'd been so excited to be included in the adult play, but looked a bit stunned now by his losses.

"Well, don't look at me. I was out ages ago," Mallory said.

She was settled sideways on the nearby sofa with pillows plumped at her back and her feet propped up, a plate of sweet biscuits balanced on her very pregnant stomach so she wouldn't have to reach.

During the game, Adam had gotten up between hands to check on her, even though she was less than six feet away. He looked ready to do the same now, but she waved for him to stay in his chair with a soft smile she reserved just for him.

At her feet, on the same sofa, sat Drake. With the table so full of players, he'd been happy to sit out. He was lost in silent reverie, the game clearly the last thing on his mind.

"Told you it would be pure butchery," Leo said, shooting a meaningful look across the table at Esme.

"Of course it was," Grace said from where she stood behind Jack's chair. Leaning forward, she wrapped her arms around his neck and kissed his temple. "That's what you all get for playing cards with a sharp."

"If I really were a sharp"—Jack stroked a hand over his wife's forearm—"I would have played for more than pennies."

"You used to play for very high stakes, remember, darling?" Grace said.

He smiled and looked up into her eyes. "The highest. It's what brought us together, after all."

"Well, thank heavens you've reformed," Esme said. "Otherwise my entire quarter's allowance would be gone."

"Half my fortune would be written on vowels if we'd been playing for real stakes," Cade said as he gazed down at what was left of his obviously dismal hand.

He sighed and rubbed an absent fist over the old war wound in his thigh. It still caused him to limp even now after nearly a decade.

Meg reached over from where she sat next to Cade. He smiled and raised her hand to his lips.

"I'd have to consider a mortgage on the estate again," Adam remarked with a rueful shake of his dark head. "Although you seemed to hold your own rather well, Sebastianne."

He nodded toward her small pile of coins.

She gave a Gallic shrug, a half smile on her pretty face. "This is not my first card game. And it doesn't hurt to have a brilliant mathematician for a husband, one who has taught me how to keep track of what's been played. Rather like his brother Jack, I imagine."

Jack's grin widened.

"Is that not right, *mon amour*?" Sebastianne said, looking toward the sofa. "Drake?"

Drake didn't look up, a faraway look in his eyes.

"Drake?" Sebastianne said again, pitching her voice so that it was low and soft, yet astonishingly clear.

Suddenly, Drake turned his head and blinked, looking right at her. "Yes? Did you win, sweetheart?"

"No, I did not," Sebastianne said.

"That's good. Let me know if you need more money." Drake frowned, the distant look coming back into his eyes. Suddenly he used the pencil in his hand to scratch something down on the small pad of paper balanced on his knee.

Rather than feel slighted, Sebastianne laughed along with the rest of them.

"What's our favorite mad genius working on this time?" Meg said in a low voice.

"A new theorem of some sort. And an invention that deals with steam-driven engines." Sebastianne smiled. "If it weren't Christmas, I would never have gotten him out of his laboratory. You know how he is when he's creating."

Everyone nodded; they all knew Drake.

"So, no one else wants to play?" Jack asked, rubbing his palms together.

"No!" they all said in unison.

Jack just laughed.

"Pardon me, my loves, but I am afraid I must interrupt your game playing," said Ava as she strolled serenely into their midst. "It is well past time we opened our presents, then went in for our dinner."

Leo smiled at his mother, her gentle voice and kind remonstrations reminding him of other occasions, other Christmases. She was just as beautiful as she'd been when he was a boy, her green eyes just as clear, her hair the same soft brown with only a few more threads of silver.

"Your timing is impeccable, as always, Mama," he told her. "We were just finished."

He and the others stood—everyone except Drake and Mallory. They both stayed on the sofa, Mallory because she didn't feel like getting up yet and Drake because he hadn't heard a word anyone—not even his mother— had said.

Smiling with patience and love, Sebastianne went to shake him out of his reverie.

Leo saved Thalia's gift to him for last, tucking it next to his hip while he opened the stack of other presents he'd received.

The room was an explosion of paper and boxes and ribbon—and noise. It seemed like everyone in the family was talking at once, exclaiming over their presents, showing them off and calling out their thanks.

He'd retreated again to the quiet corner he'd been in earlier, enjoying the small bubble of solitude. Odd really, since he was usually in the center of any action. But today he needed a little space.

Silently, he opened each present until Thalia's small gift was all that remained. He ran his fingers over the paper, taking his time as he pulled the ribbon free.

It was a book.

A copy of Jane Austen's *Pride and Prejudice* to be exact.

He opened the cover and read what Thalia had written in her elegant, flowing hand.

> *For Leo,*
>
> *Because I know you enjoy using your brain a great deal more than you care to let on.*
>
> *Merry Christmas 1817*

He laughed.

She had him dead to rights. He did act the careless Corinthian, in ways that often disguised his true self. But when a man had so many brilliant siblings, he needed some other means than being smart to set himself apart. Humor and sports had always served their purposes. And he'd always enjoyed himself in the process.

But Thalia saw through his facade.

Thalia saw *him*.

He ran his hand over the binding again and thought of her back in London, wondering what she was doing now and if she'd had a happy day.

He frowned, realizing that for all his pleasure in being among his family, there was an emptiness he'd never felt before now. Something was missing—or rather someone.

So what are you going to do about it? whispered a little voice in his head.

His hand tightened on the book.

Yes. What?

"Will there be anything else this evening, milady?"

Thalia looked over at her lady's maid. "No, that will be all. Thank you for the bedtime cocoa, Parker. And Merry Christmas."

The other woman smiled. "Merry Christmas, milady."

"Remember that tomorrow is Boxing Day. You and the rest of the staff are to have the entire day off, so no getting up early or bringing me breakfast. Mrs. Grove has set out a lovely cold repast for me in the dining room and I can brew my own pot of tea on the fireplace hearth. You've left plenty of water for me in the pitcher, so I can bathe and dress myself as well."

"I don't mind seeing to you, milady. I won't be leaving for my sister's until late morning, so it's no trouble."

"You're always so good to me, Parker. But no, you sleep in and have the whole day to yourself."

"If that is what you prefer, milady. Have you any special plans for tomorrow?"

Thalia's throat tightened. Resolutely, she pushed away the wave of melancholia that rushed over her at the thought of being alone in the house. Even Fletcher had let her know he would be away visiting an old friend. At least Hera would be around for company—unless she deserted her to go hunting for moles in the garden.

"Do not worry about me." Thalia forced a smile. "I shall find plenty to keep me busy, just as I do every year."

And she always had, since the very first Christmas she'd spent on her own after the divorce. Yet this year felt different. This year she felt her solitude more keenly than ever before.

Because of Leo.

God, I miss him.

But she wasn't going to dwell on his absence, at least not any more often than could be helped.

After bidding her maid a final good night, she poured herself another cup of cocoa, then settled back on the sofa with a book.

That's when she saw it—the present Leo had given her.

She'd resisted the impulse to open it, knowing instinctively that it was likely something expensive. Something she should return to him in spite of her agreement to accept a Christmas gift from him.

He'd given her so much already, including a huge Christmas goose, which had tasted absolutely delicious, and another mammoth load of firewood that would probably last until next winter.

She couldn't keep accepting presents from him. Still, he would be hurt if she didn't at least open his gift.

Leaning over, she picked up the box. She stroked her fingers over the luxuriously soft velvet covering, then popped open the lid.

Inside lay a strand of creamy smooth pearls, each one as big and round as a fully ripe pea. They gleamed with a lustrous warmth, delicate and profoundly beautiful.

There was a tiny note tucked to one side. Hand trembling slightly, she drew it out and unfolded it.

> *Thalia,*
>
> *I know these can never replace the memories that came with your great-grandmother's pearls, but I hope they will let you start building joyous new ones.*
>
> *Merry Christmas,*
> *Leo*

For a moment, she sat stunned.

He'd bought her pearls to replace the ones Gordon had refused to return to her after the divorce. She barely even recalled mentioning them to Leo, yet somehow he had remembered.

A tear ran down her cheek, a smothering ache rising like a clenched fist inside her chest.

Leave it to Leo to give her the one gift she couldn't possibly return. The one gift she would love above all others.

Then suddenly, she was crying in earnest, wishing with all her heart that he were here beside her rather than miles and miles away.

Chapter 28

Thalia pulled gently on the reins, slowing Athena from a canter to a walk. Leaning forward, she gave the mare an approving pat on the shoulder, pleased at how beautifully mannered she was despite all the distractions in the park.

The day was cold but sunny and the park was busier than usual, Londoners needing an escape from the close confines of their homes after a recent snow.

Children ran and shouted, while their parents strolled behind, keeping a watchful eye. Younger couples sauntered arm in arm, bundled in heavy coats and scarves, their heads together as they whispered sweet nothings to each other.

And on the air drifted the festive scents of roasted chestnuts and hot cider, with frequent shouts from vendors to buy their wares.

Thalia stopped and bought a small package of chestnuts, tucking them warm into her pocket for the ride home. The nuts would be a little treat to help ward off the blue devils, though she didn't give it much hope of succeeding. New Year's had come and gone, yet the time until Leo was due to return seemed to stretch out forever.

Her friend Jane Frost had dropped by a few days ago, diverting her for a while. But their visit had been far too brief and left her feeling lower than ever once Jane had gone.

But rather than lie abed with the sheets over her

head, Thalia had forced herself to resume her usual routine — or rather her old routine before Leo had come into her life. Curious how odd it felt now.

And how empty.

But she would make do, exactly as she always had.

Tapping her heel against Athena's flank, she set her toward home.

She slowed the little mare again as she reached the town house, the animal's hooves clattering against the cobblestones as she rode into the mews.

The groom came out of the stable to help her dismount. "You've a visitor waiting, milady. Arrived not twenty minutes past."

"A visitor? Who is it?"

"Didn't give a name. Just said they'd wait for ye inside." The servant smiled, a mischievous twinkle in his eyes.

She considered questioning him further, but turned to make her way inside the house instead.

Could Jane have returned?

Unlikely.

Or maybe it was Mathilda?

She smiled at the thought.

She rounded the corner that led to the downstairs drawing room, hoping to find Fletcher first so he could reveal the identity of her mystery guest.

But the butler was nowhere to be seen.

She was considering heading upstairs first to change out of her riding habit into a more suitable gown when a man stepped out of the drawing room into the foyer.

He turned and smiled, his green-gold eyes sparkling like gemstones.

And suddenly she was running, her pulse pounding in a frantic rhythm.

"Leo!"

She leapt into his arms, her own locking tightly around his neck. Her feet dangled inches off the floor as he held her hard against him, his mouth warm and wild on hers. She clung, pouring all her passion, all her misery at their separation, into the kiss.

But she was miserable no more, her heart swelling with a happiness so great she thought she might burst. She kissed him harder, letting his scent and taste and touch sweep through her, washing away everything but him. He kissed her back, plundering her mouth with a thoroughness that made her tingle from head to toe.

"Surprised to see me?" he said, his mouth still scattering quick kisses against her own.

"Yes. What are you doing back? I thought you'd be away for another week at least."

"I came back early. Nothing was the same without you. Did you miss me?"

"Every day." Finding his lips, she proceeded to show him just how much.

"Let's go to your bedchamber," he murmured a long, breathless while later.

She nodded, expecting him to set her onto her feet. Instead, he swung her high into his arms and moved toward the stairs.

What seemed an endless time later, Thalia lay in a state of delirious naked bliss, the sheets and coverlet kicked into tangled heaps at her and Leo's bare feet.

She supposed they ought to cover up, but she was simply too boneless to move. He'd roused her to the most amazing heights with a pleasure so intense it made her blood burn all over again just to recall.

Even now, he played a hand over her breasts, lazily fondling each one before moving lower in an arc across her stomach. Curling a finger beneath her chin, he tipped her head back and claimed her lips for a slow, indulgent kiss.

Sighing, she turned into him and snuggled closer, burying her face against his neck and closing her eyes.

"Thank you for a most excellent welcome home." He trailed his fingers over her shoulder and arm.

She smiled and kissed his neck. "It was my pleasure, believe me."

"How was your Christmas?"

"Quiet. How was yours?"

"Noisy. And crowded in spite of the dozens and dozens of rooms Braebourne has. I spent the entire time wishing you were with me."

Warmth spread like a sun inside her chest. Leaning an arm against his chest, she looked into his eyes. "Me too." She stroked a hand against his cheek, loving the smooth feel of his shaven skin. "Thank you for my gift."

"The pearls? You like them?"

"Yes. How could I not? They're beautiful."

He arched a golden brown eyebrow. "And you're not going to try returning them?"

"Not this time." Sliding higher, she pressed her mouth to his for a long, slow kiss. "You chose the one thing I couldn't possibly bring myself to refuse."

"Good." She shivered deliciously as he smoothed a palm over her bare buttocks. "I'll have to start thinking of the next impossible-to-refuse gift to give you."

"Don't."

He brushed a lock of hair away from her forehead. "Why not? I like giving you things."

"You know why not. We've talked about this before." She kissed him again with a sweet yet ardent demand. "This is enough. I don't want anything more than to be your lover. Truly."

"Well, what if I do?"

"What?" she said, her forehead creasing.

"What if I need more?" His arms tightened around her. "What if I want the right to shower you with as many gifts as I like with no one able to say a word against it?"

"But they will. You know they will."

"Not if you're my wife."

The breath froze in her lungs, her heart aching as if she'd taken a hard blow to the chest. "What?" she gasped.

His eyes warmed with excitement and he sat up, sat them both up, his arms still wrapped loosely around her. "I love you. Marry me, Thalia."

She stared, speechless.

"I realized how I felt when I was away at Braebourne," he continued. "How nothing felt right because you weren't there with me. I wanted you to meet my family, to show you off to them as my bride. I want to take you back so you can meet them now. They're going to love you. I know they will."

Gooseflesh popped out all over her skin, an arctic cold seeping into her bones. She pulled away, then knelt to reach for her robe, which was draped around the foot post. Shivering, she drew it on.

But the wool didn't make her any less cold.

"I know you weren't expecting this," he said with a frown. "I suppose I should have picked a better time and place to propose. I can still get down on one knee, if you like."

"No."

"I can put on some clothes too, if it bothers you that I'm doing this in the altogether."

"It doesn't."

He looked at her for a long moment, then crossed his arms. "Then what is it? Why do I suddenly get the idea that you're going to refuse me?" Some of the light drained out of his eyes. "Is it because you don't feel the same? That you don't love me?"

Her eyes went to his. "No," she whispered, "I do love you."

Some of the tension drained from him and he lowered his arms, reaching out to her.

But she leaned away, avoiding his touch for once.

"Thalia, what is it? What is wrong? If you love me, then say you'll marry me. Whatever other problems there may be, we can work them out."

"But we can't," she said, her voice sounding dead to her own ears.

"Of course we can. Nothing is insurmountable."

"This is." She gripped her fingers together, fearing suddenly that it was the only thing keeping her from breaking apart.

She drew a deep breath. "I cannot marry you, Leo. I cannot marry anyone."

"What do you mean?"

She stared down at her hands, unable to look at him any longer. "The terms of my divorce are quite clear. They stipulate that while my former husband, Lord Kemp, may remarry, I may not. I am barred from taking marriage vows ever again."

Chapter 29

Leo didn't say anything; he didn't quite trust himself to speak. Instead, he got out of bed and reached for his trousers, pulling them on with a few efficient tugs. He slid his arms into his shirt as well, but left the buttons undone.

Scowling, he went across to the fireplace and tossed a fresh log onto the fire, sending up a small cloud of red-hot embers.

He tapped a fist against his thigh, then turned again to face her. "There must be a way to nullify that section of the divorce decree. Do you have a copy of the document?"

"Not here. My barrister has the original at his office. And there are others filed with Parliament and the courts, of course."

"Well, I'm your new barrister from this moment forward. I'll find a way out of this for us. I know people, and my brothers know even more, especially Ned. I'll explain matters to him, see if it's possible for him to circulate a private bill in the Lords on your behalf."

"I rather doubt the Duke of Clybourne will be eager to dirty his fingers with my old difficulties."

He shot her a look. "He will if I ask him to."

"Don't. Please." She sighed. "If there is one thing my former husband is good at, it is getting his way. He took great pains to make sure I could not marry again, so I am certain whatever legalities the lawyers used to ensure his wishes, those terms are unbreakable."

"Nothing is unbreakable."

"This is. I accepted it long ago and you must now."

"Well, I don't accept it." He glared at her, raking a set of fingers through his hair. "What I don't understand is, why are you not more upset? Why do you not want to fight this?"

She didn't answer. Instead, she hugged her arms to herself.

As he watched her, his chest tightened with an unexpected dread. "You do *want* to marry me, don't you?"

The look she flashed him seemed almost helpless. "Leo, I—"

"Is that it, Thalia?" he said, his voice growing louder, harder. "Is it because you don't want to marry me? That you are relieved you have an excuse to say no?"

"No, I . . . I can't explain."

"Try anyway."

She shook her head. "Let's just go back to the way things were before. We were happy."

"Were we? So happy that I had to leave you here alone for Christmas? Happy that I can't openly claim you for my own? Can't introduce you to my family as the woman with whom I want to spend my life?"

"That's just the way it is. You knew how things would be between us when all this began."

"But that was before I fell in love with you." He went to her and wrapped his hands around her arms. "We can't go back and I don't want to. Now tell me why you won't marry me. And not the legal reason this time," he added when she opened her mouth to protest.

She closed it again and looked away.

"You said you loved me. Were you lying?"

"No," she whispered.

"Then what is it? Make me understand."

"It's because I do love you," she told him on a trembling breath, "that we can never have anything more than a temporary arrangement. I cannot allow you to waste your life on me."

"Waste my life? What nonsense are you spouting?" he demanded.

"It's not nonsense. It's . . . it's . . ." She broke off as if choked by the words, the emotions.

"It's what? Tell me now before I explode."

She looked away, her face awash with pain. "I cannot give you children. I am barren. It's the reason Gordon got rid of me. Because he knew I would never be able to give him an heir."

Thalia pushed her way free of his hold and walked across to stand in front of the fire. She was still so cold, as if her bones had turned to ice. A shiver raked through her, her chest aching with a pain so deep it felt ancient.

For this was indeed an old pain, a sorrow about which she tried never to think but that was with her constantly. It was like a quiet undertow, flowing and ever patient, as it waited to catch and pull her down when she least expected.

She would never be a mother.

She'd come to accept that fact years ago. Yet it haunted her still, lingering with an emptiness like the rooms of the third-floor nursery that would never know the clamor of tiny footsteps or the laughter of childish voices.

Another sort of quiet hung in the room, Leo's silence telling her everything she needed to know. She didn't look at him. She couldn't.

Then he stepped up behind her, laying his hands on her shoulders. "I am sorry, Thalia. Are you quite sure? Sometimes it is the man—"

"No," she said with a sharp shake of her head. "I am very certain it is me. The last time I lost . . . the last time . . . the doctor said there would be no more. And there were not."

"Lost?" he questioned softly. "A child, you mean?"

"Children." Just saying the word made her break a little more inside. "I miscarried three times during the first four years of my marriage. Then nothing for a long while until . . . until . . ."

"Yes?"

She drew a ragged breath. "I'm sorry, I cannot talk about it." She shrugged against his light hold, trying to shake him off.

But rather than release her, he turned her and enfolded her in his arms. His lips moved over her hair, her forehead. "Tell me."

She shook her head again.

"Tell me," he murmured soothingly. "What happened that last time?"

Tell him? She'd never told anyone, not even Jane and Mathilda. How could she tell him? Yet maybe if she did, it would prove there was no hope and give him reason to move on.

Then again, she would have to explain about Gordon.

A heavy shudder went through her, memories rolling over her, black as the blackest of clouds.

"If I do tell you," she said, "you must promise to do nothing. I must have your word, as a gentleman, that you will take no action based on what you learn."

"What do you mean? What kind of—"

"Never mind now. Do I have your word?" she asked sharply. Lifting her head, she looked into his eyes. "It is the only way I will explain."

His brows were drawn tight, contradictory emotions warring across his face as his need to know wrestled against his suspicions, his better judgment.

"Very well," he agreed. "My word. Now tell me."

"I need to sit down first."

"Of course."

He moved to lead her to the bed, but she refused, going out into her sitting room instead. The less intimate atmosphere would give her strength—she hoped.

Leo sat beside her on the sofa, but didn't try to hold her, intuitively understanding that she needed to do this on her own.

"Gordon and I were never a love match, but we got on amiably enough at first," she began. "He was titled and influential, charming when he put himself to the trouble to be. He was everything my mother wanted for me. For him, I had the proper lineage and the suitable dowry he required in a wife. The fact that I was that Season's Incomparable didn't hurt either. I was eighteen and pitifully naive."

She gave a hollow laugh.

"The first few months passed well enough and he was ecstatic when I found myself with child. Then I miscarried. He tried to put a good face on it, but I could tell how disappointed he was. As for myself, I was shattered.

"But we tried again. And again. Each time I lost another baby, he grew colder. Angrier and more distant. He blamed me, said I must be doing something wrong, that I must not truly want . . . a child."

She gulped down a hard breath, her ribs throbbing. Leo reached out, but she pulled her hand away, curling it into a fist.

"He started to drink and our . . . relations took on a rather unpleasant cast. He began hurting me, in small ways at first, then rougher, more deliberate. It wasn't long before he was hitting me, humiliating me."

"He. Hit. You?" Leo said on a near growl, punctuating each word. His knuckles popped as he fisted his hands.

She looked up, not liking what she saw on his face.

"Go on," he told her in a low, almost emotionless tone.

A dangerous tone.

Suddenly she didn't want to continue, afraid of what she might have unleashed in spite of Leo's promise. But she'd gone this far—what did it matter if she told him the rest?

"One night, that final time, he came home to share the news that one of his mistresses had given birth to a son. An illegitimate son, who could never be his heir. He'd been drinking, of course, and kept on drinking. He grew more and more belligerent. Yelling at me. Berating me. He hit me, as he often did when he was foxed. It had been months since we'd had relations, but that night he came at me, intending to force me into his bed."

The ache intensified in her chest, along with the cold, her fingers like ice.

"But I couldn't allow it," she said. "I had a secret, you see. Something I hadn't shared for fear that it would turn out to be another tragedy. I was with child again, only this time the pregnancy was sound. I was nearly six months along and the doctor thought everything was progressing nicely. Only that morning, he had told me there was no reason why I would not finally deliver a healthy child. I was overjoyed, but still cautious. I'd been through so much heartbreak. Years of it."

Gazing down, she stared at her hands. But instead of her linked fingers, she saw Gordon, saw the way he'd been that night, his eyes wild with drink and rage.

"I was carrying small," she went on, whispering now, "so I had been able to hide my condition. I had been planning to tell him soon, but he started ranting and I was afraid. Even when I did try to explain that I was carrying his baby, he wouldn't listen. He said I was lying. He hit me, so hard, so many times, I feared for my life. I grabbed a poker from the fireplace and struck him with it. But it only made him madder. That's when I ran. . . ."

Blood oozed in a wet smear from the cut on her temple, dripping onto the once pristine ecru silk of her evening gown. She squinted out of one eye, her other swollen shut, her cheek and lip hot and stinging where he'd slapped her. Her head throbbed, her ribs and back aching where he'd pummeled her with blows. But somehow she was still standing even as she'd curled in on herself trying to protect the precious child in her womb.

She trembled and screamed as he drew his arm back for another blow, his eyes wheeling with rage. And she knew she couldn't let him hit her again, that if she fell, she might never get up again.

The poker she'd used to hold him off dropped from her hand as she spun and ran. Ran as fast as her feet would carry her. If she could just make it upstairs to her bedroom and lock the door, she would be safe. Safe enough that it would give him time to calm down, time to sleep off enough of his drunken state that he could be reasoned with.

But she heard him pounding after her out of the drawing room, his heavy footsteps echoing menacingly off the polished black-and-white tiles in the main hall.

"Come back here, you little bitch!" he shouted.

She kept running, breath burning in her abused lungs.

Fletcher appeared, an expression of horror on his gentle face. He strode quickly forward, stepping between them as he rushed toward Gordon with his arms outstretched. "No, my lord. Stop. I beg of you."

"Get out of my way!" Gordon roared.

She heard a scuffle behind her, a grunt and a thud.

Her hand touched the stair rail and she hurried up, racing, racing with every ounce of speed and strength she possessed. She was nearly at the top, nearly on the landing that would lead her to her bedchamber, when a hard hand grabbed her shoulder. Her feet slipped as she tried to wrench herself free.

Then she was falling, her screams reverberating like thunder in her ears as she bounced and tumbled. Finally she stopped, pain blossoming through every inch of her body as she lay insensible at the base of the stairs. She heard footsteps and gasps, cries of alarm and hands reaching out.

Moments after, she knew nothing more, the world around her turning black.

"I lost the baby three days later," she told Leo in a dead voice. "A boy. They said he was perfect but too little to survive on his own. I named him David, after my father. He was buried in the family plot, but I was too weak to attend the service. I didn't leave my room for the next two months. I refused to see my friends, even though they called, not realizing more than that I'd lost another baby. That was the story Gordon told everyone. That I was ill. I suppose he was right."

She sighed. "I don't remember a great deal of that time. I slept quite a bit, barely ate or spoke. I apparently attacked Gordon the one time he came near, raking my nails down his face so badly he was afraid to return. There were whispers that perhaps I'd gone mad. Sometimes I wonder if it would have been easier.

"But finally I came back to the land of the living with Jane and Mathilda's help. They saw to everything and they held me when the doctor broke the news that he did not believe I would ever conceive again. The fall had caused too much damage. Apparently, I nearly died, though I didn't realize that at the time."

Without a word, Leo reached out and pulled her into his arms. He kissed her forehead. "I'm sorry. So sorry."

She lay against him, only then aware of the wetness dampening her cheeks. With the backs of his fingers, he brushed the tears away.

"I didn't let Gordon touch me again for three years," she said. "We lived in the house as strangers. He was remorseful at first, but as time went on, he became bitter, angry. He blamed me for not telling him that last time that I was with child. He grew to hate me as I already hated him. But he started talking again about needing an heir, told me it was my duty to provide him with a son. So I agreed to try one last time though his very touch made me recoil. But there was no baby and it was useless to hope there ever would be. That's when he decided to permanently remove me from his life."

Leo's arm tightened. "By instigating the divorce, you mean?"

She drew a shaking breath, blowing it slowly back out. "Exactly. He very skillfully arranged matters, as I have already told you, so that it would look as if I had been unfaithful to him. So that he would have the legal grounds to seek a divorce. I suppose I should be grateful he chose not to kill me, but I was too well liked at the time. Too much in the eye of Society and my friends for him to easily put me in a grave. Not without raising questions. So instead he chose to put my good name and reputation in one."

Leo rubbed his hand over her shoulder in soothing strokes. "He's the one who will be in a grave, because I'm going to put him there."

She sat up and looked into his eyes. "No, you are not. You gave me your word—"

His eyes widened, incredulous. "But that was before—"

"Your word," she said in an implacable tone. "You promised me that you would not act based on what I told you and I am holding you to that promise."

He raked a hand through his hair, then jumped to his feet, pacing. "Surely you cannot expect me to do nothing? Not after what he did to you? The man is a blackhearted fiend and deserves to pay for his crimes."

"It was a long time ago and nothing good can be served by resurrecting it now."

"Vengeance can be served. Justifiable retribution." He flung out an arm. "Or don't you care that he beat and abused you? Murdered your unborn baby? Robbed you of your friends and good name? Then tossed you onto the streets without a cent like some doxy he'd used and discarded? And don't forget remarrying. He's keeping you from that as well."

The last hints of warmth drained from her cheeks, his succinct recitation of Gordon's cruelty cutting her to the bone.

"Of course I care," she whispered, her voice raw. "I hate him more than you can ever imagine. But he is vile and vindictive and I will not have his blood on your hands. I will not have him destroy your life as he did mine. Not in defense of me."

She looked into his eyes again. "Leo, you promised."

His shoulders flexed, neck muscles bulging as his hands opened and closed into fists. Shaking visibly, he waged an internal war between his instincts and his intellect. "I should never have given that oath," he bit out. "You should not have asked me to."

Lashing out, he struck his fist against the wall, making it shake so hard it sent two paintings crashing to the floor. A little porcelain figurine dropped onto the carpet as well, but didn't break.

Hera, who had already been looking uncomfortable, shot out of the room, her claws scratching noisily against the wooden floors.

Thalia jumped as well, involuntarily drawing in on herself.

But she wasn't afraid. She knew Leo would never hurt her; he was just frustrated and angry. Young and hotheaded with rage.

However much she wished she could let him do exactly as he wanted—and believe her, it was tempting—she would never do anything that might endanger him, or worse. For even if he came to no physical harm meting out his revenge against Gordon, she didn't trust the law to see that what he'd done was justice.

She'd sensed how he might react. She should never have confided so much.

"Fine," he said after a long, tense silence. "I won't kill him. For your sake. But I won't promise anything else."

"Leo—"

"That's the best I can do. The best I *will* do."

At least it was something, she told herself. Still, she worried.

He stalked across to the small decanter of brandy she'd started keeping here for him. Often after dinner he enjoyed a drink, while she preferred tea. Pulling off the crystal stopper, he poured himself a glass, then tossed it swiftly back. She decided not to mention the fact that it was only late afternoon.

How it could be, she didn't know. The day suddenly felt endless.

"So," he said, setting his glass down with a controlled thump, "I'm going to start looking for ways around your divorce decree. Lawrence will help as well. He knows more law these days than I do anyway, so he may have some strategies I haven't considered. In the meantime, I want you to pack your belongings, just the essentials for now, and come with me to Cavendish Square. The rest of your things can be sent round later."

Her brows drew close. "My things? Why? I don't understand."

"I want you to move in with me. I would come here, but it's not as convenient and my house is a great deal larger."

Her lips parted. "Move in with you? Doesn't your twin brother live there as well?"

"What of it? Lawrence won't bother you—well, no more than he bothers anyone. If he does, you needn't see him. He and I each of us have a wing, so it's a simple matter of avoidance."

"Avoiding him would not be the issue. Leo, I cannot live with you."

"Why not? We practically live together now. And if you're worried about the scandal, don't be. Once we wed, it will be forgotten as soon as the next illicit tryst rears its tantalizing head for Society's enjoyment. Besides, my next-door neighbor, Northcote—you met him, remember— he hosts orgies, so I don't think your habitation will cause much fuss."

"Leo, we've been over this. You know I cannot marry you."

"Don't be so pessimistic. Somehow we will find a way."

An ache swelled beneath her breastbone. Perhaps it was her heart wanting to burst. "Even if we could, I still can't be your wife."

That stopped him. He gave her a penetrating look. "Why not?"

Her lip trembled. "You know why not. Weren't you listening? I cannot give you children. We will never be a family."

His expression softened. "We don't need children to be a family. I admit, I always assumed I would have children someday, but it doesn't matter. I have nieces and nephews enough to spare. They can be our children—or like our children anyway."

She blinked against the moisture in her eyes. "It isn't the same as having your own."

"Maybe not, but we'll make it enough." He went to her and drew her up and into his arms. "You'll see. We'll be happy, just us two."

She let him hold her for another long minute, then stepped away. "No, I cannot deny you the chance to be a father."

"I'm five-and-twenty years old. Believe me, I'm not all that interested in babies."

"You aren't now. But what of later? What of five years? Ten? Twenty? As you said, you're young. People change a great deal as the years pass."

His brows drew low. "If you're implying my feelings for you will change, they won't. I love you now and will love you in the future. Twenty, fifty years from now. If we do not have children, we don't."

"We won't," she said with sad certainty. "I'm sorry, but I won't do this to you. I won't rob you of this, then wake up one day to find that you regret your sacrifice. Or worse, that you resent me for the loss."

"Do not compare me to him." His voice was low, his jaw clenched.

"I'm not. You are decent and honorable, things Gordon could never be. But I will not trap you. I love you far too much."

"And if I tell you again that I do not care? That I only want you?"

She looked away, gathering her courage, locking her heart away so she would be able to say what she must. Do what was best—for him.

"I think . . . Leo, there is no point in prolonging this. We should say our good-byes now while we can part amicably. It's the right time."

It will never be the right time. Forever would be too soon.

She forced herself to continue. "I know you think you love me, but you will move on. You will find someone else. A suitable young woman who does not come with all the difficulties I do. A girl who will give you sons and daughters, who will love you and be a good wife. Be to you what I can never be."

"You think me so shallow? You think I'll just fall out of love?"

She didn't like to think so, but she had to hope. For his sake.

"Yes. That is exactly what I think."

"You're wrong. You can drive me out now, Thalia, but you won't drive me away forever. I will be back."

"Don't."

"I will. I'll bring a ring when I come and I'll make you take it. I'll have you for my wife if it's the last thing I do."

He stalked from the room, fury rolling off him in waves. She listened as he dressed, his boots hitting the floor with hard thuds as he shoved his feet into them.

When he reappeared, he glared at her. Then he pulled her into his arms, kissing her with a passion, a savage hunger and desperation, that mirrored her own.

But it was over far too soon.

Pushing her away, he strode to the door, slamming it at his back.

Chapter 30

"Hell and damnation, there has to be a way to revoke this accursed decree!" Leo smacked his hands down on the wide mahogany table, sending legal tomes and piles of parchment sliding onto the library floor.

Lawrence looked up from where he sat at the other end of the long table in front of his own huge stack of books and documents. "I'm sorry, Leo. We've looked at this from every possible angle and I can't see any way to break it. I know the barrister who drafted it. Unfortunately for you and Lady Thalia, he's damned good at his job. Too good. I took the liberty of asking him, discreetly, of course, if it could be challenged, but the bloody thing is airtight. I've looked it over myself, again and again, and I think you're going to have to face the fact that it's inviolable. Lady Thalia cannot remarry."

Leo dropped back down into his chair, his spirits as haggard as he knew he must look.

In the month since he'd slammed his way out of Thalia's town house on that dreadful, cold, wet afternoon, he'd spent his time combing through every law text and legal precedent he could lay his hands on.

When he'd had no luck on his own, he'd written to Lawrence for his help. Without asking questions, his twin had traveled back early from Braebourne to lend his aid. But to Leo's fury and frustration, even Lawrence's brilliant legal mind could not find a solution.

"And Ned's had no luck either?" Lawrence said quietly.

Leo shook his head. "He made a couple inquiries in the Lords about a private bill. He even briefly chatted up the prime minister. But it can't be done. Apparently Kemp has too much influence. He would stop any attempts to change the decree, even if the law was on our side."

"Which it is not."

He struck his fist against the table again, causing another couple of pages to slide to the floor. "I wish to God I hadn't promised Thalia not to kill that miserable bastard. What I wouldn't give to get my hands around his neck again. This time I wouldn't stop squeezing until he'd taken his last breath."

And though he hadn't confided in anyone, not even his twin, he'd seriously considered driving to Kemp's estate to confront him about his vile abuse of Thalia. Demand that Kemp somehow free her from the terms of their divorce. But the man would just laugh and turn him away. He knew it as surely as he knew his own name.

What had stopped him—the only thing really—was his fear that he might actually kill Kemp. He was angry enough, frustrated and outraged enough, that it would be easy given the right set of circumstances.

Lawrence sent him a wry smile. "It would solve your problem if Kemp went to an early grave. But Lady Thalia is right. Killing him wouldn't end with you and her living happily ever after. Not if you're hanging from the end of a noose on Tyburn for the murder of her former husband."

Leo grunted, then turned to stare blankly out the window. A long silence followed.

"She sent Athena back last week," Leo said dolefully.

"Who is Athena?"

"A horse. A mare I gave her before Christmas. She was training her for Esme to ride this Season."

"Esme has a horse. And every other breed of animal known to man, come to that."

"It was just an excuse to get her to accept my gift. I bought the mare for Thalia because she fell in love with her at Tattersall's. I thought once the horse was installed in her stables, she wouldn't have the heart to return her."

He'd hoped she wouldn't return any of his others gifts as well. But more than two weeks ago, a package had arrived by messenger.

It was the pearls.

He'd drunk himself into a stupor that night.

"She won't see me either. I've called, but Fletcher won't let me through the door. I could barge in, of course, but he's an old man. I don't want to hurt him."

He drew a ragged breath.

"When was the last time you slept?" Lawrence asked.

Leo shrugged. "Don't know. I can sleep later."

"You should sleep now. You're dead on your feet. I haven't said before, but you look like hell, Leo. Worse than hell actually."

"That about sums it up."

Because he was in hell.

Hell without her.

"Go upstairs to your room." Lawrence gave him a look as if he understood exactly what he was feeling.

And maybe he did. They were twins, after all. Identical in more ways than just the cut of their faces.

"I will. I just want to look all this over one more time."

"Leo, you know it's not going to do any good."

"I'm going to look it over one more time," he repeated through clenched teeth.

For a moment, Lawrence looked as if he was going to argue. But he nodded instead. "All right. Let's look. One more time."

"So what do you say, Thalia?"

As if from a great distance, Thalia heard her name. She blinked and looked up, startled out of her reverie. "What?"

Quietly, Mathilda set her cup onto the tea table between them. "I asked what you thought. Would you like to go shopping tomorrow in Bond Street? We'll go to all the stores like we used to and you can buy anything you fancy."

Thalia focused on her friend, realizing the tea in her cup had gone cold. She too set her cup aside. "You know that I am no longer in the position to buy anything that I fancy. But I'm happy to accompany you and lend my opinion on your purchases."

"It won't be any fun if I'm the only one buying," Mathilda said with a little pout. "Let me treat you to something. It will be my pleasure."

Thalia sent her friend a brief smile. "You are all kindness, but you know I cannot accept."

"At least a hat. Or some gloves? Surely you cannot complain about either of those?"

"No, really. I do quite well on my own."

Mathilda raised an elegantly coiffed brow.

"I do," Thalia insisted. "Honestly, I want for nothing. Besides, I have little need for new finery, since I so rarely go out. I could show it off to Hera, but somehow I don't think she'd be all that impressed."

She forced a laugh, but Mathilda didn't join her.

Instead, Mathilda frowned. "I should have had you to Lambton for the holidays—"

"You asked me. I said no."

"Yes, but I ought to have insisted. I guess I was rather under the impression you were hoping a certain admirer would return to Town."

Thalia looked away, the misery that was her constant companion these days snapping its jagged little teeth.

But she didn't want to think of Leo. She spent the majority of each day trying very hard *not* to think of him. It was one of the reasons she had sent Athena and the pearls back to him. She couldn't bear to see either one of them, couldn't stand the memories of Leo that they roused within her empty, broken heart.

"I . . . well, perhaps at the time," she said.

"And now?"

She curled her fingers into a fist beneath her edge of her skirt. "Now what?"

"Are you and he still . . ."

"No." Her voice sounded sharp. Sharper than she'd intended.

She moderated her tone. "Lord Leopold and I are no longer seeing one another."

"Ah." Mathilda leaned over and reached for a lemon biscuit, nibbling the sweet cookie as was her habit when she was uncomfortable. "When did that happen? You didn't say."

"No, I didn't."

"I'm sorry, Thalia. Did he end it?"

"No. I did. It was time."

"Really? But the two of you seemed so happy the last time I saw you together. I thought . . ."

Thalia forced herself to look into Mathilda's eyes, careful not to let anything show in her own gaze. "What did you think?"

"You seemed different around him. And the way he looked at you. I thought perhaps the two of you were in love."

Her heart gave a hard pump as if she had taken a blow. She glanced away again.

"Whatever we were, nothing could come of it. You know I cannot remarry."

"Marry? Were things so serious that you talked of marriage?"

She squeezed her hand tighter, her nails digging into the tender flesh of her palm. She welcomed the pain.

"Tilly, I know you mean well, but I do not wish to talk about it. About him. Tell me again how Tom is doing in school."

Mathilda studied her for long seconds, then sighed. "Very well, I won't pry further. But you know you may always come to me."

"I do."

She reached for her cup and dumped the cold tea into the silver waste receptacle, then poured herself a fresh cup. She raised the hot tea to her lips. It drove away a little of the cold inside her. A cold that had never really gone away, not since the day Leo left.

"Now, Tom," she said again, striving for a lighter tone. "How is he doing?"

Chapter 31

April flowers blossomed in a vivid riot of color. Trees adorned themselves in new green finery like girls preening for a ball. Warmer air drove away the lingering cold. And all around, the city hummed with a renewed vitality that could mean only one thing—springtime had arrived.

But Leo noticed none of it as he strode along the crowded streets, his muscles tight with a frustration and despair that went bone deep.

His every effort to find a way out of Thalia's divorce decree had met with failure. Every road he took led to yet another impasse, another new defeat. He wasn't used to losing; it wasn't a situation in which he often found himself. But finally, against even his own instincts, he'd had to accept the truth.

Thalia would never be able to remarry.

Not that she would have him, even if Kemp weren't in the way.

He'd tried over the past couple of months to reason with her, to convince her that her inability to provide him with children didn't matter. But she was sure it would—maybe not now, but someday.

She'd been hurt too much in the past to believe. He could not get through the wall she'd built around herself.

They'd seen each other again nearly six weeks ago when he'd gone to her town house. It galled him that he hadn't been able to bring an engagement ring as he'd promised.

He'd expected Fletcher to refuse him entrance as he had so often before. But this time had been different. This time he had been invited inside and left to cool his heels in the drawing room.

She'd joined him a short time later, looking every bit as beautiful as ever, although she seemed a little thinner, and tired.

As tired perhaps as he was himself.

"You have to stop this, Leo," she said in an emotionless voice. "Stop writing to me. Stop coming to my door. We have said all there is to say. I have made my wishes quite clear. We are done."

"Do you love me?"

She'd shown no reaction, though she had refused to meet his eyes. "Whether I do or not no longer matters. This is the final time we will see one another. I will no longer accept your letters and if you call upon me—"

"Yes? If I call here again?"

Finally, she looked at him, her eyes hard as flint. "If you call once more, I will be forced to make sure you cannot ever do so again."

"Really?" He crossed his arms. "And how do you propose to keep me away?"

"I won't have to. I will sell the town house and leave London."

"What?" His jaw had grown slack with shock. "But this is your home."

"I will find another home. I will leave quietly and move very far away. There will be no chance of our ever crossing paths again."

He hadn't thought his heart could break any more than it had the day she'd ended their affair.

He had been wrong.

So he'd left, securing her promise that she would remain in her London house and giving his that he would not contact her again.

To his despair, he had kept his word, unwilling to take the risk of her disappearing forever. He needed to know he might catch a glimpse of her every now and again— even if only from a distance.

His family was in Town, the Season in full swing. Esme had been presented at court and had a spectacular coming-out ball. So far she seemed to be enjoying herself, eligible gentlemen eagerly lining up to dance attendance on her. Whether she truly wanted their attention—or any proposals of marriage—remained to be seen.

For her sake, he was doing his duty as older brother by attending the usual dinners and parties and other obligatory entertainments. But for the first time in his life, he couldn't drum up any of his old boisterous enthusiasm. Even the nights he spent making rounds with his friends were falling flat. How could they not when half his mind was always in another part of the city, wondering how Thalia was? Wondering what she was doing and with whom she might be doing it.

His boots beat out a hard rhythm against the pavement, his hands clenching and unclenching as he strode along. He was in a foul humor and judging by the wide berth he was receiving, his fellow passersby knew it.

Christ, he wanted to hit something.

Badly.

Which must be why his footsteps had taken him to Gentleman Jackson's without his even being fully aware of his destination. He stared at the front entrance for a few minutes, then went inside.

He was well-known here at Jackson's—just as Lawrence was—and had no difficulty securing a sparring partner in spite of his unanticipated visit.

Yet two rounds and twenty minutes later he was no closer to working off his anger than he had been when he'd arrived.

He smacked his sparring mufflers together, wondering if he would take more satisfaction fighting bare-knuckled. But Jackson frowned on his patrons' not taking appropriate safety measures and even more on those patrons' bruising and bloodying his staff—and themselves.

He was about to start another round when he heard a voice that froze every muscle in his body. Blood seemed to boil in his veins, hatred washing over him like a blast from a furnace.

Pivoting on his toes, he fixed his eyes on Lord Kemp. Then he smiled.

It would appear fortune was favoring him today after all.

He strode away from his boxing partner, the other man giving him a worried look, as if he didn't like the expression on Leo's face.

But Leo had forgotten him already, his entire focus centered on Kemp.

Ever the bully, Kemp was alternately punching and taunting the man who'd been assigned to spar with him. Jackson didn't employ lightweights and his men knew how to fight. But they kept a sporting attitude and were instructed not to lose their tempers even when confronted by hotheaded clients. Kemp was taking advantage of that, getting in shots that were far from gentlemanly.

Then again, as Leo well knew, even though Kemp might hold a title, he was no gentleman.

He watched for a minute as Jackson's man got in a fine uppercut to Kemp's jaw. But moments later he took a pair of jabs to his stomach and another to an area in his side that was already beginning to bruise.

The man shuddered and moved back, gloves up as he tried to shake off the pain.

"That the best you can do?" Kemp jeered. "My mother could provide better sport with one hand tied behind her back. Tell Jackson to get me someone else. Someone who'll give me a challenge rather than wasting my time."

"I wouldn't bother Jackson with this," Leo said, planting his gloved fists on his hips. "His men fight hard and fair, but none of them are going to give you what you want."

Kemp swung his head around, a pugnacious sneer on his face. He stared at Leo for a minute before recognition set in.

"Well, if it isn't Thalia's brash young cub. Byron, is it not?"

"That's right."

Kemp smirked. "How is my wife these days? Still amusing herself by robbing the cradle?"

"More like continuing to congratulate herself for getting away from you."

Kemp's expression darkened, Leo's verbal jab clearly striking home. "So? Have you come to learn from your betters, Byron?"

"If I were, I wouldn't be interested in fighting you."

"Fight me?" Kemp puffed out his large chest, then laughed. "You are amusing, if nothing else. But you are wasting my time. I need a real man to fight."

"Still hiding behind excuses so you don't have to face me? How's the throat by the way?"

Kemp's chin jutted forward, all humor wiped away. He glared malevolently. "You want a beating, whelp?" He jerked his head toward the sparring area. "Then come and get one."

"What do you say we make this more interesting?"

Kemp paused. "Interesting how?"

"A bare-knuckles match. No gloves. Just you and me. I did hear you say Jackson's men weren't giving you enough of a challenge."

A few of those men and several patrons had gathered round, listening with undisguised interest to him and Kemp. Leo's earlier sparring partner stepped forward, his heavy brows knotted with concern.

"My lord," he said in a low voice, "I would advise you not to embark on such a course. Jackson doesn't hold with bare-knuckle matches, not for his clients. There is far too great a risk of serious injury. If you wish to spar, use the mufflers."

"That's right, Byron," Kemp advised, his upper lip curled with derision. "Listen to the man. You're going to get hurt."

But as far as Leo was concerned, he wasn't the one in danger of getting hurt. Kemp was a cruel, arrogant brute and he was going to relish wiping the smug grin off his face.

"Advice noted," he said to Jackson's man. "But I believe I'll take my chances." Bringing one of the gloves up to his mouth, he loosened the strings with his teeth and pulled it off. He worked the second free with his hand.

"So, Kemp? Game for a real man's fight, as you call it? Or are you afraid it'll be too rough for you?"

For a fraction of an instant, Kemp hesitated; Leo could read the uncertainty in his eyes. Kemp was a bully, and bullies liked to be sure they had the upper hand.

But then Kemp's natural pride reasserted itself; he was obviously confident that no one could best him, especially Leo.

Besides, Leo thought, they had an audience, one Kemp wouldn't be able to win over to his side so easily this time. Kemp had played the mature pragmatist during their last confrontation. This time if he retreated, he would look scared, pure and simple.

Kemp smirked again and held out his gloved hands so his servant could unfasten the ties.

"At least let me wrap your knuckles, my lord," Jackson's man insisted. "And yours as well, Lord Kemp."

"Very well," Leo agreed.

It wouldn't do him any good if he broke his hand on the bastard's hard head with his first hit.

A few minutes later, he squeezed his fingers open, then closed, testing the strength and flexibility of the cloth strips wound tightly around his hands. Across from him, Kemp did the same.

Voices buzzed as bets were placed by the men who'd gathered to watch the coming action. In all the time he'd come to Jackson's salon, Leo had never seen it so crowded.

He brushed all that aside, concentrating on his plan, anticipation surging through his nerves and veins.

Then Kemp stood before him, heavier than him by at least two stone and far nastier, likely looking to any casual observer as the more fearsome opponent.

But Leo had the advantage; he had fury on his side.

He had right.

For each blow would be a blow of justice for Thalia.

Each drop of blood spilled would be in honor of the losses she'd endured, the pain she'd suffered and been unable to take recompense for herself.

He smiled and beckoned Kemp forward with a hand.

Kemp glanced around, posturing for the crowd; then

he struck, his fist connecting in a hard blow against Leo's jaw.

Leo's head snapped back.

Distantly, he heard laughter.

But he barely felt the punch, ice-cold vengeance and molten hot rage burning too deeply inside him for the pain to take hold.

With a gimlet stare, he turned his head and spit out a mouthful of blood onto the floor. Then he looked at Kemp and smiled again, his teeth slick and red with menace.

The fight was on.

Before Kemp even knew what was coming, Leo struck, pounding his fists into his exposed gut in a hard, fast volley of blows. The breath wheezed out of Kemp's lungs, his face turning white, then red as he struggled for air.

But even as he managed to draw in the next breath, Leo struck again, hitting him one-two in the face, then again in his side in the same tender spot where Kemp had earlier been pummeling his sparring partner.

Kemp wavered, then held up his fists protectively, moving backward and away with several heavy, lumbering steps. He shook his head, trying to clear it so he could regain his equilibrium.

Leo came at him again; this time Kemp got in a pair of punches, striking him in the face and the stomach.

But rather than draw away, rather than take a moment to catch his own breath, Leo pursued. He hit, then hit again, striking whatever vulnerable parts of Kemp that he could reach. His muscles ached from the reverberation of the blows running up his arms, his hands turning slick with fresh blood.

Again, he barely felt the pain, pressing his advantage, every strike a victory for Thalia. He wanted Kemp to know how she'd felt. He wanted him to cower and beg, in fear for his life as she'd been for hers.

"Not like hitting a woman, is it, Kemp?" he said in a voice only the other man could hear. "I'm not so easy to beat and abuse, am I? How does it feel to be whipped like a beast? How do you like being the victim this time?"

Kemp's swollen eyes widened with understanding and fear. And hate.

But no remorse.

Leo saw that as clearly as he saw the bruises spreading over Kemp's flushed skin.

Leo really let loose then, raining Kemp with blows that the other man could not avoid or have any hope of returning. Kemp made one last feeble attempt to hit back; then he went down, sprawling at Leo's feet in a miserable, moaning heap.

Leo nearly followed, wanting to hit him again and again and again until there was nothing left that was worth striking anymore.

But Thalia's voice rang out in his head, reminding him of his promise. His vow that he would not give in to the basest parts of his nature.

He spit again, on Kemp this time, as a sign of his utter contempt.

Then he turned away.

Chapter 32

"Lady Frost to see you, milady," Fletcher announced in low, dignified tones.

Thalia looked up from her sewing, then hurriedly secured her needle in her embroidery and got to her feet. "Jane! What a wonderful surprise. I didn't know you planned to drop by today."

Jane Frost walked into the room on a whisper of lavender silk, her glossy brown curls artfully arranged beneath her chip-straw bonnet decorated with silk flowers that had been dyed to match her gown.

Five children and fifteen years had thickened her a bit through the middle. Even so, she still managed to look as bright and lively as the girl Thalia had first known the year they'd made their come-out together.

Jane hugged Thalia, Jane's gardenia-scented perfume drifting sweetly in the air. She looked and smelled like springtime.

"I was thinking about you this morning, so I decided to pay you a call," Jane said, moving to take a seat.

"Tea, Fletcher, if it wouldn't be any trouble," Thalia told him.

"No trouble at all, milady."

She waited until Fletcher had departed before resuming her own seat. "So, what news have you come to share?"

"What makes you think I have news?"

Thalia lifted a knowing brow.

"Oh, pooh, there's no hiding anything from you. You can always read me like a book."

"Good thing the story is always so entertaining. Well, out with it."

Jane straightened the lines of her skirt. "Maybe we should wait for the tea to arrive first?"

"No, now. It's not bad news, I trust?"

"No, quite the opposite. At least I assume you'll feel that way once you hear."

"You have my complete attention." Thalia laced her fingers together in her lap and waited for Jane to begin.

"Well, apparently there was quite a row at Gentleman Jackson's boxing salon yesterday afternoon. The whole town is abuzz. Jeremy filled me in on the details over breakfast this morning. Or at least everything he heard last night at his club."

Jeremy was Jane's husband. He was one of those men who claimed to disdain gossip but who always knew all the latest on-dits.

Thalia frowned. "Oh? And why would I be interested in a fight at Jackson's boxing salon?"

Jane leaned forward, her eyes sparkling. "Because it involved Lord Kemp."

Thalia stiffened. "Did it?"

"Don't fly up in the boughs. I know you hate even hearing his name mentioned and with good reason, but you're going to like this. He was challenged to a bare-knuckles match, then literally beaten senseless."

"What!"

Gordon had always taken great pride in his pugilistic skills, boasting of his prowess on many occasions. He cowed other men and he liked it. Just as he'd once cowed her.

"Indeed. The fight was a brutal affair and despite Lord Kemp getting in a few good blows, he lost badly. They say the other man is nearly as good as Mr. Jackson himself. He beat Kemp right down to the ground, then spat on him when he walked away."

Thalia stared, unable to say a word.

"Jeremy told me that Kemp had to be carried home

insensible," Jane continued. "Reports from the doctor say he suffered three broken ribs, a fractured jaw, a loose tooth and two black eyes. Oh, and a dreadful headache, although that seems to be improving, more's the pity. About time that dreadful bounder got his comeuppance."

Some man had beaten Gordon? Beaten him so badly he'd been unable to walk out on his own?

An odd tremor rose in her stomach. "Jane, what is the name of the man who fought him?"

"Why? Are you thinking of sending him a thank-you note?"

"His name?" she repeated.

"It's Byron. Lord Leopold Byron." Jane studied her for a long moment, then cocked her head to one side. "You have the most peculiar look on your face."

"Do I?"

"Why do I get the feeling there's something you haven't told me?"

Thalia sighed. "I meant to, but then I didn't because it's over."

"What is over?"

"The affair I had last winter."

"*You* had an affair?" Jane's eyes turned round.

Thalia nodded. "Yes. With Lord Leopold Byron."

Thalia sat staring out the window of her study for a long while after Jane left.

She'd told Jane about Leo, but not everything. Even now it was hard to speak of him. His absence was a painful void in her life, a hollow emptiness that nothing and no one else could fill. The weeks they'd spent together seemed like a happy dream, brief brilliant moments that outshone all the rest.

He'd fought Gordon for her—and won.

Part of her was grateful.

Another part was afraid.

He shouldn't have done it, whatever the outcome.

Gordon would not soon forget.

She wished she could run to Leo, wrap him in her arms and tell him how much she loved him. How much she missed him. Warn him to be careful and not to fight any more battles on her behalf.

Maybe she should write him a letter?

But no, it would only open up the barely healed-over wounds again. If there was any hope of letting him move on, of convincing him to let her go once and for all, then she needed to stay away, even if it killed her.

Maybe she should leave, as she'd once threatened she might. Sell the town house and go deep into the countryside.

Derbyshire.

Or even Wales.

Somewhere distant. Somewhere he wouldn't think to look.

If she really wanted to separate them, she could always go to the Continent. But the thought of being that far away from him, of not even being in the same country any longer—why the very idea had the power to drive her to her knees, to rob her of what little strength she had left.

Simply put, she feared such a permanent parting would destroy her.

No, she would say nothing. Leo had proved his mettle against Gordon. He was a grown man, who was clearly more than capable of looking after himself.

She would not worry.

She would let him live his life. And for his sake, she would live hers—alone.

"Oh, don't say you won't join us, Byron," said one of his friends nearly two weeks later. "Pritchett's is the best new gaming club in London. The play is unparalleled and the women just as sweet. You've got to come. The night won't be the same without you."

The rest of his five friends all made noises of agreement and urged him to join them on their continued revels. Lawrence was not among them, having gone off with a cadre of his legal associates who had wanted an evening of their own out on the town.

Leo knew he ought to carry on making merry with his cronies, but it was late and he'd had enough of pretending to enjoy himself for yet another night. He had no appetite for gambling and even less interest in fending off the overly perfumed advances of the club's doxies who offered their bodies for sale—no matter how "sweet" they might appear.

There was only one woman he desired and she was out of his reach.

Inwardly, he scowled.

Outwardly, he forced a smile. "Sounds tempting, lads," he lied, "but I shall have to postpone that particular pleasure for another time. Right now, I'm off for home."

"Home? Surely not?" another one of the group complained. "It's barely one o'clock. The best part of the night is just beginning."

"True. But unfortunately I am promised quite early tomorrow at a breakfast fete with my mother and sister. I don't fancy showing up bleary-eyed and nursing an aching head from too little sleep and too much drink. No, you fellows have fun and I'll join you another time."

They made a couple more halfhearted attempts to change his mind, then finally gave up, waving him off down the street to locate a hackney. He didn't have his carriage. He'd ridden to dinner earlier with three of his friends; then they'd all continued on to a party afterward.

They were right, though. He had turned into a sad dullard of late. Rather than carry on with his usual routine, all he really wanted to do was sit and wallow in his misery. Thalia had told him he would get over her. That he would forget her and find another woman to love.

But she was wrong.

Other women no longer interested him.

As for forgetting, he could as soon forget to breathe as he could ever rid himself of her memory.

He swallowed the bitter thought and kept walking, letting a passing hackney drive by. He would catch the next one. Or the one after that.

Despite the late hour, the streets still teemed with people, bursts of talk and laughter filling the air while the scents of summer drifted lazily past.

He was crossing from one street to another, an alley immediately to his left, when a pair of men emerged suddenly out of the darkness and blocked his way. He moved to go around them, but they prevented him again, crowding him deeper into the mouth of the alley.

They were big, rough-looking sorts. The kind more generally suited to the wharves than here farther in the heart of the city.

"If it's money you're after, I'm afraid I only have a couple of pounds," he said. "I'm not in the mood for a fight, so it's yours if you'll go on your way."

Rather than reply, they hurried forward and seized his arms, then dragged him farther into the alley—or tried to at least.

He elbowed the first and shook the second off with a kick to the shin, freeing himself. But when he turned to escape, he found the way blocked by two more toughs, each of them larger than the last. A glance behind him revealed two more who strolled up from the alley itself.

He fisted his hands, realizing he was surrounded. "Why do I get the feeling this is no ordinary robbery?"

Before he could let out a shout in hopes of attracting attention from helpful passersby, they were on him, shoving him forcefully into the depths of the alley before unleashing a storm of fists.

He did his best to defend himself, punching and kicking any of them he could reach. He got in some good hits, sending one of them crashing down onto the rough cobbles. But there were too many to battle all at once and the blows rained down like hammers.

Pain exploded in his head and face, chest and back and stomach. He fell to the ground, curling into a tight ball to protect whatever he could. Blood dripped down his face, pooled in his mouth, his ears ringing. Hazily, he wondered if he was going to die.

Then finally, after what seemed forever, the beating stopped. He thought they would leave.

Instead, one of them leaned down, his mouth near Leo's ear. "Lord Kemp sends his regards."

He heard their laughter as they walked from the alley. Then he heard nothing more at all.

Chapter 33

Thalia was eating breakfast in a sunny spot in the dining room three days later, enjoying a dish of newly picked strawberries and fresh cream, when a quiet knock came at the door.

It was Fletcher.

"Pardon the interruption, milady, but you have a caller."

Her brows arched. "At this hour?"

It was eight o'clock, far too early for any ordinary visit. She couldn't imagine anyone who would come to the house at this time of day unless . . .

She laid down her fork, her pulse suddenly racing. "It isn't Lord Leopold, is it?"

A faintly peculiar look came into Fletcher's eyes. "No, ma'am. It is his brother, Lord Lawrence Byron."

Lord Lawrence? Why would he of all people want to see her?

She puzzled briefly, then gave a nod. "Show him in, please."

Even though she had met Lord Lawrence before, seeing him came as something of a shock when he walked into the room. He looked so precisely like Leo that for a second she found herself wondering if it was Leo after all. But on closer inspection, she saw the subtle difference between them again, the slight variation in the coloring of his and his brother's eyes.

He bowed, then straightened to the same impressive height as his twin. "Lady Thalia, good morning. My pardon for intruding upon you at such an early hour."

"That is quite all right. Fletcher, another place setting, if you would be so good. Please, sit and take some breakfast, Lord Lawrence."

"No, I couldn't."

"Tea, then, at least."

He inclined his head. "All right. If you insist."

Lawrence eased into the chair on her left while Fletcher laid fresh china.

The servant withdrew.

Taking up the teapot, Thalia poured, then passed him the cup and saucer.

He took a single sip and set it aside.

"So, Lord Lawrence, to what do I owe the pleasure?"

His golden brown eyebrows drew tight, his mouth unsmiling. "This is not a social call, I am afraid. I have come to speak with you about my brother."

"Oh?" Her heart gave several more hard beats.

Had he come to warn her off, concerned she might be thinking about resuming her relationship with Leo? Well, he need not worry on that score. She had relinquished any hold she may have had on Leo and had no plans to resume it.

She looked at Lawrence's expression again and felt her heart stutter for a different reason entirely. "What is it? Has something happened?"

His face grew sterner. "Leo was set upon by a gang of ruffians three nights ago and beaten quite severely. He was left in an alley and not discovered until several hours afterward."

She gasped, her blood turning to ice. "Oh, my God! He isn't—"

"No, he's alive. But he is gravely ill. He has been asking for you. I have come to take you to him if you will accompany me?"

For a second she couldn't think, her throat tight, ribs aching in an agony of disbelief and horror.

Leo hurt?

Leo possibly dying?

She blinked away the sudden moisture that stung her eyes and came to herself again, tossing her napkin onto the table as she stood.

"Of course," she said. "I shall come with you immediately. Just let me inform my butler where I am going and we will be off."

"Thank you, Lady Thalia." He looked relieved and abruptly exhausted as if he had not slept in days. And so disturbingly like Leo that the tears threatened again. Holding them back, she went to make ready.

Leo lay in a haze of pain, trying his best not to move. Even his skin hurt where it made contact with the soft cotton sheets and silk coverlet. Time moved forward in strange fits and starts, some moments slow and intensely vivid, while others simply weren't there at all—just gaps of black nothingness that he knew he would never get back.

Yet even in the darkness, the pain never left. His injuries ran like a patchwork of misery all over his body. Bruises and breaks. Cuts and swelling. He could see out of only one eye, the other swollen completely shut. He could move his jaw enough to take a little water or broth but nothing more, which was fine since he had no appetite.

He wouldn't have worried, certain he would heal, if it were not for the deep, persistent ache in his back and the blood in his urine.

Internal organ damage, he'd heard the doctors murmur. Bruised kidneys. Broken ribs.

He was, he realized, in rather a bad way.

They'd wanted to bleed him, but he'd been lucid enough to refuse. Lawrence had supported his decision, had them bind his ribs as tightly as breathing would allow and leave a few restorative tinctures. They gave him laudanum as well; it was the first time in years he'd taken it and he was grateful for anything that would blunt the razor's edge of his suffering.

Someone was always with him, keeping vigil at his bedside. His mother. One of his sisters, brothers or sisters-in-law. Even Adam had been there at one point.

Yet there was one person missing. The one he longed for the most. The one about whom he dreamed.

His sorrow.

His salvation.

Thalia.

He'd come awake near dawn with her name on his lips.

Lawrence had been there, looking haggard and more concerned than he had ever seen him look. They'd talked, though he couldn't quite remember about what.

Then he'd been lost again, slipping into the darkness, seeking comfort in dreams of her.

A soft hand smoothed his hair, cool fingers ever so gently caressing his forehead and one small uninjured area of his cheek. A faint floral scent drifted on the air, warm and feminine and hauntingly familiar. He must be dreaming again to imagine that Thalia was here.

Or maybe I've died and this is heaven, he thought as he felt her lips whisper over his own with the lightest, sweetest of touches.

And in that instant, there was no pain.

"Oh, Leo," she murmured brokenly. "Oh, sweetheart, look what they've done to you."

She took his hand. Something wet and warm fell onto his skin.

He forced his eyes open—or rather the one lid that wasn't swollen shut—and found her bending over him like an angel.

"Thalia," he whispered, his voice hoarse and strained from disuse.

He looked more closely. Had she been crying? Her eyes were very brown, moist and luminous, distressed.

"Shh," she hushed reassuringly, stroking her fingers over his hair again. "Don't talk. Go back to sleep."

"Am I dreaming?" he said after a moment. "Are you really here?"

"Yes, I'm really here. Your brother Lord Lawrence came to get me this morning. He told me what happened."

Another tear slid down her cheek.

"Don't cry. I hate it when you cry."

"Then I won't." With the back of a hand, she wiped the tear away and smiled. "See? All gone." She went back to stroking his hair. "Is there anything you need? Are you hungry or thirsty?"

He shook his head, ignoring the pain the movement caused. "The only thing I need is you."

"You have me."

But for how long?

He tightened his grip on her hand, pulling her down to sit on the bed. With extreme care, she settled next to him.

"Don't go," he said.

"I'm right here."

His chest began to ache, lungs straining beneath his broken ribs. "Swear you won't leave."

"I'll be here when you wake," she said.

But what if she wasn't? What if she went away, disappeared as she'd once said she might? What if this was the last time he saw her?

"Swear," he demanded.

"Shh, I swear. Don't upset yourself. I'll stay for as long as you want me."

He searched her eyes for a long minute, then let himself relax again. But he didn't ease his grip on her hand. "That means forever, you realize? Because I'll always want you. I love you."

"And I love you. Sleep now. Just sleep."

But he didn't want to sleep. He wanted only to lie here and look at her. Memorize each beautiful line and graceful curve of her face.

There was something else, though. Something he needed to tell her. Something important.

"Did Lawrence tell you?" he asked.

"Tell me what?"

"That I made a will."

A shudder went through her. "You don't need a will," she said fiercely. "You aren't going to die."

"I could. I heard the doctors."

"Whatever you heard is nonsense and doctors are quite frequently wrong about such things. You're only twenty-five years old. You just need to rest and recover, that's all."

"Still, if I don't get better—"

"Of course you're going to get better. I won't let you do anything else."

"But if I *don't*," he said insistently, "I want you to know I've made provision for you."

"Provision? What do you mean?"

"I'm leaving you my fortune."

Her eyes rounded. "That's impossible. I don't want your money."

He ignored her statement. "When we parted a few months ago, I know you turned me away out of some misguided notion that I would be happier without you. That I would have a better life if I moved on. But I won't. I can't."

"You may not think so now." She glanced down at their joined hands. "But you'll realize I'm right someday."

He squeezed her hand. "I won't."

She looked up again.

"I love you and I'm not going to stop. Not ever," he said. "There is something you should know about Byron men."

"Oh? And what is that?"

"We live wild lives until we find the right woman. Once we do, we hold fast and never let go." Pausing, he drew a breath. "I know we cannot marry, but it doesn't matter, not to me. In my heart, you are already my wife. Am I your husband?"

"Leo," she murmured.

"Am I?"

For a long moment, she said nothing. When she spoke, her words were as solemn as a wedding vow and just as meaningful. "Yes. In my heart, you are my husband."

He gave a faint nod, satisfied. "And a husband provides for his wife, even after his death."

"You are *not* going to die. Stop saying such things."

"I couldn't rest easy, not without knowing you were provided for. You'll never want for anything again, Thalia. Everything that is mine is now yours."

"I told you, I don't want your money. All I could ever want is you."

Tears welled in her eyes, then overflowed.

He reached up and brushed his thumb over her cheeks, ignoring the pain that went through his back and chest at the movements. "Kiss me and tell me you love me, wife."

"I don't want to hurt you."

"You won't," he lied.

"I love you, husband. More than I've ever loved anyone in my life. More than I will ever love anyone again."

Her lips met his, soft and gentle and infinitely sweet. He closed his eyes and drank in her touch, her warmth, knowing if this was the last, then he would die happy.

Slowly, the blackness returned, pulling at him again, drawing him down and away. He tried to resist, hearing her voice calling him, as if from a distance. But he couldn't hold on; the darkness was just too powerful to resist. Like a great ocean wave, it swept over him into nothingness.

Chapter 34

Thalia startled awake at the touch of a hand on her shoulder. She looked up to find the Dowager Duchess of Clybourne's clear, gentle green eyes resting upon her, a concerned smile on her lips.

"Why don't you go get some proper rest in one of the bedrooms?" Leo's mother suggested softly. "I can watch him for a while."

"No, I'm all right," Thalia said, shaking off her sleepiness as she sat up in the chair at Leo's bedside. "I promised him I would be here when he wakes."

The dowager studied her intently. "As you wish. I shall join you, if you do not mind the company."

"Of course I do not. Here, let me get you a chair."

"No, no. I can do it. You are tired and I am not yet in my dotage, even if I do have eight grown children and more grandchildren than I ever dreamed I might."

Ava Byron pulled a small side chair near and sat down.

Both their gazes moved to Leo where he lay in the bed.

It had been three days since Thalia arrived. Three long, sleepless days and nights filled with endless worry and creeping despair. Rather than improving, Leo's condition had worsened until a mournful pall hung over the room.

But she'd held her fears at bay, refusing to believe that he would not come through the worst. Despite a bone-deep exhaustion, she'd refused to leave his side, tending to him through the dark, endless hours.

Finally, early this morning, his condition had improved. His rapid heartbeat slowed to normal and the color had come back into his cheeks; they'd been white as death for the past couple of days.

She'd held back tears of relief when he'd roused long enough to take a bowl of beef tea, then again as he'd drifted into an easy peaceful slumber for the first time since she'd arrived.

The doctor had visited a few hours later and shaken his head with happy amazement. He'd pronounced Leo definitely on the road to recovery. Quiet cheers had gone up throughout the entire household.

Even with the certain knowledge that Leo was no longer in danger, she'd stayed with him. She'd given her promise and she would not break it.

She and the dowager sat silently for a time, each content to simply watch Leo sleep.

His mother was so kind—all the Byrons were—far kinder than she had ever expected her to be. She had been uncomfortable at first, waiting for harsh looks and cruel words of indignation at their finding Leo's former lover tending him at his bedside. But the Byrons had been all gentle smiles and shared commiseration. None of them had questioned her presence. Not one had treated her with anything but respect.

"You love my son very much," Ava said, her soft words breaking the silence.

Rather than looking at the dowager, Thalia gazed at Leo, caressing his beloved face with her eyes. Her chest swelled with so many emotions that they seemed almost impossible to contain.

"Yes, I do," she said simply.

"And he feels the same about you. Lawrence told us. It explains a very great deal. Leo has not been himself these past few months and I had wondered what was wrong. I don't believe I have seen him smile once since I arrived in Town, and of all my sons, Leo is the one who is never without a smile or a laugh. I think you broke his heart."

Thalia swallowed past the lump in her throat. "I didn't mean to."

"I am sure you did what you thought best, but for all your good intentions, you have made him quite miserable."

"He wants to marry me, but it is not possible," she said dully. "Did Lord Lawrence tell you that as well?"

"He did. Along with the fact that he and Leo and Edward all tried to move heaven and earth to find a way past the legal impediments of your divorce decree, but to no avail."

Thalia's gaze flew to the dowager's. "The duke tried to help break my decree? And Lord Lawrence? I did not know."

Ava Byron nodded. "Leo was quite distraught when he realized he could not free you. But it makes no difference to his feelings. Lawrence told me what Leo did with his will. He also told me he overheard the two of you talking and that Leo considers you his wife, even if you cannot legally wed."

Thalia's hands tightened in her lap. "Lord Lawrence should learn not to eavesdrop or tell tales."

"Now, now, do not be overset." The dowager reached over and patted her hands. "He only tells me things because I am his mother. Normally, he is quite circumspect. By the way, he loves you too, like a sister."

"I didn't think he greatly approved of me."

"He loves his brother and wants him to be happy. You make him happy. I want Leo happy again as well."

She met the dowager's eyes. "So you don't mind if your son and I live in sin?"

Ava frowned. "Well, I admit, it is not an ideal situation and there will be many who disapprove, but I am not one of them. You will find the rest of the Byrons feel the same, in the immediate family at least. We're used to making waves. What's a few more?"

All Thalia's defenses crumbled at the dowager's show of support. "Are you sure, ma'am? I would never wish to shame him."

"Yes, so I can see."

"And I cannot give him children," she said, her voice low and rushed. "He says he does not care, but he is young. He may change his mind."

"If there is one thing my son knows, it is his own mind. And his own heart. Do not try to make it up for him." Ava sent her a soft smile. "As for children, I am truly sorry, since I can see how it pains you. But perhaps God will bless you after all. Nothing is ever as certain as we like to think."

Thalia smiled back. "I pray you are right."

Ava leaned forward and kissed her cheek. "You are a sweet girl. I can see why he loves you."

Silence descended again as Thalia worked to hold back sudden tears.

On the bed, Leo shifted, his eyes opening slowly. "Thalia?"

She leaned forward, taking his hand. "I'm here. Right here."

He studied her with concern. "You look tired."

Jubilant to hear him so lucid, a laugh burst from her lips. "So do you," she said, with a smile.

His gaze moved past her. "Mama?"

Ava was beaming. "Hello, dearest. How are you feeling?"

"Better." He paused as if considering. "Much better."

"I'm so glad. We'll talk later. For now, I'll leave you and Thalia alone."

He waited until his mother left the room, closing the door behind her. "Why do I have the feeling I've missed something?"

Thalia stood and leaned over to straighten his sheets. "Your mother and I have come to an understanding."

His brows furrowed. "What kind of *understanding*?"

"She has given her approval for us to live in sin."

"Really?" His brows shot up this time. "And how do you feel about that? The two of us, living in sin?"

Leaning down, she brushed her lips over his. "Fine. Wonderful. If that is what you want as well."

"Of course it's what I want." He laughed, then groaned, clutching his abused ribs. "Come here."

"Where?"

He reached for her hand. "Here on the bed. If my mother doesn't mind us being together without the sanction of clergy, then I doubt she'll mind us sleeping here together."

"But I might hurt you."

"You couldn't," he said, urging her to stretch out next to him. "Not unless you go away again."

Carefully, she climbed onto the bed, curling close to him. Then she kissed him again, light as a feather. "Don't worry, my love. From this day forward, I'll be with you. I'll never go away again."

Lying together, heads close on the pillows, they went to sleep.

Chapter 35

"Are you certain you feel up to this? We can always go another time," Thalia said.

Leo took up the reins from where he sat next to her in his curricle. Over the past six weeks, he'd made a remarkable recovery, his health improving quickly and steadily until only a few aches and bruises remained.

He gave her a knowing look. "No turning coward on me now. I promised long ago to take you to Gunter's for ices and to Gunter's we shall go. Don't you want to shock the old harpies?"

"I believe we shocked everyone quite enough when I moved into your town house."

She brushed a gloved hand over her new cerise-and-cream-striped silk afternoon dress with matching spencer and chip-straw bonnet. Now that they were as good as married in all but the eyes of the law, Leo had insisted on buying her a new wardrobe. He'd gifted her with Athena again as well as a lady's touring carriage. And lastly a diamond tiara so beautiful it had made her gasp. It was for evenings at places such as Holland House or entertainments with his family. He was pampering her in the most lavish of ways, and having lost all her former resolve, she was letting him.

Still, there were looks and mutterings wherever she went—not that that was anything new. But now that Leo was back on his feet, the sight of the two of them together would just add more kindling to the fire.

"Tilly told me the most dreadful rumor the other day.

Apparently people are saying that you and Lawrence are sharing me."

He laughed. "Anyone with half a brain would know that was a ridiculous lie."

"Because you and Lord Lawrence are too honorable for such lurid shenanigans?"

"No," he said, chuckling again. "Because I don't share!" Leaning over, he pressed his mouth to hers for a heady, heart-hammering kiss.

She kissed him back, forgetting all about the fact that they were right out on the street where anyone might see. And honestly she no longer cared. She was just too deliriously happy. Happier than she'd been in her entire life.

Her nerves were humming when he finally let her come up for air.

"Shall we continue on to Gunter's or do you want to go back inside?" he asked in a husky voice.

"Gunter's," she said after a moment. "Your ribs are still tender. I don't want to risk reinjuring them."

"I could always lie quietly and let you do all the work," he whispered into her ear. "You've learned to do amazing things with those hands of yours. Not to mention your very clever tongue."

She met his eyes. "I had an excellent teacher. Now, are we going to Gunter's or not? I'm suddenly in the mood to scandalize some old tattlemongers."

With another laugh, he flicked the reins and set the team and curricle in motion.

"One black currant ice for you, my love," Leo said as he took the dessert from the waiter and passed the painted china cup to her. "And maple hazelnut for me."

As was the custom in summer, couples remained in their carriages while they indulged their sweet tooth and took note of the others gathered to do the same.

Her head held high, Thalia ignored the frequent surreptitious glances that came their way and concentrated instead on savoring the cold treat and Leo's wonderful company.

As she'd told him on that long-ago day at Tattersall's, it had been years since she'd visited Gunter's. Despite the expected disapproving looks from some haughty matrons, it was good to be back. And she realized to her surprise that she really didn't care what anyone thought. Her life was her own to do with as she liked.

She gave a little chuckle, feeling liberated.

"What is funny?" Leo asked.

"Nothing. I'm just happy. And the ice is good. I'd forgotten how delicious they are."

"Then I am glad we came."

She smiled and ate another spoonful.

A slight breeze rose up, the cooler air refreshing on a late June day. The waving feather on a lady's hat caught her eye and she glanced toward it.

That's when she noticed its wearer, a pretty young woman with pale blond curls and roses in her cheeks. She looked very young and very innocent.

Too innocent.

She frowned and looked away.

"What's wrong?" Leo asked.

"Nothing." She ate another spoonful of her frozen black currant confection.

Leo raised a chiding brow. "Again, what is wrong? No secrets, remember."

Inwardly, she sighed, wondering if she should tell him. Wondering now how she could not.

She'd seen the girl a couple of weeks ago when she and Mathilda had gone shopping on Bond Street. They'd all been at the same modiste and she'd been unable to keep from overhearing two of the shop assistants discussing the "delicious" fact that Lord Kemp's new fiancée, Lydia Duxworth, just happened to be in the dressing room right next to his former wife, Lady Thalia Lennox.

Thalia had taken pains to make sure she and Miss Duxworth did not meet that afternoon. Still, she'd observed the young woman long enough to realize that Lydia Duxworth was shy, sweet and obviously far too easily controlled by her rather domineering mother.

Money. That must be the reason for the engagement—

not that Lydia necessarily realized that. Gordon could be charming when he put his mind to it. He might even have convinced young Lydia that he loved her. And perhaps some small part of him did. Still . . .

Thalia had not been the only one whose reputation had suffered due to the divorce. For years, matchmaking mothers of the *Ton* had steered their daughters away from Lord Kemp. However rich he might be, no respectable family wished to align itself with a divorced man. And such things as having a wife with good lineage meant a great deal to Gordon, so he had waited rather than marry beneath him.

But now after more than six years, it would appear that, with the right amount of money, he was being allowed to buy his way into an advantageous marriage again. Finally, he would be able to have the wife and sons he craved.

And poor Lydia Duxworth was his choice.

Thalia looked at Leo, aware he was waiting.

She stifled another sigh. "I'll tell you if you promise not to get upset."

He cursed, heavy lines creasing his forehead. "What is it?"

"You're getting upset."

"Of course I am. I remember the last time you wrung that kind of promise out of me and it turned out to be something that definitely made me upset."

"Fine. Then I won't tell you. You've only just recovered and your health is still in a precarious state."

"My health is fine. Although I may have an apoplexy if you don't cease these infuriating delays. Just tell me. I'll decide afterward how upset I want to be."

She looked at him again, then handed the cup with the last of her uneaten ice to a passing waiter. "Do you see that young woman over there?" Subtly, she nodded toward Lydia Duxworth.

"The little blonde, you mean?"

"Yes."

"What of her?"

"Apparently, she is Lord Kemp's new fiancée."

"What!" he exclaimed, loudly enough that several heads turned in their direction. Thankfully, Lydia Duxworth's was not among them.

"See? This is why I didn't say anything before. Just his name is enough to rouse your ire."

"Of course it is after everything he's done." He fisted his hands, his knuckles popping from the strain. "I don't know why I let you and Lawrence convince me not to hunt him down the moment I was out of my sickbed."

"And the rest of your brothers," she reminded. "We all agreed that a direct confrontation between you and Gordon would do nothing but escalate the enmity between you, and potentially put you in harm's way again." Reaching out, she took his hand. "I nearly lost you because of him. I won't risk losing you again. Let the law take its course."

"And if it doesn't?" he asked blackly.

"It will. Have faith. Your brothers are doing everything they can to find the men who assaulted you. Once they do, at least one of those men is bound to name Gordon as the villain who hired them."

"But he is a peer and as such cannot be prosecuted for anything less than murder."

"What he did to you was attempted murder. If that is not enough cause, then we will find some other means of seeing justice done." She paused. "Of course, you could always just let it go."

His jaw tightened. "You think I can just forget—"

"No, not forget, or forgive. Just put it behind you. We have the rest of our lives ahead of us. I am tired of letting Gordon's hate intrude on our happiness."

Leo looked across to Lydia Duxworth. "And what of that girl? She looks utterly naive. Do you really think she has any idea what he is or how he treated you? Do you imagine he'll turn saint and be kind and loving to her?"

She frowned, having already given those same questions some serious thought. The answers troubled her greatly. So much so, there had been nights she had not been able to sleep.

"He might," she said. But even she didn't believe it.

Leo gave her a hard look. "And if he doesn't? Do you really want that on your conscience?"

"No, of course not. But what can we do? Even if I could find some way of speaking to her, she'd never believe me. Everyone would tell her that I'm just trying to get back at Gordon and making up stories designed to discredit him. I don't want her to suffer any more than you, but I don't see what I can do."

Leo fell silent, considering. "Maybe you don't have to do anything," he said after a moment. "Maybe someone else can do it for you."

"The florist is here with the flowers, milady," Fletcher told Thalia a week later. "Where shall I have him place them?"

She turned from where she was penning a letter at the small lady's writing desk in the drawing room and looked at the elderly butler.

Although Leo and Lawrence already had a butler, she'd brought Fletcher, Mrs. Grove and Parker with her when she'd moved to Cavendish Square. Fletcher had been promoted to serve as her personal majordomo with main butlering duties on the days the other butler was off. So far the new arrangement seemed to be working well, although the situation belowstairs in the kitchen—what with two cooks instead of one—was not proving as easy. But she was determined to work through it. When she'd moved from her town house, she and Leo had agreed that none of the staff—either hers or his—would be given notice.

She was, however, considering asking Mrs. Grove to come with them to Brightvale once they removed there in August. The shift would hopefully soothe ruffled feathers on both sides.

"Oh, good," she told Fletcher as she laid her pen aside. "The arrangements are for tonight's dinner. The epergnes with the roses and lilies go in the dining room. The hollyhocks and irises in the entry hall and here in the drawing room."

She had to admit she loved the luxury of having fresh

flowers in the house again. Leo was extravagantly generous and happy to let her buy anything she desired. Even so, she tried not to overindulge.

But she couldn't resist the temptation of fresh flowers, especially given the excellent excuse tonight's meal provided. His family was coming over for a quiet evening in. They were to have dinner, then cards, games and music. She was quite looking forward to it, particularly the music and the games, which she hadn't enjoyed in ages.

Leo and Lawrence had left a couple of hours ago to see to some business across Town. She didn't expect them back for a while.

Once Fletcher bowed himself out to see to the florist, she returned to finishing her letter.

Ten minutes had passed when she heard raised voices in the entrance hall.

"Excuse me, my lord, but as I told you, Lady Thalia is not receiving."

"I am sure she'll make an exception for me," came a booming voice that sent chills down her spine. "Out of my way, Fletcher. I wouldn't want to have to hurt you."

She stood, gripping the back of her chair. She glanced toward the fireplace and the poker, then noticed the silver letter opener on her desk. She wrapped her hand around it and slid it into her pocket only seconds before Gordon strode into the room.

He stopped, then swept his gaze over her, his eyes malevolent with disdain—and simmering anger.

It was a look she knew well.

"Thalia. Come up in the world again, I see. You must be better than I remember to convince him to let you move in here. Where is your young protector? Or is he still recovering from the injuries he suffered after his unfortunate run-in with those street thugs?"

Gordon smirked, gloating and cruel; she knew that look too.

"Lord Leopold is quite hale and will join me any moment. He will not be pleased to see you, so I suggest you leave now before he arrives."

Smiling, Gordon sauntered forward, idly surveying the room.

Inside her pocket, her fingers tightened on the letter opener.

He stopped, leaving about six feet between them. "I'll go when I get what I came for."

She lifted her chin, refusing to let him intimidate her. "And what is that?"

"As if you don't know." His voice grew deeper, more menacing. "You interfering little bitch."

"Get out of my house."

Lifting her voice, she called for the footmen, but they didn't arrive. Had he done something to them?

She pulled out the letter opener and held it in front of her like a weapon.

He laughed. "You think that's going to stop me? You didn't learn much, did you, from when we were married?"

"I learned plenty, including what a vile waste of a human being you are."

"Is that what you told her? I want to know."

"Who?"

"Who?" he repeated, his words louder, then louder still until they were nearly a shout. "*Who?* Miss Duxworth, of course. She broke off our engagement this morning. Turned me away with barely a word of explanation. I want to know what you said to her. I want to know what lies you put into her head."

"I didn't tell her anything. I've never even met her."

Actually, it had been Mathilda and Jane who had told her. Mathilda and Jane who had gone to Lydia Duxworth and explained to her exactly how much danger she would be in if she was foolish enough to marry Lord Kemp. Apparently their entreaties had been effective.

"Someone told her something to make her change her mind. Whatever the source, the information had to have come from you."

"Then it cannot have been lies. Whatever her reasons for reconsidering your suit, she is well-off to be away from you."

A red flush of fury crept up his neck and into his face.

He took another step forward. "Two years I spent cultivating that relationship. Two years ingratiating myself to her parents, to her friends, so that she would say yes when the time was right. Now, in the matter of a few days, you've undone all my careful planning. All my hard work. She was the perfect one to marry. The right one to give me the heir you were too weak to provide."

His eyes bulged, his chest and shoulder muscles taut with rage. "I could kill you. I *should* have killed you years ago when I had the chance. It would have been a hell of a lot easier to just put you in a grave when I had the chance. Maybe I'll do it now."

"Get away from her, Kemp!"

It was Leo. Lawrence stood at his side.

Slowly, Gordon swung around. "The valiant savior returns? What are you going to do, Byron? Hit me again?"

"Hitting you again would be a pleasure. Now step away from her."

"You dare to give me orders, puppy?" He pointed at his chest. "Me? A peer of the realm. You may think that family of yours gives you protection, but it wouldn't if I decided to pursue charges against you for assault."

"If anyone is going to pursue charges, it would be me." Leo pointed a finger. "You are the one who barged into my house uninvited. The one who attacked my servants and threatened the woman I love. Now, I'm giving you one last chance to be gone, or I'll toss you out myself."

Kemp gave a harsh laugh. "Just try. You are nothing, you know. Just some trumped-up younger son who hasn't learned to respect his elders. I see that beating I arranged for you didn't drum any sense into your head after all."

Leo arched a derisive brow. "You're the one who lacks proper intelligence, Kemp. I heard you blaming Thalia for having had a hand in ending your engagement, but you're directing your anger at the wrong person. You see, *I'm* the one who saw to it that Miss Duxworth was given a thorough appraisal of your character. That she knows exactly the kind of cruel, callous bastard you are. That she's aware how you abused and tormented and lied about Thalia—a woman whose name you aren't even fit to speak."

Kemp opened and closed his mouth, his fists clenched, arms trembling at his sides.

Leo took a pair of steps forward. "Miss Duxworth's going to tell everyone in the *Ton* about you and this time they'll believe the truth. She's going to whisper in the ears of every girl of marriageable age and warn them to run as far and as fast from you as they can. You'll become a pariah, so tainted and condemned that no decent woman will have you. You'll never marry again. Never have that heir you want, Kemp. Just illegitimate bastards who won't be able to inherit your title or your estate."

Leo leaned closer, as if imparting a secret. "All your clever plans and machinations, your cruelty to Thalia, it will have been for naught. In the end, you will have nothing. And should Miss Duxworth fail to finish you off, Kemp, rest assured that my family and I will not."

A roar came out of Kemp's mouth, his hands clenching so hard it looked as if his fingers might break. His skin turned the color of a ripe apple, red and shining with a film of sweat from throat to hairline, eyes bulging in his head.

"You impudent whelp," he said on a shout. "You think you can best me? I'm going to destroy you and I'm going to destroy her too." He jabbed a wild finger toward Thalia. "By the time I'm through with the pair of you, you'll wish you'd—you'll wish—you'll—*urgh*—"

Suddenly he froze and clutched at his chest, his words turning to a wheezing sputter. He staggered, his lips wide, gasping as if he could no longer draw breath. His fingers clawed at his waistcoat, his cravat. He let out an odd, gagging moan, then crashed in a heap onto the floor, where he moved no more.

There was silence in the room as Thalia, Leo and Lawrence all stared.

She was the first to recover, hurrying to the door. "Fletcher," she called. "Fletcher, fetch the doctor, now!"

"Thalia," Leo said quietly.

Turning back, she found him kneeling beside Gordon. "There is no need for the doctor," he told her.

"Of course there is. He's collapsed. Whatever he's done, we cannot leave him like this. He needs someone to attend him."

Leo exchanged a look with Lawrence; then he stood. "No, he doesn't. Thalia, Kemp is dead."

Chapter 36

"Are you all right?" Leo asked Thalia several hours later as they settled together onto the sofa in the sitting room that adjoined their bedchamber.

Hera had joined them, the little tabby cat curling into her new favorite spot in the window seat. She'd made a bed out of one of Thalia's old woolen shawls, and not having the heart to dislodge her, Thalia had let her keep it.

"Of course," Thalia said. "It has just been an eventful day."

"We ought to have canceled dinner."

"No, I am glad your family came over."

Even though the evening had been a quieter one than originally planned, without the games and the music, she'd been pleased to have the company. The confrontation with Gordon and his unexpected death had been shocking and unsettling.

The doctor had been called after all to examine the body. He'd pronounced Gordon dead of an apoplexy. His heart had simply stopped. Word had been sent to Gordon's next of kin and the body moved to Lord Kemp's town house.

Thalia supposed she ought to feel bad about his death, yet her strongest emotion was relief. The long ordeal was over. Gordon was gone and would never plague her or Leo again.

Leo wrapped an arm around her shoulders and hugged her close, kissing her forehead. "Shall I ring for tea?"

"No. Unless you want some?"

"Brandy, then?"

"Definitely not."

"It might help you sleep."

"I'll sleep well." She caught his skeptical look. "Really. I will."

"Very well." He kissed her again, pausing before adding. "You know what this means, don't you?"

"What what means?"

"You're free. In the eyes of the law, you're a widow now."

She sat up, turning to look at him. "You mean—"

"Yes. We can marry."

Her heart picked up speed, a sudden, terrible pressure spreading through her chest. "You're right."

A short pause fell between them.

"Then why aren't you smiling and throwing your arms around me?" he asked. "Don't you want to get married?"

"Of course I do. It's just . . ."

"Just?" he coaxed, his eyebrows drawn into a frown. "Just what?"

"It's only that maybe *you* don't. Not really. Maybe you're just saying this because you're an honorable man and it's the expected thing to do."

She drew a quick breath and rushed on before he could reply. "All the old difficulties remain. I'm still older than you. I cannot give you heirs. And I will never fully escape the taint of having been a divorced woman. It will always be there even after Gordon has long been in his grave. People will always whisper about us and try to bring you shame. Because of me. Maybe you should give yourself some time to make sure you don't have second thoughts."

A thunderous expression came over Leo's face; he was angry in a way she'd never seen him. "Thalia Geneva Lennox, I have always held your intelligence in high regard. Now I'm not so sure. After all that we've been through, I thought you understood. Clearly, you need reminding.

"Do you love me?" he said.

"That is beside the—"

He gazed into her eyes, his own a vivid combination of green and gold. "Do. You. Love. Me?"

Her heart throbbed beneath her breasts, her throat tight. "Yes. More than I thought I could ever love anyone."

"And do you believe I love you?"

As she looked deeper into his eyes, a quiet calm stole through her veins. "Yes," she whispered, "I do."

"Good." He gave a satisfied nod. "Then there is only one more thing to say."

Before she had any inkling what he meant to do, he slid off the sofa and knelt on one knee before her. He took her hands in his. "Lady Thalia Lennox, I give you my heart, my happiness and my life without reservation. I have no second thoughts and never will. Say you will be my wife, not just of my heart, but in all ways. In every way. For the rest of our lives together."

This time she didn't hesitate. Instead, she threw her arms around his neck and kissed him. "I'm sorry I was being silly. Yes, my love! Yes, I will be your wife."

He deepened their kiss and pulled her tight against him, making her blood sizzle and her senses whirl. She laughed suddenly against his lips, overwhelmed by a joy that knew no limits.

Then he was laughing too, deep and exultant and happy.

Climbing to his feet, he bent and swept her off her feet, cradling her high against his strong chest.

And she knew in that moment that everything would be all right, so long as they had each other.

She tugged his head down for another fervent kiss as he strode into the bedroom, then sighed in bliss as they sank into their own private heaven.

Epilogue

"One final touch and you'll be ready," Mathilda Cathcart declared one month later as she slid a sapphire hair comb into place in Thalia's sable locks. "That is your something borrowed—and I do want it back, by the way, since it was a gift from Henry. The diamond and gold shoe buckles from the dowager duchess are your something old. Your gloves are new and your gown is the blue. You have everything you need for a perfect wedding."

Thalia arched a brow and smiled. "I believe a groom is required as well."

Tilly grinned. "Well, lucky for you, he's been pacing a hole in one of the duke's best Aubussons this hour past. His brothers are under strict orders not to let him come up here, since he absolutely cannot be allowed to see you before the ceremony."

"It seems a bit ridiculous considering our living situation."

"Which is why you spent last night here at Clybourne House. A little separation is good. Builds anticipation for the wedding and the night to come. Lord Leopold is going to be bowled over; you're so beautiful.

"Is she not the most beautiful bride, ladies?"

"Exquisite," Mallory said with a wide smile as all the other ladies assembled made heartfelt murmurs of agreement.

Mallory had just returned from the upstairs nursery, where she'd been feeding and tucking her infant son into his crib.

She took a seat now among all the other Byron women—Meg, Grace, Claire, Sebastianne, Esme and Ava. Thalia's friend Jane Frost was in attendance as well and would serve as one of Thalia's two matrons of honor—Tilly, of course, being the other.

It was Thalia's second wedding, yet everything felt brand-new, as if she'd never been married. But rather than being nervous, she was brimming with excitement, because this time was special.

This time she would be taking marriage vows for all the right reasons.

This time she was pledging herself to the right man.

The man she loved.

She did hope Leo would think her beautiful. Rather than white, she'd chosen a gown of sky blue silk that billowed around her ankles when she walked. The bodice and half sleeves were sewn with Belgian lace. The dress also had a sheer overskirt that was just as ethereal as the rest of the ensemble. Her hair was swept high on her head, yet simply dressed with only the hair combs she'd borrowed from Tilly and a lace veil that matched her gown.

Esme came forward and handed her the bridal bouquet, made from lily of the valley and forget-me-nots. The fragrance was sweetly intoxicating.

Thalia thanked her sister-to-be with a smile.

She was still getting to know her new family and liked them all. But Esme held a special place already, perhaps because of her love of animals—she adored Hera—or maybe it was because she was the youngest and saw the world through fresh, enthusiastic eyes. Esme had also been unconditionally supportive from the instant she and Thalia had met, coming up to give her a deep, warm hug as though they'd been friends for years.

"Perhaps I shall be able to do this for you soon, Lady Esme," Thalia said. "Are you quite sure there were no handsome suitors who caught your eye this Season?"

Esme laughed. "Very sure. Several gentlemen were handsome, but none took my fancy. Frankly, I shall be glad to get back to my animals and my painting at Braebourne. There is nothing like the countryside this time of year."

"Maybe next Season, then?"

Esme gave a noncommittal shrug. Unlike most girls, she was in no hurry to marry.

"It is time, my dear," Ava Byron told Thalia, sharing a happy smile with her. "Ready?"

Thalia nodded and listened to the strains of music winding up the stairs. Tightening her fingers around her bouquet, she followed the other women from the room.

Leo waited next to Lawrence, whom he had chosen to serve as his best man. His heart hammered, his gloved hands slightly unsteady.

"You have the ring?" he asked his twin in a low voice.

"Yes." Lawrence sighed. "It's right here in my pocket, where it's been the other ten times you've asked. Relax. She'll be here any minute."

"Easy for you to say. Just wait until it's your turn."

Lawrence gave a gentle snort. "I guess I'm in the clear, then, since I have no interest in taking a wife. Not for years, not until I'm old and gray."

"You won't say that once you meet the right woman. Once you do, you'll wonder how you ever managed without her."

"We'll see."

The music began moments later and they both turned toward the door.

Leo forgot everything but Thalia, his heart filled to bursting as he watched her walk toward him. He'd thought her beautiful before, but today she was radiant, her dark eyes shining with happiness and love. Then her small hand was inside his own, the minister prompting each of them to recite the words that would join them as one before the world.

"I do," he repeated.

"I do," she said, never looking away from his eyes.

He slid the diamond ring that had somehow appeared in his palm onto the third finger of her left hand.

"I now pronounce you husband and wife."

Family and guests clapped, cheers bursting to life around them. But all he cared about was her. Wrapping his arm around her waist, he pulled her near.

"Leo," she said on a breathless laugh, "everyone is watching."

He grinned and bent his head. "Good. Let them watch. Because I want to kiss my bride."

And then he did, quite thoroughly, before one and all.

Read on for an excerpt from
Tracy Anne Warren's next novel,

Happily Bedded Bliss

Coming soon from Signet Select

Lady Esme Byron hiked her sky blue muslin skirts up past her stocking-clad calves and climbed onto the wooden stile that divided Braebourne land from that of their nearest neighbor to the east, Mr. Craycroft.

Craycroft, a widower near her eldest brother, Edward's, age of forty, was rarely in residence and never complained about her trespassing on his land, so she was free to use it as if it were quite her own. Not that Braebourne didn't provide plenty of beautiful acreage to explore—it did, especially considering that her brother owned nearly half the county and more besides. But Craycroft possessed a lovely natural freshwater lake that sat a perfect walking distance from her family's house. The lake attracted a rich variety of wildlife, so there was always something fascinating to sketch. Plus, no one ever bothered her there; it was quite her favorite secret place.

She jumped down onto the other side of the stile, taking far more care of the satchel of drawing supplies slung over her shoulder than she did for her fine leather half boots. She wobbled slightly as she sank ankle-deep into the mud. She stared at her boots for a few seconds, knowing her maid would give her a scold for sure. But she was always able to talk dear Grumbly around, so she wasn't worried.

Grabbing hold of the fence, she unstuck herself one

boot at a time. She scraped the worst of the mess off into the nearby grass; then, with a swirl of her skirts, she continued on to her destination.

She sighed blissfully and turned her face up to the sun.

How good it was to be home again after weeks in the city.

How wonderful to be out in the open again, free to roam wherever she liked, whenever she liked.

A tiny, guilty frown wrinkled her brow, since technically she was supposed to be back at the estate helping entertain the houseguests visiting Braebourne. But all seven of her siblings and their families were in residence, even Leo and his new bride, Thalia, who had just returned with celebratory fanfare from their honeymoon tour of Italy. With so many Byrons available to make merry, she would hardly be missed.

Besides, her family was used to her penchant for disappearing by herself for hours at a time as she roamed the nearby woods and hills and fields. She would be back in time for dinner; that would have to be enough.

An exuberant bark sounded behind her and she glanced around in time to watch her dog, Burr, leap the stile and race toward her. She bent down and gave his shaggy head a scratch. "So, you're back, are you? Done chasing rabbits?"

He waved his golden flag of a tail in a wide arc, his pink tongue lolling out in a happy grin, clearly unapologetic for having deserted her a couple of minutes earlier to hunt game in the bushes.

"Well, come along," she told him before starting off toward a stand of trees in the distance.

Burr trotted enthusiastically at her side.

Several minutes later, she reached the copse of trees that led to the lake. She was just about to step out of their protective shelter when she heard a splash.

She stopped and motioned Burr to do the same.

Someone, she realized, was swimming in the lake. Was it Mr. Craycroft? Was he back in residence?

A man emerged from the water—a man who most definitely was not Mr. Craycroft.

And who was most definitely *naked*.

Her eyes widened as she drank in the sight of his long, powerfully graceful form, his skin glistening with wet in the sunlight.

A quiet sigh of wonder slid from between her parted lips, her senses awash with the same kind of reverent awe she felt whenever she beheld something of pure, unadorned beauty.

Not that his face was the handsomest she had ever glimpsed—his features were far too strong and angular for ordinary attractiveness. Yet there was something majestic about him, his tall body exquisitely proportioned, even the unmentionable male part of him that hung impressively between his muscled thighs.

Clearly unaware that he was being observed, he casually slicked the water from his hair with his fingers, then walked deeper into the surrounding area of short grass that was kept periodically trimmed by the groundskeepers.

She shivered, her heart pounding wildly as she watched him settle onto the soft green canopy of grass and stretch out on his back. With a hand, she motioned again to Burr to remain quiet. She did the same, knowing if she moved now, the beautiful stranger would surely hear her.

One minute melted into two, then three.

Quite unexpectedly, she heard the soft yet unmistakable sound of a snore.

Is he asleep?

She smiled, realizing that's exactly what he was.

She knew she ought to leave; this was the perfect chance. But then he shifted, his face turning toward her, one hand resting at his waist, his knee bent at an elegant angle.

And she couldn't leave.

Not now.

Not when she was in the presence of such artistic majesty—as if the universe itself had given her a gift. How could she refuse the opportunity? She simply had to draw him.

Without giving the impulse so much as another moment's consideration, she sank quietly onto a nearby rock that provided her with an excellent view of her subject. Burr settled down next to her and laid his chin on his paws as she extracted her pencil and sketchbook from her bag and set to work.

Gabriel Landsdowne came abruptly awake, the late afternoon sun strong in his eyes. He blinked and sat up, giving his head a slight shake to clear out the last of the drowsy cobwebs.

He'd fallen asleep without even realizing. Apparently, he was more tired than he'd thought. Then again, that's why he'd come here to Craycroft's, so he could spend a little time alone, doing nothing more strenuous than taking a leisurely swim and lazing away the day. He could have done the same at his own estate, of course, but the place always put him in a foul mood.

Too many bad memories.

Too many unwanted responsibilities to ignore.

His usual crowd would laugh to see him doing something as prosaic as taking a solitary afternoon nap. On the other hand, he was out of doors naked, so they would most certainly approve of that.

Smirking, he stood up, brushing an errant blade of grass from his bare butt. He was about to cross to the stand of bushes where he'd left his clothes when he heard a faint rustling sound behind him. He turned and stared into the foliage.

"Who is it? Is someone there?" he demanded.

The only answer was silence.

He looked again, but nothing moved; no one spoke.

Maybe it had been the wind?

Or an animal foraging in the woods?

Suddenly a dog burst from the concealment of the trees, its shaggy wheaten coat gleaming warmly in the sun. The animal stopped and looked at him, eyes bright and inquiring but not unfriendly. He seemed well fed but was of no particular breed, a medium-sized mix of some sort. Part hound and part something else.

"Who might you be, fellow?" Gabriel asked.

The dog wagged his tail and barked twice, then spun around and disappeared into the trees once more.

Just then, Gabriel thought he spied a flash of blue in the woods.

A bird?

The dog must have sensed it too and had gone off to chase whatever it was.

Shrugging in dismissal, Gabriel turned and went to retrieve his clothes.

"It's high time you were home, my lady," Grumbly scolded as Esme hurried into her bedroom a couple of minutes after the dressing gong rang. "I was on the verge of sending one of the footmen out after you. Och, and look at those boots. What new mischief have you been about this afternoon? Tromping in the mud."

"Oh, don't carry on, Grumbly," Esme said, using the maid's old nickname given to her when Esme was still in apron strings. "I went for a walk, then stopped at the stables afterward to check on Andromeda. Her wing is still healing and she needs food and exercise twice a day."

Andromeda was a hawk Esme had found in the woods last month, shot with an arrow. She'd nursed her through the worst and hoped the bird might be able to fly again with enough time and care.

Mrs. Grumblethorpe *tsk*ed and turned Esme around, her fingers moving quickly to unfasten the buttons on Esme's dress. "You and your animals. Always worrying over some poor, misbegotten creature. Rabbits and birds, hedgehogs and box turtles. You're forever dragging something back, to say nothing of all the cats and dogs and horses."

Three of Esme's cats—all strays she'd rescued—lay snoozing in various locations around her room, including a big orange male, Tobias, who was curled up on a cozy spot in the middle of her bed. Her maid didn't approve, but she'd given up that battle long ago.

Burr, who had trailed in with Esme when she'd returned, lay stretched out in front of the unlit fireplace hearth. He snored gently, clearly tired after their recent adventures.

Esme thought again of the splendid naked man at the lake and the drawings of him that were now inside her sketchbook.

A flush rose on her skin.

She thought too of how he'd almost caught her as she'd been leaving. Good thing he'd assumed the noise she'd inadvertently made was Burr.

Good old Burr.

Who was the stranger? she wondered not for the first time. Certainly no one who lived in the neighborhood. She would have remembered a man like him. Peculiar, though, that he seemed oddly familiar, as if she had seen him somewhere before. She'd thought and thought and just couldn't place him.

Oh, well, it would come to her—or not. She wouldn't concern herself. After all, it wasn't as if she were likely to see him again, let alone be introduced.

She didn't have time to ruminate further as Grumbly removed her dress and half boots and sent her over to the washbasin to tidy herself for dinner.

In far less time than one might have imagined, Esme stood clean, elegantly coiffed and attired in an evening gown of demure white silk—presentable for company once again.

She'd hoped with the Season over, she might be able to put all the entertaining behind her for the year. But then Claire had decided to host one of her autumn country parties, inviting the usual gathering of friends and family, in addition to a few new acquaintances from London.

Esme sighed inwardly, wishing she could spend a quiet evening with just the family, then retire early with a good book.

Instead, she straightened her shoulders, fixed a smile on her lips and headed downstairs.

"Might I procure a beverage for you, Lady Esme?"

Esme glanced up from where she sat on the end of the

long drawing room sofa and looked into the eager gray eyes of Lord Eversley.

Only minutes before, the gentlemen had rejoined the ladies after dinner, strolling in on a wave of companionable talk, the faint lingering aromas of cigar smoke and port wine drifting in as well.

Esme had been listening with only partial attention to the other women's discussion of fashion when the men entered and Lord Eversley approached to make her a very elegant bow.

He'd been seated next to her at dinner, his conversation both pleasant and interesting. He was attractive, personable, well-mannered and intelligent—in short, everything any sane young woman could want in a husband. Plus, he was heir to an earldom and a fortune that was impressive even by her family's standards.

Eversley had been one of her most attentive suitors this past Season and his presence here obviously amounted to Claire and Mallory's rather badly disguised attempt to further the relationship. A little nudge in the right direction, she could hear them saying, and wedding bells would ring.

She ought to be cross with them. Really she should. But she knew they only meant well. They just wanted her to be as happily married as they were. If only they would believe her when she said that she wasn't interested in a husband.

Not right now.

Not for a good long while if she had any say in the matter.

Luckily, her oldest brother, Edward, was in no hurry to get her off his hands, content to let her remain here at home for as many years as she liked.

The time would come when she needed to marry. Until then, she would have to find ways to avoid the overtures of interested young men, even ones as thoroughly eligible as Lord Eversley.

"Thank you," she said in answer to his question, "but I already had tea."

"Ah," he said, linking his hands at his back. "A stroll,

then, perhaps? The gardens here at Braebourne are quite splendid, even by lantern light."

"Indeed they are. Again, I am afraid I must refuse. Another time perhaps? I have walked a great deal today, you understand, and my feet are far too weary for another outing at present."

Her feet were never weary—everyone in the family knew she could beat paths through the fields like a seasoned foot soldier—but Lord Eversley didn't need to be apprised of that fact. Hopefully none of the others were listening and would give her away.

Yet apparently someone else *was* listening. Lettice Waxhaven—another of the London guests, who happened to have made her debut along with Esme this past spring—leaned forward at just that moment, a fierce gleam in her pale blue eyes. "Yes, where were you this afternoon, Lady Esme? We were all of us wondering, what could be so fascinating that you would vanish for the entirety of the afternoon?"

Esme hid her dislike for the other young woman behind a tight smile. Why her mother and Lettice's mother had to be old childhood friends who had been unexpectedly reacquainted this Season, she didn't know. It was because of the renewal of that friendship that Esme found herself far too often in Lettice's company.

"I was just out," Esme said. "Walking and sketching."

"Really? Pray tell, what is it you sketch?" Lettice asked as if she were actually interested—which she was clearly not.

But Esme wasn't thinking about Lettice's false sincerity. Instead, she was caught up in memories of the beautiful naked man by the lake and the drawings of him that she'd done while he slept. Suddenly she was grateful for the room's warmth, since it disguised the flush that crept over her neck and cheeks.

"Nature," she answered with a seemingly careless shrug. "Plants and animals. Anything that takes my fancy at the time."

And oh my, had the glorious stranger taken her fancy.

"Lady Esme is quite the accomplished artist," Lord Eversley said with enthusiasm. "I had the great good fortune to view a few of her watercolors when we were last in Town." He smiled at her, clearly admiring. "She is a marvel."

Lettice's mouth tightened, her eyes narrowing. It was no secret—at least not to Esme—that Lettice had long ago set her cap at Lord Eversley and that so far he had failed to take notice of her. Esme would have felt sorry for her were Lettice a nicer person.

Lettice blinked and rearranged her features into a sweet smile, as if realizing that she'd let slip the well-practiced air of kind innocence she wore like a mask. "Oh, I should so like to see your sketches. Perhaps you might show them to us?"

"Yes, Lady Esme," Eversley agreed. "I too would greatly enjoy a chance to view your newest work."

"Oh, that is most kind," Esme said, hedging. "But I suspect you would find my efforts disappointing."

"Impossible," Eversley disagreed. "You are too good an artist to ever draw anything that could be deemed disappointing."

"You give me far too much credit, Lord Eversley. What I drew today amounts to nothing of importance. Just a few random studies, that's all."

Nude studies of an unforgettable male.

Sleek limbs corded with muscle.

A powerful, hair-roughened chest.

Narrow hips.

Taut buttocks.

Impressive genitalia—at least *she* found it impressive, considering it was the first real, flesh-and-blood set she'd ever seen.

And his face . . .

Planes and angles that begged for an artist's attention, rugged yet refined, bold and unabashed.

Captivating.

"Truly, they're mostly rubbish and I have no wish to offend anyone's eyes with the viewing," she said, hoping Eversley would take the hint and let that be the end of it.

Instead, he persisted. "You are too modest, Lady Esme. Why do you not let me be the judge?"

"Who is modest?" her brother Lawrence said, joining the conversation. A few others turned their heads to listen as well.

"Lady Esme," Eversley explained. "Miss Waxhaven and I are trying to persuade her to show off the sketches she did today, but she is too shy."

Leo, Lawrence's twin, laughed from where he sat next to his wife, Thalia. "Our Esme? Shy about her art? That doesn't sound likely."

"Yes, she's usually raring to share," Lord Drake Byron agreed.

"That's because even her bad drawings are better than anything the rest of us can do," Mallory said before she shot a glance over at Grace. "Except for Grace, of course. No offense, Grace, since you are a brilliant artist too."

Her sister-in-law smiled. "None taken." Grace looked at Esme. "Do let us see, dear. I know we would all enjoy a glimpse or two of your latest efforts. I particularly love the landscapes you do."

Cheers of agreement and encouragement rose from those gathered.

Esme's chest tightened. "No, I couldn't. Not tonight. Besides, my sketchbook is upstairs. There's no need for all this bother."

"It's no bother," Edward said. "We'll have one of the servants fetch it." He glanced over at the butler. "Please ask one of the maids to collect Lady Esme's sketchbook and have it brought here to the drawing room."

"Right away, Your Grace." The servant bowed and exited the room.

No! Esme wanted to shout.

But it was too late. Any further protestations on her part would look odd, causing speculation about why she was so adamant that no one see her sketches. When her siblings said that she had never before shown a great deal of modesty concerning her work, they were right.

This could still work out fine, so long as she didn't panic. For the most part, her sketchbook contained renderings of birds and animals, field flowers, trees in leaf and the landscapes for which Grace had shown a partiality. The sketches of the man were at the back of the book. So long as she was careful, she could show the innocent drawings in the front—and only those.

All too soon one of the footmen walked in, her blue clothbound sketchbook in hand.

She leapt to her feet and hurried across to take it before anyone else could. "Thank you, Jones."

Quickly, she clutched the sketchbook against her chest, collecting herself. Then she turned to face the waiting company.

"Here we are," she said brightly as she crossed to resume her seat. "Since you all wish to see, why don't I just hold up the drawings rather than passing the book around?"

Slowly she cracked open the book, careful to go nowhere near the back pages. She thumbed through, looking quickly for something she hadn't already shown her family.

"Ah, here we are," she said, relieved to have found a new sketch. "I drew this of the hills toward the village earlier today."

Actually, she'd drawn it last week.

She held up the book, fingers tight on the pages.

Murmurs of appreciation went around the room.

"Lovely," Lady Waxhaven said.

"Astounding," Lord Eversley pronounced. "As I said before, you are a marvel, Lady Esme. Show us another."

"All right."

Bending over the book again, she found a new sketch. This one of her dog Burr lying under a tree.

She held it up, eliciting more positive remarks and smiles from everyone—everyone, that is, except Lettice Waxhaven, who looked as if she wished she'd never started this.

That made two of them.

She showed one more of farmers in the field, then closed the book, holding it on her lap. "There. You have all had your art exhibition for the evening. Now, enough. Please go back to what you were doing before, talking and drinking and enjoying the evening."

"Esme is quite right," Claire said with a broad smile. "Let us make merry. Perhaps a game of cards or some dancing? I should dearly love to hear a tune."

"That sounds wonderful, Duchess," Lettice declared, openly enthusiastic. Her gaze went to Eversley. "Do you dance, my lord?"

"Indeed," he said. "Mayhap you could play for us, Miss Waxhaven? You're quite accomplished on the piano-forte, as I recall."

Then he turned to Esme. "Lady Esme, what about you? Would you care to take to the floor?"

Lettice Waxhaven's face drained of color.

Esme actually felt sorry for her—and rather cross with Lord Eversley for being so obtuse. She stood, intending to refuse him. But before she could, Lettice stalked forward and deliberately bumped her shoulder, though Lettice did a good job making it look unintentional.

The sketchbook flew out of Esme's grasp, pages fluttering wide before the book spun and landed on the floor.

She moved quickly to retrieve it, but Lettice Waxhaven's loud gasp let her know it was already too late. Everyone else was turning and looking, the page with the beautiful naked man lying open for them all to see.

Breath froze in Esme's chest and she couldn't seem to get enough air, her thoughts spinning as she tried to think of an explanation for what she'd drawn.

"What in Hades' name is that?" Lawrence said, his voice loud enough that she jumped.

"I believe we can all see *what* it is," Leo answered, his face wearing the identical look of shock and outrage as his identical twin's. "The only thing I want to know is how we're going to kill him."

"Kill who?" Esme squeaked, suddenly finding her voice.

Leo's and Lawrence's gazes shot to hers, while the rest of their family and friends looked on.

"*Northcote,*" Leo said, spitting out the name as if it were a curse.

"Our neighbor from Cavendish Square," Lawrence finished.

s0514